SEEING RED IN GRETNA GREEN

SEEING RED IN GRETNA GREEN

MIDLIFE RECORDER
BOOK FOUR

LINZI DAY

Also by Linzi Day

Midlife in Gretna Green

Painting the Blues in Gretna Green

Ties that Bond in Gretna Green

House Party in Gretna Green

Coming in 2024

Code Yellow in Gretna Green

Published in the United Kingdom in 2023
Midlife Recorder series. Book 4

ASIN: B0C6R2HT6Q
ISBN: 9798858221838

Cover Design: Axe Designs
Book Formatting: ESG

*For Caleb Owen, without whom the Red Celts would be a **lot** less Red.*

And to Jacqui Travers for Caleb and so much more: wine, lasagne, boxes, her fabulous sense of humour, and puppies. There have to be puppies—right?

To Simon Travers too, I suppose, for Jacqui and, oh yeah, for being my friend for 48 years and making really excellent wine.

ACKNOWLEDGMENTS

I'd like to thank those readers who have shown such unexpected love for my books, especially the ones who share with ME any typos they find in them. But please remember British spelling varies from USA norms. While Amazon can't do anything about typos, I can and I do. Special thanks to Marisa Richardson, who is a complete star at this.

linziday@gmail.com will always find me.

To James, my rock and my rainbow, for more reasons than I could ever write here. But I know, he knows >2

My profound gratitude to the friends and experts who helped with aspects of research, historical queries, and randomly odd author questions. I'm indebted to them for their expertise, patience, and good humour throughout. Peter Branney, Sheryl Murawsky, Lynn Ross, Judith Stuart, Jacqui Travers, and Caleb Owen.

More gratitude to everyone on my support team, especially, Axe for my pretty covers and Krista, my efficient and hilarious editor.

Special thanks to Pope Clement VIII without whom ... very little would ever be written ... by anyone.

As always, my deep appreciation goes to my FABs—my Freaking Awesome Beta-reading team for all that they do to help make this a much better book for everyone.

This book's team was **Carolyn, Divya, James, Jan, Nives, Robin, Rossi, Sheryl, Simon, and Wendy.** I'm so appreciative of you all.

And now we will all benefit from my MVPs—my Magnificent Volunteer Proofreaders. Thanks to them, you have hopefully enjoyed a smoother reading experience. The first MVP team included **Betsy, Dasha, Holly, Katie, Louise, Lynn, Marisa, Rachel, and Vanessa.**

I'd like to send a special heap of cake-flavoured gratitude to my new friend, Betsy Nortrup, who went the extra mile in so many ways to make this a much better book. You saved me from future blushes. Weird, huh, Betsy?

AUTHOR'S NOTE

I gave away free Bonus Epilogues for the first three books to subscribers to my newsletter. You can simply read them online in your browser if you wish or download them to your device.

I've always tried to include enough information so anyone who hasn't read them won't be confused by anything in this book. But as the series progresses it's getting harder to do. There's also a new novella *House Party in Gretna Green* available on Amazon between Ties and this book which you may have missed.

The free bonuses are **still available** if you'd prefer to read them and catch up before beginning this one.

Get your bonus epilogues from <u>linziday.com/newsletter</u>

PART ONE
WEDNESDAY

Allow the fire that drives you to burn brighter than any flames around you.

Many fear getting their wings for the first time. But consider the butterfly. If it had remained a caterpillar, would it not grieve when all its peers flew away, so free and elegant? The struggle is brief, but your rewards are infinite.

Finding your Inner Fire: How to Claim your True Self by Peggy Hwybon

(Warmly recommended by His Majesty Mabon ap Modron)

CHAPTER
ONE

Wednesday, 24th February, 2021—Gateway Cottage—Gretna Green, Scotland

In my mind, I heard the rich, plummy tones of the celebrity who narrated a reality show I loved back in the days when I had time for television. Before my life spiralled into the current whirlwind of daily magic-filled chaos.

"And here's Niki McKnight, chilling out with coffee at the table in her warm, cosy kitchen. Today, she's relaxed, unusually well-dressed and poised. We haven't seen those stylish red boots before. They must be new. A new hairstyle too. Doesn't her vibrant, rainbow-hued hair with its spiky cut give us a clue about her confident, outgoing personality?"

The narrator's voice continued in my head, "Look. Her luggage is packed. Oh, and she's holding her adorably fluffy, newly groomed Bichon Frise, Tilly, close to her heart. We can see how eager they are to depart on this trip."

Then I imagined the trailer for today's episode of *The Gretna Green Gateway* voiceover: "After Sunday's celebration of Dola's 1400th anniversary, yesterday was just one month since Niki became the thirteenth McKnight descendant to stand as the Recorder. Now she's about to take a well-deserved break with her Prince Charming in the Red Celt realm. Can't we all see how much she's looking forward to it?"

That fictitious observer would be as wrong as it's possible for anyone to freaking be.

From the outside, to my imaginary narrator, who obviously had no psychic Gift, it might appear I wanted to go. But my inner child was currently a bad-tempered toddler about to have a screaming, foot-stamping tantrum. It shouted, "Won't! Shan't! Not going! NO!"

Tilly whined softly. I put her on the floor and picked up my coffee mug. It was empty just like my self-confidence bucket.

"Right, Dola, I've changed my mind. It's silly to go to the Red Celt realm so early. There's an awful lot to do here. Fi's only had a couple of weeks to get settled in. It's too soon for me to go gallivanting around the kingdoms. I'm sure that's what Gran would have said. She said 'gallivanting' a lot, didn't she? And has Finn fully recovered from the Vikings trying to kidnap him? I don't think so. And Rosemary starts in a few days. I ought to be here to help her settle in."

Complete silence from Dola, the entity who was my sentient house and now also held the post of the Recorder's equerry.

Was I talking to myself? Did I care? Nope.

I was going to line up my excuses anyway.

"Everyone's had a difficult time, between all those bondings, the problem in the Pict realm, and this forthcoming sentencing of John Fergusson. Let's not forget all the women who've filed petition requests against King Troels. How many do we have now? Fifty-something?"

I blew a breath out in frustration.

"It's quite the wrong time for me to take a holiday. My intuition is telling me not to go. What the hell was I thinking? I'm staying here for now. I'll go for John's judgement and the main St. David's Day thing. The Book said that's what the Recorder normally does. But it isn't until the end of the week. It'll give me longer to make sure everything is running smoothly here."

Silence.

I fingered Agnes's locket nervously. It contained miniatures of Agnes and a younger version of Mabon. I'd decided to wear it so I wouldn't lose it, but I also hoped if I wore it openly, someone might recognise it. If all else failed, I'd have to buttonhole Mabon because I needed to know what it meant.

"Dola, you OK?"

My phone buzzed on the kitchen table. I turned it over and pressed the green button happily.

"Hey, I was just about to call—"

My best mate Aysha was in efficient lawyer mode. "Listen to me carefully, girl. Dola says you're bottling out. This is not the time to lose your nerve. So, you won't. You will breathe. You will find the courage you seem to have mislaid. You will go and stay with Dai. It will be fine. You won't vomit from nerves. It only feels that way. Drink the hot chocolate Dola's about to give you. Then get your butt to the Gateway and meet Prince Charming. You deserve some happiness and fun, Nik. Go and at least find out if he can supply you with either. If you don't, I will phone Janet and give her your address. Do I make myself clear?"

The line went dead.

"She had to go into court, Niki; please drink this." My empty coffee cup disappeared as Dola replaced it with an elegantly curved porcelain Winnie the Pooh-themed mug. Overlaid onto the iconic pastel watercolours was the text, *You're braver than you believe, stronger than you seem, and smarter than you think.*

No, I damn well wasn't. I was a bundle of limp tagliatelle tied in a knot.

The mug of hot chocolate had the distinctive aroma of brandy emanating from it. Oh crap. If Dola was feeding me brandy before lunch, I was in a bad way.

I picked it up with shaking hands and sipped slowly, breathing in the soothing brandy fumes. The thing was, I truly had a niggling feeling this visit wouldn't go well, and I'd be needed here. My tummy was unhappy. Perhaps it was just nerves? Either way, Aysha wouldn't believe me.

Dai, Prince Dafydd ap Modron, heir to Mabon, the king of the Red Celts, had invited me, specifically as myself, not as the scary Recorder, to spend some time with him. He'd said I should come before the St. David's Day festival being held in the Red Celt kingdom and reacquaint myself with him and his realm before the formal celebrations on the first of March. He'd told me he'd finally be able to answer my many questions once we were in his "lovely mountain home."

I'd jumped at the chance. Right now I couldn't imagine what planet I'd been on when I'd swiftly emailed back saying, Yes, please, Niki and Tilly would be delighted to accept his invitation.

I must have been insane.

I sipped.

I breathed.

Dola's warm contralto voice said, "This may be what is called a panic attack. The internet offered a trusted friend, a soothing drink and some breathing exercises as solutions. So … do you feel better now?"

I laughed. "I'm pretty sure the trusted friend is supposed to say, 'There, there, sweetie, just breathe; it'll all be fine.' I don't think threatening me with my ex-boss is supposed to be the main thrust of the usual anti-panic attack regimen."

There was a moment's silence before, in a smaller voice, Dola suggested, "It appears to have worked, though?"

I'd decided my reluctance to go wasn't intuition; it was simply nerves. So I'd have to woman up. What a stupid phrase that was.

Then Dola said, "Everything you said before was inaccurate. You are going to Pant y Wern for the events and Mynydd Cefn y Ddraig, where Dai lives. His house is called Pencoed. Mabon's phone usually works there since you upgraded it; yours should too. Your earbuds will work. Take a Dolina with you for your room, and do not forget, if there are any problems, you can be back here in seconds."

Ad'Rian had named his Dola device his "Dolina," and the name seemed to have stuck as we'd all taken to using it. But all I'd heard were a lot of Welsh words I didn't recognise except Pant y Wern.

The name of the Red Celt's capital had struck my six-year-old self as the funniest thing in the world. How could a town be called after my underwear? Oh, how I'd giggled. Mabon patiently explaining it wasn't Pantywern but Pant y Wern, three words that, in Welsh, meant a swamp and a valley had done nothing to suppress my amusement. OK, in the spirit of full disclosure, it still amused me, just perhaps on a different plane from my six-year-old understanding of what panties covered. Swampy valley indeed.

I'd need to leave before Aysha made good on her threat. I probably only had the time she was in court. Aysha didn't make threats; she made promises you'd rather she didn't deliver on. The first time she'd threatened me, we were undergrads. She'd said if I didn't stop living in my ratty, but so comfortable, favourite sweatshirt, which, according to her, was a holey disgrace, she would turn it into a kite.

I hadn't believed her.

She'd run it up the building's flagpole the following night. Not technically a kite, but I got the message—even nineteen-year-old Aysha did not make idle threats.

I stood, gathered my luggage and Tilly again, and

the doorbell rang. I ignored it. Dola dealt with the doors. It was usually a courier who hadn't read the address properly and was looking for some other cottage. Everyone who should have access just came through the small wrought-iron gate after Dola opened it for them and made their way around the side to the Gateway.

"Niki, there is a visitor at the door asking for you. She was a friend of your grandmother's. She has visited me before."

"Huh, OK." I put all my luggage and Tilly down again and headed to the door.

A tiny, older woman, perhaps late seventies or early eighties, smiled at me. She looked unremarkable in every respect except for her dark eyes, which were piercing as she surveyed me.

"Ah, Niki," she held out a hand, which I automatically reached out to shake, "how lovely to put a face to you finally, child. My condolences on your loss."

There was a strange static charge to her weak handshake, similar to the one I'd noticed when I shook Rollo's hand. Was this some new ability I didn't understand? I'd have to ask the Book.

I expected her to introduce herself. Instead, her head twisted, and she looked at me out of one eye. It was an odd birdlike gesture. Her other eye watched the lane. "It's about the Community Centre, dear, and the Fergussons. The bequest in Elsie's will for the new central heating, you know?"

She turned, looked fully towards the gate and shuddered slightly as though she'd seen someone she didn't like.

I looked too, but the small lane along the front of the cottage was empty.

"I'm Tina. May I come in for a moment?"

The base of my neck tingled as a strange sensation moved up my spine. I hesitated, debating between explaining I was just leaving and seizing the opportunity to delay my departure. Cowardice won, and I stepped back, holding the door open. "Of course, please."

I led her through to the kitchen, where, on the previously empty worktop, a kettle and various storage jars now waited. It seemed I was to pretend to be normal. Could I remember how to do that? I guessed we'd see.

The woman was bird-boned and fragile. I pulled a chair out for her. "Please make yourself comfortable. Can I offer you anything?" I gestured vaguely at the kettle. I could remember how to make drinks the old-fashioned way, couldn't I? Gods and Goddesses, of course I could. I hadn't become so spoilt in just a month, had I?

But my back wasn't just tingling. It was almost itchy now.

"Thank you, child, a cup of tea would be lovely."

After I switched on the kettle, I half-turned towards her and caught something out of the corner of my eye.

Nope, it had gone.

Twisting back to face the kettle so my visitor wouldn't see me do it, I carefully curled a tendril of power into my half-closed fist.

"How do you take your tea?" I smiled pleasantly and focused closely on her. I looked with what Ad'Rian had always called "my other eyes." I talked to the curl of power I'd drawn in my mind while I looked at her.

Huh! I hadn't seen this since Ad'Rian's daughter, Fionn'ghal, impersonated my assistant Fi during my first week in my new job. "You can drop your glamour in here, please."

She laughed delightedly, a tinkling, melodic laugh I knew well. An Alicorn laugh. She was from the Fae royal house?

"Oh, by Lugh, you're good. Very good indeed. It took your grandmother almost four years, you know. And it was only because I had to return to Fae for a wedding, and she had the opportunity to see me in the Gateway with the power at her disposal."

She shook herself gently, and now a slim, attractive woman who appeared to be about my own age stood in front of me. Her skin of deepest lilac and silver blue-violet eyes identified her as Fae. She looked strangely familiar, and I tried to retrieve the memory that might tell me who she was.

"I'm sorry about all the nonsense, but, honestly, this village has eyes and ears around every corner. They've nothing better to do than spy on people, and that damnable Troels pays most of them. I'm Ti'Anna; the locals know me as Tina."

Taking in my confused expression, she offered, "De'Anna's sister, dear. L'eon's aunt."

Now I knew who she reminded me of. The first bonding I'd ever done in the Gateway had been her nephew L'eon to his partner Kaiden. This woman had a look of L'eon's mother De'Anna. I just hadn't known De'Anna had a sister, had I?

I smiled at her. "Sorry I'm being slow. I didn't realise you lived here?"

How did I have a Fae living in the village and not know?

Ad'Rian had never mentioned it, even Fionn'ghal hadn't said she had an aunt here. What the hell? And how to ask it politely. Thoughts of politeness brought my manners out of hiding, and I made her the cup of tea. Turned out, spoilt Recorder or not, it was like riding a bike.

We settled at the table, and I picked up the remains of my drinking chocolate. "So, what may I do for you? You said you needed to speak about the Fergussons, or was that just misdirection too?"

"Oh no, Recorder. By Lugh, that's real. You must not permit them to execute Jamie. Not yet, anyway."

Should I know who Lugh was? I'd heard his name before from someone in the Pict realm, Aysha's Lewis or Hugh, maybe?

"Who's Lugh? And, as far as I know, no one plans to?"

Her forehead creased into the slightest frown. Fae faces often expressed less emotion than the other races. "You don't look stupid, and you must have strong powers to see through my glamour so quickly…" she trailed off.

A few weeks ago, I might have fallen for her obvious fishing expedition, but wimpy Niki had grown up a little, at least when Dai wasn't involved, so I laughed.

And waited.

With a small huff, she said, "Oh, well, it was worth a try. You're not like Elsie, are you? How annoying."

My phone vibrated with a message.

> Dola: She used to gain much information from your grandmother. Shall I ask Ad'Rian about her? He is in his study by his Dolina device.

Niki: Yes, please. Specifically, why is she really in Gretna Green? Does she live here? Can I trust her?

I should ask Ti'Anna the same question and then compare the answers. Gosh, I was getting more sceptical and suspicious the longer I lived here. I strengthened my shields. Ad'Rian always said I had tight shields, and I didn't trust this woman. I didn't distrust her, either. But better safe than sorry, as my gran always used to say, even if she didn't seem to have acted on her own advice with Ti'Anna.

"Ti'Anna, I don't wish to be rude, but I was about to leave." I gestured at my luggage, still in the middle of the kitchen. "So, could we speed this up? Why do you think the Red Celts intend to execute Jamie, and what's your interest in him? Oh, and who is Lugh?"

I was getting better at this asking questions lark, wasn't I?

CHAPTER
TWO

"Child, I think you—" She cut herself off. "No, not child. That's rude if I don't appear to be eighty-five, isn't it? Recorder, have you made an official appearance, with your grandmother perhaps, at any previous sentencings?"

I shook my head.

"Have you consulted the Book or my liege lord Ad'Rian or even King Mabon ap Modron about the format of them?"

I shook my head again. My best friend was a lawyer. I hadn't thought I needed to look up how a sentencing hearing went. Was I being an idiot again?

"There are very specific rules. You may wish to acquaint yourself with them."

She did the bird-like head tilt thing again, but this time, I saw she was using her Fae sight. Don't stare straight at the thing you don't understand. Sometimes peripheral vision shows you more. The change in her eyes from their usual silver-blue colour to the white of a royal Fae using their power was the real giveaway.

I kept my shields tight and waited her out.

She let out a small breath, not quite a sigh. "They will obey all the rules, but once they have fulfilled the requirements, they carry out the sentence with extreme swiftness. I understand Mabon claimed him on behalf of all the realms because John is an oathbreaker. There is no arguing with that. Oathbreakers can't be permitted to live when they've put millions of lives at risk." She paused, still using her Fae sight on me. Now she sighed openly. "You have excellent shields. Quite unlike both Elsie and Leyla, so you don't take after your mother, either. But you remind me of someone."

I waited some more. I wasn't about to help a Fae I didn't know, especially when I had no idea if I could trust her. But as she was obviously checking me out, I used my Gift on her. She was concerned and worried about something. It seemed sincere. But with an unknown Fae, I couldn't be sure. The Fae might be the reason the old homily *once you can fake sincerity, the rest is easy* even exists.

I took a shortcut. "Can I trust you?" The Fae didn't lie. They obfuscated, they avoided, they misdirected, and they would bend the truth to its snapping point, but they didn't lie. So her answer to my question might speed this along. I needed to be out of here before Aysha finished in court.

Her horrified expression, unusual to see on the often inexpressive faces of the more senior Fae, was revealing. How long had she lived here? Had she picked up human habits?

Her mouth opened, then closed. I waited. In the pregnant silence between us, the muted vibration of my phone sounded loud. I glanced at the text.

> Dola: Ad'Rian says, 'As far as you can throw her.'

> Niki: What?

> Dola: We established that was the English phrase he wanted. He thinks it means 'she's not untrustworthy per se; however, he couldn't describe her as trustworthy. But she is still Fae enough not to lie, so phrase your questions with care.' I am obtaining more information on why she lives in the village. She never dropped her glamour inside me before.

I looked back at Ti'Anna, who slowly said, "Quite unlike Elsie. Well, Recorder, in this specific matter, regarding the vital importance of Jamie being spared, at least for a short time. No, not a short time, spared for just long enough. Yes, you may trust me."

"OK. Then tell me the what, when, why, how, where and who please?" I glanced at the time on my phone. "And with no intention of being rude, I am now late."

She sipped her tea. "The village needs the bequest from Elsie's estate. They also need a functioning solictor's office. If Jamie were to be executed by the realms, then Caledonia would never know, would they? So, at this end, it could and probably would take years to sort out all the tangles with the legal practice his great-grandfather founded. Certainly, there are rules to protect clients and their assets and bequests. But I have consulted... others ... and those Scottish laws might leave a lot to be desired if you need reliable lawyers and swift disbursements."

"OK." I didn't know what I expected, but a Fae concerning herself with my gran's bequest to the community hall for a new heating system wasn't one of them, and it didn't feel important. I could buy them a new system if they needed one. Gran had left me loads of money. How much could central heating cost?

"If the heating situation is desperate, I'd be happy to help in the interim?"

She almost sighed. "That's not the point, dear Niki. Elsie and I understood, in a tiny village, it's not wise to appear to be wealthy. But a bequest in a will is a perfectly acceptable way of giving back to the community after a long life. I do the same every time I die."

I gaped at her, sipped my drinking chocolate, and tried to catch up. "Every time you die?"

"Oh dear, if you must leave soon, you will need to listen quicker. I mean, of course, each time I appear to die, and then I inherit my cottage as my niece, or goddaughter or granddaughter—it varies. Like vampires, you know, dear?"

"Vampires?" Was I losing the plot here?

"In those wonderful books. It's what they do. Sticking to the point, please, Recorder. Persuade the council to spare Jamie. Then he can come back here, sell the family legal practice in an open, above-board manner, which will prevent any delays in the disbursements. It will also reduce gossip and specu-lation, and then he can," she made air quotes, "'move to London, or Las Vegas or Lima.' Whatever works. I don't care. But I do care that Fergusson, McPherson and MacDonald are put back on a solid footing. Moving the probate with two partners missing, espe-cially as John is the current managing partner, will take far longer than if Jamie is allowed back here to sell the firm. The other partners will probably buy him out. If he disappears, it could take years to have him declared dead. It's a small town. They're the only solicitors. The village needs them, the adjoining towns need them, and you *and* the village need a swift probate on Elsie's will. I am charging you to ensure your gran's last wishes are carried out."

Well, when she put it that way ... but why would she think John's sentencing had any connection to Jamie's?

"Ti'Anna, you may have incorrect information about Jamie. At my ascension, I realised John had never tested his son before appointing him. Mabon made the prior claim immediately over John on behalf of all the realms for oathbreaking and dereliction of the Knight Adjutant's duty for thirty years."

Ti'Anna inclined her head.

I continued, "But the decision about Jamie is mine. It's up to the Recorder and the Gateway power. I decided not to involve the human courts, so Jamie is currently undergoing treatment by the Fae. He won't even be put on trial in the realms until the Fae pronounce him fit. So he can't be executed yet. But if you're concerned, I'll mention it to Mabon."

There, I'd been polite. Now I needed to leave.

Or not.

Because ten minutes I didn't have to spare later, she'd made herself perfectly clear. I thought my only important role up here was being the Recorder. I was wrong. Apparently, I also had duties as one of the wealthier inhabitants of the small village I now lived in. Gran had taken her responsibility seriously; so did Ti'Anna.

The community had needs. They were good at claiming grants and other funds, but the new central heating wouldn't be installed without Gran's legacy. There was a toddlers' play group, a young mums' club, exercise and slimming groups, yoga, tai chi and other classes, and a seniors' coffee and social group. All of them needed the heating to work in this community hall.

As a city dweller, these sorts of things had always been what Aysha and I called S.E.P. or Someone Else's Problem. But now I was the someone else whose job it was to help fix the damn problem.

Ti'Anna and I exchanged contact information as she left, saying, "Don't hesitate to contact me if you need advice to expedite this."

She shook herself at the front door, and an elderly lady hobbled back out just in time for Tilly to chase past her to the iron railings, where she barked furiously at the local greyhound she'd taken against. He was dragging his grumpy owner behind him as usual.

"Spies, all of them," Ti'Anna hissed as she limped away down the lane.

I finally reached the Gateway with my luggage, my dog, and something masquerading as my nerve.

Dai was waiting in the Red sector and gave me a wide smile.

"I'm so sorry. I *was* ready on time, but I had an unexpected visitor."

He grinned at me. "If you invite me to the centre, I can take your luggage."

I was making such a mess of this. "Prince ap Modron, I invite you and Dru to the centre of the Rainbow." Dru bounced through. Tilly demanded I put her down so she could greet him properly, and the blue gate opened behind us with a loud thud.

"Careful, Tom." A large wheeled cooking range nosed into the Blue sector, followed by a mobile market stall. Both were being pushed by the almost identical red-headed twins, more usually called Twirly and Whirly—two of Autumn's favourite people. She adored their kurts or vampire bread.

"Sorry, Will, it got away from me." Twirly glanced around and added, "Whoops, our apologies, Recorder."

The wheeled contraption made its stately way to the centre. Both men paused and bowed. "My lady, Your Highness, we're off to set up for Dewi Sant. Get there early for a good spot, you know."

Dai grinned at them. "Sounds like an excuse not to go home to me, lads."

"No, we are going home, but after Dewi Sant. OK to go through, my lady?" Whirly enquired.

"Of course, gentlemen, I'll be along for a kurt once you're set up."

Twirly reached into the stall and retrieved a bag, which had Tilly dancing madly on her back legs as he passed it to me. He reached under again to a different cupboard and retrieved another one, I guessed without the spice mix, which he threw to Dru.

"We always make a few spares before we leave. Does she need one of her own, my lady?" He smiled down at a dancing, begging Tilly, who promptly sat down in her best what-a-good-girl-I-am pose and nosed at the bag I held.

"No, she'll share mine, thank you. Unlike Dru, she loves the spice mix." I rummaged in my bag for coins, but Whirly shook his head. "No need, my lady. Take it as a gift for the passage."

I thanked them both, and as they headed towards the red gate, they paused. Twirly smiled at Dai. "*Gwnewch y pethau bychain mewn bywyd.*"

"*Gwnewch y pethau bychain mewn bywyd,*" came from Dai in return.

I couldn't even separate the words in my mind, but they sounded Welsh. "What does that mean?"

Dai said, "'Do the little things in life.' It was Dewi Sant's motto. You probably call him St. David. He's the Red Celt's patron saint. He said it on his deathbed, apparently."

"OK? Because?" I frowned in confusion at Dai and then totally forgot all about the little things as Twirly and Whirly shook themselves in exactly the way Ti'Anna had. In their places stood two typical Red Celt men. They were the same height and size but with the black hair, bright blue eyes and white skin of the classic Welsh man. I gasped.

"Did you not realise?" Dai enquired.

"Are they Fae?" But as quickly as I'd asked, I answered myself, "No, ignore me. They feel nothing like the Fae." Their energy was darker and denser than the Fae's bright psychic presence. Swiftly, before they could get through the red gate, I turned my Gift on them. Their auras were unusual, and their shields were solid rock walls—that was becoming a pattern, wasn't it? I couldn't get much more than different, mutable and potentially dangerous—but not to me.

Dai watched me. "What do you think they are?"

"If I had to guess, I'd say werewolves, but that's ridiculous. I've just been reading too many fun paranormal books again. But they treat the dogs like equals, and they feel mutable, changeable, not set. So I don't know. What are they?"

He laughed tightly, but under his laughter, I got a vague sense of shock. But he avoided my question. "Well, Angus will be delighted to see them."

I thought about Angus, the man Dai and I had seen one day in Aberglas in the Pict realm. He'd met a Red Celt woman at one of the festivals and proceeded to court her, marry her, and get her pregnant. Then moved from his native Scotland to Pant y Wern because his wife didn't want to be away from her large Welsh family. She'd had pregnancy cravings for Whirly's kurts. So I'd seen Angus regularly in Aberglas, the Pictish capital, when Twirly and Whirly were there. He'd collected bags of the sweet bread for his wife almost daily.

"Hmm, do you really think so? I'm not so sure. How long will it take him to get to the square, pick up fresh kurts and get them back to, sorry, what's his wife called? Anyway, to get back home?"

"It's Peggy and about ten minutes. Why?"

I grinned. "I think he'd rather have an hour away from his mother-in-law and his heavily pregnant wife. It's a difficult stage. Aysha was a nightmare when she was seven and a half months preggers with Autumn. I could have throttled her daily."

He grinned at me, watched me share my kurt with Tilly, and reached for my luggage. "You might be right. Shall we go?"

"Sure. How are we getting there?"

THREE

Three thousand nine hundred and two.

I was trying *hard* not to be a whiny bitch, but this was beyond ridiculous! My new red boots leaked, my thigh muscles were crying like teething babies, and Tilly shivered, whimpered quietly and tried to bury her face more deeply inside my scarf. I wrapped it more securely around her. If Willow hadn't given her a magical fluff and buff, she'd have been wearing her usual fur coat and probably bouncing around happily. But we'd both wanted to look nice for our short break at Dai's.

Four thousand and eighty-six.

Yeah, about that "break."

I hadn't realised, "You're both very welcome in the spare room of my beautiful mountain home. The views are to die for," meant it was at the top of the damn mountain and back in time about a hundred years.

Before snowmobiles, or cable cars, or civilisation.

I couldn't transport there because I'd never been before. I might die before I ever got to appreciate the fabled view. In this snow, I couldn't see ten feet in front of my face. Words failed me. Well, no, they bloody didn't! But the only way I'd prevented myself from spewing a stream of profanity, including many F-words and even some of the worse ones, was by imagining Autumn here with me.

It was too cold to talk. Dai had made that clear when I'd tried several times to start a conversation. He'd shaken his head and gestured ahead of us. My breath froze in the air, and Tilly and I shared both ends of my scarf wrapped around our glaciated faces.

The unbelievable freaking cold up here. The incredible freaking stupidity of the man who thought, "It's just a-ways over there," was a reasonable manner in which to describe a three- or four-mile upward trek across snow and ice in a forty-miles-an-hour headwind.

My eyes gave up about a mile back and now streamed constantly with the cold. I kept catching odd rainbow-coloured flashes ahead and to the left. But I couldn't wipe my eyes to see what might have created a rainbow in this whiteout—also because I was carrying Tilly and my tissues were in my bag. I'd been wearing it cross-body before the headwind had blown it around to my back also about a mile ago.

Four thousand two hundred and seventy-one.

Dai walked in complete silence, about four paces ahead of me, carrying my suitcase. His single comment so far had been, "Now you know why I was always grateful when you summoned me down the mountain."

I'd offered to go home and pack my stuff into a more sensible tote bag when I realised we were walking to his house, but he'd picked up my case as if it weighed nothing and marched off.

The atmosphere between us was uncomfortable, but I couldn't pin down what made it so miserable. Was he angry I'd been late? He hadn't seemed it. He'd been smiley and happy in the Gateway, but now he was marching off like an Arab sheik and leaving Tilly and me to trail behind him like two of his wives. Dru had disappeared, probably to get out of the miserable bone-numbing cold.

I wanted these few days to go well. I needed some answers. He'd said he could give them to me at his "lovely mountain home." He hadn't mentioned the uphill hike to get there. If he had, I wouldn't have worn cute new boots and jeans. I'd have worn five layers of thermal leggings, waterproof socks and my Doc Martens.

I knew I had trust issues with men after Nick. But

I'd known Dai since I was a kid, and the crush I'd had on him when I was eleven had inspired me to open up to the man. He'd been kind and understood I was struggling to settle into my new role when everyone else expected me to just know what I was doing.

But then, when he'd had dinner at the cottage with Autumn and me, he'd been strange and evasive. He'd hurt and confused me. I'd allowed myself to hope some time together would make everything less awkward. A research trip to the Red Celt realm to see how much I remembered from all my childhood trips here might clarify things. I wanted to find out what kind of man Dai had grown into. He'd been evasive during our weird dinner in Galicia, but he'd told me he could answer all my questions in his own home.

Four thousand two hundred and ninety-seven.

Yes, I was counting. When I got to five thousand, I planned to transport back to my warm civilised cottage and have a long hot bath to thaw out. Tilly would probably join me in the bath—it was large enough for us both. I stroked my shivering, distressed dog and sent her messages about *not far now, baby, just hang on.* And *it'll be OK. There'll be chicken and a fire, I promise. And if there isn't, we'll go straight home.*

Dai had said it would take no longer than an hour and a quarter, possibly less—that was four and a half thousand seconds. The fact I even knew this should show you the lengths, including random mental arithmetic, I'd gone to just to prevent myself from either exploding in fury or bursting into tears. He had 5000 seconds, which included a generous margin for error, but it was all I could stand in this hell-hole wilderness of whiteout. I was a city girl, dammit!

Four thousand five hundred and sixty-two.

My main consolation was, once I got to Dai's damn house, I'd be able to transport there any time I needed to. I'd NEVER have to make this horrible trek again. I moaned softly.

Everyone has an internal thermostat. Apparently, some people are rarely cold, and others don't complain when the thermometer hits stupid highs. The Caribbean end of Aysha's family had been amazed when, on a holiday in our twenties, I'd coped fine during a heat wave when the temperature and humidity hit almost the same triple digits.

But I hate the cold.

With. A. Passion.

I'm almost certain my toes dropped off about half a mile back, but at least my fingers had stopped throbbing, or maybe they were gone too.

Four thousand, six hundred and—

"Here we are."

I stopped dead and tried to wipe my streaming eyes as Dai pointed towards a low-lying, stone hut-type structure. I didn't care. If it had a wood-burning stove or even just a fire, it would be my new favourite place. Then the building wavered, and my vision of the hut faded. Was it an illusion? Like an oasis?

OMG. I must be in heaven, or Valhalla, or paradise. Honestly, I'd never been certain there was a proper afterlife, but if there were, I'd often doubted I'd ever get there.

The mountain was a nasty place to die. I hoped it wasn't Mabon who found my body. It would upset him. But if this was what death by exposure felt like, it beat a shark attack any day of the week. At least I seemed to be in one piece.

I sipped the hot mulled wine and sank below the warm water of the hot tub, gazing around in amazement. This place was unbelievable. Tilly barked once, softly. It was her "I feel better now, Mum; is there chicken?" bark. I'd always hoped you could take your animals with you to heaven or whatever version of the afterlife this might be. I sighed happily, my struggles over, and sank beneath the water.

OK, perhaps that had all been delirium caused by my sheer relief at being out of the snow.

What actually happened was we made it through the door and into a small, dark, cramped corridor. Dai opened a cupboard door and handed me, oh the blessed relief, a large, warm towel.

"Don't try to get warm or dry—it doesn't work. I know a better way. Just strip off and put your swimsuit on. You brought it, didn't you?"

I gaped at him. I had, because, like an idiot, I'd thought I was going on a holiday, not an endurance challenge, but I nodded.

"Good, give Tilly to me. I'll dry her off and warm her up." His hands as he reached for Tilly were warm, almost hot in fact. I couldn't even feel my own fingers or toes; I must ask him what brand of gloves he recommended. Tilly went to Dai happily and was soon swathed in another warm towel.

He pushed me into a small but modern shower room and said, "Hurry. You need to thaw out," and pulled the door closed on my questions.

When I came out, he'd shepherded me, steering me by my elbow from behind as if I were a shopping trolley, through to a covered, glassed-in terrace. Then he picked me up and simply dropped my stumbling self into the hot tub.

Later, I had vague memories of being fed soup

and a sandwich, and Dai showing me to my room. The bed was large, with a warm duvet.

Tilly and I snuggled together under it. My final thought was this is a great start to our holiday, isn't it? But at least it can't get any worse.

So much for being psychic then, Niki?

PART TWO
THURSDAY

Find a trusted mentor who has already traversed the path ahead of you.

Do not dismiss their advice lightly unless they have a great deal of scarring.

In that case, you may want to be more prudent than they were—but still give their counsel full consideration. Vital life lessons can be learned from others' scars.

Remember, never making a mistake is the biggest mistake of all. Caution is not a good teacher.

Finding Your Inner Fire: How to Claim Your True Self by Peggy Hwybon

FOUR

Thursday, 25th February—Pencoed—Mynydd Cefn y Ddraig (Dragon's Back Mountain)—Red Celt Realm. Dark O'clock.

It was pitch black when I woke. I felt human again, although I was hungry and desperate for caffeine, with an intense, thumping pressure headache behind my eyes.

The house was quiet, but once I got out of my room, light spilled through a doorway. I headed towards it and entered a modern kitchen, spacious and well designed, if a little clinical. The down-lighters reflected off sparkling worktops. I was looking for the coffee maker when Dru's head popped out of an adjoining door. Mabon's magical immortal companion, Drudwyn, who normally chose the form of an enormous Scottish deerhound, had been my horse when I was a child. Since my recent power boosts from the Gateway, we'd had simple mental communications.

"Hey, lad," I whispered.

Huuuunnnngry echoed inside my head.

"OK, where's your food? And the coffee maker?"

Dru emerged, stood by a kettle on the worktop, and gazed at the cupboard above it. I opened the cupboard: instant coffee and tea bags, along with some empty storage jars. I sighed, put the kettle on, and turned back to him. "Your food?"

He padded back through the side door, and I followed him into a utility room with two large fridge freezers. He stood by one of them. Opened, it proved to be completely full of what I could only identify as "meat." The entire bottom shelf was filled with a lump of something red, which Dru was gazing at hopefully. "This?"

Haaalllf.

"You mean you can have half of it?"

He simply nosed gently past me into the fridge, seized one side of the meat in his powerful jaws, and pulled. Huh, it had already been cut into two pieces before being stuffed into the fridge.

I held on to the piece that was obviously supposed to stay in the fridge and let him take his share. On the top shelf were several cooked chicken breasts. Aww, Dai had asked me what Tilly ate. There was several days' worth of her kibble in my suitcase, but the moment I looked at the chicken breast, I heard her claws skittering on the tiles behind me. How do dogs do that?

I chopped the chicken to appease Tilly. She was probably as hungry as I was. The moment the kettle boiled, I opened the jar of instant coffee. Yuck! I wasn't just being a spoilt Recorder. I hadn't drunk instant coffee since my student days and had forgotten just how unlike real coffee it was. But, adding insult to my pain, this coffee was stale. I chipped rather than spooned granules into a mug, then sipped. Even for instant, it didn't taste right. I found the sell-by date on the jar. 2014. Dai obviously did not drink coffee. I grabbed my phone to check in with Dola and get myself something drinkable.

No signal.

I pulled power.

Actually, I didn't. Nope, no power here either.

I tried again, but I was pulling on nothing.

I swiped at my phone, looking for the wi-fi network.

More nothing.

What the hell? Dola had told me I'd be in contact up here, hadn't she? I ran the conversation back through my mind. When I'd said I shouldn't leave with all the things that were happening, Dola had specifically told me my earbuds and my phone would work.

Maybe all the snow had affected the connection? Oh well, Dai would be up at some point and tell me how to access whatever connection there was and where I could find a coffee machine. In the nearest shop, I was beginning to suspect, but there wouldn't be anything open at six a.m. I'd have to hold out. In the meantime, I was starving. In the utility room, the other fridge held normal stuff, including, oh yeah, eggs and bacon.

I was assembling breakfast items when I heard, "Up early you are." Dai's Welsh accent was more noticeable than usual. Perhaps he wasn't awake yet.

"Hey, good morning, I think I missed dinner. Sorry I passed out. The walk was insane. I only planned to rest my eyes for five minutes, not sleep for hours."

He gave me a warm smile. His short, thick, dark hair stood on end, but he looked good. His eyes, so like his dad's, but the darker blue of lapis lazuli, twinkled at me as he said, "Let me make us some breakfast. I see you fed Dru."

"Yep, and Tilly. It's only the people who haven't eaten. I couldn't find the coffee maker?"

Dai looked at the mug of coffee on the table. "What's that?"

"Oh, it's instant. I was desperate, but it's seven

years out of date, stale and nasty. So, I'm ready for the real thing now?"

"That's all I've got."

"Oh." Dola to the rescue then I hoped. "Is the wi-fi down because of the weather?"

"No wi-fi either."

"What about the phone signal? My phone's got nothing."

Dai drew in a breath and, in the careful voice you might use to a panicked animal, said, "There isn't any wi-fi up here. Or phone signal either. That's why I asked you about magicking my phone, remember?"

I frowned. Without coffee, my brain was obviously on a go-slow. "But my phone already runs on the Rainbow Network. And it's still not connecting up here."

He shrugged. "I'm not great with tech. That's Rhiannon's arena. She always has a signal, but I don't know how she does it."

OK, so no drinkable coffee and no connection to anything. But I'd brought a Dolina. It ran purely on the magic of the Rainbow Network. It would work anywhere the power could reach. "Are you really OK with making breakfast?"

"Of course, I'm not a fancy cook, but I make a mean breakfast."

"Cool, I'll go and get dressed." I gestured pointlessly at my dressing gown and bare feet as though he hadn't noticed I wasn't dressed yet. As I returned to my bedroom with Tilly at my heels, a rising discomfort unsettled me, but I wasn't sure why.

I retrieved the Dolina from my case and prodded it. There wasn't an on/off switch. It didn't need power or a wi-fi connection, it just worked—usually. But it showed me a dead screen. Softly, I said, "Dola? Come in, Dola. Are you there?" the way they did with radios in old movies.

Nothing happened.

I felt panicky. Surely it wasn't simply being without the power? For heaven's sake, I'd lived without power for the first forty-one years of my life. A few days couldn't be the end of the world. I was on holiday. I should chill out. A little unplugged time would do me good.

Transporting was part of the McKnight Recorder's gift. I didn't need the Rainbow Network to do it. So I'd transport down to Pant y Wern, buy a coffee machine, and the world would make sense again—right?

But the niggling feeling in my tummy said —wrong.

I grabbed my jeans and a new thing: a pretty combination of bra and thermal vest. I hadn't worn it yet, but after yesterday, extra warmth seemed a good plan. Throwing a nice and also cosy shirt on over it, I glanced in the too-small, too-high trendy stainless-steel-framed mirror. The top of my hair looked colourful—I'd just have to hope about the rest of me.

It wasn't cold in the house. As I put boots onto my perfectly warm feet, I realised there must be underfloor heating. How peculiar! Why would somebody have something as up-to-date as underfloor heating and yet no decent coffee or wi-fi?

The kitchen smelt of good things when I got back there. I put the kettle back on and decided I'd rather have tea than more undrinkable coffee. Tea went with breakfast, didn't it? My question to Dai revealed he'd have a tea too, with milk and one sugar, please.

The light had changed in here, and I finally noticed the whole back wall of the room was glass. The sun was coming up, and the sky was lightening. "Hey, the snow stopped. It was insane yesterday. Does it do that often up here?"

Dai smiled at me. "It wasn't the best welcome for you, was it? Yes, we're snow-covered up here pretty much from November until March, sometimes even April. But normally we just hunker down while it's actually snowing. Yesterday was unusual."

I made a non-committal sound as he dropped cutlery too noisily next to the two mugs of tea on the shiny glass kitchen table and asked me, "Anything you don't eat?"

"No, whatever's going will be great, thanks."

This was all a bit stilted, wasn't it? But I didn't know how to relax myself. I felt strangely off. My Gift was niggling at me, and I really needed to check in with Dola and make sure everything was alright.

As Dai obviously didn't need my help, I picked up the hardback on the table. It was stamped with Proof Copy and the title *Finding your Inner Fire: How to Claim your True Self* by Peggy Hwybon. Intrigued, I leafed through it, laughed and settled in to read.

Dai took it out of my hands and put a placemat in front of me instead. The book disappeared. Wow, protective or just rude? Should I have asked if I could touch it?

"Sorry, was that private?"

Dai gave me a quick surprised glance. "No, the publisher sent it to me requesting a quote for the jacket. But the woman's an idiot. Da will send her something polite. But you wouldn't want to read while you eat, would you?"

I bit back my instinctive response of, "Well, I often do," and instead smiled politely. I'd need to remember I was a guest. Guest manners, Niki, find some.

The breakfast smelt appetising. He was obviously trying to be hospitable. He just hadn't yet grasped I ran on coffee. It would all be better once I'd acquired a coffee maker—wouldn't it?

Once we'd eaten, and it was a more civilised hour, I'd pop down to Pant y Wern and Mabon's castle home. I had an appointment with Glynis, Mabon's castle manager. He'd made me smile when I asked him about her. He'd said, "Don't call her a house-keeper; she's a CEO crossed with a general."

I looked forward to meeting her. She'd have coffee, wouldn't she? Glynis had acted as an informal therapist to a lot of Troels' victims. When I took over from Gran, she'd encouraged many of the women Troels had raped to file paternity cases. The various authorities in the realms had shown no inclination to deal with any of their accusations. Glynis had thought arbitration requests to the Recorder peti-tioning for support payments for the children might be a way to shine a light on the problem.

I'd learnt all this from Fi when she'd told me about her own experience and subsequent single motherhood. She said Glynis had been wonderful with the women and offered informal support groups and much more.

I needed to gather any information I could before announcing the Recorder's decision about whether I would hear those petitions. I hoped Glynis could clarify some things for me, so I'd be more comfort-able about the right way to proceed without stressing the women unnecessarily.

Dai put two plates on the table. Wow! Now here

was a breakfast for a hungry woman. I smiled happily at crisp bacon, poached eggs, browned sausages, baked beans, a slice of golden fried bread, and something that might have been a slice of black pudding finished with rolled oats or maybe an over-done potato cake.

I dug in. It was excellent. "You *do* make a mean breakfast, thank you." I cut into the potato cake, and something oozed out. "OK, what's this?"

Dai glanced over at my plate, where my knife poked a green, spinach-like goo. It smelled odd. Fishy.

"It's laverbread."

"It doesn't look like bread—it's green."

He laughed. I ate some sausage and slipped a bit to Tilly. It was good. "Is this one of those hazing things? Tell the stupid visitor it's actually food?"

Still laughing, he said, "No, very traditional laver-bread is. Ask my Da. He loves the stuff. He'll put it in anything, but it's nice with eggs. Truly."

Cautiously, I pushed a small amount onto some egg and tried it. He was right, it *was* good with eggs. For some reason, it made me think of Rollo. Perhaps it was just the seaside smell of it. I had some more with my sausage. "Is it safe for dogs?"

"Once it's cooked, yes. Dru likes it too but not raw."

"What is it when it's raw?"

"It's laver, edible seaweed."

I was really glad I'd already swallowed it. But to be fair, it was an interesting umami taste. I bet it dissolved into soups and stews and left intriguing flavours in its wake. I said this, and Dai huffed a laugh. "You sound just like Da. Don't get him started on campfire meals and how laverbread was the only thing that made squirrels or rodents into a nice dinner back in the first millennium."

The sun was coming up. I checked my useless phone. Still no signal, but it was almost eight o'clock. I gazed out of the window and admired the snowy peaks as they gradually became more visible in the distance. I'd just have to deal with being stuck here for another hour. Maybe in the meantime I could get to the bottom of all the things Dai hadn't been able to tell me during our dinner in the Galician realm?

"Well, I'm here, and you said you'd be able to talk if I came." Out of my jeans pocket, I pulled the piece of paper from our dinner in Galicia when he hadn't even been able to remember the questions I'd asked him. There were eight questions on it. I handed it to him.

"Do you want to make a start on these?"

A look of panic crossed his face, but he took a breath and reached out for the slip of paper just as Dru let out one abrupt bark and arrived at the kitchen table.

"*Cachu*, sorry, Nik, I need to go. I should only be an hour, two at the most. Just relax, help yourself to anything you need, and I'll be back as soon as I can. We'll get to these then."

I would behave like a grown-up. Was it only me who thought Dai had a lot of convenient interruptions in his life? But to be fair to him, he felt sincere, and my shoulders remained quiet.

"No problem, I have an appointment with Glynis this morning, anyway. Shall we meet back here at lunchtime?"

But he shook his head. "You can't get down the mountain right now; it's not safe. Stay here. Stay inside. Do not go out." He sounded serious, stern even.

"Is Pant y Wern in danger?"

"No, it'll be fine in town. Stay inside, Nik. Just wait. I won't be long." He stuffed the last sausage on his plate into his mouth and grabbed a jacket from the back of a chair.

I stood up. "Where are you going?"

"Over to Dragon's Back."

"I thought this was Dragon's Back?"

He looked hassled. "It is. Well, it's more Dragon's Shoulder. I'll just be on the other side of the mountain." He pointed.

He gave me a brief hug. I relaxed into it and sniffed subtly, but he didn't even smell right. There was the coal smoke scent but no woody aroma. He was hot as always, though how did he stay so warm all the time?

"But if Pant y Wern is fine, why can't I keep my appointment with Glynis? It's rude not to let her know, and with no phone, I can't call her. I can be back before lunchtime. I have responsibilities too, Dai. This is an important meeting."

"You'll have to re-schedule. It's not safe."

"But why? If it's OK in town, and I'm going to be in town, at the castle."

He swore in Welsh, then rounded on me, anger on his face. In a too-loud voice that held an undertone I didn't like, he said, "Just bluddy stay here. Stay inside. Don't open the door. Don't go outside. It's safe here. I'll be back."

He followed Dru and left swiftly, entering some numbers on a keypad by the door as he went. As the door clicked shut behind him, I heard several short beeps and one long one. Had he armed the house alarm? I promptly tried the back door, but it was locked.

What the hell?

How had we gone from a pleasant, if slightly uncomfortable breakfast, to me being imprisoned in a house on a mountain like a naughty teenager?

With no damn coffee, no damn wi-fi and hot fury building inside me.

CHAPTER
FIVE

The room was cramped with a crackling fire, a small round table, a desk, two large book-cases, a filing cabinet, two upright wooden chairs, and no room for anything else.

Glynis, Mabon's castle manager, was small. Shorter even than my five-foot-nothing, but unlike me, she had a sturdy build. Not fat, not even plump. It looked like solid muscle under her pale skin. I struggled to pin down her age. She could have been anything from early forties to early sixties. Her energy felt fiftyish, but her unlined face didn't match my assessment. Her unruly but still dark reddish-brown hair framed lively brown eyes and a pleasant face. She smiled politely at me, bowed, and held out her hand.

"Recorder, I wondered if you'd make it down the mountain."

"Oh, down was the easy bit. Making it up there was the challenge!"

I expected a smile from her, but I got a confused frown. "Sorry, did I say something wrong?"

She shook her head slowly. "Did you get a lift down, then?"

I'd simply transported into a space behind one of the castle's storage sheds I remembered from my childhood. Luck had been with me, and nothing had changed. The only thing I'd bothered with my sudden arrival had been a Highland coo who must have become separated from the herd.

I'd waited almost two and a half hours for Dai with my headache and caffeine deprivation getting worse by the minute. Then I'd sworn and used my transportation power to get to Pant Y Wern. The moment I landed and had a phone signal, I'd time travelled back and shaved my wasted hours off so I could attend my appointment with Glynis and get back before Dai realised I was even gone. The moment I reconnected to the Rainbow Network, my Gift stopped nagging at me.

When Dai left, I'd initially sat and fumed, devising suitable punishments for an idiot who hadn't thought to buy any coffee in the last seven years. Then I'd marched round the house trying to burn off my anger and confusion. Dai's home was beautiful and much bigger than it had initially appeared. Not in the magical way my cottage or the Gateway were, but because it was only a single storey at the front, where we'd entered last night.

But at the back, the architect had used the natural slope of the landscape. The house sprawled down the side of the mountain with three floors. There was a large terrace with a glassed-in inner part where I'd been in the hot tub last night. The outer section was open to the elements and currently under several feet of snow.

It was all spotless and modern, but I didn't think Dai had completely moved in yet. The fabric of the building was gorgeous. A lot of glass and multi-height rooms, but none of the soft furnishings had arrived yet. The inside was bare and sharp-edged, still waiting for rugs, fabrics, lamps and personal touches.

I decided I had no obligation to explain myself to Dai. He'd triggered me when he'd ignored my questions, dismissed the idea I might know a safe way to Pant y Wern and issued instructions like a sergeant-major to a recruit. He'd been weird and controlling with all his "you have to stay inside, Niki, and be safe" admonitions.

But mostly, I'd just needed a drinkable coffee.

Whoops, I'd got lost in my thoughts, and Glynis

was waiting patiently for an answer I couldn't give her. *Get it together, Nik, or she'll think you're crazy.*

Tilly came to my rescue by poking her head out of my tote bag as she woke. Her breakfast of slightly too much chopped chicken and several pieces of my sausage had put her straight back to sleep.

Once Glynis had finished cooing at her and making all the usual *she's so fluffy* noises, she'd forgotten her question, and I pressed on with mine. "Did Fi speak to you?"

"Yes, my lady, she told me you're prepared to deal with Troels. If the tales are right, and the livestream as accurate as the TEK said it was. If Troels really tried to hurt this little cutie, I can see why you might not be as blind to his—" she stopped as if unsure how to continue.

I said it for her, "His half a century pattern of raping but not bothering to pillage?"

Glynis seemed to let out a sigh of relief. "Oh, thank Mother Modron, Fi's right, you're not like Elsie."

I'd put up with this from Fi because she'd worked with Gran for over twenty years. They'd been close, and Fi had been adjusting to a lot of changes. But I didn't know this woman. What was that saying? I can be rude about my family, but you better hadn't be—at least within my hearing? Honestly, if one more person said I wasn't like Gran, I might lose my patience. It had been funny at first, but the refrain was becoming tedious.

I put a little steel into my tone. "I probably am, you know. She was my grandmother, and I'm definitely a McKnight."

An uncomfortable expression crossed her face, and I reached out with my Gift to see why. Something I'd only experienced before with the senior kings happened. As I reached out, she met me halfway. She was trying to read me too. I strengthened my shields. "Was there something particular you wanted to know?"

"My apologies, my lady. I'm making a mess of this. You're not what I expected. Can I offer you tea?" She gestured at the table with a teapot, milk jug and sugar waiting on it. I wanted to be polite but not enough to drink any more tea today.

Wow, I had been really stressed because I'd forgotten to ask Dola to send me coffee. Gods and Goddesses, Niki, find your brain.

Thinking quickly, I said, "No, thank you, I left my coffee somewhere. Let me just take this call and collect it." I opened the camera on my phone. "I put it down just outside. Pour your tea, and I'll be right back."

Once through the doorway, I hissed, "Dola?" into my earbud.

"Give me a 360 please, Niki."

I swung the camera in a circle around me. On a stone ledge just outside the door, an enormous take-away cup emitting the characteristic caramel and coffee fragrance arrived.

"I owe you, girl. Thank you from the bottom of my caffeine-deprived heart."

"Niki, can we talk please before you go back up the mountain? It was distressing not being able to reach you. I am looking into why you were off-grid, and I have some other information."

"Of course, I'm sorry, but let me go back in before Glynis thinks I'm even stranger than she already does." I felt guilty. I'd been so angry with Dai, I'd forgotten everything except my appointment with Glynis and hadn't contacted Dola. I was all over the place this morning. "Listen in and message me if anything's urgent—OK? We'll catch up as soon as I've finished this."

"Recorders are often eccentric. I would recommend yet again you cease attempting to conform."

Huh. She might be right. I'd been making progress on not having to be polite, cautious Niki all the time. But Dai's odd energy had thrown me off. *Stay here. Be quiet. Be safe. Do as you're told.* It had all made me feel less like my more powerful Recorder-ish self. The one I'd begun to like and enjoy being.

I walked back into the small room. Glynis half-stood at the table, and I pulled out a chair and looked at her until she said, "I'm sorry, my lady. Please sit, be comfortable."

Everyone had made this woman sound like a powerhouse. Even Mabon was cautious not to offend her, and Fi respected her. Why was she being so tentative and apologetic with me?

She took a deep breath. "My lady, I'm an empath and used my talent on auto-pilot. I did not mean to offend."

I wasn't judging her. After all, I'd been doing the same myself.

I locked my personal feelings and private business away behind my shields the way Ad'Rian had taught me so many years ago. On the surface of my mind, I left my emotions about Troels, the Vikings, my experiences with the Recordership so far, and my worries about all these women and how I could help them. I hoped my anger at Dai wouldn't leak through.

I laid my hand on the table and asked, "Quid pro quo?"

"Sorry, what?"

"Shall we read each other?"

Shock blazed on her face. I said, "What? If you're an empath, you must be able to recognise others with talent? Mine is a bit different, but ..." I waited.

Almost stuttering now, she said, "Since I moved

back here, only Rhiannon, and no one reads her. Well, no one who lives to tell about it."

"But I'm not her. I don't mind sharing. I was only startled at being probed without discussion or consent."

She flushed. "I didn't get any information except your lack of caffeine and your concern about your dog. Your shields are tight, my lady."

I smiled. "I know. Ad'Rian was a wonderful teacher, and I started very young." I'd never been a woman who boasted, but something about Glynis confused me, and I wanted to find out what. I waggled my fingers on the table.

She reached out, and when she took my hand, I schooled my face into an impassivity that would have made Ad'Rian very proud.

What the hell?

"Are you? … How are you …? I mean, is what I'm sensing correct? Are you truly part dragon?"

SIX

The door to Glynis's office swung open with a bang. Tilly jumped up, letting out a happy woof. "Ah, Nik-a-lula, there you are. Sensed you were around, but couldn't bluddy track you down, could I? Glynis, good morning to you, very fine you look today."

I stood up and was enveloped in a bear hug from my favourite man in the world. His scent of fresh pine, autumn leaves and wood smoke soothed me and allowed me to breathe more freely. I hugged him back hard and then just leaned on him.

He held me away from him and considered me carefully while Dru and Tilly licked noses and completed their greeting ritual. But what was Dru doing here? He'd only just left with Dai on this timeline.

Mabon stared at my chest, then, with a tiny gasp, grasped my elbow just as his son had done the previous evening. He steered me towards the door, saying, "Excuse us, Glynis. Need a word with the Recorder. Bring her back shortly, I will."

I dug my heels in and reached back to the table for my coffee. This day had not yet contained enough caffeine for me to proceed with the plan I'd hatched when I'd put the locket on yesterday.

Mabon steered me along the corridor to a room I knew well, his private day chamber. It was about twenty times larger than Glynis's overstuffed office.

Like Ad'Rian's study, Mabon's private rooms in the castle hadn't changed in the almost thirty years since I'd last visited him. There was still a welcoming crackling fire, still his large, comfortable armchairs. He steered me into one by the fire. Honestly, I was a little tired of the ap Modron men treating me like a shopping cart. Move her here, move her there. However, I sat, folded my hands around my warm coffee and watched as the dogs settled together in front of the fire.

The room's scents of leather, wood smoke and damp dog started to soothe me.

In a gentle voice, which, to my intuition, held a lot of underlying tension, he pointed at Agnes's locket. "Where did you get that, *bach*? See it I would, please?"

"No."

Astonishment crossed his face. "Nik-a-lula!"

"Don't you Nik-a-lula me, Boney. I've had just about enough right now. It's not yours. It's a McKnight family heirloom. You know exactly what it is, and if I give it to you, you won't answer my questions. Oh, you'll be lovely, and you'll muss my hair and hug me and make me feel better. But I won't get any of the information I need. And I really need your help with Dai. And I have questions about Dru and Glynis and Troels and ..." I wound down like a tired clock.

I couldn't be angry with Mabon. He was giving me his kicked puppy expression. All sad eyes and tilted head. I always fell for it. I'd been a sucker for an unhappy Mabon, even when I was a child. He'd say, "Now your gran would be very cross with me if we ate any more ice cream today, so let's not." And we hadn't.

But I'd given this a lot of thought. All these people—Mabon, probably Ad'Rian, and possibly even Dai—had some of the answers I urgently needed that the Book couldn't or wouldn't help with. Not solely about Agnes, but after my confusing dream, you can bet I'd added her to my list.

"Your Majesty, you haven't been available for almost a week. The Recorder has questions. If I let you look at the locket, I won't get any answers, and you know it."

I needed to seize my opportunity and stop him from being my lovable mentor and honorary dad and make him give me some answers.

He sat in the adjoining armchair in front of the fire. Noticing I was still cold, he passed me a throw from the back of his own chair.

"What's your main question, my lady?" My title meant he was taking this seriously—well, good. I was serious, and I wasn't happy with any of the ap Modrons right now. Well, except Dru, of course. Dru was adorable, but how was he here when he'd been out with Dai and I'd time-travelled back? Surely he should still be up the mountain?

Mabon just waited, watching my face carefully.

"I have about six urgent ones. I've been trying to reach you since Dola's birthday party on Sunday. Sending me cute gifs and funny memes instead of answering my questions needs to stop. I'm delighted you're enjoying your phone, but, I need information please. Shall we start with how is Dru here?"

At my question, Dru stopped licking Tilly's paw, raised his head and woofed softly. *Boooored, shooouting.*

"Why wouldn't he be here?"

"Because your son took Dru out with him. Or maybe Dru took your son out with him. Oh, I don't know. Dai got up in the middle of breakfast, told me it wasn't safe to leave the house. He locked me in—" I cut myself off as I heard my voice rise to a stressed, screeching pitch and breathed in.

I tried again, "Your son didn't just lock me in, Boney. I told him the Recorder had an important meeting, and he still wouldn't listen and tried to lock the Recorder in his house. Isn't that a crime?"

I stopped to breathe, but Mabon was frowning now.

"He told me to reschedule my meeting with Glynis. Although he didn't have any suggestions about how I might actually do it stuck up the damn mountain with no phone signal. He said it wouldn't be possible to get down the mountain today, and it wasn't safe outside. I should cower in the house. Then he left me, locked in, with instant freaking coffee. *Stale* instant coffee."

My voice had risen again—crap, I needed to get a grip on myself. I swigged my coffee, which blessedly was still hot.

Mabon laughed now. The bastard laughed.

"Well, you ignored him, as any woman with a backbone would, and you have coffee." He sniffed. "A caramel macchiato, even. Been days since I had one. Forget I do, how good they are until I smell them."

I offered him my own cup, which was so much

bigger than a Venti, I'd no clue what to call it. I'd never drink it all before it went cold, so why be petty?

Oh, damn it. No!

He was doing it to me again. Was Mabon's superpower getting people to be reasonable?

He drank deeply before handing it back to me, then he gave me a long, assessing look and seemed to shake himself. "How far can you push the time turning thing now?"

I prevented my mouth from dropping open with a real effort of will and just stared at him. "The Book says people don't or shouldn't know about that?"

"Trusted, I've been by the power and a few Recorders over the years, so how long can you borrow?"

I shrugged. "Not sure. Hours. Eight or ten is the longest I've done. But if the power lets me do it, then it's fine."

"Ask the power what time you need to leave here to get back to the house before Dai loses his bluddy mind."

I did. I pulled a little power—how wonderful it was to do it again—and asked.

"It says I can take the time we need to calm me down and get my answers, but as I'm already time travelling right now, I'm not to leave this room. I don't quite understand why. But it does, and it's clear. If I stay in here with you, and we don't affect anything or anyone else, we're fine."

"Now ask it if you can take me back with you when we're finished, because I have some important meetings today?"

I did. The power was unbothered as long as we stayed privately in Mabon's day chamber and didn't involve anyone outside of it. It was fine with me taking Mabon back to the current time once we'd finished.

Over the next five minutes, Mabon summoned various members of his staff. He sent my apologies to Glynis and told her I'd have to reschedule as something urgent had come up. I caught up with Dola and told her I'd be here a while, then warned her I'd time travel back to earlier, so she didn't worry or get upset as she had done once before.

Food for us and the dogs arrived, along with logs for the fire. Mabon locked the door, told his steward we were not to be disturbed on pain of pain until he opened it again. The steward backed away carefully, assuring his king he would remain undisturbed.

"Ask Dola for two more macchiatos, would you?" He frowned at the enormous cup I held. "Normal size, *bach*. More we can always get. Now start with the most important things. Answer everything I can, I will. Then you will allow me to hold the locket. A deal do we have?"

I looked at the size of the coffee cup. "Is there still a bathroom in here?"

His wonderful laugh rang out as he pointed to a familiar door at the back of the chamber.

"My first time-stealing rodeo this is not, *bach*."

Hmm, interesting, had he and Agnes...? I cut my thought off and concentrated on the things I needed information about. "So how is Dru here when he left the house up the mountain," I consulted my phone, "about twenty minutes ago with Dai?"

"Stay where or when he doesn't want to, Dru won't. Just like you, he is. If Dai was being annoying, Dru would just come back here. Peas in a pod, you two always were."

"Is Glynis part-dragon?"

"No, *bach*." I breathed a sigh of relief, which cut off sharply when he added, "A full dragon, she is. And it's why she came home to work for me, of course."

My face must have shown everything I was thinking. In his gentlest tone, he asked, "Is her dragon-kin status the most important thing you need to know right now? Or should we put all the dragon questions into one bucket?"

He sipped his macchiato and watched me carefully. "Talk about the dragons, we must. Furious about John Fergusson, they are. Submitted requests to me for one of their own to supervise his sentence.

Not an unreasonable thing. The Fergussons' negligence, not just John but his father and grandfather too, may have hit the dragons the hardest. Fair it is to ask for retribution. But messy eaters they are, so it will have to be Rhiannon."

I gaped, and, for the life of me, I couldn't close my mouth as I tried to process his statements.

He took pity on me. "So, add it to the Dragon Bucket too, hey?"

I just nodded helplessly.

"So what easier questions might you have for me?"

I swallowed hard, and my suddenly dry mouth remembered it had coffee. I sipped and considered. There were more important questions for the King of the Red Celts, for sure. But the thing that kept getting in my way was the emotions Dai had churned up in me. I hated how he'd tried to make me feel powerless again. "What is Dai's damn problem?"

He laughed. His wonderful warm, infectious laugh rolled over me and warmed my frightened, unhappy insides. "Oh, *bach*, by the Goddess, my mother herself, that's a question, isn't it? More specific could you be? Which problem? Such a glorious abundance to choose from the boy has."

He was right. What was my biggest problem with Dai? Oh yeah, I knew! The ridiculous dinner we'd tried to have in Santiago while the *Carnaval* went on all around us, and he couldn't answer a single question I'd asked. Or even remember I'd asked them. Then this morning when I pulled the questions out, he'd looked panicky and run away again.

"His inability to answer even simple questions, or even to remember them seconds later. His inability to lower his shields. Or admit he even has them. His stupid paranoia about Dola, even though he made the mistake, not her. His total lack of understanding that a Recorder can't and won't just sit up a mountain like a child who needs to be left in a playpen. *He locked me in, Boney!*"

My last words came out on a wail, and I was mortified when a sob followed them.

In seconds, I was in his arms. And, yes, he was mussing my hair, and damn him, yes, I felt much better. I gave in and sobbed. Eventually, he gave me his handkerchief, and when I looked up at him to apologise, there was an expression I didn't recognise on his face. I reached out with my Gift, but before I could sense a thing, he'd put me back in my chair.

"Guilt, *bach*. Guilt is what you'd find if I let you, and some of those things I'm guilty about aren't mine to share. But some of the sins you mentioned, I think I may have created. Sorry I am." He gestured at Agnes's locket. "As she herself often said, I do not consider all the possible out-comings before I take action. But fix them, I will. Give me a few days. So let's add it to the Dragon Bucket and move to the next thing."

But I couldn't do that. I trusted Mabon's word, but Dai hadn't even resonated as the same person to me since I came back. When we were kids. No, when I was a kid, and Dai looked like one even if he'd been about ninety at the time, we were close, and he'd been fun. Last week, yesterday, and even this morning, he'd been so angry and awkward. I said some of this to Mabon, and he just looked sadder.

Eventually, he said, "The story isn't mine to tell. You know, a concussion I had?"

Dola had described it as a severe head injury that took months to recover from, but whatever. "Dola mentioned it in passing when she was explaining about the house shields you gave her that go into the past and the future after ..." I trailed off. Had Dola ever explained after what? I didn't think she had. I must ask her.

Mabon just nodded. "Sometimes, forget I do, my own brainwaves and ideas. It's why I was so angry your gran blocked your memories. Not remembering is a terrible thing. Wish it on my worst enemy, I wouldn't. Leave it in my hands, *bach*. Then the boy can explain himself to you. Proper that would be, don't you think?"

He was sincere, so I moved on. "Can I trust Glynis? Not the dragon thing, the Troels thing. She's masterminded all these petitions landing, you know. We're almost into the sixties now, possibly more, and Fi warned me several hundred more are coming if I can get Glais'Nee's help."

"Glynis, hmm, tell you if *you* can trust her, I can't. But trust her, I do. An odd life she's had, but she's a strong woman with a good heart and a solid sense of wrong, right, and justice. She even knows they're not always the same thing. Advanced thinking, that is."

That was high praise from Mabon. Dola's voice came through my earbud, "Seventy-four."

"Sorry, there are seventy-four petitions against him now. The petitions are all paternity claims, because Glynis is clever, and she knows the Recorder wouldn't be able to hear the other cases." I breathed in. "The surely many hundreds more rape cases, according to Fi, that led to seventy-four women who thought they could file paternity suits."

A flash of red light exploded from Mabon, and I focused on him. Whoa! His usual white and silver aura was totally overwhelmed by the red sparks of his anger. It was easy to forget I was dealing with a God King ruled by Aries when he was being my kind mentor, but he was incandescent now—literally. His feet weren't just sparking; they were on fire! He didn't like Troels any more than I did. So why the hell hadn't he done anything about him?

SEVEN

I gave Mabon's flaming feet a resigned smile and did what I'd always done when he lost control. Kept it light. I pointed down, "That's a lovely rug, Boney. Let's not set the pretty flowers on fire, hey?"

Dru stood and butted him with his head, and Tilly clambered up onto my knee and barked sharply once at Mabon. He rummaged in his pockets.

"Sorry, *bach*, I know you don't like them, but the smoke will mostly go up the chimney, and it's the only thing that works once the sparks flare up. Fight fire with fire." He lit a cigarette and inhaled long and slow, and sure enough, all the fireworks and flames surrounding his lower legs calmed.

I remembered he'd gone into my garden for a cigarette when he first understood what my gran and Jamie had done to me. Did his anger always come out on behalf of other people? Before my ascension, it had been me, and now it was the women Troels had abused?

"Boney, it's your own castle. Of course you can smoke if you need to. But if you're so angry about it, why has no one done anything to stop him?"

This was the bit that completely baffled me. "My research so far would suggest it's been going on for more than forty years. I don't know how the hell the man has time to do anything else. People must have been aware?"

Mabon looked calmer as he drew on his cigarette. "Troels now, we're into history there, aren't we then? The Red Celts don't have the power we once did. We couldn't take on the Viking kingdom without our queens. And need the ap Modron power I do for our own realm. Have to think of all my people. Banned Troels from coming here ever again I did, once Glynis explained it to me. But I can't prevent women from going to Viking. Rights they have, you know."

"OK, that's you, but there are other royals?"

He gave me a thoughtful look. "These men, rotten apples, come and go, you know? Thought we did, if we killed him, someone far worse like Halvor might take the throne. Assassinate Rollo, Halvor would have. Only way to the throne for him. And it hasn't affected Ad'Rian. He frightened Troels. Bet, I would, not even one of those names you have are Fae?"

He was right, they weren't. I'd ask Ad'Rian what he'd done to protect his women.

I looked at my watch. "Well, we don't need to talk about it today. But I need your counsel on him and Rollo soon. I can't stop thinking, or maybe I mean worrying, about Rollo. HRH is interfering there, and she rarely gives a toss about anyone. I don't know why she's involving herself in this. And I'm going to need to talk to *all* the monarchs about Troels very soon."

Mabon reached over and picked up a book from a short pile. I recognised it instantly, *Ruling Regally*. "Breanna sent this with an invitation to a book club. I was about to tell her I was busy. A reader, I'm not. But her note said to speak to you before I refused." He held the book out to me, looking confused.

"I know it well. It's hilarious. You might enjoy it. But the book club is only a way for you all to talk about Troels without him accusing everyone of conspiring." Hmm, might that be a part of why they hadn't all ganged together to stop Troels? Mabon had mentioned history and being accused of conspiracy used to be a serious thing, didn't it? The realms had a lot of old-fashioned legislation still on their law books.

Mabon leafed through the book with an unhappy expression on his face. I remembered what had changed Ad'Rian's mind swiftly when he'd asked me if he should come. I added, "It's in the Gateway; Juniper is catering it. Ad'Rian is coming."

Now he gave me his best crooked smile. "Oh, well now, you, Ad'Rian and Juniper's food, come then, of course I will. But I don't read very well. Never had the time to do it, really."

I had a brainwave, grabbed my phone and searched, YES! I sent a screenshot to Dola with my message.

> Niki: Can you put this audiobook on his phone and make sure Mabon listens to it before Breanna's book club?

> Dola: Yes, but it will not be easy.

> Niki: Start him off with the funny bits then?

> Dola: OK.

"Dola's going to help you read it. Audiobooks are wonderful, Boney. I recommend them."

He looked thoughtful then picked up the next book on the pile, the same one I'd tried to read at breakfast in Dai's kitchen this morning.

"Would Dola's plan work for this one too? Publisher needs a recommendation from the king for the cover. I don't think I know the woman, but Hwybon is an ancient Welsh name. Know her family I probably do. Wouldn't want to offend them."

I shook my head and took the book from him. I explained how proof copies are pre-publication and audiobooks come later. Mabon gave me a sad smile, and I had a wicked idea. "Would you like me to read it for you and message you something to send to the publisher in your name?"

His grin was blinding as he nodded so furiously, his curls bounced. I put *Finding your Inner Fire: How to Claim your True Self* by Peggy Hwybon in my bag. Dai had pissed me off when he'd snatched it away so rudely. Anything he didn't want me to read should move to the top of my TBR pile. It might teach me something about these confusing dragons.

"So, Nik-a-lula, have I earned my moment with the locket yet?"

"Two more quick things, then, yes."

I told him all about Ti'Anna's request that I prevent Jamie from being executed for the sake of the legal practice and the central heating. "I didn't think we could try Jamie yet. He's still being healed, and you left it up to me, didn't you?"

"I did, yes. But the Fae isn't wrong. If the boy wants to, he has the right to see his father's sentencing. If the healers think he's up to it. Blood can run hot, and things sometimes happen ahead of the right time. But forewarned by a Fae is forearmed. Leave it with me you can. My word on it. They won't kill him on Friday. After then, well, we'll all need to talk. The decision on him is the Recorder's. Agreed on it, we all did at your ascension."

I undid the locket, watching the naked hunger in his eyes. I'd never seen him look so eager for anything. "One last question about her, Boney?"

"What?" His eyes sparkled in anticipation.

"What was your nickname for her?"

"That note you've found, have you, in the Book?"

I laughed and nodded.

"And how many answers do you know?"

"All of them I think except the ekename."

He gave a low whistle. "So, tell me, what *is* my favourite sweetmeat?"

"I think it's Simnel cake."

His eyes widened. "Taking a grip, you are, on the role in a way few of your ancestors did. Why is that now?" He tilted his head as if to make clear this wasn't a rhetorical question.

"I like to read. I take the Book to bed with me most nights."

He nodded. "Her nickname, forgotten I had we used to call it an ekename. I called her Senga."

"Senga?" I thought about it.

Senga? Senga? Why did I ...?

Then I giggled. "And was she? Backwards, I mean?"

He gave me his wicked, crooked smile. "Not the way the modern parlance would have it. No. A smart girl, she was. But, yes, she lived her life backwards and forwards with the time travel and the transporting. There were no movies then to give her ideas. She worked it all out for herself. Liked to read, she did. Just like you."

"Her notes in the Book are a nightmare. She put conditions and requirements on releasing any information. It's infuriating."

"A powerful seer she was. Tried asking it if she left any notes specifically for you, have you?"

"For me?" How the hell could a woman dead for nearly four hundred years have left notes for me?

"Think about it, *bach*, but for now, earned a moment of joy, I have." He held out his hand.

"Do you want me to take you back in time before or after I lend it to you?"

"I can borrow it?" His face crumpled. Hell, I felt awful for making him wait. But I'd got a lot of answers in a short time, and I wouldn't have done that without the bribe of Agnes's locket, would I?

"Provided we set a time to discuss the Dragon Bucket and you come to the book club to help out with the decision about Troels, what if I leave it with you until St. David's Day? Sorry, Boney, I'd give it to you, truly I would. But there are so many of Agnes's prophecies, and they're mostly incomprehensible at worst or only half-understood at best. The Recorder's Office might need it."

I couldn't give it away. It was a McKnight family heirloom. But I couldn't take it straight off him, either. This felt like a workable compromise.

He nodded solemnly, and I handed it over.

At first, he clasped it in his fist, resting his hand against his cheek. Then he released his grip, and his finger traced the shape I'd thought must be a numeral.

Watching the movement of his finger, though, I had a different idea. "Is that, or rather, was it once an infinity symbol?"

He smiled now. A small, wan smile, but a smile all the same. "She was all about infinity. She'd love those Avengers movies. Loved all the crazy stuff, and she was behind even more. Like it better now, she would, I think. Very little fun stuff back then. A woman centuries ahead of her time, she was, for sure. You know this symbol was always on the locket, and yet, some years it was after her death when I first saw other people using it."

Then, with great care, he opened the heart-shaped locket and was suddenly still. I barely breathed myself, but he impersonated a statue.

Dru was on alert. Even Tilly put her head up. I nudged my Gift. Something was wrong with the locket? What was wrong? I hadn't damaged it, had I?

As he stroked the miniature of my ancestor's face, his own held a soft expression. I'd seen it once before when I asked him about the odd colour my earrings had gone during my ascension. He'd told me about an ancestor of mine who'd owned a necklace of rainbow gold.

Carefully, with his thumbnail, he flicked something inside the casing, and a little heart-shaped door opened. I leaned forward for a better view as he let out a huge laugh. Still laughing, he said something in Welsh far too fast for my extremely limited understanding of the language.

He grinned at me. "She was a one. Unique back then, she was. Becoming very like her in many ways, you are. She found her courage much younger than you. But she didn't have your gran's memory block to contend with, did she? And she ascended too young to the Recordership. How did you find this? Asked for it, I did, after she died. But Elspeth the Witch said she couldn't find it."

"Elspeth the Witch? Do you mean bitch, or did I have an ancestor who was an actual witch?"

He laughed. "No, she was a bitch for sure, but not a witch. Although they burned her as one. Stupid, cruel, unpleasant woman. It was all witch trials back then, and none of the poor women were witches, of course. The real ones were all safe in the realms." He gazed happily down at the locket, running his finger tenderly over the outside.

"Seriously? How could they burn a Recorder? I mean, why didn't she just transport?"

"Elspeth convinced herself the power to transport came from the devil. Superstitious time it was. Refused to do it. And she hated the Book. Said it gave her too many words. I've always blamed her for the decline of the Recorder's Office. But no one expected Agnes to die, and Elspeth was the untrained heir."

"I always wondered which idiot told the Book not to teach us anything we didn't specifically ask. It took me ages to work out why I couldn't get a sensible answer to anything my first week."

Gently, Mabon observed, "Took you a whole week, did it? Elspeth was when, oh …who knows, but after Agnes. Not quite the mid-sixteen-hundreds? So, in four hundred years, give or take, none of your foremothers corrected the mistake? Why would that be?"

"Maybe it was more like ten days? I don't know … perhaps they didn't like to read?"

Then I realised he'd spoken in normal English. He must have been struggling with even more emotion than he was showing. I stood up and held my hand out. "May I see what made you laugh?"

But he closed his fist protectively around the

locket and looked up at me beseechingly. "St. David's Day, you said? Return it then, I will."

I didn't have the heart to fight him. I moved us both back in time and left him alone with the memory of his love.

I must have been trying to do the being in too many times at once thing again because the power wouldn't let me go back to Dai's at 10.30 a.m. when I'd left. It was almost 11.30 a.m. by the clock in his lounge when I got there.

I'd been with Mabon for hours after I'd taken us both back in time. I'd almost gone straight back to my cottage. I didn't want to be up Dai's damn mountain, but Dola said everything was quiet at the cottage, so I'd womanned up. It really was a stupid phrase.

The long living room was empty when I returned. Phew.

Then I saw them through the incredible corner window at the end of the lounge. Full height and set into the brickwork of the house as though the glass had organically grown out of the stone was a three-storey window. And up there, flying, yes, flying over the house, were two dragons.

A Bichon, the Recorder and Dragons, Oh My!

They were graceful and compelling to watch in flight. I stood frozen, still holding Tilly, who was fascinated by them too. The edge of another beautiful rainbow sparkled, but as I tried to focus on it, like the one I thought I must have imagined in the snow yesterday, it disappeared.

And I screamed.

Tilly barked crossly.

Dai now stood between us and the window. His face was red, his expression angry, he appeared to be shouting and was waving his vape device at me. I clicked my earbud to turn my music off. Oh, yeah, he was yelling.

I remembered the promises I'd made to myself when I'd read *Good Grief* for the first time. In the future, I would give people a chance to make any points they wanted to, provided they stayed civil. Then, if I disagreed with them, I'd simply say "no, thank you." If I'd used the strategy with Nick, I wouldn't have ended up with the hideous glossy table in my kitchen or many other things, including him, that I'd never wanted in my life.

The idea Dai was triggering my "dealing with people like Nick" strategies concerned me, but I was here now. I'd better handle it. I swallowed and ran the quick breathing exercise *Good Grief* recommended for those moments when panic threatened.

At least he'd stopped yelling. "So what do you have to say about it?" Dai asked loudly, with an undertone of fury in his voice. I used my Gift to work out what his problem was. But, as usual, I got nothing useful. Only the rock walls of his shields.

I tried words. "I think you're being unreasonable, and I don't know why. But until you calm down and stop shouting at me, I don't see how we can discuss whatever's upset you."

"Whatever's upset me? There was a flaming avalanche." Oh, was that why Glynis asked how I'd come down the mountain and looked confused?

"I *told you* not to leave the house, *not* to go outside, *not* to open the door to anyone. How the hell did you get out, anyway? I know I locked the doors."

So he'd intended to lock me in! It hadn't been an oversight?

It was as if he didn't realise I could transport. But he must, mustn't he? Although I couldn't think of any time I'd done it when he was around. But he'd known Gran? And Mabon knew, and, oh, this was stupid, and it wasn't the point.

Part of me wanted to tell him how ridiculous and unreasonable the idea of locking a grown woman in the house was. Also dangerous. What if there had been a fire, for heaven's sake? The other part saw how red his face was and how scary he looked and wanted to be safe at home—now.

I was lousy at this type of confrontation. Tilly was wriggling to be put down, but I re-seated her firmly on my hip.

I thought longingly of my quiet kitchen. Why hadn't I gone straight home? My stomach was unhappy and didn't want to be here anymore. I didn't *think* it was my Gift. But how would I know for sure?

I held up a hand. He asked, "What?" but his harsh tone didn't invite conversation.

I tried anyway, "I can't do noisy arguments, shouting or drama, Dai. Either calm down, or I'm going until you do."

He crossed to stand between us and the door. "You're not going anywhere until you explain why you ignored my instructions and apologise."

I tightened my grip on Tilly. When Nick had done this to me, I'd always clammed up as I struggled to get my words out. But I'd practised drawing boundaries and making simple statements to wrap around the "no, thank you" statement, breathing between them if necessary.

As calmly as I could manage, I said, "I am the Recorder. I don't owe you an apology. You owe me one for attempting to detain me against my will." I was pretty sure trying to imprison the Recorder was actually a crime in the realms. And he had locked me in. Describing it as his lovely mountain home changed nothing. Anywhere is a prison if you don't want to be there. I took in a breath.

He took a long pull on his vape, but it didn't seem to calm him. He was still shouting, doing what Nick had always done. Carried on talking over me like my words didn't matter. But I'd learnt it did matter, if only to me, to get those words out.

"I don't have to take instructions that come with no explanation anymore. I told you I had important appointments today. I told you I couldn't stay here and be completely out of touch. I told you I have responsibilities."

One look at his darkening face told me this was pointless. It wasn't changing anything.

I reminded myself sternly I couldn't grow up to be Kick-Ass if I kept losing my nerve. Except it wasn't losing my nerve that was frightening me right now. It was the storm of fury brewing inside me. Deep breaths. Stay calm. But the angry tempest threatened to erupt. It tore at the fragile threads of my self-control.

I bit down on it, breathed through my nose to keep my voice steady, and even managed to put a little more volume into it. "You ignored me. As you can see, I'm fine. Now when you're calm, we can talk, but if you carry on shouting and not listening, I'm going until you have your temper under control."

He was still shouting, perhaps even louder. "You had no right to ignore me." He didn't seem to have heard a word I'd said. But then he surprised me. He'd heard the last bit, at least.

"You can't go anywhere. You came here for us to talk. Stop being ridiculous, Niki."

Oh, that freaking did it.

Something snapped.

It might have been my last nerve.

How many times had Nick said something similar? *Stop being ridiculous. Be sensible. Be reasonable. Calm down.* And I was never the one who was shouting.

I pictured my kitchen and thought, GO.

As I left, he shouted, "There's been a bluddy avalanche. There's no way down right now. You can't just run away."

I landed in my warm, cheerful kitchen, put Tilly down, sat at my kitchen table and burst into shaky sobs.

EIGHT

A door closed, and footsteps came down the corridor from Finn's room. They stopped and retreated. Shit, I shouldn't sit here blubbering like an idiot.

I headed to my bathroom to wash my face. The link in my bathroom mirror, which I'd only now realised must have been the very first Dolina ever created, came alive.

"Are you OK, Niki? I was worried last night. It is silly, but I have become accustomed to your presence, and when I could not reach you, I asked Mabon if he had any information."

"What did he say?" I reached for one of the many clean, fluffy white towels Dola always made sure my bathroom was stocked with.

"He explained Dai has no internet connection at his

home. There is no network in most of the mountain regions, but Dru seemed to think you were fine and sleeping. I did not intend to give you incorrect information. I have often reached Mabon when he was at Dai's."

I delved into the drawer below the bathroom countertop for the tube of eye gel. It said it helped with puffy eyes. Let's try it. "Did he mention his damn son's over-controlling tendencies?"

"No, but he told me you'd headed back to Dai's. It surprised him to learn I could not reach you there. Mabon said his phone usually works there. At least outside the house it does."

Something tickled my intuition, or was it just suspicion? I tucked it away for later. "Yeah, like an idiot, I went back. Then I left again. What time is it?"

There was a brief pause. "It is currently three p.m. Do you want to tell me about it?"

"Three p.m.? How can it be three p.m.?"

"Did you forget the time difference between the Red Celt realm and here?"

"Oh, yeah. Sorry. OK, three p.m." No wonder I'd been awake before sunrise. Time zones were a mess.

"Tell me about it, please, Niki. Aysha thought you would be fine if you went, but you seem unhappy."

So I gave her the quick version of my horrid day. And I felt better for getting it out. Dola wasn't like Aysha; she didn't get angry on my behalf. She said helpful things like, "I shall contact Glynis to reschedule and look into why you were unable to connect to any networks at Dai's. I know Rhiannon has a connection in the region. Perhaps we might add her phone to my network."

I couldn't see Rhiannon allowing it, and was certain if I asked her, her reply would end in "off."

"If you are feeling better now, a problem has begun in the Gateway."

"It has? What?" The seven-pointed star tiles inset into my bathroom mirror changed from reflecting my face to showing me the Gateway. It looked peaceful. Fi was at her desk; Finn was walking through the Green sector from my cottage and looked over at the yellow gate as he passed it. He'd used his private entrance instead of taking his usual route through my kitchen. Bless him for giving me privacy to cry it out.

Several people I didn't know were crossing from the Pict's Blue sector to Green. All the travellers glanced across at the yellow gate as they moved through the Gateway. Then the sound came through the speaker in my mirror.

"What the hell? What's that noise?" It was a rhythmic, loud thumping sound, as though someone was hammering steadily on the door.

I pulled my phone out and texted Rollo. As I did,

Dola said, "I have some information from Rollo." But I'd already sent the text.

> Niki: Any idea what's happening on your side of the Gate?

> Rollo: He has some men trying to chop into the Gate. I let Dola know.

> Niki: Sorry, I was up a mountain. Red Celt realm. No signal.

> Rollo: If I can do anything, shout.

"Dola, have you discovered any more than the fact Troels has people attacking the door?"

I looked around for the Book as I walked back to my bedroom. There it was.

"Any advice on what I should do about people trying to chop the yellow gate down?" I opened the Book as I asked.

It flipped a single page. **Act swiftly, decisively, and conclusively. No one should remain unpunished for attacking any part of the Gateway. EVER.**

The widely known penalty for ANY infringement upon or damage to the Gateway's space or even any ATTEMPTED attack is instant DEATH.

Well, hell. And it was using caps. Then more pages flipped, and I was looking at an old-fashioned page. No, an ancient page. Like something you might see in a glass case in a museum. It was probably an agreement, given the bunch of signatures at the bottom. I counted seven, two of them with small sketches next to them. But I couldn't read any of it. Then at the bottom were words I recognised, Rex and Regina. The letters were ornate with large curly capitals. *OK, this might be in Latin.*

I took my best guess. "Is this the original agreement to use the Gateway? Who are the signatories, and is there a date?"

Yes. The kings and queen of the realms in 1205.

I scrutinised it with interest. Other than the first name, which could say Will, and seemed to have a small sketch of what might be a lion's head next to it, the others looked like chicken scratches. Oh no, that one might say Ad'Rian—although I was only basing it on the two letters I could make sense of might be an A and D, and they were followed by an apostrophe.

I took the Book's point. "So they all agreed not to harm the Gateway, and the penalty for breaking the agreement was death. And this agreement has never been rescinded. Is that what you're saying?"

It flipped one page and gave me a big green tick emoji.

"Niki, someone may have told Troels you would not be here for a few days."

"But, Dola, that makes no sense. How would they get a message to him?"

"The Recorder usually attends *Dewi Sant*. It may simply be a guess, but it appears suspicious it began about twenty-four hours after you left. It seems even more suspicious you were in a communication black spot. But I have no proof. There has been no electronic communication in or out of the Viking realm I am aware of except from Rollo, and he was warning us."

"OK, well, the Book says I need to act decisively, so I'm going to the Gateway." Then I paused. "What is *Dewi Sant* again? Twirly and Whirly mentioned it?" I transported straight to the centre of the Gateway. Tilly's cross bark followed me as I left—oh well, she'd have to find her own way. At least it wasn't snowy here.

Dola replied through my earbud, "It is the Welsh name for St. David's Day."

I stood in the centre next to the anvil on its throne and asked the power what it needed. I rose into the air. Not again! I sent the power a clear message: *if you want me to do that, you have to wait one minute.*

I reached out to the anvil and thought, *lock all the Gates and raise all the barriers except green.*

To Fi and Finn, I said, "Sorry, guys, but stuff's probably about to get weird. I'd be more comfortable if you were safe in the Green sector behind the barrier in case the power flies around. Or maybe go over to the cottage for half an hour, but I need to deal with this now. Decide quickly please."

They looked at each other, and Finn said, "Green, stay for the show, OK?" And Fi nodded.

"Can one of you grab Tilly please? I forgot her. A Bichon-shaped rocket should arrive any minute."

Finn's laconic "will do" drifted up to me as I rose into the air. As soon as they reached the green sector, I raised the glass barrier. I didn't even know why I was being so cautious. But I knew I didn't want any more nasty surprises today.

Unhappiness, fear, and anger met me as I lowered my shields. I'd never known the power to be like this. It was anxious and frightened, and for a change, I was the one soothing it.

I knew how to soothe. I'd had plenty of practice with Autumn.

I dropped my shields completely and sent it waves of warmth, support, love and assurances. We would deal with this.

We were strong together.

We would fix whatever it was.

No one would hurt it.

The swirling, unhappy energy calmed and flowed more normally.

What's the matter? What upset you? We can fix whatever it is. Just tell me.

It gave me back a wave of confused feelings. It couldn't reach me to alert me. I didn't take the Book with me. Then it showed me some little mini movies of what I sensed were its brothers and sisters. Other gateways lost from the network over the centuries through wars, violent attacks and bloodshed. The power hated violence. Bloodshed all over it was the worst. It showed me its siblings dying.

Their ends *always* began with people chopping at their doors.

Whoa—OK.

I thought quickly. I wasn't killing people, whatever the Book had said, especially not people I didn't know who'd only been given an order by King Slimeball Troels. But I would send a clear message. The most important thing seemed to be to calm the power. It needed me to make the chopping stop so it could heal itself.

Thinking quickly, I organised my priorities. Calm the power by stopping the attack. When I'd secured the Vikings from Aberglas, I'd fooled them into entering a glass cage. I'd worried there might not be enough air in the cage for them all. There had been, but now the thought gave me an idea.

I sent the power an image, and then I ran a short movie scene in my mind. I hadn't visited Viking yet, but the power sensed what was on the other side of its own gates. There was a boundary around all the gates, which was why it got warmer before I reached the actual doorway. The power controlled the boundary areas, not the realms.

The power swirled with purpose. Its anxiety muted now we had a plan.

I'd been so focused on calming the power, I hadn't even freaked out about floating in the air. But, unusually, I wasn't even very high. The power supported me right above the anvil and concentrated its efforts on the yellow gate. Something clicked in my head. I sensed rather than heard a whooshing noise, and the thudding on the door stopped.

Finn high-fived the air. He was going to love this when we got a look at what the power had created.

The power sighed in my mind and sent me an enormous sense of relief, quickly followed by bright, fiery rage.

I rose higher as the power separated itself into its component colours as it had first done at my true ascension. The Red, Orange, Green, Blue and Violet strands reached the matching doors,

I looked down. HRH sat on her plinth on the throne with one paw extended to touch the anvil. I could have sworn she was trying to comfort it.

"You OK, Your Majesty?"

"I am well. I don't understand your action, but it appears to have worked, and I can sense no dead bodies on the other side. Several unconscious ones, but none dead, yet. Such a shame. Death can be such an efficient teacher for the living."

I looked up again. Indigo and yellow strands floated in the air. The yellow strand was wider and far fuller than the indigo one. And it continued to grow.

A narrow band of the indigo power headed down to the cat of its own volition. A smaller amount than she'd received last time, but she wriggled, straightened her spine and leaned her head into the stream as she preened in the flow.

Then an odd thing happened.

Out of HRH came a stream of bright yellow power. It mixed into the now large swirling ball of yellowish power in the centre of the Gateway. Perhaps it was an illusion, but the ball seemed to grow larger. Had the power swapped with HRH? Given her indigo power for the yellow she'd obviously been keeping somewhere?

Thin yellowish streams returned to the centre of the Rainbow through all the doors. Those streams converged on the large swirling ball of yellow in the centre, which had grown and was now almost the size of a normal room.

What was the power *doing*?

I was missing stuff here. But the power didn't seem to need anything from me except for me to hang in the air above the anvil. I closed my eyes briefly, shuddered at how often I ended up in the air, tried not to sweat through my deodorant and waited.

When the indigo stream to HRH cut off, she sat still on her raised plinth and spoke in a deeper voice than her usual one, but not the crazy, stoned, gravelly one she'd used the last time the power fed her. "Recorder, use the star. Summon Rollo."

"Prince Hrólfr? Bring him here, you mean? Now?"

With thinly veiled impatience in her voice, she gave me the impression she was doing me an enormous favour by providing an explanation. "Yes, he was always to be involved, but this is sooner than even I anticipated."

What was I missing? Why was I *always* missing something? I was the Recorder, damn it. Wasn't someone supposed to tell me this stuff?

"Use the phone I encouraged you to give him. Warn him to move to somewhere he cannot be observed. We would not want Troels to know about this."

"We wouldn't? Why wouldn't we?"

HRH sounded so smug about the phone. And yet both she and Dola had urged me in different ways to connect Rollo to the Rainbow Network. HRH with his phone and Dola with the Dolina device she'd talked me into giving him.

I was about to object to HRH's interference when the power thrust Rollo's image at me and dropped me down to touch the anvil.

"Dola, message Rollo right now, please. Ask him to get to a private place and tell him I said to prepare for lift-off."

As I dropped, the anvil rose to meet me on its plinth. I fumbled, trying to remove the Recorder's star from the chain around my neck. Eventually I got it off, held it above the anvil and dropped it into the star-shaped hole on the top. I didn't feel the usual click in my mind when it landed. The power was pushing at me. It wanted Rollo here.

My reluctance to summon Rollo until he confirmed he was somewhere private was strong. As annoying as HRH could be, when she was specific, it was wise to pay attention to her.

Dola's voice came from several speakers in the centre and through my earbud, "Prince Hrólfr is ready."

Still hanging above the anvil, I stretched to poke the tree rune for the Vikings. "Prince Hrólfr of the Vikings, I summon you to the Gateway."

Nothing happened.

I reached down again to check the star was

nestled in its holder. Perhaps I hadn't placed it as carefully as usual—because, you know, hanging about up here in mid-air really helped with accuracy.

The star looked wrong. I'd never noticed before, but the sides were subtly different. But from above, it was clear it hadn't settled properly into the indentation on the top of the anvil because it was upside down. I flipped it over and tried again. "Prince Hrólfr of the Vikings, I summon you to the Gateway."

I felt twin pulls, the usual one on the Gateway power, and another strong pull on my own Gift. What an odd sensation. That had never happened before. But then, without fuss or ceremony, as if everything was perfectly normal, Rollo arrived in midair.

He dropped about eight feet and made a perfect superhero, three-point landing. In a crouch, one leg extended, one knee bent and fingers splayed on the Gateway's floor. I didn't even hear an oomph.

Be still my beating, Marvel-loving heart.

He'd bypassed the Gate and the Yellow sector completely! I didn't know anyone other than the Recorder could do that. Even Mabon had never done it.

CHAPTER
NINE

Rollo turned and took in the entire Gateway. He gave me the impression that *arrive and conduct full reconnaissance before acting* was a perfectly normal sequence of events for a Thursday afternoon in his world.

He stood in one supple movement and bowed to me, then gave me a head-tilt WTAF expression as he realised I was dangling in mid-air.

Fi and Finn were still in the Green sector with Tilly. Rollo did the guy nod thing to Finn and bowed to Fi before looking back up at me as I floated above the anvil.

"You called, my lady?" His grin was infectious.

I couldn't stop myself from smiling down at him. He looked much better than he had the last time I'd seen him. But then his uncle had just tried to kill my dog, so it wasn't surprising this was a better day. He'd taken being catapulted into the Gateway in excellent spirits.

"Actually, the power summoned you, Prince," I stopped myself from calling him Hrólfr, remembering he'd said he disliked it and asked me to call him ... "Rollo. It asked me to fetch you. It says this could, or perhaps it means should, be yours." I pointed at the large churning ball of yellowish power which continued to grow.

The power was still retrieving parts of itself back from the realms, but I didn't understand why. Or what it might mean. I needed to ask the Book about this. I tried to send the power an enquiry. *What are you doing with the yellow energy?* But all I got back from it was a sense of a child holding on to toys and shouting "MINE," which didn't help me at all.

HRH strolled across the anvil's surround and sat amidst the beautiful rainbow flowers made of power.

Rollo gave her his usual greeting, "Great One." He bowed low. "What do I need to know?"

"We are finished with knowledge, Rollo. Now is the time for choices."

He quirked a brow at her, but his tone was respectful as he inclined his head. "About what?"

"Your future. Child or man? Surrender or claim your throne? Rule or withdraw? Assert control or continue to placate? But right now, your most important choice is fast and hard or slow and steady."

I almost giggled at the astonished look on Rollo's face. I firmly reminded myself I was the Recorder, and giggling at unintentional innuendo from a cat was probably beneath my dignity.

But an expression I could only describe as deliciously male crossed his face. He caught my eye as he said, "Be gentle with me, my lady," before turning back to HRH. "Both have their advantages, Great One. Which would you advise?"

She gazed up at the now enormous ball of yellowish power. "Yes, this may need both. Give me your hand."

Without hesitation, he held his hand out to her, and five of the power flowers attached themselves to his fingers and thumb like little barnacles. Exactly the same way they had when he'd first seen them. Last time he'd seemed to be in a world of his own and hadn't even heard me talking to him.

So I addressed HRH, "They did that to him before. What's going on here?"

The flowers turned a brighter shade of yellow than the ball of energy, and the power spread up Rollo's left arm in a golden glow.

"Last time was a test, Recorder. This is the real thing. It is preparing him for that." Her head turned to the swirling ball.

"OK." I swallowed. I was in over my head *again*, wasn't I? "And?"

"By my tail, woman, use your Gift. Ask the power. Stop waiting to be spoon-fed. You are better than this. Be what you could be."

Whoa, OK. She sounded stressed. I'd never heard her sound anything close to worried before. But I'd already asked the power and got nowhere. So, as she'd suggested, I tried my Gift.

Rollo was blissed out and communicating with the yellow power.

HRH was excited. Really?

Yes, I checked again. Excited or maybe anticipatory. I wished my vocabulary was better because there was fear and some other proprietorial emotion coming from the cat too. But mostly I sensed eagerness in her, and I didn't know one word that could describe that particular combination of emotions.

I tried the power again. It had focused and was less agitated now. There was a determination in it, as though it was protecting something bigger or more important than today's events. But what?

Annoyingly, none of it told me what the hell was going on.

I sighed. It would be really nice just for once to understand all the crazy shit that seemed to be my life now.

Rollo slid to his knees, his hand still up above his

shoulder, held on the anvil's surround by the power flowers. His skin always had an undertone of gold, but with his fingers still encased by the pulsing, glowing blossoms, he was actually turning to gold now. The golden wave of power had reached his shoulder and spread across his excellent torso.

HRH said, "Your turn is coming, Recorder; begin slowly, or you may break his mind. Treat him as carefully as you do that dog of yours."

And with her words, the power lifted me higher, and the yellowish ball of power rushed to me, surrounding me. But there was a darkness in the energy I didn't like. It was toxic, polluted. Exactly the way Troels had made me feel when I'd inadvertently received a stream of pornographic images from his mind at my ascension.

Strangely, it echoed how Dai had made me feel earlier when he was shouting without cause this morning.

The swirling power was repugnant. Not liking any part of the power was an unfamiliar experience for me. Indigo energy sometimes had a greasy component. But the Gateway power I normally worked with was clean, light, bubbly. I wanted to retreat from this yellowish stuff, or at least push *it* away. Even to the most casual glance, it was a different shade of yellow than the glorious golden energy that filled the flowers on the anvil's throne.

Even now, the energy was spreading further over Rollo's body, turning him into a kneeling version of an Oscar statue.

Were the flowers on the anvil surround and the ones attached to his fingers filtering the yellow power before they gave it to Rollo?

I dug in my heels and mentally rebelled against the Gateway's insistence I give the yellow power to Rollo. Now.

I fought it hard.

But it pushed the power through me. I shuddered. It felt wrong.

As the power reached Rollo, he went, if that was even possible, more statue-like, and then he let out a blood-curdling scream.

The obvious pain, horror and disgust in Rollo's scream brought me to my senses, and I remembered I was the damn Recorder. Breathing too quickly, I gathered the revolting yellowish power back from around him and sent it upwards towards the still revolving ball.

The Gateway power felt more tentative now. Perhaps it realised it had gone too far, or perhaps my anger with it was getting through. It told me Rollo MUST take the power. I must give it to him.

I sent, *NO, I WON'T*.

It recoiled. I tried softer words and attempted to convey the sense of wrongness the ball of energy held. Humans couldn't absorb corruption like that and remain untouched.

I tried thoughts. *It's dirty. Tainted. He isn't. I won't turn him into Troels. How do we clean it first?*

Everything stopped.

The yellowish power slowed its frantic swirling. Now you could clearly see there was a green tinge to it, with brown edges and nasty little blobs inside it. The colour was sickly-looking. It was nothing like the pure golden power that now coated Rollo.

The power was confused and asked me what to do.

I was too high in the air and couldn't think. I needed to check on Rollo. Although the cat didn't seem distressed, so he was probably fine.

But the tainted energy and my helplessness suffocated me, and I couldn't stay up here. I pushed against the power, sure I was right about this. I'd always been confident in my ability to sense energies. This yellowish power was wrong.

I put my foot down, literally, demanding the power return me to the ground. Once there, I pulled a small amount of it into the palm of my hand, shuddering at the sliminess of it. I crossed to HRH and looked straight into her eyes. "No. I'm not giving him this. Check it yourself. It isn't right."

Total silence. Her mouth opened. Swift, agile, and astonishingly long, her tongue darted out like a serpent's, tasting the power with a quick flick. Then, surprise clear in her tone, the cat said, "You are correct. Astonishing. We must cleanse it."

I didn't know how to clean power, but I knew how to change energies. While the power and HRH debated clever ideas, I could at least try what had worked for me in the past.

"Dola, somewhere in the things you brought from my former home, there is a small cardboard box with sage sticks in it. Could you send it over here, please?"

The box appeared on the anvil's surround, and I opened it and breathed in deeply. I chose a bunch of white sage and lit it, wafting it around myself, then around the cat, who sneezed but then breathed in. And, finally, around Rollo. Then I stood under the swirling ball of power, wafted the sage stick and allowed the smoke to drift into the ball of energy.

From the Gateway came a happy sense of recognition. This was something it knew, something that used to happen, but the power had forgotten it. Well, smudging or burning sage as a cleansing practise for negative energies was an ancient ritual. Possibly my ancestors had done it. They probably hadn't bought their supplies online, though.

After about ten minutes of this, although the energy was less aggressively offensive, it still wasn't right.

I sighed. Then the open box caught my eye, and, as I saw the small sticks of wood in the box, two things clicked loudly in my brain. It might not be the answer to this current problem, but it was also the mysterious wooden component of Dai's scent. The one I'd never been able to identify. Well, damn! How dumb had I been?

The Palo Santo stick caught the flame. Where would be safe for me to put the still-smouldering sage down?

Fi called, "Niki, I can help. I know how to do this. Need another pair of hands?"

When I dropped the green barrier, Tilly arrived immediately and nosed at Rollo, who was still on his knees, but he was curled in on himself now.

Were we running out of time?

Fi took the sage from me, and, rather than extinguishing it, she moved it anti-clockwise and mumbled what sounded like a blessing under her breath. Finn stood back by the barrier. Obviously, this was eight steps past far-too-weird for him. Then he strode purposefully towards Fi's desk and retrieved the purple peril, the device that checked power levels. He showed me the readout, and I stopped and breathed in slowly. All the stress and the need to argue with the power, which I'd never done, before must have nudged my power draw away from the prime.

I breathed. My power being off-kilter wouldn't help anything.

Finn held the peril high above his head into the edge of the yellow cloud of swirling energy. "Nasty. Can you fix it?"

He held the display under my nose. The yellow energy was showing an error reading. When Finn moved it back towards me, the display changed to show my normal 16007 power level. As he moved it back into the bottom of the ball of yellow power, it errored out again.

Nope, I had no idea how to fix that.

CHAPTER
TEN

I n what I now thought of as my Recorder's voice,
I demanded, "Where is the Book?"

I put out a mental call. When I'd finally worked
out the Book could follow me around, I'd stopped
worrying where I'd abandoned it. The blue leather-
covered family heirloom appeared on the corner of
my desk.

I checked with the power: *Can you keep the yellow
energy in here for now? Is it safe?* I got a *yes*, and a
picture of all the gates remaining locked.

"Your Majesty, is he alright?"

The cat licked around Rollo's ear. "Act with
despatch, Recorder. But I will stabilise him."

At my desk, I asked Dola for a coffee and waited
until the Book changed to its red open-for-business

colour before I asked my question. "Why is my Gateway full of yellow power?"

Attacking the Gateway breaks the Vikings' agreement with the power. The part of itself it gifted to Rollo's ancestors when they first took the yellow throne has been retrieved.

It is Regnal power and gives a person the right to rule. Much of the yellow power was scattered around the other realms by Troels. The power has recouped it too. And plans to return the power to the correct vessel.

OK, I actually understood that. Go me.

I sipped my coffee, very conscious of the gigantic ball of power above me. It was a hell of a lot of power. How would it even fit into Rollo? Would he be OK?

The Book, as it so often did, answered my unspoken question. Pages flipped, and text slowly appeared.

You hold a hundred times more power than that. You survived. He will have to grow to wield it—as you are.

I looked at the vast ball. Gods and Goddesses, did I really? A hundred times more? No damn wonder I'd had a killer headache. But to use HRH's metaphor, the power had hit me fast, hard, and with menaces.

I finished my coffee muttering, "My caffeine level

is far too low, still." I needed a simple question to ask. "How can I clear the taint out of this yellow power?" That might work.

The Book flipped to a page that wasn't about the power exactly. The title read **How to cleanse.**

It would do. I wasn't fussy. I saw one of the new-style pages.

Cleansing spaces, touch HERE

I touched it. Suggestions included everything we'd already tried, along with eucalyptus branches and lively music.

Cleansing auras, touch HERE

Cleansing edibles, touch HERE

Cleansing spell ingredients, touch HERE

Cleansing sources of magic, touch HERE

I refused to be distracted by spell ingredients. Spells? Really? I'd come back to that when we weren't holding a man I liked, possibly against his will. I tapped to read the cleaning of magic.

Pages and pages of small text in tightly written handwriting arrived. Hell, this might take a while. I didn't think we had a while.

A mug of strong black coffee I hadn't requested arrived on the desk. On it was a diagram. The caption said, *Necessity may be the mother of invention...*

I twisted the mug around and read *...but desperate women can turn coffee into solutions.* I laughed and turned it back to the beginning of the graphic. It looked like something a mad inventor had devised, but I grasped what Dola was suggesting.

I pulled a little power and tried to find a simple way to convey filtration and purification to an ancient power source. I tried sending various pictures. One of a water filter. Another of air filtration.

I was still holding the Palo Santo. Breathing the smoke soothed me, and then it reminded me of Dai, which didn't. I handed the smouldering stick to Fi.

I checked on Rollo. He was still in the same kneeling position, but his energy seemed better. The golden power sank into his skin, and more built up and sank in. There was a cycle going. The flowers from the anvil surround must have been acting as a kind of filter? I glanced at the toxic yellow ball, which was no smaller, and thought, yep, we're definitely going to need a bigger filter.

HRH was monitoring Rollo. "Any other ideas, Your Majesty?"

She put her head on one side. "If the power will trust me, I may be able to clean it. Channel some to me, as you did with the indigo energy."

The power had no objection, so I sent her some of the tainted power. It still felt repulsive.

Then I stood open-mouthed in surprise.

HRH drew the power from me as she always did.

But there was no eagerness as there always was with the indigo power. She was all iron will and control.

As she pulled from me, power streamed out of her spine, but the exiting power came from different vertebrae or maybe even different chakras. It was a glorious effect as the power split into separate threads. There was green, red, blue, a lot of blue, in fact. Maybe that was why the yellow power looked greenish?

Some orange came from the cat now, but no violet or indigo. The effect was like a mini version of the album cover of *Dark Side of the Moon* but with the cat instead of the prism in the centre. I snapped a quick photo. This was a memory I wanted to keep.

I focused on what she was doing to see if I could help her, and in my mind, I heard her angry mumbling. *Thieving cowardly rabbit. You didn't just rape them, did you? No, you stole their power too, didn't you? Try to keep what's not yours, would you? The boy should have had this years ago. Well, he's getting it now, or my name's not the Mistress of Dread.*

She was so furiously angry, I nearly laughed. But as I looked at the power with my Gift, I got a horrible, sinking, unpleasant inkling of what she might mean and shuddered. Looking at all the blue power, I thought about Fi and the other Pict girls. I remembered Breanna saying, "I can't afford any more pregnant chambermaids."

I hadn't had a damn clue, had I?

After several minutes of this, HRH slumped to the anvil's surround. "I can do no more. I hoped it would be enough to demonstrate the idea. Ah, I see it was. Excellent."

I followed her gaze to where the power itself was now doing the same to the large ball of still murky yellow power. It split, and thin streams headed towards the green and red doors, coating the insides of them. The blue door opened, and Caitlin walked through it. It closed swiftly behind her, and I felt it lock again. And the blue energy began coating the inside of the Pict doorway.

She stood stock still and surveyed the whole Gateway. "I tried the door, but it was locked, then my hand tingled on the handle and it opened for me. Odd sensation."

"Perk of being a Knight, Caitlin. Don't touch anything yet."

She nodded and rushed towards Rollo.

I repeated, "Do NOT touch him. He's fine. You might not be if you touch him. The energies are all in a mess right now."

"Ma had Ad'Rian on the Dolina, and he said the Gateway was under attack." She looked around, her assessing gaze shrewd, exactly as Rollo's had been when he landed. "Seems fine." She pointed at the ball of power, which now looked much cleaner than it had before. "That's a Recorder problem. Right?"

I nodded absently and assessed the yellow power.

"I even checked my phone in case you needed me." The aggrieved tone in which Caitlin said this made Finn and me laugh.

"Not serious enough to make you use your phone, Cait," Finn got out between his gusts of laughter.

"I think we're almost done here. Give me a minute to monitor the power. Get a coffee or a beer or whatever you want for whatever time it is in the real world."

"It's mid-afternoon," Caitlin informed me.

Gods and Goddesses, we'd been at this for hours. I was ready for bed, and it wasn't even tea-time. I shooed her out of my way. The yellow energy ball was slightly smaller now, and it had changed colour. Almost totally an attractive golden yellow. It looked like sunlight flowing around the centre of the Gateway instead of its previous toxic gas appearance.

"Finn, have you got the peril?"

He came over and stuck the small purple device into the yellow power. It read 571.

In unison, we said, "Prime number."

"But does it mean anything?"

Finn asked, "Dola, what's the wavelength of yellow light?"

"570-585 nanometres, Finn."

"Might just be showing us it's all yellow now. Looks better."

I thought he was right, and so did the power because I rose into the air and was suspended above the anvil again. This was getting so old, so fast.

Weirdly, Rollo appeared taller and leaner slumped against the anvil's surround with one arm in the air. That couldn't be comfortable. Even as I had the thought, the flowers released his fingers, and I swiftly directed the power to cushion his head. The stone floor was hard. Almost as soon as I removed the cushioning energy and settled his head as gently as I could, he opened his eyes and looked confused to find himself on the floor.

HRH told Rollo, "You were communing with the power. My advice would be stay precisely where you are. The next bit might be less pleasant."

He sat up groaning, "How much less pleasant?"

HRH stared at him.

Rollo looked as if he was struggling to focus properly. He gave me a querying look.

"Sorry, don't know. I've never done this before. The power needs me to give you that." I gestured at the glowing golden ball. "From my experience, I'd advise you not to fight it, and, if you can talk to it as you were doing," I gestured at the flowers, "every-thing seems to go easier. If you know how to drop your shields, it reduces the pain a lot—well, it did for me."

His energy reached out to mine. Was he saying something? Could everybody but me do this mind-speech thing? I didn't know what he was saying, but I tried to send him reassurance. "I won't leave you alone until you feel yourself again. My word on it."

"Do you mean, if I just give in, it will go better for me?"

Whoa! That stopped me dead. It sounded like something the horrible Troels might have said.

I focused on him. When I looked closely at him, he seemed different. Older and more serious.

"Hell no, Rollo. If you don't want this, say so. We've cleaned it, and the power keeps telling me," I gestured at the enormous ball of sunshine above our heads, "it's yours."

I glared at HRH. "And didn't you say this power should have been his years ago?"

"No, Recorder, I did not. I may have thought it, but since when could you ...? Oh." She turned her bright green eyes on me. Then, as if she'd settled something to her own satisfaction, she said to Rollo, "It is time to choose your path."

Speaking more to the cat than me, Rollo asked, "Is that the yellow regnal power?"

She blinked slowly at him.

Huh – he knew what it was? Only the Recorder who was out of the loop then.

"No. I don't want it." Rollo's voice held absolute certainty.

HRH blinked her clear green eyes at him again. Were they communicating?

"There's nothing I want less than the Viking throne, and you know it." He gave her a seated half-bow.

I felt it then, even before I saw it. Power I hadn't pulled swirled, and a full rainbow of it wrapped Rollo from head to toe. I opened my Gift fully. What the hell was going on now?

All my Gift could show me was a private communication was taking place.

The power retreated.

There were several moments of absolute stillness, and then Rollo stood. He found a smile from somewhere and repeated his earlier comment with a wicked twinkle in his eye, "Be gentle with me, my lady."

I frowned at him. "Please sit down. You won't fall as far. And I don't want any confusion afterwards. Do you truly want this?" I gestured at the yellow power, which now felt clean and almost bubbly with sunshine. It wasn't unpleasant to be around anymore. In fact, it was nice. Soft, silky and warm.

"There's nothing I want less, but the price for my

cowardice would be too high for the others. I've agreed to hold it securely and temporarily. I consent, Recorder; I clearly consent. Do what you must, but I'd rather meet my future on my feet."

I caught Caitlin's eye, hoping she'd understand I meant her to prepare to lower the stubborn idiot to the ground. She just gave Rollo an approving nod and frowned at me in confusion. Finn whispered in her ear. Her face cleared, and she gave me a thumbs-up behind Rollo's back.

I tried to be gentle with him. But the power rushed to him like an over-eager, loyal golden retriever who finally saw his master after a long absence.

I fought to slow it, to try to give him a chance to assimilate it. I battled with the yellow ball. It was wriggly and fighting hard to escape my control. HRH sat on her plinth, her green eyes glowing with a strange light I hadn't seen in them since my first day in the Gateway.

In her smuggest tone, she said, "What is that song the children sing? Oh yes, 'Let it go, Recorder, let it go.' You shouldn't hold it back. It's been away from its true line for too long and needs to return to its home."

So I released it as gently as I could, the stupid theme song an earworm in my head now. I squashed any thoughts of frozen mountains as I did so. I'd had quite enough of those this week.

As predicted, Rollo passed out cold. Finn and Caitlin lowered him to the floor.

Poor bastard, I knew exactly what power shock felt like.

Once the last of the yellow energy disappeared into Rollo, the power tidied up efficiently. It collected the extra power it had stripped out of the yellow ball from the doors. As it merged it all back into itself, I still sensed anger from it. But I wasn't sure what about. The power had never been angry before. I wondered if the Book would know why?

But I had the ominous feeling I'd need to find out and soon.

CHAPTER

ELEVEN

After a short debate on what we should do with Rollo, I got a firm grip on him and transported him to my guest room. We landed in a heap on the double bed. Which would have been embarrassing, but he was unconscious, and all my instincts told me he'd stay that way until morning. I still didn't fully understand what had happened between him and the yellow power. But it had clearly been a coiled path he'd trodden through the labyrinth to a choice he could live with.

I had a list of pertinent questions for when I had some peace to consult the Book. But for now, I needed to ensure his safety. In my recent experience of hard life changes, they were often followed by a long sleep and waking up starving hungry. Vomiting or weeping were optional.

Caitlin and Finn volunteered to walk over to the house with Tilly. While they were en route, I surveyed what Dola called her blue guest room with an unhappy frown.

This wasn't the pleasant guest room Aysha and Autumn used. That one was warm and friendly. This was the spare, spare room. Finn had been the last person in it before Dola made him his own Foxhole, as Caitlin insisted on calling the TEK's apartment. But Finn liked dark colours and womb-like spaces. Honestly, he probably didn't even notice them, provided his laptop worked.

Rollo's energy was more outward-looking and mature than Finn's. For some reason I couldn't justify in any rational way, I knew this golden-skinned man on the bed didn't like dark or gloomy spaces.

I sighed and dug an earbud out of my pocket. "Dola, can we do a quick and dirty update on this room, do you think?"

"Why do you want me to dirty a clean room?"

There was a pause while I waited, and then, "Oh, OK. I see. Yes, I have spare energy for minor improvements. What would you like?"

I put one hand on Rollo's forearm and stood quietly, breathing and thinking. I tried to sense what might help someone who'd endured a difficult life step with grace and good humour. He'd had a tough few hours, and I wanted him to wake up with a sense of safety, warmth and welcome.

While I considered the problem, I'd been stripping off his boots, belt and several knives on autopilot. Well, he was fully clothed. OK, he was as fully clothed as I'd ever seen him. I put my middle-class reservations about a half-naked man unconscious in my guest room aside and concentrated on his comfort.

"A door through to the adjoining bathroom, so he has some privacy. Thank heavens you updated it to white on Monday. It wouldn't surprise me if he throws up when he wakes. I did, didn't I? Or was that before I passed out? Anyway, a door, please, Dola." I tapped my Gift again, considering how horrific it might have been for poor Rollo if it had still been the horrid pink bathroom. Power shock and that black-and-pink monstrosity felt like a double whammy he didn't deserve.

"Change the colour of the bedding and the curtains; make the curtains, duvet cover and pillowcases yellow and the sheet white. Clean, fresh cotton. Something lighter and more neutral on the walls. A cream or sand colour, but a warm shade, not a cool one. Put a Dolina in here please, and can you monitor him and alert me instantly if he vomits or appears distressed while he's unconscious?"

A Dolina appeared on the bedside table. As I

watched, the blue lamps changed to white ones with yellow shades, and the bedside tables changed from a gloomy, old-fashioned dark brown wood to a modern light birch. It was both creepy and fascinating to watch.

Rollo was a big guy, but he looked taller than usual in this space. As I struggled to get him fully onto the bed, I said, "This bed needs to be bigger, if it's not too much trouble, Dola."

"Stand back please, Niki," came out of the Dolina.

It was too intimate in here, and I heard Tilly's claws skittering down the corridor. "I'll go and see Caitlin and Finn. Shout if you need me for anything."

I met them in the kitchen. "He's fine. Dola's redecorating the room for him, and he's out cold. Do you guys have any idea what the yellow power thing was all about?"

Finn frowned at me. "Thought you'd tell us. Bit random."

Caitlin asked, "What started it all? Ma said they were attacking the Gateway. How did you stop them, and why didn't you call me?"

Gods and Goddesses, it felt like it was days ago. I slumped into a chair at the table. "Dola, can I have an enormous glass of wine, please?"

I started laughing.

They both gave me concerned looks. Finally, Finn said, "Niki, you stopped them chopping at the door. How? We were stuck in Green and couldn't see anything?"

Caitlin was gaping at me. "You trapped them in the Green sector, but you didn't call me?"

"Oh, let's not go there, Caitlin. I've had a long-ass bitch of a day, and yesterday was one of the most miserable of my life." My breath caught in my throat and stopped me speaking. *You will not cry again, Niki; you will shape up.*

I breathed. "I dealt with it. Those two stayed safe, OK? But please don't push me today, KAIT. I might snap and cry again, and I'm an ugly crier. Three times in one day is two too many."

Now she looked concerned and dropped her hand onto my shoulder. "But you went for a …" she paused, apparently searching for an inoffensive word, "short break with Dai. Why was it such a miserable day? Did he upset you? Did you upset him back? Did you zap him? Is he OK? He can be annoying."

Oh, bless her. I loved the way she assumed I'd fought back instead of running away. Even though running away was precisely what I'd done, wasn't it? I wasn't proud of myself for that.

If I said yes, he upset me, what might she do to him? But it wasn't her business or her problem. So I told her about the forced march through the snow and passed that off as being responsible for my unhappiness.

Finn's patience had run out. "The Yellow Gateway?"

I started laughing again, and before he could totally lose his shit with me, I stammered out, "A... a...air...lock"

His face split into a huge grin. "Like in Oxygen Not Included?" I shook my head. "OK, what about ..." He went on to name many, many computer games that used airlocks as part of the game mechanics, and I kept shaking my head.

"Like Ripley in *Alien*," Caitlin stated. "Sigourney was so cool in those old movies."

I grinned at her and nodded. "But this was way less cool because there was no vacuum outside. The power created an airlock-type structure on the other side of the yellow gate and sucked the air out of it. As they started to pass out, it opened the door. They crawled out, and it sealed itself and removed the air again. From the visions it sent me, I'm pretty sure no one was seriously injured. But the power was so frightened and then so angry. That's when it started collecting all the yellow power from all the gates into the Gateway."

I told them all the things the power had shared with me about its fellow Gateways dying, and how it always started with someone chopping the door down. They were my Knight Adjutants. I thought they had a right to the information I had in case they could shed any light on all of it.

Looking thoughtful, Caitlin asked, "Can I tell Ma about this? Nope, wrong question. May I tell the Queen about it?"

"If she agrees to keep it to Gateway personnel, Mabon, Ad'Rian and Rollo for now, yes. And provided she'll share any ideas she has with us?" I had a lot of respect for Breanna. I needed to catch up with her myself and ask about those pregnant house-maids. Or had she called them chambermaids? Was there a difference?

"How did Ad'Rian know?"

"Ma said one of his warriors, a sensitive, shared a vision with him. The airlock makes sense of what the guy said. I'm not sure he'd ever seen one, so his vision didn't come across clearly. He said, 'A small metal box rendered Troels' lumberjacks unconscious.'"

Wow, if Troels had sent lumberjacks with their strong shoulders and sharp axes, no wonder the power had been distressed. I'd check on it first thing in the morning, but now I wanted my bed. This day had been waaaay too long already. I stood up to say goodbye to Caitlin, and the odd expression on her face stopped me.

"You OK?"

Finn looked at his sister, and maybe he saw the same thing I did. Unhappiness in her eyes. "Come visit the Foxhole, Cait."

She gave him a grateful half-smile but said, "Gonna have a word with Niki, then I'll be along."

We sat in silence until we heard Finn's door close at the end of the corridor.

I reached out with my Gift, only checking her surface emotions. She wanted to be sure Rollo was OK. She was concerned about him. Her feelings towards him confused me. There was complete trust there. But also something else—betrayal? No, perhaps it was abandonment.

"Niki, can I check in on him? He's like an older brother to us both, you know. And he's gonna be right in the firing line now. Troels is a vicious, dirty fighter."

She was telling the simple truth, huh? Why had I always thought she was hiding something personal, probably connected to Rollo inside the iron-bound wooden chest I'd found in her mind? I wished I hadn't been so driven by my ethics now and had looked a little harder. But it had been fae-locked, so it hadn't felt like it was any of my business. Perhaps I could just get her to talk about him.

"Sure, come on, I'll show you." We walked the opposite way from my bedroom down the corridor to the guest rooms. I tried to find a way to ask for more info without prying.

But before I could, she said, "I didn't even know this was here. This cottage is bigger than you think."

I laughed, opened the door, and ushered her in. Dola had done a great job. It was a bright, sunny room now. Much nicer for Rollo to wake up in. Caitlin stopped dead inside the door. She looked all around with wide eyes and an open mouth and then snapped her jaws shut.

She walked to the bed and knelt by it to smooth Rollo's hair. Then she pried open his eyelid, felt the pulse in his neck, nodded to herself, and turned to me. "He's fine. Bit of help here?"

I walked in, unsure what she wanted. "Let's get him on his side, for safety." So saying, she efficiently manipulated his arms, pulling him onto his side facing the door, and held him there. "Stuff those pillows behind him, please."

She'd done this before!

Caitlin gazed down at Rollo, concern still showing on her face. I tried to reassure her. "Dola is monitoring him. She'll wake me if there's a problem."

She nodded, and as we headed back to the kitchen, in a cautious, carefully casual tone, asked, "When did you visit his flat?"

I stared at her. "He has a flat? He said he had a longhouse."

"His flat in Edinburgh. Not been myself, but you obviously have."

As we reached the kitchen, I dropped into a chair at the table. "No, I haven't. I've not been to Edinburgh for a few years." I suppressed memories of a weekend there with Nick. He'd wanted to stay at one of the posh five-star places. He hated the quaint, pretty hotel I'd chosen and whined about it during the entire trip. "What on earth made you think I had?"

She observed me as she pulled out her phone. Poked it, swiped, muttered, swiped some more and finally held it out to me with a set of photos showing. "He sent those to Finn and me after he redecorated the flat. Was years ago now, after he made the big change at work."

I gazed at a photo of a bedroom that, apart from an enormous white wrought-iron bed frame, was virtually the twin of the one I'd asked Dola to create for Rollo ten minutes ago.

CHAPTER
TWELVE

Apart from an unconscious Rollo, I finally had my house to myself, but I was too tired to eat. Tilly was already snoring softly on the end of my bed. The bed looked so cosy, it drew me towards it. I set the remains of my glass of wine and the Book on the night table.

I didn't care what time it was in the real world. In my head, it was several months past bedtime. I chose a pair of full-coverage pyjamas in case I had to get to Rollo in a hurry. It was a little unfortunate they were from an era when Autumn had been obsessed with the movie *Frozen*, but they covered me respectably.

I mean, I love those romance books where the heroine "completely forgets" she's wearing a tiny, see-through negligee as she dashes along draughty corridors on her midnight mercy mission to the hero's room after his gunshot wound as much as the next red-blooded woman. But in real life, I'd prefer not to flash a guy who might be concussed or power-shocked.

When I caught sight of myself in the mirror, I stopped dead and peered down at my chest. Aysha had told me Autumn had chosen these and insisted her mother buy them for me. Olaf the snowman's grinning face in the middle of the pyjama top had three words around his head: *Just Be You*. I wondered if Autumn had picked them only for the *Frozen* theme. Olaf was her favourite character. Or had she been drawn, as I now was, to the words?

What could happen if I was just me? What if I let go of all the stuff that kept getting in my way? Let go of my need to be polite and have people think well of me? If I wasn't being polite, I'd have transported out of Dai's while he was still asleep and come here to grab some real coffee. Was it pure coincidence HRH had mentioned the theme song when she told me to give the yellow power to Rollo?

Let it Go and Just Be You. I considered those words for a long time until Tilly's cross sneeze told me it was time to get into bed.

Snuggled in bed, I waited while the Book's cover changed from deep blue to its red open-for-business colour. "What was the enormous ball of yellow power all about? Did you call it ruling power?"

A page flipped and I read, **It was the yellow realm's regnal power.**

"Regnal power?" Yeah, I'd gathered that much earlier, but what did it mean? "How does it work?"

One of the new-style pages appeared.

Regnal power and its origins, TOUCH HERE

How the Gateway uses it, TOUCH HERE

Additional regnal power outside of the Gateway's control, TOUCH HERE

How regnal power passes to the next ruler, TOUCH HERE

The options continued down the page. This was a big subject. How on earth had I not heard of it before today? But I started at the beginning to be sure I understood what I might have to deal with.

The regnal power has always existed. Historically, it is the reason certain monarchs were described as touched by a Goddess or appointed by a God. The power landing on a ruler might appear to ordinary people like the hand of a higher power.

Huh! During Queen Elizabeth's jubilee, there had been a documentary about her coronation. There was a part in the ceremony where Knights of the Garter surrounded the young queen holding golden curtains. They cloistered her with a senior bishop and some precious, rare anointing oil for a private moment to consider her lifelong oath. Hadn't the documentary said something about she went in a princess and emerged an anointed queen, and the crown was merely an external symbol of the change of rank?

I moved on to the second option: **How the Gateway uses it, TOUCH HERE.**

The monarchs make solemn vows to protect the Gateway. In return, the Gateway shares regnal power with them so they cannot be deposed or forced to abdicate.

Wow! So the power was in the process of dethroning Troels? I couldn't say I blamed it. If someone sent a team of lumberjacks to attack me, I wouldn't be giving them any help either. I'd rightly consider them an enemy. No wonder the power had been all riled up today.

The third option drew my finger towards it. **Additional regnal power outside of the Gateway's control, TOUCH HERE.**

Some of the oldest monarchs were brought to power by their own Goddesses. The goddess Áine is the Fae's kingmaker and bestows her own power along with the violet power upon the Fae kings on the Gateway's behalf. They have private ceremonies for this. Ad'Rian received his directly from Áine.

During Valentine's week, Ad'Rian had gone all grey and shaky when the Hobs invoked Áine. He'd said something about her being the Goddess who gave a monarch the right to rule, hadn't he? I remembered struggling to grasp the name because it had sounded as if I should spell it Onya.

There was more, and my eyes moved swiftly down the page.

The Red Celts and Mabon also have two sources of regnal power. Their original source came from the Goddess Modron, the Great Mother and Mabon's progenitor. The second part comes from the Gateway as usual.

Mabon ap Modron and Ad'Rian Alicorn have always been most respectful of their right to rule in conjunction with the Gateway power.

Wow again! No wonder those two were the most powerful kings by a country mile. It wasn't simply the length of their lives, but they also had twice the power sources of the other monarchs.

I gazed at the page. Did I need any more information right now? I was exhausted. As if the Book had picked up my thoughts, the line **How regnal power passes to the next ruler, TOUCH HERE** appeared to sparkle.

I tapped it.

In the normal course of events, the dying ruler passes their regnal power on to their heir in a private ceremony as they near death.

Breanna, for example, received hers from her mother, Berin, moments before her death. The

transfer of the power often speeds the death of the donor because the power is connected to the life force of the ruler. This ability to offer a speedy, pain-free passage to the next world is the last gift of the power to a loyal ruler.

This all sounded serious and important. How had I not known any of it? Was it one of those things people didn't speak about? A sort of taboo subject? Or merely a very private one?

If a ruler breaks faith with the Gateway, the power can, as it did today, retrieve that which belongs to it by force. This is a rare occurrence. By removing the power's support, the ruler's appearance will change to reflect their real age. They will appear as they would have if the power hadn't delayed their aging.

I'd thought Troels looked remarkably vibrant and healthy for a man of his age at the bondings, hadn't I?

I'd grasped the basics, but I still didn't know why the yellow power had been so foul, contaminated and the wrong colour. I asked the Book. The pages flipped for a long time. It felt for all the world as though the Book was thinking about the easiest way to explain it. Eventually, it settled on a short page.

Troels and his half-brother Jonvar, Rollo's father, were profoundly different men.

The power should never have passed to Troels,

but the circumstances of Jonvar's death in Viking meant it happened privately before anyone could intervene. Troels avoided the Gateway for months. Removing his regnal power later might have cast the Viking realm into civil war. Rollo was an infant at that time.

The power now sees it should have acted sooner.

But it didn't answer my question about why the power was so polluted, did it? I skimmed a lot more history until my eyes slowed on the text.

Regnal power is the personification of its user. If the power goes to the true ruler, it cannot become fouled. But if it is stolen, used for evil, or abused, and if the holder of the stolen power avoids the centre of the Gateway, its misuse can be concealed.

Your summons to Troels for your public ascension was the first time the power had been in direct contact with him for more than three decades.

What? Surely my gran must have called him to the centre of the Rainbow at some point? For Viking weddings? For meetings of the royals? For … something?

Then I thought about all the people during Valentine's week who'd told me my invitation to the centre was their first—other than for their own wedding vows. People travelled around the edges of the centre on their way from one gate to another. But being invited to or lingering in the centre at the anvil had been rare during my gran's Recordership. And the centre was where the power was strongest.

"Dola, if Troels has been married four times, where did those bondings take place? Do you know?"

My Dolina came to life instantly. "Troels has never been bonded, to my knowledge. Although it is not unusual for the Vikings to prefer a private wedding at the autumn equinox in their own realm. Consider how many couples you bonded from each realm, and yet, only seven from the Vikings. The lists I sent to your gran have always been weighted the same way since Troels took the throne. There were many more Viking bondings during King Jonvar's reign."

"OK, thanks. I think I've calmed down enough to eat now. Is there anything light?"

Some cheese, fruit and cold meat arrived for me, accompanied by a small glass ramekin of chicken. Tilly woke immediately. Her cute little black nose was a food-seeking sensor even before her eyes opened.

I nibbled as I went back to the Book and asked it some questions about Rollo. What he might need from us. He'd said he didn't want to be king, but how was the power classifying his status? If he had the regnal power, was he the king now? Apparently not. He had to accept it properly. Right now, he was holding or conserving it. The Book struggled to define "properly," but I remembered my fight to fully bond with the Gateway power. Was this similar? I'd look into it further when I was awake. But the last line caught my attention.

The power has made its support for Prince Rollo clear. The Recorder should render assistance if she can.

It took me forever to get to sleep. I was over-tired, and the peculiar events of my too-long day kept re-running in my mind. Mabon's unusual frankness, Dai's unreasonable shouting. All the weirdness with the yellowish power. Whatever I'd thought this job might entail, I'd never imagined trying to cleanse a room-sized ball of toxic, tainted power.

And what did I need to do now the Gateway had insisted on giving the regnal power to Rollo?

I slept fitfully, disturbed by dreams of Agnes in the Gateway, a huge cat prowling by her side.

I lay in the dark and considered my unsettling memory of Troels at my ascension. When the Rightful King of the Vikings himself and his current queen, Randi, were the only royals who hadn't shown the new Recorder the respect of a bow. The warm look in Rollo's eyes as he'd bowed low. And HRH's interest in him. What was she up to? It felt more personal than one of her usual wagers. Maybe she simply liked him? Nope. I shook my head even as I considered it. There must be some potential personal gain behind her interest in him.

Should I have known at my ascension things weren't right with Viking? But how could I have known? I'd only been in the role for three days. I hadn't even undergone my true ascension then.

Mabon helped me get back my memories just *one* day before my announcement to the realms. And my childhood memories hadn't helped me at all with the complex politics. I'd been nervous meeting the royals for the first time. I should give myself grace. I was doing my best. It was all any of us could ever do, as my headmistress had so often told me.

I fell asleep with the Book open on my chest.

PART THREE
FRIDAY

A certain type of person focuses their energies on correcting and criticising others. Avoid becoming one of them. They are usually individuals who possess limited authority but use it excessively. This can lead to unnecessary outrage over imperfectly sharpened pencils, inadequately washed coffee cups, or enquiries about who ignited the photocopier.

They often end their days with only the power to proscribe how far their window is opened. Their entire world will then revolve around the window being opened either too much or too little.

As for you, cease denying your own power, jump out of the window while you still can, and fly, my darling.

Fly high, fly free. Spread your wings for the pure joy of it.

Finding your Inner Fire: How to Claim your True Self by Peggy Hwybon

THIRTEEN

Friday, 26th February—Gateway Cottage—
Gretna Green

"Niki, Prince Hrólfr is up and in the new white bathroom."

I jolted awake, disturbing Tilly and dumping the Book on the bed as I sat up. Tilly grumbled at me as I scrambled out of bed.

Dola continued, "He does not appear to need assistance."

I got up anyway and hustled through to the kitchen, flipping switches as I walked. Rollo, in a strange house, could follow the light trail, as I had myself yesterday at Dai's mountain home.

Goddess, was that only yesterday? No damn wonder I was still exhausted.

HRH was waiting. I opened her cupboard on

autopilot. What a well-trained cat servant I'd become. But as I reached to get her food, she said, "I'd prefer to wait for breakfast, thank you, Recorder. The power yesterday satiated me. Tuna has become uninspiring unless I'm ravenous."

A large silver mug of black coffee arrived on the kitchen table. I pounced on it and drank. Dola had really nailed delivering my first cup at the correct temperature for drinking.

The navy-blue text on the mug said, *People who need coffee before they can talk to others are saying they're unpleasant to be around if they're not under the influence of drugs.*

I considered this, remembered my lack of coffee yesterday morning and my new Just Be You resolution. "Not necessarily, Dola. It could equally well mean far too many people are just assholes who deserve a slap, which I might give them if I'm not loaded up with the magic of caffeine. It's my drug of choice—there are many worse—and I'll stand up for my right to drink it."

Rollo stood cautiously in the kitchen doorway. I gestured him to a chair. He sat down and stared longingly at my coffee. I empathised with his expression and pushed it over to him, trying not to stare at his six-pack abs, which his leather waistcoat did nothing to hide. What was his objection to wearing clothes?

Not that I was complaining ... oh my, no. No complaints here.

"Dola, may we have..." I had no idea how he liked his coffee. Perhaps Dola did. He had a Dolina, didn't he? She usually bribed people with coffee. "A coffee for Rollo, please?"

"Of course. Good morning, Rollo, which of your many favourites would you like this morning?"

"Good morning, another one exactly like this, please." Hmm, a coffee lover with manners; he kept surprising me. He appeared to have survived the night well, a little drawn around the eyes but still young, hot and wonderfully distracting at breakfast.

Seriously, Niki, he's too young for you. Don't turn into one of those women, I chided myself. But was it really in poor taste if I simply enjoyed the exceptional view? I wasn't harming anyone by simply admiring his glorious golden skin and chiselled muscles ... was I?

I assessed his health, refusing to be distracted by his plump lower lip. He was ... I sighed at my lack of self-control and did a re-set. "How are you feeling? Any headache?" That felt like a safe place to start.

But he wasn't listening; he was gazing at his coffee mug, which, as he'd requested, was exactly like mine. I took mine back and finished it off.

Rollo read his coffee cup. "Thanks, Dola, but this message is wrong. It doesn't mean that at all. It means other people are horrific to be around if I haven't had enough coffee. It should say, *Coffee: saving the lives of the dumb, the annoying and the obnoxious since the sixteenth century.*"

I choked into my mug.

"Sorry, Niki, no offence meant. My filter doesn't click in until my third cup."

I was still laughing, but in between my snorts of amusement as I worked out his reference to the sixteenth century, I managed to get out, "Nope. I said exactly the same thing before you arrived. Well, not as amusingly, but the same meaning."

He gave me a doubtful look, as if he thought I was being polite. "Dola, Rollo doesn't believe me."

As he watched me closely, my own voice came out of the Dolina on the table saying, "Not necessarily, Dola, it could equally well mean far too many people are just assholes who deserve a slap, which I might give them if I'm not loaded up with the magic of caffeine. It's my drug of choice—there are many worse—and I'll stand up for my right to drink it."

He managed to swallow his mouthful of coffee before his own laugh burst out of him. It was a great laugh, and as it settled into a grin, it showed his dimples. This was the first time I'd ever known him to be relaxed enough to laugh, which bothered me.

I said, "I thank that pope on a daily basis. Can't remember his name, but he was a hero. Actually, wasn't it you who told me about him, Dola? Didn't you say an ancestor of mine knew the chap?"

"Yes, Niki, it was Agnes. You should ask the Book. And it was Pope—"

Rollo joined in, "Pope Clement VIII—imagine thinking Clement was an interesting enough name to have eight of them. And weren't there three or four antipopes also called Clement?"

I frowned. "What's an antipope? I've never heard the word."

Chagrin crossed his face. "Sorry, I tend not to think before I speak if I'm relaxed. I didn't mean to lecture."

I waved my hand. "You're absolutely not; I'm interested. I love learning new stuff, so what *is* an antipope?"

He sipped his coffee and watched me carefully, as though, again, he didn't quite trust my words. "It's what they call the contenders for the Bishop of Rome who try to take the position away from the duly appointed pope."

"Like the Catholic church's version of a coup?"

"No," he shook his head, "these guys literally set themselves up as pope in opposition. They were often senior archbishops who thought the other guy was doing it wrong and set up their own pontificate. One of them was antipope to about three or four of the approved popes, and he had a huge following." He stopped, still watching me closely.

I waved my hand. "Well, go on, don't force me to research it on my own."

He laughed again. I was proud that the day after a scary power download, he was relaxed enough in my kitchen to laugh and chat. Yesterday at Dai's, I'd been sure it must be my fault that everything was so awkward and stilted. I'd wondered if I'd forgotten how to enjoy breakfasting with a man. But what if it wasn't me who'd been the problem?

Both our coffee cups refilled themselves, and, almost in unison, we both said, "Thank you, Dola."

I waved my hand again at him, and he gave in. "You know how, in the Galician church, the emperor appoints the pope?"

I nodded. Hadn't Fi told me this last week? I'd meant to look it up.

"Well, around 1000 AD maybe—dates aren't my best thing. The Catholic church in your world was arguing about whether the pope should change things. One side thought future popes should crown the emperors and not the other way around. It caused something of a split, and they had two conse-crated popes. One for and one against. Google 'papal supremacy' if you really care and aren't simply being polite."

My face must have told him I was genuinely

interested because he added, "You know, one of the first ever firework displays in Europe was at a papal inauguration. But that would have been before Clement, our coffee-blessing pope's time."

"Fascinating. I had no idea. I need to get up to speed on the Galicians. My gran had little contact with them, but the emperor was sweet at the bondings, and I want to build a better relationship with them. Fi, being the new Director of Trade, should keep him happy for a while."

Rollo grinned at me. "Oh yeah, Alphonse is always the salesman. But he cares about his people, and, unlike some, he's not afraid to admit when he's wrong. Although I don't envy his kids; he's planned their entire lives out."

There was an unhappy look in his clear hazel eyes now, and I regretted being a part of putting it there and tried to lighten the mood. "If you'd told me yesterday when I was recovering from frostbite, I'd start today learning about ancient religious history and enjoying it so much, I wouldn't have believed you. Could you eat breakfast?"

"Yes, please, Recorder."

My eyes dropped to HRH, who sat on one of the chairs. She was doing her damned furry invisible ornament thing again so she could listen in. I glared at her. "You will either teach me how to see through it the way I can with Ad'Rian's look-away spell, or I'll ban you from my kitchen."

"If you can predict accurately what I want for breakfast, Recorder, then I will teach you."

Rollo laughed. I reached out with my Gift, and HRH, as expected, batted my mental enquiry away. "Do you promise not to lie about it?"

"Recorder, are you impugning my honour?"

"Hell yes!"

"Very well then, my word on it."

"Dola, can I have smashed eggs and far, far too much smoked salmon please?"

A noise, it could have been a rusty laugh, came from HRH. "Well played, Recorder. I shall teach you once we are in private. But we have business with Rollo first."

Rollo asked, "Smashed eggs?"

"When I was a kid, there were words I couldn't say. Scrambled was one of them. I used to feed Her Highness here," I glared at the cat, "from my own breakfast. Once I got my memories back, she told me she'd been confident the real me was still in there somewhere because I offered her scrambled eggs and salmon during one of our first negotiations."

"Your memories back?"

I glanced at Rollo. Why had I assumed the news would have made it around the realms? "Didn't you hear the story?" He shook his head. "Sorry, gossip seems to spread like wildfire among the realms. I thought you would have known."

He shook his head again. "Not to Viking, it's the outlier. Did you have a concussion?"

"No, my gran blocked my memories and sent me to live with my mother. My peculiar mother packed me straight off to boarding school, and a bunch of messed-up decisions drove me into a life that shouldn't have been mine. But because Gran had blocked the fact the Gateway even existed from my mind, I didn't know any better."

I sighed as his face showed astonishment and sympathy. "Sorry, probably more information than you wanted. I'm not awake either."

He shook his head. "Not at all. I was considering how we all think our own sad story is the most difficult. Then we hear someone else's and realise everyone has their own problems, and you have to get over them and get on with life. Ugh, I sound like a fortune cookie."

I tested his energy with my Gift. He felt good, better than I'd expected. "What's your sad story, Rollo? I have so much information to catch up on. I know nothing about you except what I learned giving you the power yesterday."

Cautiously, he asked, "And what was that?"

"The power likes you. But that doesn't tell me anything about you, the person, I mean."

His dimples emerged again, and in his clear hazel eyes, green flecks sparkled as he smiled. "Mine is a story worthy of Charles Dickens. A poor orphan taken in by his wicked uncle. His inheritance stolen and his life controlled. Cue the sad music." He played an imaginary violin. "But in the spirit of all great tales of redemption, it appears the power thinks I should have another chance to do the right thing. Problem is, other than being dead, I can think of nothing I want less than to be the King of Viking. I didn't accept it." His voice tightened towards the end of his sentence until he almost spat the last three words.

I saw with interest he used breathing techniques too. Then, in his normal voice, he finished it out, "I need to find a better solution. One that won't screw me over or leave everyone I care about in Viking hanging out to dry."

Wow. Handsome and loyal. When I'd been in arbitration with the Picts and trying to work out what the Vikings were up to, everyone said Rollo was a good guy, and his word was his bond. I should probably cut him a break and lighten this up.

"I feel your pain. I didn't want to be the Recorder either." I gestured around the table. "Now I'm the referee between a cat with an attitude problem and a house with a wonderful heart who hasn't yet discovered the healing power of forgiveness."

HRH said, "Meow."

"Just saying the word 'meow' doesn't fool anyone here, you know. You're in a strange mood today. Did you need something?"

She stretched her elegant neck. The narrow green collar she always wore was crooked, and I reached out to straighten it. She glared at me, but I could have sworn she was amused. "Recorder, would you prefer me to point out it's healthy to have a superior attitude? It's only individuals whose own attitude shows a lamentable paucity of courage who have a problem with it? Now, I wish to discuss the arrangements and tests for Rollo."

Rollo and I looked at each other, and both slowly shook our heads.

"Great One, what tests would these be?" Rollo enquired.

She stretched up to the tabletop in a single fluid movement and sat in front of us, a seamless blend of grace and poise. She curled her tail around her front paws and surveyed us both. Today, the always intense, luminous green of her eyes radiated an ethereal glow, and the leopard-like rosette pattern in her coat almost glittered. "We must test his power, Recorder. One would not want it erupting uncontrollably at the wrong moment, would one?"

She had a point. So much power must change the

man even if he was putting a handsome, I mean a brave, face on it.

I nodded. "OK, but let's get breakfast inside us first because I've learned to eat when I can in this job. You must be starving, Rollo. I always have been after a power boost, and if we have to test what the power gave you, then you should know using it burns through food quickly. What would you like?"

He tilted his head and smiled, his dimples showing. I'd always been a sucker for dimples. "Is this a party trick? Do you know what I want to eat, too?"

I reached out with my Gift and got a clear picture of mornings in greasy spoon cafes after long nights out. "Rollo would like a large, full Scottish breakfast please." I shuddered. "He even wants the black pudding, the haggis, and the square sausage thing with it."

Rollo laughed again. "It's one of the things I miss most in Viking. I try to mostly eat clean, but you can't beat a *braw* full Scottish. They got me through my masters, and I still had one about twice a week for all the years afterwards when I stayed in Edinburgh."

"You even picked up the Scottish word for 'lived,' I see. It confused the hell out of me when the locals asked me, 'So where did you *stay* afore here?'"

He gave me a genuinely amused smile that went straight to my core, and I rushed into speech before I blushed. "How long were you there? After Uni, I mean?"

"Almost ten years." The cheerful expression on his face turned sour. "Then my uncle made it clear I'd better return home permanently. Well, he meant to Viking, which is not and never was home, but …"

HRH's food arrived, and I pushed it over to her. It looked as though the words I'd had with Dola about making me go hungry so the cat could have my breakfast were working. I'd pointed out it wasn't the cat she was punishing but me, when I only got to eat the toast after I gave the cat the eggs and salmon.

"May I have chicken for Tilly please? And for me, the egg thing with the sauce but with—"

Dola interrupted me, "—with the yummy bacon, not the nasty spinach, yes, Niki. I will remind you *again*, the dish is called eggs Benedict."

"I know, Dola, but I like winding you up. And I enjoy reminding you what a horrible shock it was when you gave me eggs Florentine with all the green stuff instead of the Benedict when I'd asked for the *nice* egg thing with the sauce."

Silence and then Dola said, "Ha, ha. A joke. I am most amused. Listen to me laughing." There were several seconds of complete silence before she continued, "I am sure the goddess does not care whether you eat your spinach." A multi-vitamin capsule arrived on the table in front of me. Even she was in a strange mood today.

When Rollo and I finally stopped laughing, sounding more like herself, Dola said, "Please check your phone, Niki. I am uncertain about the correct answers to give after yesterday's unprecedented events."

FOURTEEN

Mabon still hadn't worked out how to change the current silly identifier Dola had given him.

> Mabon the Dragon Wrangler: Is Gateway closed for a reason? Need passage to the Fae Healers with Dai. Urgent it is. Remember royals and others will want access too for the sentencing, 3pm today your time.

Shit, I'd forgotten it was today. Well, not forgotten exactly, but it felt as if it was still Thursday to me. I was becoming worse than Ad'Rian at knowing which day it was. And I'd been so weary last night, I'd left the Gateway closed. Travellers were doubtless cursing me.

But why was Dai going to Fae for healing? Mabon had said he'd speak to Dai and "fix things"?

What the hell had he done to him? It never occurred to me he'd do anything so drastic it required a trip to the healers. I'd imagined a conversation more along the lines of, "Now, lad, this isn't how we treat women we like …"

Another damn mess to sort out. I checked the time on Mabon's message and told him I'd be there in five minutes.

Then I chilled out and considered what to do, while I ate one-handed and checked the next message. I was being very ill-mannered. Living alone had given me bad habits. I looked up to apologise to Rollo, but he was scrolling on his own phone and looked relaxed. Excellent, that made things easier. And after Dai took the book off me yesterday, I was childishly pleased I wasn't the only one who thought reading at the breakfast table was perfectly reasonable. I must read the dragon book and send Mabon the quote he needed.

> Ti'Anna: I can't come round. The spies are everywhere. I require your assurance you are now familiar with the procedures for today?

> Niki: Not yet. Been too busy. But Mabon told me Jamie won't be harmed today.

Ti'Anna: Have you reminded him of his assurance today?

Niki: No? He gave me his word on it.

Ti'Anna: Please do so now and confirm same to me.

Gods and Goddesses, was the woman paranoid? Was there more to this? It seemed a heck of a lot of fuss about some central heating for a community hall.

I sighed. Did I need to work on setting boundaries *again*? That task could take a number and get in the queue. I was already juggling all the balls I could keep aloft for one day. John's sentencing, Rollo's testing, making sure the Gateway was ready to open to traffic, finding time to meet Glynis, and, oh, all the normal Recorder's day-to-day workload. Dola and Fi might need to pick up some of the slack.

A message from Aysha flashed up in my notifications. She hoped I was enjoying my break. I'd deal with her later. She'd think I was having a lovely time if I ignored her. I'd need to tell her about the hopeless mess with Dai face-to-face, or she'd keep saying I was being unreasonable. Stale instant freaking coffee. I was *not* being unreasonable.

"Sorry, but did you say stale instant coffee?"

I hadn't realised I'd said it aloud. Rollo's quizzical expression made me smile.

"Whoops. Not intentionally. Sorry. I've had a shit week."

He grinned at me. "Well, if it included stale instant coffee, sounds enough to ruin any week. I thought it was one of those swear word substitutions. You know how when people say 'sugar' when they don't want to say 'shit'? I was trying to work out what stale instant coffee might be a substitute for."

We were both laughing uninhibitedly when Finn and Caitlin walked through from Finn's Foxhole into the kitchen. They looked shocked to see us up, laughing and at the table with empty plates in front of us.

"Nice outfit, my lady." Caitlin smirked at me. I looked down at my pyjamas. "I'm only taking your mother's advice, Caitlin."

"Erm, Ma doesn't breakfast in pyjamas?"

"No, but she'd like to. She told me she should have started exactly as she meant to go on. Immediately after her coronation, she should have curled up on the couch in her most disreputable sweatpants. Made it clear to the staff, if the crown was in the drawer, they and their outdated beliefs could submit their notice if they wished. But what they couldn't do was be paid by her and criticise her personal choices in the privacy of her own Broch." That reminded me, "has Mrs Fosdike taken to her retirement?" I raised an eyebrow, and Caitlin looked abashed.

"Sorry, Niki, only meant … it's not like you. But yeah, Mrs F has rustled off to pastures new. They threw her a retirement party. The new Broch manager starts on Monday. Ma is happier."

I pulled my top away from my body so she could read the Just Be You and appreciate Olaf's silly smile. "I will be too. Meet the new me. But you're here early. Do you need something?"

Finn said, "Cait stayed at mine last night. The couch thing turns into a bed. Handy. Ignore her. She's worried about him." He looked Rollo up and down. "You OK?"

While they caught up with Rollo and Dola delivered them bacon sandwiches, I headed to my bedroom to get changed. I'd need to look like the Recorder today. Caitlin, damn her, wasn't wrong. Lounging around in my pyjamas wasn't like the woman I'd had to become since taking the Recorder role. But having a normal breakfast, laughing and making a fun start to the day with Rollo had been so refreshing and different. I'd enjoyed it.

Back in the kitchen, wearing my Recorder's robe, even if I had thermal leggings and jeans under it to counteract the expected cold of the Red Celt realm.

With some makeup and my new spiky rainbow-coloured hairdo, I felt good.

I found Rollo alone.

He'd also dressed and now wore a denim shirt under his leather waistcoat and jeans instead of his leathers. It was an improvement for my blood pressure. At least I could glance at his torso now instead of having to keep my eyes above his chin. But, sadly, it was a … what was the word for the complete opposite of an improvement? A dis-improvement? A depressing moment of reality arriving in my kitchen? Mostly I felt like a kid whose favourite plushy had been put firmly into the cupboard.

Seriously, Niki, get a grip, woman. This is the heir to a realm, not a cute toy. But … he's such a nice person too.

I sighed then saw Rollo was staring at me with a querying expression. I smiled and tried some manners. "Have my Knights gone?"

"Yes, a while ago. Finn wanted to update the portal and do something about the complaints from Galicia. He can't work out what's happening with their connection. It's unreliable. I said I'd help if you had other stuff to get to before my tests begin?"

"Sounds good. Do you like rollercoasters? Do you drive fast?" I was trying to work out if he was likely to throw up if I transported us both backwards half an hour and over to the Gateway. Maybe he should walk over. He looked baffled, and his mouth opened and closed a few times.

In the meantime, I asked, "Dola, are you stealing clothes or retrieving Rollo's own?"

"He has a Dolina now; it makes things easier. I am monitoring his longhouse. All is quiet there, and no one yet knows he is here. His staff have decided he is visiting a friend."

Rollo, with a wicked grin, answered my earlier question, "Yes and yes, probably too fast."

"You should be fine, then. Let's go. See you over there, Dola."

I grasped Rollo's right hand with my left, wincing at the static charge that always seemed to be present when we touched, and lifted Tilly with my right arm. I pictured the time on Mabon's message, cut it to two minutes before my five minutes would have elapsed, and thought, GO.

The world went yellow.

I opened my eyes in a strange room.

Rollo gasped. There was a Dolina on the bedside table and an enormous bed in a wooden frame.

Shit!

Tilly whined softly. I shushed her in my mind and stroked her shoulder. Rollo gazed about himself and whispered, "This is my longhouse in Viking. Was this supposed to happen?"

I shook my head.

He gestured me to an alcove behind the door, opened it quietly and stuck his head out. Closing the door and speaking at a more normal volume, he told me, "We're alone. The staff will still be at breakfast in their own quarters. Very odd sensation. It felt exactly like when you summoned me. What happened?"

"I'm not certain, but let's get out of here, unless you'd prefer to stay?"

He shook his head firmly. "Can you spare two minutes, though?"

"Sure." I sat on a chair by a solid wooden table currently serving as a desk and tried to make sense of what might have happened. The power we'd used to come here hadn't felt like mine. Mine was either green or rainbow-coloured if I used the Gateway power to time travel. But this transport had felt yellow. I had no idea what it meant, and then an idea pushed itself forward from the back of my brain and waved at me.

I'd need to check the Book. In the meantime, I looked out of the window. But the view didn't give me any sense of Viking. One way, fallow fields stretched across the landscape with a dusting of snow. In the other direction was a choppy-looking stretch of water, probably a river.

With quick, efficient movements, Rollo opened a large classy-looking leather tote and stuffed things in it. Clothes and toiletries removed from the adjoining bathroom joined everything else. Then he moved me aside and released a lever under the desk and pulled. The furniture wasn't solid as it had appeared, because a deep, suede-lined drawer came out as he pulled. In it lay a small box and a wide arrangement of weapons. The box and a selection of the weapons went into the bag too.

Next, he grabbed a black nylon backpack and loaded it with electronics: his laptop—a top-of-the-range MacBook, nice; various cables; an e-reader; a tool pouch; and, finally, several tablets.

He obviously planned to stay away for a while. Or maybe he didn't want to leave these things here unprotected. The Dolina by his bed was pretending to be an elegant photo frame. Clever. It showed a retro-style photo of a man and woman with their arms around each other. The man looked like Rollo and about his age, but the woman? I looked closer. Wow, she was beautiful and familiar with long, silvery-violet hair and eyes and surprisingly dark violet skin. Not the deepest purple of Ad'Rian's and Glais'Nee's, but even so, she must have been quite mature when she married Rollo's dad. Well, old for the Fae was quite different to old for humans.

I turned with the Dolina in my hand as Rollo came over. "Sorry, didn't mean to pry. But your mother was lovely, and you look just like your father. The Book told me his name was Jonvar?"

His face cleared of expression, but he nodded.

"And your mum?"

"Le'Anna." Again I watched as he did a breathing exercise. "It's very close to a similar Viking name, and, apparently, she wore a Fae glamour outside the longhouse to appear more Viking. That photo is the only one I have of her true face."

He picked up the Dolina as though to pack it when Dola's voice said, "I have stored it for you, Prince Rollo. Take the photo, but leave the Dolina here so I can monitor your home, please."

Rollo removed the photo and tucked it carefully into the backpack. Before he'd even returned the Dolina to the nightstand, it displayed the photo again. Go Dola. Rollo straightened. "Ready when you are, my lady."

I managed not to fan myself, but it was a challenge. He'd had the same effect every time he said *my lady* instead of my title. The first time when he came through to the Gateway for the bondings, I'd had what felt like a hot flush. He gave the *my lady* title a certain inflection that definitely got to me.

"I didn't think, did I? Is it harder for you to transport if there's more weight?"

I shook my head. "Weight isn't a problem, but thoughts are. Empty your mind please, Rollo. I think you may have been thinking about this," I gestured around the room, "when we transported."

With a guilty expression, he said, "I'm so sorry."

"Not your fault. How were you to know? But think only about the outside of the Scottish entrance to the Gateway and 8.07 a.m. today, please." I didn't want to transport him directly into the centre until we'd worked out what his power was doing. Also, two quick transports, and he might throw up. Caitlin's favourite flower pot would be handy if it happened.

He nodded, and the world went rainbow-coloured. Phew!

When we arrived, he asked, "So you can transport yourself? Like something out of *Star Trek*?"

"Pretty much."

Finn and Caitlin strolled down the path towards us, Finn finishing the last of his bacon sandwich as usual. He had the timing of his saunter from the cottage down perfectly to fit in a walking breakfast.

Rollo started to say something, then closed his mouth and gave me an assessing look.

Caitlin's eyebrows rose as she scrutinised Rollo. When nothing happened, she said, "Slagging hell.

You transported, didn't you? And he didn't throw up, did he? Why do I still do it?"

Rollo glanced at me, and the humour on his face came through in his voice as he commented, "You never did like speed, Cait."

"What's that got to do with the price of throwing knives?"

CHAPTER
FIFTEEN

Back inside the Gateway, I opened the gate, and Mabon strolled through alone. His usual bounce was absent this morning. I met him in the Red sector and gave him a hug. "Sent Rhiannon to get Dai, I did. Still snowed in up there."

While we waited, I opened Ti'Anna's message and handed the phone to Mabon. Only a few weeks ago, he would have acted as if I'd passed him a hand grenade with the pin out, but now he scrolled competently. After giving me an enquiring look before he pressed share, he airdropped Ti'Anna's contact details to his own phone and opened a message window.

I was amazed. I mean, sure, I'd hoped he'd get the hang of it—but this was much faster than I'd dared to hope. "You're doing really well with your phone."

Like a small boy with a pet frog, he waved his screen under my nose. "No need to do the writing, is there? Always my downfall, the typing part."

He tapped the phone and said, "Send a message to Ti'Anna." He paused, then continued speaking, "The Recorder informed you I had given her my word. No more should you need ever. Mabon ap Modron. Send." He gave one satisfied nod before adding, "Right now, *bach*, important business here before company arrives. A bad father I've been."

Then he noticed Rollo, sitting at the conference table chatting to Caitlin. "Do I want to know about that? A good man, Rollo. Does he need anything?"

"I think he's OK for now. The power, the Recorder and HRH are on the case. When we've sorted your problem out, we'll talk about him."

"Right you are. So Dai …"

"Uh-huh, Dai?"

"When he was a child, he couldn't keep his mouth shut. Kept wandering off. Caused a few … problems. Incidents, you might say."

Something about the way he said "problems" suggested starting wars and blowing stuff up rather than setting off a few out-of-season fireworks or coming home wet and muddy.

"Took him to Ad'Rian I did, and he did a few of his tweaks. Just enough to stop the child blabbing family business to all and sundry and make him easier to keep track of."

I didn't know what my expression might have said, but he rushed on, "No, not like your gran, *bach*. Truly not. But a bit tired we got of having to ask my mother to step in to find him. Always good about it, she was. But as she said herself, it would get annoying after a hundred years. And, after the problems with Rhiannon as a child, well, she had the right of it, did my mother. Couldn't argue with her logic. Better to do something about it."

Mabon's mother was the Goddess Modron herself. She was the source of the Modron House name. Mabon's name simply meant Son of the Great Mother. If he needed an ancient and powerful Goddess's intervention to find a lost child, where the hell had Dai been hiding?

"I feel like I'm getting the extremely short version of this, Boney, but it's none of my business, so, sure, go on."

"So Ad'Rian did his few tweaks, and then I got injured again, and, well…" He actually blushed. "Truth to tell, *bach*, forgot about it, I did."

"Forgot?"

"A funny time it was, lot of bad things happening. Anyway…" He drew in a long breath and waved his hands as if to say *what's done is done*. "All I can do now is fix it. So get him to Ad'Rian quickly, I must."

"Quickly? After all this time, it's suddenly urgent … because…?"

He patted my shoulder. "Actually, Nik-a-lula, might be your doing. It might be … I know you wouldn't have … oh, bugger it."

I had absolutely no idea what he was trying to say. The only other time I could remember Mabon stuttering was when he'd had to tell me—oh shit. No!

"I did this? How? W-what h-happened? And w-when? I didn't. Did I?" Now I was stuttering. I gathered my courage. I breathed. "What did I do, Mabon?"

"Angry you were, yes?"

"I was furious. But *what* did I do?"

I remembered the last time Mabon had been this upset. I hadn't properly secured the latch on Dusha and Diamant's paddock, and Diamant had injured his hoof. Ad'Rian and, consequently, Mabon had both been distraught. But not as distraught as I was once I saw the effect it had on Ad'Rian. It was the first time I'd ever seen a Fae go the grey colour that indicated shock.

I'd sworn I'd never be careless with an animal's safety again. Fortunately, the injury was minor. But the horrified fear in my stomach that I could have been the reason Diamant injured himself more severely or—monstrous thought—died, had left a scar on my soul. I'd been careful, cautious, responsible Niki with all animals ever since.

"Wondering I was if you used the power on him? Accidentally, of course. You were a ways past angry when you got to the castle. But now, all of Ad'Rian's tweaks are breaking down. Dai's ... well, *bach*, he's broken and a touch crazy right now."

I sagged with relief, and he must have seen it in my face. "What?"

"No. Not me." I shook my head. I felt bad for Dai. It might explain a lot. But I was only human, so I also gave an enormous sigh of relief. "I couldn't use the power up the mountain. There wasn't any. No wi-fi, no power, and no damn drinkable coffee. But, thank the Goddess, whatever caused it, it wasn't me."

"But Dai said you transported out. So you could use power? For some reason, he didn't think you could transport from there? Stupid boy."

"Well, yes, I did. But that's the McKnight Gift. Think about it, Boney. Take my gran, she could transport home from Manchester. I didn't understand it back then, but she did. And she couldn't use the power anywhere outside the Gateway, could she?"

Mabon nodded but looked confused. So I rushed on, feeling light-headed with relief. "My word on it, there was no power and no access to any in Dai's house when I was there."

He looked thoughtful now. "Good to know. What

the bluddy hell caused it then?" He shook his head, looked confused, and finally said, "Ad'Rian will sort him out." His phone vibrated, and he glanced down at it. "They're here, Recorder, if you wouldn't mind."

The red door swung open with a bang, and a voice said, "Sorry!"

A remarkably ugly, large, triangular-shaped, dark red head poked in. It had a lot of teeth. Sharp, pointy teeth. It was followed by a long red neck.

It had spines on it.

Then, smoke came from its nostrils, and my mind split in two.

The sensible half ran back to the centre, raised all the barriers and cowered under my desk, cuddling Tilly and screaming, DRAGON! The other half stepped forward and, in my best Recorder voice, said firmly, "No smoke or flames permitted in the Gateway, or I'll have to put you in a glass cage where you can fumigate yourself."

The neck came further in, and from outside the doorway, I heard a familiar snarky voice. "Ah, Recorder, you'll have to excuse us. No time to change, and I couldn't handle Dai in my other form. He's flipped. Mabon said it was urgent. The smoke is a nervous thing. The dragon part doesn't like buildings."

It took me a second to process, but then I stepped forward, peeped cautiously through the door, and looked up. "Rhiannon?"

And an entire pack of dominoes cascaded in my head as a lot of formerly confusing things made sense.

"Yes?"

I walked through the door and into the Red Celt realm and looked up.

And up.

And then a bit further up.

Sitting astride a somewhat twitchy-looking, huge, glossy, dark-red dragon was Rhiannon ap Modron. Her bright blue eyes sparkled with humour. Her long dark hair was piled onto the top of her head and secured in a messy updo with a dark red spiky comb.

Slung across the base of the dragon's neck near its shoulders—well, where I thought shoulders should be, anyway—between the spines was an unconscious Dai. He looked uninjured but unconscious. Gods and Goddesses, I was surrounded by unconscious men this week. But I couldn't see Rhiannon's legs, which quickly distracted me from Dai. Ooh, I was wrong. She wasn't sitting astride it; she was sitting *in* the dragon.

No. That wasn't right either. I squinted to get a

better view. A long way above me was Rhiannon's upper half. Her lower half appeared to *be* the dragon.

I closed my jaw with such a firm snap, it reverberated through to the base of my skull. I focused on her face and politely enquired, "Want a coffee or anything? It's cold today."

Rhiannon said, "Thanks, that'd be great. Vanilla latte if poss."

I damn well knew she was Aysha's soul sister!

CHAPTER
SIXTEEN

In a remarkably short time and with great efficiency, Mabon, along with several of his burly boyos carrying Dai, were on their way to the Fae healers.

I was insanely curious about what had happened with Dai. He'd looked fine. If Mabon hadn't told me otherwise, I might have thought he was sleeping. I was so relieved there hadn't been any access to the power in his house. At least I didn't need to fear I'd had anything to do with whatever pushed him over the edge. That would have been freaking perfect, wouldn't it? The first time I'd stood up for myself to a bullying man, and I ended up half killing him. Goddess, I sounded self-centred.

I wanted more information. But no one was offering me any. Mabon had said, "Don't know, *bach*.

Need to wait for Ad'Rian's say-so we will. Dai was raving when I got there. Mostly about you. Started on me too, he did. Used to see it in battle sometimes. A man's mind snaps when it can't handle any more. Fix him up, the healers will."

I thought I ought to be worried about Dai, but, oddly, I wasn't. Ad'Rian would fix him. I wasn't proud of it, but I'd just discovered I wasn't a kind enough person to be concerned about a man who'd intentionally locked me in his house. And then tried to do it a second time. If it made me a self-centred bitch, so be it. But someone who would have succeeded in holding me hostage if I hadn't been able to transport was not at the top of my list to send get well cards to.

I'd rather be a bitch than a hypocrite. Was I becoming uncaring? Honestly, being a little less caring about people who mistreated me didn't seem like the worst thing in the world.

Rhiannon had drunk her latte and left after calling, "See you at the sentencing. I'm saving you the head. Wear red." And the dragon's head disappeared with Rhiannon still on its back? In its back? Part of its back? How the heck did that even work?

Seriously, I needed information. Who could I ask? Hmm, the Book maybe?

· · ·

I looked at my phone. It said 9:45 a.m. The entire day stretched ahead of me, but I felt like I'd worked half a day already. My cheerful mood after my fun breakfast with Rollo had evaporated quickly.

The adrenaline rush from discovering ourselves in Rollo's longhouse and then having a dragon in my Gateway probably wasn't helping. I considered eating a second breakfast hobbit-style, not because I was even hungry. But because hot buttered toast felt as though it would taste exactly like a big soothing hug about now, and I could really, really use one.

"Finn, stick a notice on the portal please saying the Gateway will be closed." I thought about it. If I closed even for ten minutes, it would buy us hours in here if we needed them with the time-slip thing in the centre. "Briefly at 10:30 a.m. for essential maintenance. OK?"

There was no response from Finn. I turned to look and saw Rollo had his hand on Finn's back between his shoulder blades. My TEK looked unhappy. I shot over to him, "You OK, Finn?"

He turned his greenish-white, unhappy face to me. "Dragons," was the only thing he got out before he shuddered.

"Yeah, they are very weird. But she's gone now. Are you OK?"

I caught Rollo's eye and gave a querying shrug. I had absolutely no clue what had freaked Finn out.

That he didn't like dragons was obvious. But this looked almost like a phobia. What was I missing? How could I help? Rollo massaged Finn's tight shoulders.

A vanilla Coke and a foil-wrapped chocolate biscuit landed on Finn's desk. He picked the can up. And laughed.

I could barely believe my eyes. He'd gone from shaky to shaking with laughter in barely a heartbeat.

His can of Coke said, *Join my exclusive dragon-loathing club*. There was a graphic of a black arrow wrapped around the can alongside the words.

The biscuit was an orange Club and said McVities. Didn't Jacobs used to make those biscuits? I shook my head. I obviously wasn't myself yet either. But Finn was still laughing and showing Rollo the can. Then Rollo started laughing too.

I walked over. Finn held the can up to show me. When I simply gazed at it in confusion, he said, "It's Bard the Bowman's black arrow."

"Okaaay?" Actually, Bard the Bowman sounded familiar. From a movie maybe?

Rollo interjected, "From Tolkien."

Oh, Gods and Goddesses, we were in fanboy territory, weren't we? I faked a smile. Anything that cheered Finn up was fine by me.

Seconds later, Finn said, "The announcement's up."

He looked better. I asked, "Are you OK? You can take a minute."

"It's OK if I'm expecting it. But the head. Ugh. Poking through the door. In *my* Gateway."

I grinned. His Gateway, huh? Aww, my TEK was taking full possession of his role. I patted his shoulder.

Finn said, "Rollo's got an idea about the Galicians' bandwidth issue. OK to focus on it for a bit?"

"Sure. I don't need him until ten-thirty. *He's* the essential maintenance."

Rollo grinned at me, tucked an earbud in, and I heard him speaking in a rapid undertone.

I tapped my own earbud and said, "Well done, Dola. But who the hell is Bard the Bowman?"

There was a silence. Then she said, "He killed a dragon in a popular movie. And there were some books."

"Yeah, Rollo said, but how did you know it was what Finn needed?" It seemed completely illogical to me. Brush off all his fears with a can of Coke and a biscuit?

More silence.

"I do not know, Niki. I simply did. But I will consider the answer and get back to you."

I'd once thought knowing what people needed might be Dola's superpower. But this example of it felt like a huge step up from sending me hot chocolate when I was frightened. I'd ask the Book.

Caitlin and Fi arrived together at my desk.

Caitlin spoke first. "My lady, have you studied up on the sentencing yet? I've only been to a few myself. None as important as this one. Absolutely everyone is coming. I have to be there anyway for Ma, but did you want me to come with you? Said I'd let Ma know."

"It's fine. I spent a lot of time in the Red Celt realm when I was a kid. You go with your mum. But what do you know about dragons?"

"Messy little bastards, and some of them are crazy. Rhiannon's OK." She lowered her voice. "But Finn hates them, and he's terrified of her. Ma doesn't like her either, but she's always been cool with me. Why?"

"I didn't realise they were sort of like centaurs?" Caitlin looked confused, and I wondered if she knew what a centaur was. Actually, were they a mythical Narnia thing? No, Mr Tumnus was a faun, not a centaur, wasn't he? I tried to clarify my muddled thought process. "Half person, half whatever?"

"No, dragons aren't. At least I don't think so. More like shifters, I think, but with a half form. Ask the Book?"

I nodded, and with a sly expression, she added, "And can you tell me what it says? I've always wondered about them. Tried to ask Dai once when he was working with them, but he just gave me an odd look. Is he gonna be OK, do you think?"

"He'll be fine. Mabon wasn't worried."

"Yeah, but I'mma not sure what would worry him."

I'd noticed whenever Caitlin reverted to the Pictish habit of adding an A onto random words, there was something going on, and I wondered what was bothering her. "Clear and present danger, or people he cares about being injured worry him. Trust me on that. What he told me made it sound like a PTSD-type thing. But he's confident Ad'Rian will fix him."

She nodded and headed towards the blue gate to tell Breanna she'd be going with her, I assumed.

I retrieved the Book, intending to ask about dragons, and moved over to the conference table accompanied by Fi and Tilly. On the way, I surveyed Finn's desk. He always used multiple screens, his monitor, phone, laptop—whatever was handy—but today it looked like a damn Apple store.

I stopped. Where had all the extra screens come from? Rollo reached out and poked several of them. Ah, OK.

"Finn, my desk and monitor are free for an hour if

191

you're running out of space. And there are the spare desks too. No need to be squashed."

Finn ignored me. He had noise-cancelling on as usual. But Rollo, who wore a single earbud, exactly what I preferred myself: connection to the screens but also awareness of the world around me, met my eyes. "Thanks, Niki. It won't take long with us both on it, but, yeah, not enough space. There's something odd going on, but it's at their end not ours. You haven't got a pencil, have you?"

I grabbed him one out of Fi's beautifully organised top drawer, then watched as he gathered all his long, blond multi-shade hair to the back of his head in one practised motion, twisted it and secured it with the pencil. It wasn't the first time he'd done that! But that wasn't the interesting thing. The interesting thing was how very different it made him look. Older, more serious and much less hot Viking and far more hot geek. Huh.

He moved next door to my desk. I quashed wholly inappropriate, warm feelings about him sitting on my chair. What the hell was wrong with me? I wasn't some stupid teenager, and women who publicly lusted after men annoyed me. Could it be weird middle-aged hormones? No. Since when wasn't it normal to notice a hot guy? And he was an extremely hot guy. Muttering, "Noticing is one thing,

Niki. But you're pushing it. Chill out, do some damn work," to myself, I arrived at the conference table.

"What do you need, Fi?"

"I wondered if you required me to come to the Red Celts with you?"

That surprised me. Did she want to come? It didn't sound like a fun afternoon. But I was being self-centred again, wasn't I? She must have worked with John. He'd been Gran's Knight Adjutant for the whole time she'd worked in the Gateway.

"Did you want to go?" I glanced at her. So far, in the admittedly not quite three weeks I'd known her, I'd formed some impressions of Fi. None of them included her even being capable of blind fury. But fury was exactly what was in her eyes now. Scary angry. But about what? I tapped my Gift, but the anger was so white-hot, it was simply anger with no more info.

Words then, try words.

She hadn't even been that angry when we'd talked about Troels having raped her. What the hell had John done? I'd thought he was just an incompetent, buck-passing, lying old buffoon.

Outwardly calm, Fi said, "Oh, I'm going. My mother is coming through for it too. I only wondered if you wanted us to come with you? There'll be space in the box if you don't mind."

The lovely Mrs Glendinning was coming too? Why?

"Fi, I'm obviously missing stuff here, sorry. Is it yet another of those things I should know but don't? Why's your mum coming?"

Fi gave me a level look. "Do you know much about the druidic beliefs and ceremonies?"

"Druids? Er, nope, not really. Trees and robes, sometimes standing stones and, erm, nature? Yeah, nope. Why?"

Her eyebrows squished into a monobrow. "You might want to ask the Book."

"Sometimes, the Book should be the last resort, not the first. It's brilliant and magical and what have you, but it can't tell me how people feel. Which is why I'm asking you." I folded my hands on the conference table and waited.

It worked, go me!

She said, "The Red Celts are, broadly speaking, still Druidic."

"OK." I nodded. Mabon had taken me to an oak grove when I was a kid and told me oak trees were sacred to his subjects.

"Druids believe in reincarnation. They also believe sins committed during a life can be atoned for in the next one." Fi watched me carefully.

But, yeah, it made sense. I nodded. I mean, weren't we all constantly trying to do better?

Whether in this life or the next was a small step to me.

Fi was on a roll now she saw I was listening. "Mabon claimed him as an oathbreaker on behalf of all the realms."

I nodded. "Yes, at my ascension."

"So, if someone is to be executed, there's a Druidic ceremony called sentencing where everyone they hurt, harmed or damaged tells them what they did wrong. John's sentencing isn't about handing down a sentence. We all know the kings and queens have tried him and judged him guilty of being an oathbreaker. Oathbreaking isn't a crime anyone in the realms ever survives, so he'll die this afternoon. The sentencing bit is us all pronouncing our verdict on his life."

She paused, but I was following her, which was a blissful change. In this job, I mostly hadn't followed anything anyone tried to tell me the first time around.

I nodded again, and when she didn't carry on, I added, "Uh-huh."

I was already aware of all this. The penalty for breaking an oath was death. John had also appointed his son to the role of Knight Adjutant without ever bothering to check he could see the power. He hadn't taught him anything about the Knight's vital role. So Jamie thought he could drive a bulldozer over my cottage, "a shack," he'd called it, and the Gateway.

It would have left all the citizens of the realms stranded with no access to each other's world, which went against everything the Knight Adjutant was supposed to stand for. Major oathbreaking.

John's trial and the quick vote on his guilt from all the royals had taken place at my public ascension. Mabon had taken John into custody and said I should decide what to do about Jamie.

I told Fi all this, and she simply nodded. I offered her the part which still confused me. "But why the hell is everyone going to watch? It seems gruesome."

Fi shook her head. Obviously, I still hadn't got it. "To make clear his full crimes against the realms." She started ticking off points on her fingers. "Their inhabitants." She stuck her thumb out. "The other Knight Adjutant candidates he left hanging out to dry without even testing them so they couldn't get on with their lives." A finger joined the thumb. "All the magical creatures he didn't protect or even believe in because he couldn't see them. The dragonkin, the unicorns, the percys." She reached the end of her left hand and stuck her right thumb out. "Even the vicious little piskies."

Fi paused for thought. "And, of course, the Gateway, your gran herself and the Recorder's Office." She looked sadly at her single pinkie finger still folded down because she didn't have anything or anyone to attach to that one. But, wow, it was a lot of damage caused by a single middle-aged idiot.

I told her this, and she nodded vehemently. "It's an opportunity for everyone to tell him his failings so his soul can improve on his journey. And he can do better in his next life."

"Okaaay?"

"Druids value threes: Goddess, God, worshippers. Granddaughter, Mother, Daughter. The Triskele, the Celtic knot, the triad, all threes. The injuries will be stated in threes as well."

Fi was embracing her teacher status now, but it was what I needed. "Dola, can I have a black coffee, please?" I raised an eyebrow at Fi.

She said, "A lavender-mint tea please, Dola." Lavender and mint tea? I kept my shudder to myself.

"Corby's coming, and hopefully her sister and her wife too, if they can get out of the salon. And Glynis will be there, of course, with some of the girls and—" She paused as our mugs arrived and turned hers around to read it.

Her mug said, *A hug in a cup.*

Mine said, *Fool me once, shame on you; fool me twice, shame on me. Fool me three times, shame on us both.*

Ancient Druidic saying via Stephen King.

"But why?" My question burst out of me as I bit back a laugh at my mug. I immediately felt rude.

"Sorry, Fi, I'm not getting it. What did John have to do with it all? I mean, I get the breaking his oath thing, sure. But why are random people like your mum coming?"

She paused, sipped her tea, looked at her mug, and smiled. "Have you ever heard the saying about all it takes for evil to win is if everyone else doesn't do anything, or something like that?"

"Sure. *The only thing necessary for evil to triumph is for good men to do nothing.* That one?"

She nodded. "That was John. He didn't kill anyone. But he let many people die. He didn't sexually assault anyone, but he refused to do anything about the droit de seigneur trade, which resulted in hundreds of rapes. He told me I was too young to understand. I had a little boy who had the horrible Troels as his father, but I was too young to understand!"

She shuddered. I reached for her hand. "I'm so sorry, Fi; I didn't mean to upset you."

She completely ignored my sympathy and, in a low angry voice, continued, "He left your Gran in ignorance about a lot of important things. When my grandmother died, my lady Elsie asked me why on earth I hadn't brought her through to live with me and my mum at the end."

She had to stop again, and a small sob broke through.

I was so out of my depth here. I wondered whether to hug her, but then she turned those blazing eyes to me again. "While your gran was on holiday, John told me my lady Elsie had said no to my gran coming through. One-in, one-out, of course? But he'd *never* even asked her!"

I'd never understood the one-in, one-out rule properly. I'd have to look into what else my gran might have screwed up with it.

"Later, my lady Elsie said, 'Of course an exception could have been made.' The one-in, one-out was a guideline; it wasn't carved in stone. John told me it was a *law*. The lying sack of shite. He was the Knight Adjutant, so I trusted him. I never believed a word he said after that, but your gran said she was stuck with him, and we'd have to work around him."

Fi swallowed hard. "Then you came and changed everything *in a week*." Her voice had risen to a parrot screech now.

I finally understood why the only thing she'd said to me on her first day back was, "It's all changed. How has it all changed?"

With a sob in her voice, Fi said, "Your gran should have just fired Fergusson. But she didn't even know she could."

Well, crap.

But Fi hadn't finished. "So, no, Niki. He committed no 'crimes' himself. Well, nothing we could charge him with until you uncovered the oath-breaking. But he allowed a lot of horrible, miserable, viciously cruel, heartless things to happen on his watch." She paused to breathe and looked as if she might break down.

"Dola, can we have some mead for Fi's tea please?"

The bottle of mead arrived, and I uncorked it and hovered it over Fi's mug. She nodded. I waited until she sipped it and got herself back under control.

I was also beginning to understand why Breanna always sounded like she was spitting whenever she said John's name. As the Pictish queen, she'd have known about Fi's gran being forced to stay in her realm and away from her loving family as she approached the end.

"Some people, like Mabon, Breanna and Inge, stepped in and stopped some of his worst crimes of omission. But if they hadn't …" She shuddered. "He kept my gran alone and away from us until her death, because he couldn't be bothered to fill in the paperwork for her to stay with us in the village. You'll hear this afternoon, anyway. I need to go home and collect my mum. Dad's made a basket for John. So is it OK if I take the afternoon off?"

"No, I don't think so."

She scowled at me.

"I mean, of course you can go—but please

consider it as work time. It's a Recorder thing, isn't it? And you work in the Gateway? No need to waste half a day of holiday time on it."

I was dreading what would happen this afternoon now. What the hell had I started when I fired him?

Then Fi, with steel under her now-soft tone, said, "No, thank you. I'm very sorry, Niki, but I'd prefer to take a half-day of holiday, so I don't have to behave like a member of the Recorder's staff. I think it will be better that way. This afternoon I need to be my son's mother, my mother's daughter and my late grandmother's representative. Threes, you see?"

I thought I was finally starting to see. Tears of frustration pricked at the back of my eyes. Oh, Gran, you were always such a fighter. Why the hell didn't you fight for these people?

CHAPTER
SEVENTEEN

The Gateway bustled with travellers headed to the Red Celt's realm. Almost all offered subdued greetings in place of their usual cheery ones.

A group of women came through from the Pictish realm and simply stood and waited in the Red sector. It was only when several more women came through from Galicia, and another group from Caledonia joined them from the Green sector, I realised they were waiting for friends so they could all arrive as a group. Some of them carried baskets, and I overheard Glynis's name.

The sectors were wide and spacious. The women weren't blocking traffic, so I left them to it as they looked around, searching for their missing friends.

The atmosphere was becoming oppressive, so I was relieved when my phone said 10:30 a.m.

When I called, "The Gateway is closing for a short time for essential maintenance. Pick your gate, ladies, please." Several of them looked at each other in panic, but then two women ran up the Green sector from the Caledonian gate, calling, "Sorry, sorry."

Once the group had moved through to the Red Celt realm, I touched the anvil and closed the gates before I sought Rollo, who still sat at my desk.

"Shall we see what you gained yesterday, and if you're fit to go home before anyone notices you're missing?"

He frowned but stood up and, after speaking to Finn, made his way over to me in the centre. "How do we do this?"

"I have no idea. I was expecting HRH to arrive with a plan. She usually does."

We waited.

We looked at each other.

We looked around.

I said, "OK. It's up to us then. Do you sense any difference in yourself? Apart from our unscheduled trip earlier, I mean?"

"Oh, yes. I feel both liberated and resistant."

"Resistant to what?" Such an interesting word. He appeared completely relaxed. Obviously, he had a good front. I tapped my Gift. It gave me the same mix of fury, anger and frustration I'd picked up from him on our very first phone call when he wanted me to allow the Viking bond mates to come through for their ceremonies.

I wondered anew how on earth a man who wasn't just strikingly handsome but was also fun, intelligent and interesting could be sexually frustrated? Were the Viking women blind? I also sensed again the desperate sadness he'd had before. It was still there, along with a vast empty pit where his happy vibes should have been.

Surely he wasn't short of willing volunteers? As I thought this, his head swivelled round, and he looked straight at me. "How could you be sure they were willing in Viking? Tell me that."

I goggled at him. Had he just read my mind?

"Yes," he said. "I seem to be able to do that now."

My cheeks felt as though they were the colour of strawberries.

He gave me a kind smile and a sexy wink. "Breathe, Niki. I was flattered. Truly—and confused."

"Confused?" The heat radiated from my flaming red face. I looked around, but everyone else seemed to be busy. I sighed with relief and prepared to apologise, grovel even. OMG, the things I'd thought at breakfast. Shit! How long had he been able to do this?

205

How utterly inappropriate. How absolutely bloody mortifying.

Rollo's tone was warm. "Yes, confused. I've no idea why you're beating yourself up about it? You weren't being rude, or unkind, or unpleasant. Why did you think you shouldn't look at me? Is it because of the difference in our ranks?"

"Ranks?" What difference in our ranks? WTF was he talking about?

He laughed. "I'm still doing it, you know. I'm not sure how to turn it off yet. I meant you being the Recorder, and me not even wanting to be a prince, never mind take the Viking throne. What sane man would want to? But it's a huge difference in our ranks."

I didn't always understand the realms' perception of rank. But rank had absolutely nothing to do with why I didn't think I should lust after a hunky twenty-something.

I did the only thing that made any sense to me. I ignored it until I thought of something intelligent to say and, in the meantime, offered a prayer to the Goddess Miseria asking her to cool my glowing red face quickly.

I straightened my already straight Recorder's robe. "Well, this is super embarrassing. Shall we focus on what else you can now do before I have to open the Gateway again? And I'll work up a proper apology when my face isn't on fire."

Twenty minutes later, the answer seemed to be nothing. He couldn't do anything. He saw the power still, but couldn't do anything with it. Autumn had a better connection to it than he did.

He couldn't pull power, direct it or cover his hand with it. It was the same whether I used the Gateway power, or if I separated the Gateway's yellow power out from the rainbow for him. When he touched the flowers made of power on the anvil's throne, they no longer attached to him. They did shiver, as they had when Mabon and Ad'Rian had stroked them, but that was all.

When I pulled power and directed it to him, it dispersed in mid-air before it reached him.

I'd taken a quick break and asked the Book, "What am I supposed to do with Rollo? Am I supposed to be helping him use his power?"

The Book remained still. Eventually, it produced a page that said, **Render any help you can. At this time, it is not yet clear what might be necessary.**

Which felt like a generic error message and the Book's equivalent of a game developer's, *Whoops! Something may have gone wrong. No, we don't know what yet, but, relax, someone is probably working on it—almost certainly right now.*

Rollo shot me a surprised look. "Do you game, Niki?"

So he was still reading my mind. And then it occurred to me my shields were far more open than usual. I'd had to keep them low to connect with the power, test his abilities and help him. In fact, they'd been almost fully down since yesterday because I'd probably been subconsciously monitoring Rollo while he slept last night.

I should close them down now. He was fine, at least physically. Perhaps my brain was back online too. Because I might be mortified that his half-dressed body was distracting, but I wasn't in the least bit embarrassed that I'd always enjoyed online games. Gaming wasn't like thinking what an incredible sight his chiselled torso was at breakfast, was it? *Oh, FFS, stop it, Niki. He's reading your mind, remember?*

There was a low, masculine chuckle, and before the embarrassment overwhelmed me again, I pulled my shields tight and closed them.

Rollo squeaked.

He really had squeaked, and when I swivelled around to see what had happened, under his golden tan, he was pale and shook his head like a dog with water in its ears.

Then, with the first note of panic I'd ever heard from him throughout this entire experience, he asked,

"What did you do? It's like the light went out inside my head!"

"What do you mean, the light went out in your head?"

What had I done? What light?

I reached out with my Gift, but his blind panic was overwhelming. For such a strong guy, he looked shaky.

I waited, but he couldn't seem to string words together.

I dropped my shields to ask the power to help him, or at least tell me what I'd done, and he took in a gasping breath.

"Please don't do that again. It was horrible."

Closing my shields had made him panic?

HRH arrived. Of course she did. She couldn't have come earlier when I needed her advice, but now something interesting was happening, and here she was. How she'd turn Rollo's meltdown into a wager would be worth watching.

She jumped onto the anvil's surround, and her voice was odd, softer than her usual sneering one. "Give me your hand please, Rollo. And breathe normally."

She extended a paw to his hand, but her eyes never stopped assessing me, although she appeared to be looking over my head. "What? I didn't mean to do whatever I did."

"Really, Recorder. 'How was I to know?' You still believe you can use stupidity as a valid defence? Close your shields, please."

I glanced at Rollo. I didn't want to give him unnecessary pain if the cat was simply experimenting.

HRH batted at his hand with her paw. "I am here. All will be well. Allow me to test it."

Rollo nodded at me. I closed my shields. Tight.

His face paled again, and I saw the cat pulling some of the yellow power out of him. She licked it. Which was strange.

Caitlin arrived. "Everything OK, Niki?"

The cat glared at her. Caitlin took an involuntary step backwards, then resolutely stepped forward again. "Recorder?"

I got a strong sense Rollo didn't want Caitlin to observe whatever this was. "No, it isn't. But it's a Recorder problem, not a Knight one, thank you, KAIT."

She nodded and moved back to Fi.

HRH said, "Open your shields precisely five percent, Recorder."

I had no clue what five percent of my shields

meant, so I cracked them a little and watched her until she nodded. Rollo was still too pale.

"Take the Recorder's hand please, Rollo."

He caught my gaze with his tawny eyes in a way that asked, *OK with you?* I reached out my hand. He took it and smiled. I wanted to shake my own hand. The strange static charge was still there whenever we touched. "What is that?"

Rollo said, "Oh, you get it too? Thought it was only me. I didn't want to mention it. Seemed like the kind of dumb thing people say in a movie."

I laughed, but hadn't I thought something similar myself?

The cat was in full-on science professor mode now. "Continue with the contact, but close your shields, Recorder."

I did as I was told. What else would I do on Friday morning except follow commands from a feline goddess and entertain the Gateway staff? I damn well knew they were all watching us. Oh, yeah, and hold hands with a Thor look-alike who made me tingle. My life used to be boring. It sure as hell wasn't anymore.

Rollo looked paler. I glared at the cat. She was licking yellow power again. "What are you *doing,* Your Majesty?"

"I'm testing his connection to the yellow regnal power. To see if it is linked to this problem."

OK then. Was this like when I didn't realise I hadn't accepted the Gateway power properly, and Mabon and I worked out I needed to breathe it in? I'd had killer headaches until the Gateway and I properly connected. Was Rollo's darkness like my blinding headaches? My sympathy for him ramped up several notches. That had been a nasty, painful week.

"Recorder, do not close your shields if you can avoid it. Ten or fifteen percent open should be sufficient."

I nodded. "OK, I'll do my best." I opened them a bit more. Rollo looked happier.

HRH gave Rollo her imperious stare. "Hear me well now, kingling. You must fully accept the yellow power swiftly. Stop resisting it. Do it within the next three days. If you don't, there will be a painful price to pay. Remember, accepting the power is *not* accepting the throne. You agreed to hold it safe, but you're keeping it at tail's length. You need to integrate it fully. It will not bite."

She paused and watched him carefully.

"Everyone except the imbecilic Troels knows you don't want the throne. But the power has made its inclination clear. You have been charged with keeping the regnal power safe and healthy. It does not preclude you from passing it on to whomever you think should rule in your stead. But rejecting the power is not an option. Viking will fall if you do. Integrate it."

He'd been pale before, but Rollo looked horrified now. His eyes were enormous in his face, and the dark circles under them stood out in stark contrast to the white of his usually golden skin.

"You may leave us, Recorder."

I thought about objecting—it was my damn Gateway—but I wanted a coffee, so I nodded. She seemed to understand what was happening, which was more than I did. "Rollo?" When he looked at me, I said, "Tell her about this morning and our unplanned trip. It might be relevant."

As I left, I heard HRH say, "Now, Rollo, first remind me about your paternal grandfather. What was his breeding? Because something is keeping your fae blood suppressed, and it ought to be helping you here."

Huh, was he like Kaiden? No, because Rollo knew his mother was fae. Kaiden hadn't had a clue. What had Ad'Rian called Kaiden? *One of the lost ones?* I gave up. Lunch seemed like a good plan. Somehow, I was getting the idea I wouldn't want to eat after this afternoon's sentencing.

CHAPTER
EIGHTEEN

E ven though Fi had insisted on taking the afternoon as a holiday, it still turned out to be quite the office outing. I'd left Tilly in the cottage with Dola and Rollo.

Fi, her mother, Corby, and I headed towards the red gate to Pant y Wern. Traffic in the Gateway was still brisk, with travellers from almost all the realms heading through to the Red Celt capital for the sentencing. As we were leaving, Finn rushed up holding his livestream camera.

I said, "No, Finn, I don't think so. I have an unhappy feeling about this afternoon. Take whatever footage you want, but nothing goes out via the portal without the Recorder's express approval. OK?"

For the first time ever, Finn shook his head at one of my instructions.

I waited.

Finn said, "Oughta go out to everyone. Ma says doing things in the dark is how John did the damage. No one could question him. Don't want us to be like him. Livestream shows the truth."

That was more words than usual from Finn. I held up my hand to show I was thinking it through.

I tapped my earbud. "Dola, your thoughts?"

"Finn may be correct. John was a poisonous fungus. Fungi grow in the dark. You believe in allowing people to understand why we have taken our decisions, don't you? Shining a light on facts stops gossip and conspiracy theories. I think we should send it to all the realms, even Viking. The royals sentenced John to death. It was the correct decision. We should show everyone why."

Dola had obviously shared her thoughts through Finn's earbuds too, because he was nodding so hard, he looked like his head might come loose. Finn pointed at his earbud and said, "That."

They had a point.

I said, "OK, but I want a five-minute transmission delay and trigger warnings before anything too horrible. Do we allow minors to watch the livestreams?"

I wasn't a great believer in trigger warnings. Sometimes I thought they were just spoilers for a good movie. But if the emotions I was picking up from the Gateway travellers today came to fruition, it might scar for life any kids watching it. I'd never recovered from Bambi's mother being killed. I wouldn't upset the kids. The adults could make their own decisions.

I heard Dola's, "No, Niki. We segment the audience. This will only be available to adults." Finn gave me a thumbs-up.

Pant y Wern was ridiculously crowded when we arrived, and the Highland coos really weren't helping anything or anyone. Why weren't they down by the river as usual? I liked the Highland cows. The Red Celts called them Hairy or Heilan Coos. They were big and silly and fluffy with wonderful curving horns. But the small, tame herd—or fold, as a group of Highland cows was correctly called—had lived on the riverbanks when I was a child. I'd loved feeding them with those little cattle cubes the cow herders kept for them so they got enough minerals. But now they appeared to have invaded the town.

We all eventually forced our way out of the red gate with the Red Celt's dragon insignia on their side of the beautifully maintained doorway. The realms took pride in their gates, from the Picts' beautiful iron, three-legged triskele to this one with its sinuous dragon. The dragon's head was above my eye level. I followed the curving line of its back down to the tail, which coiled around the bottom of the door. Even with the dragon's partially spread wings, it didn't convey the scary reality of the real thing.

The Gate connected to a small lane inside Mabon's castle walls, which fed into the main square. I'd been here often as a child. My gran had never cared if I went alone to visit Mabon.

But today it was gridlock.

People and coos were everywhere, unable to move along to the square. There was no way through the throng, and the group of us couldn't slip nimbly through as I'd always done as a child. The crowd wouldn't have disgraced a major football game. It was overwhelming, with too much angry emotion in the air, and I tightened my shields.

From behind us came a call in a deep, authoritative voice, "Make way for Her Majesty Queen Breanna."

Breanna, Caitlin and a group of the Broch guards drew alongside us. Caitlin scooped us into their party, but the progress was still ridiculously slow, and all the people were still too close. The combination of body odours, tobacco smoke, and an excessive use of perfume made me queasy. The sheer weight of all the people so close gave me panicky feelings. I've never liked crowds.

I consoled myself—once I'd seen where we were

going, I could transport directly next time and avoid all this stinky, oppressive madness.

From behind us came another loud cry, "Make way for the Imperial Emperor and Empress. Their Majesties, Alphonse and Sabella, require access."

Breanna drew us all slightly to one side. As I gave her an enquiring look, she said, "We normally wait in the Gateway and come through together. It's easier for the guards if they can wedge us in the middle. Ours will take the front, and theirs will bring up the rear. But we were late today, and I thought they'd gone ahead."

Alphonse and his wife, Sabella, reached us, along with their son, Alejandro. Natalia and their new son-in-law, Tomas, were still on their honeymoon. Natalia had put up a fight to marry her bond mate, only to discover they had a seven-fold bond, which even her stubborn father couldn't argue about. At least not once Autumn helped the emperor to see the bond. I hoped the newly-bonded couple were having a wonderful holiday. Alejandro's handsome face was sulky and scowling as he greeted Caitlin.

The guards exchanged hand signals and gathered us into the middle of a protected bubble. With guards waving pointy things to encourage people to move, I had space to breathe. I didn't see any injuries. The threat seemed to be enough, and much swifter progress began. Like when you follow an emergency vehicle with its lights and sirens on, the path ahead of us cleared. We came to a large wooden double doorway, and Breanna took my arm to usher me through as the guards peeled off to allow the rest of the group into the hallway with us.

Alphonse came forward, his arms open to hug Breanna, and Empress Sabella greeted me. "So sorry, my lady, terribly rude of us. But the guards are so strict, so *difícil*, they can't protect us if we stop to chatter. How lovely to see you again! How is your adorable goddaughter? What a gift she gave me, allowing me to see Tomas and Natalia's bond. Her manners and mode were *encantadores*, just *perfecto*. A wonderful smile she has too."

Apparently, the empress didn't need to breathe between sentences. She chattered on and on about flowers and ribbons, and who had finally caught Natalia's bouquet after the small fight, until finally Breanna rescued me.

"Let's take our seats, Sabby. I'm sure if you invited the Recorder to tea, she would come and have honey cake and sunshine once we get through slagging February. But for now …" she took the empress's arm and moved her firmly towards the stairwell, "…we need to make room for the next arrivals."

Finn gestured towards the stairs. "This way, my lady, I know where your box is."

I had a box? Yeah, Fi said there would be room in the box, didn't she? I couldn't wait to see it. A box sounded fun.

A couple of years ago, Aysha's accountant told her she should have a box at the opera. If she used it for corporate entertaining, there were tax breaks for her law practice. Being Aysha, she'd promptly booked a box at one of the Manchester theatres for pantomime season and invited various clients and their kids. "Well, opera is fine for the old guard and their silly games, but, seriously, Niki, who wouldn't rather take their kids to a panto? It's a great stress buster."

It had been so popular, she'd done it every year since. So I'd been in a posh, velvet-lined, curtained box with a splendid view of the stage before.

Yeah, this one was nothing like that.

This one was constructed of old stones, the walls covered with nightmare-inducing woven hangings. I'd probably call them "famous trials and sentencings throughout the centuries." It was like having old-fashioned freeze frames of the gorier CSI episodes embroidered and hung on the walls.

They'd used a lot of red embroidery thread or wool or whatever they made them with. It was all mostly black and white for the buildings, grey for the sky, and then red. Red dragons, red blood—lots of blood spread everywhere—and Red Celts. Yeah, just a ton of red.

The rest of my large stone box contained bench seating for my guests, I assumed, and two thrones. Actual gold-painted thrones. With deep red cushions, thank goodness. The guys in the cheap seats got a wooden bench and were grateful. There was a single entrance door at the back of the room and a fireplace on a side wall with a large crackling log fire. The thrones faced a deep full-height window embrasure with currently closed green shutters.

It was apparently the Recorder's box. Finn told me the Pict royal box was next door. All the realms had their own boxes. This was a part of the castle I'd never visited before.

We all settled. I sat on the throne feeling ridiculous, but Fi had given me a firm look, "It's tradition, my lady," which put me in my place. I'd offered Mrs Glendinning the other throne, but she insisted it wouldn't be proper. She agreed to borrow one of the throne's many cushions for her hard bench seat, though.

And we all waited. I wished I'd asked the Book some more searching questions. And I really wished I'd brought a coffee. Even with the fire, it wasn't warm in the room. I felt like a poorly barbecued chicken leg. My left side, close to the fire, was grilled to golden, and my right side was still raw and freezing.

The general atmosphere was subdued. I was trying to think of a polite conversation starter when the shutters swung open, surprising me. A draught of icy air flowed in. I was glad of those thermal leggings now and my cloak.

I stood and looked out of the window, which led onto a narrow balcony, as Finn said, "Ma would never let us do that. Not seemly."

"Well, you're not a child anymore. I'm not your mother, and I don't care. Recorders are allowed to be eccentric. Dola tells me I need to cease feeling the need to conform. So over to you, Finn."

He grinned and stuck his head and then his camera out for a panning shot. "Wanted to bring the drone. Cait said the dragons'd eat it."

I looked out, but there were no dragons. Only the busy main square of Pant y Wern with its black and white buildings curving along the inside of the castle walls. They usually looked attractive. But the white plaster was grubby at the end of winter, and the black wooden supports had faded to dark grey after the harsh weather. The people whitewashed and painted in April so it would be fresh for the celebration on May Day. I recalled excessive paint smells and tinkling bells to remove the last of the winter energy for weeks before the dancing and scents of wood smoke at Beltane. But today the flags of all the realms fluttering in the brisk, icy breeze gave it a festive feel.

To my left, Caitlin, ignoring her mother's injunctions, also hung out of the window of the next box along. With all the shutters open, it was clear the window frames and shutters that faced onto the square were painted in each realm's colour. I couldn't remember ever seeing them before. Was it a new thing? Or maybe the rainbow colours were the new part?

The boxes were in the same order as the Gateway doors. So my green one was between the Picts and the Vikings' empty yellow-painted box next door, which would mean Mabon's was the one on the end with Galicia next to his. Mabon's box also seemed to be empty. I couldn't be certain because the curve of the building wasn't tight enough for me to see in, but it looked empty.

Between the farthest violet shutters at the other end was Glais'Nee. He gave me his wonderful smile and a discreet wave.

"Why all the flags at a sentencing? Are we celebrating justice or what?"

Fi and Corby were deep in conversation and didn't hear me. Finn, as usual, was in his own world. But Mrs Glendinning smiled at me. "They'll be for the St David's Day celebrations, rather than for today."

She continued in a conversational tone, "And the blood shouldn't reach high enough to splatter them. Of course, if it's one of the males, they probably will have to change the flags, but if it's Rhiannon, well, now, her aim is legendary. I've only witnessed her once with the man who murdered all those women. The fae healers said he wasn't sick, just evil. But they'll probably start with the thieves today, to get everyone settled down."

She sighed happily, as though discussing a forthcoming movie treat, and I stared at her. She was kidding, wasn't she? But the emotions I was picking up from the crowd said she wasn't.

Through my earbud, Dola asked, "Has it started yet?" I switched on my phone camera so she could see nothing was happening yet. "Pan down to the stocks, please, Niki."

In the middle of the square was a large, round, open space. Surrounding it was a mass of people. There were no visible barriers, but everyone seemed to know the middle area must be kept clear. I couldn't see a crowd respecting a boundary without sturdy barriers in Manchester. But in this square, it was as if everyone saw the same invisible circular line. In the centre was a wooden structure, which could be stocks.

"How do they know they can't push in any closer?"

I was talking to Dola, but Mrs Glendinning didn't realise and answered me happily, "Dragon wingspan, Recorder. If they get in too close, pain follows. A dragon's wing can give you a nasty clip around the ear if you're in its way. My lady, did you want Fergusson's head?"

I looked at her in horror. "No! Why on earth would I?"

"It's yours by right. Rhiannon will save it for you."

My head spun. Yes, Rhiannon had said something about a head. Had I thought she was kidding? No, I didn't think Rhiannon did that. But my brain couldn't make the connection to a person's head being an object anyone could have "a right to."

Mrs Glendinning wasn't finished with me. "If you truly don't want it, would you cede your right to me?" She waggled her lidded, woven willow basket at me. And then, with complete incongruence, she offered, "I could swap you for some lemon cupcakes?"

I gaped at her.

She was a lovely woman, middle-aged, middle class, Scottish. Well, Pictish originally, but truly Scottish now. What the hell did she want with a head, any head, never mind John's specific head?

I had to know. Didn't I?

"Why? What would you do with it?"

"I'd bury it near my rhubarb. We dug the hole in case you said yes. Rhubarb thrives on nitrogen-rich soil. Then, when it's rotted, I'd clean the skull, spray it a good Pict blue and grow black-eyed Susans through its eyes. I have a spot for it on my patio."

I remembered when I'd invited her to Dola's birthday party, there had been a weirdly-shaped hole hadn't there? And this was an awfully specific plan.

I definitely had to know. "Why?"

She swallowed, glanced around the room, saw no one was paying any attention to us and leaned in to me. "In memory of my mother, Susan."

I tuned in to her. My Gift gave me anger, grief, frustration, and, most of all, a sense of injustice. This was what Fi had been trying to tell me earlier. This matter was far from resolved in her family's hearts.

I thought it was a ridiculously creepy idea, but if it would give the Glendinnings closure, then it was also simple. I didn't want John's head. Mrs G had been wonderful to me since I was six years old when she'd been a volunteer at my school and helped me with my speech problem.

I looked into her kind eyes. "I cede my right to you. Do I need to do anything else? Or is that enough?"

"Just let Rhiannon know, my lady." She grasped

my hand and squeezed tightly. In a voice choked with emotion, she said, "Thank you, thank you so much. It will help us all heal."

I'd just realised why all the family cake recipes Fi gave Dola for her birthday hadn't included my favourite lemon cupcakes. Mrs G had needed them for this bribe. I murmured, "I need coffee."

Mrs Glendinning shot me an enquiring glance as I spoke. But when I gestured at my earbud and phone, she wiped a tear from her eye and returned to looking expectantly down at the square below.

Dola said, "I could send one to you, but could you move somewhere private? I am concerned about Rollo. He is distressed. Tilly was trying to comfort him, but now she also appears unhappy. I'd like to channel your voice through the kitchen Dolina, to calm them both."

Crap, I'd closed my shields again to get through the crowd. I lowered them to about half power. Immediately through my ear bud I heard, "Oh, thank the Allfather, you're back. We need to find out what's happening with this power connection. It's … not good when I can't reach you. Apologies, I may have briefly stressed your dog, but she's wagging her tail again now."

"Fi, have I got time to pop to the bathroom?"

She looked up from her chat with Corby and nodded. "There'll be several minor sentences carried out before John." She pointed at the door. "The doors on this side of the passage are the royal boxes, and the ones opposite are bathrooms. Look for the green one."

This was all beautifully organised. I quickly got myself into the bathroom with the seven-pointed Recorder's star on it and a green door handle. Huh, a simple system.

"Dola, do I need to come home?"

"No, Niki, Rollo is fine now. I would recommend you continue doing whatever you did. Show me where you are, and I'll send you coffee."

I did the usual 360 turn for her. It was an upmarket bathroom with a chaise in one corner, a full-length mirror by the sofa, and half-height mirrors above the vanity. The beautifully fitted wash basins were set in a glossy green tiled surround. The lighting and the hand towels were both soft, everything sparkled, and a gentle whiff of something light and floral floated in the air.

As I watched, a cardboard take-out cup with caramelly-coffee aromas appeared on the vanity. It was deliciously warm in here. The hot water pipes running around the walls might be helping. It made me want to curl up on the chaise with my coffee and wait this ceremony out.

"Dola, if I speak, can Rollo hear me?" Unlike Dai, Rollo had the same laidback attitude as Finn towards Dola. It made life much easier.

"Hey? Thanks, Niki. Sorry, I lost my cool there for a few minutes." He still sounded stressed.

"Sorry, I forgot and closed my shields. The atmosphere here is so horrible. Everyone's eager for the show. I feel like they're all going to take their knitting out any minute. Even Fi's mother, who's the nicest woman usually, has a glint in her eye I don't like. She wants John's head, and I don't mean that metaphorically. I mean, she literally asked me for his skull!"

He laughed. "Ugh! Shades of the guillotine. I've thought the same myself many times. Vikings are so different—with a few notable exceptions, a quick death in battle and a speedy transfer to Valhalla is the thing. I'm all for a fair fight, and I wouldn't mind if they just chopped his head off, but these Druidic ceremonies are barbaric, in my opinion. But it's their belief system, so ..." he trailed off before he insulted another realm.

"Thing is, I'd like my shields closed. The eagerness for blood coming off them all is creepily unpleasant. If this doesn't work, I'll have to deal with it, but I'm wondering if I can open a sort of pipeline exclusively to you so you don't get stressed until we work out what's happening, but I can shut the rest of the bloodthirsty masses out. I've probably only got a few minutes to test it before Fi comes looking for me. Any ideas?"

Dola interrupted, "Niki, do you mean like using port forwarding on a wi-fi router? A unique, secure connection between the two of you?"

Rollo's wonderful rich laugh rolled through my earbud. "I think she's got something there. I'm trying to open Port 22 in my brain. Not words I thought I'd ever hear myself say. No idea if it'll help."

He might be right. He was definitely a geek under those oiled muscles and leathers. Port 22 was a secure, protected link to another computer. Brains were computers, weren't they? I wondered if, like so much in my new life, if I believed it would work, it just would?

I pulled some power, glad of the privacy of the private bathroom, and tried to do what Rollo suggested: open a secured private connection. Something clicked in my brain. It was a disconcerting feeling.

Rollo must have felt it too, because he said, "Something changed. I feel much steadier. I can't work out what's causing it, but it's very dark in my head when you shut off. Try closing your shields now while we at least have the voice connection, hey?"

I did.

"OK. Closed." I waited. The relief of shutting out all the excitement, bloodthirsty thoughts and darker emotions was immediate and immense. My shoulders came down about six inches as I stopped hunching against all the people who wanted to see blood fly around the square.

Inside my head, I heard, *I'm still here, I think. At least the light's still on.*

"Phew. And I feel a lot saner."

Can you hear this?

Yes.

I said, "Well, it's odd, but pretty cool. When I was a kid, I read a book about twins who could do it. I really wanted to be able to read someone's mind. I mean, the McKnight Gift is great, but it mostly gives emotions. I'm happy it seems to work for you. Once I get this afternoon over with, we'll get you properly connected to the yellow power. Still OK at your end?"

"I really am sorry to be so much trouble."

Bless him. He hadn't asked for any of this either. "Don't worry. I'm going back in. I have my phone—if it goes wrong, or you start panicking, message me."

I reapplied my lipstick—with this many royals around, I should make an effort—and wrapped my cloak firmly about me before I braved the icy corridor and headed back into my box.

NINETEEN

As soon as I opened the bathroom door, the laughter coming from all the boxes greeted me. Laughter was good. I rushed back. "What did I miss?"

Everyone stood at the window, giggling, laughing, and pointing as a long stream of flame shot across the sky, and more laughter followed it.

I pushed forward, making a space in the window enclosure for myself. "What's happening?"

Finn finally noticed me. "Got it all on vid, my lady. You gotta watch it back later." He dissolved into helpless giggles like a twelve-year-old. What the heck had I missed?

In the centre of the square was a wiry-looking man in his late thirties. He was secured into the stocks, and a wide selection of vegetables were strewn around him. Above him was a sturdy little reddish-brown dragon, its wings spread protectively. OK, considering its wingspan, the dragon wasn't small at all. It simply looked that way when compared to the one Rhiannon had allowed to poke its head into the Gateway this morning.

When a turnip hit the dragon's shoulder, its head turned, and flame belched. A man in the crowd squealed, batted fruitlessly at his burning trousers and then dropped and rolled.

"Somebody *TELL ME* what the hell is going on, please?"

Fi finally noticed me and, between her gusts of amusement, said, "The chap is a highwayman. Generous Gary, they call him. He steals from the rich and gives to … well, everyone else."

"Gary the Highwayman?" I started laughing myself.

"Well, his name's Gareth, but they call him Gary."

"Yeah, OK, why is that dragon …" What the hell *was* the dragon doing? Protecting him? "What is it doing?"

Fi was laughing so helplessly now and almost hanging out of the window as a woman landed a dreadfully rotten tomato on Gary's shirt in an underarm throw. When the dragon's head swivelled, the woman turned and ran, and the dragon caught her right on the bottom with a long, well-aimed stream of flame. She squealed like a stuck pig. The dragon roared.

Comments flew, "Serves her right, so it does," and "Save the veg, she should, for the *pen pidyn* what deserves them — her bluddy, lousy son."

They were all crazy. I gave Finn my best you-are-my-Knight-Adjutant-and-I-require-information look. "Report, Finn. What the actual …?"

Finn pulled himself together. "He's technically guilty but a fan favourite. Gives away most of what he steals. The dragon," he gestured, as though I could somehow miss the dragon outside the window, "is his sister." Then he dissolved back into incomprehensible laughter again. Even Finn?

I gave up. They were all insane.

I glared at the ridiculous throne, drank my coffee, and thought longingly of my warm, quiet kitchen. Then I considered the women who'd filed petitions against Troels and pictured him in those stocks. I didn't think any of the dragons would defend him. Until my staff rediscovered the minds they appeared to have mislaid, I'd visit Glais'Nee. I would find out if he would help with my brainwave, which might save the raped women from the ordeal of having to give evidence at the arbitration.

• • •

There was more laughter inside the Violet box as I tapped on the door with House Alicorn's unicorn horn symbol. Glais'Nee himself opened it and stepped back, waving me in. He was classically handsome, with high, pronounced cheekbones, a great jawline and a wide, generous mouth currently curved into an enormous grin. His skin was almost as deep a purple as Ad'Rian's, showing he was ancient and powerful, and his bright silver-blue eyes indicated he was a skilled practitioner of the Fae magics. Those eyes sparkled with amusement as he drew me to the window.

It was much warmer in here, as though there was a heat shield across the window, so the cold wasn't flooding in as it had in my own box. Fae magic for the win.

"Glynis defends her brother and takes the opportunity to settle a few scores at the same time. You should not miss this perfect justice."

Glynis? The dragon was Glynis? OK, I was starting to understand some of the humour. Glynis, the stroppy Dragon, and Gary, the Generous Highwayman. It would make a fine plot for a sitcom.

"I am informed the spiteful woman with the flaming posterior has a son. When he abandoned his wife and two small daughters without food or funds, she espoused the position that her daughter-in-law must deserve such treatment. Gary provided foodstuff and other necessities for her and the woman's grandchildren. What is the saying in your world? Let she who is without sin cast the first tomato? But if she is not without sin, then her butt will burn in the fiery pit?"

Now I started laughing.

Glais'Nee said, "Ad'Rian will be here shortly. He is—"

At his tentative touch on the door to my mind, I opened it for him.

"Ah, I see you are conversant with the problem. My liege lord is helping with Prince Dafydd's healing. It should not have been overlooked. You did well alerting the king to the problem. He and Ad'Rian will be along later. I am holding the room. No, the fort? Yes?"

I needed to get used to everyone knowing everything, wouldn't I? How many times had I thought gossip and information spread like wildfire in the realms? Glynis set someone else on fire, and I wondered what they'd done?

I smiled. "Yes, it's holding the fort."

Then his face grew serious. "Recorder, are you aware you have an interloper?"

What?

What the hell was he talking about?

He tapped his own head. "You have a soul-to-soul

connection you did not instigate. Are you apprised of it?"

Oh, wow—he could see it? Soul-to-soul—was that what the Fae called Port 22? *Rollo, would you say hello to Glais'Nee, please? He's concerned I didn't know you were there.*

I felt Rollo send a low, respectful bow to Glais'Nee. This was all getting a bit odd for me. But Glais'Nee took it all in his stride as he, both out loud to me, and in my mind to Rollo, said, "Oh, all is well. I know the Recorder is still working on her mental potentials, and I was unsure if she was aware. My apologies, cousin. I would have known better if I could have seen it was you, but the Recorder was," he gave me a querying look, "shielding your identity?"

Cousin? Well, Rollo's mother had reminded me of someone in that photo in his longhouse.

"It's a long story, Glais'Nee, and I'd welcome your advice, but before I forget, I had one quick query first about your genetic assessment abilities. Have you heard about the petitions against Troels?"

He shook his head.

"Can we do it the quick way so you don't miss all the fun?" I glanced out the window as Generous Gary was released and another chap took his place.

Glais'Nee frowned at me, so I tapped my third eye and added, "I don't know how to instigate the mental connection again. Ad'Rian or Mabon usually do it for me."

His face cleared, and he paused with his own finger just above the skin between my eyes. I nodded, then remembered they liked to hear it out loud. "I consent, thank you."

In no time, I'd brought him up to date on the petitions. I shared the information from Fi about the other two hundred women who wouldn't even file a petition because they didn't want to relive the events leading up to their pregnancy. And Glynis's role in the concerted push to bring Troels to justice.

I shivered. It was suddenly icy in here. Fae anger could be cold rather than hot. What had I done?

"I didn't mean to upset you, Glais' Nee. My apologies for—"

"My anger is not with you, Recorder. It is with everyone who was cognisant of this and did nothing to prevent it. I now understand why you are shielding the prince. We may need a council of war."

"Yes, Breanna had a brainwave. Would you speak with Ad'Rian and come to her book club?" He frowned at me. I took the shortcut that seemed to work on everyone else. "She's holding it in the Gateway, and Juniper is catering it. Ask Ad'Rian about it, please?"

His wide, wonderfully generous smile was back in place now. The room warmed again. "Ask Juniper if she will make her special Just Deserts please. If she will, I shall attend, Recorder. I will think on what you shared; may I convey it to His Majesty?"

"You mean something called Just Deserts and not just some desserts, right?" I wanted to be sure I asked for the right thing. You never knew with the Fae.

"Yes, one of my favourites has been renamed, to Just Deserts. I save it for a good day."

I had no clue, but if it got Glais'Nee to the book club, I'd request it. "OK, and please tell Ad'Rian about the paternity petitions—I've been so busy. I planned to fill him in when I rode Dusha last week, but we were distracted by Dola's birthday gift and it slipped my mind."

A kerfuffle outside the window caught my attention, and I glanced out to see Jamie being dragged towards the stocks. "Oh hell no, Mabon gave me his word." Panic rose up my throat. I took in a huge breath, partly to calm my fear, and partly in case I had to shout.

"His word about what, Recorder?"

I attempted to explain the problem clearly to Glais'Nee. The lump in my throat didn't help. "Jamie is only here because it is apparently his right to be present at his father's sentencing. But I have the claim to decide what to do with him. We still need Jamie. Mabon gave Ti'Anna and me his sworn word Jamie would be safe."

In the square, this time people weren't holding vegetables; they were holding rocks.

At the window, I drew in another huge breath.

I remembered my promise to Ti'Anna.

The information the Book had given me was clear.

I leaned out and bellowed at the top of my lungs, "NO! STOP! The Recorder forbids this. I claim priority. Mabon granted it. The right is mine. STOP!"

Almost everyone in the square looked up—except the guard, who was diligently leading Jamie ever closer to the stocks. Jamie didn't look as though he was even aware of what was happening. What the hell was he doing here? Just because he was entitled to come didn't mean he should have. Who'd made this stupid decision? Surely he should still be with the healers?

Panic rose in my throat. Ti'Anna had been worried about this happening. Was she a seer? If I used the power, my secret that I could use it outside the Gateway would be out. It was much too high a price to pay. But what could I do? Scream like a banshee?

"You, guard, your King and the Recorder forbid it. Hold!"

He completely ignored me. Was he deaf?

I yelled to the crowd, "STOP HIM!"

Metal rasped behind me, and through the large

window, right past my head, flew a spear. It impaled itself in the crack between the cobbles, and the haft stood upright about eighteen inches in front of the guard's face. He stopped and looked around in shock.

The crowd pointed up to the window at me.

Clearly, in case he was lip-reading, I held my hand up, palm out, in the universal symbol for stop and enunciated, "No." I shook my head and slipped off my cloak so he could see the Recorder's robe and the seven-pointed star at my throat.

He bowed, and my knees started quivering.

TWENTY

I thanked Glais'Nee for his help as we walked out of his box together.

"I am at your service, Recorder. Excuse me, I must retrieve my spear before some vagabond attempts to make off with it and dies screaming. I would not wish to upset Bright Justice. Dike herself blessed that spear for me to ensure it worked only for good. I will leave you now and make certain your own and King Mabon's wishes are clear and the son is held safely. I shall take him home with me and return him to the healers until the time for his own trial arrives."

I tapped my earbud. "Dola, where the hell is Mabon? He would have been forsworn if I hadn't almost lost my voice bellowing like a madwoman at an idiotic guard. Next time you speak with Ad'Rian —who's also missing—will you ask him if Ti'Anna has the power of the seer? Because, if she has, I should listen more carefully to her damn warnings."

"They are both delayed, Niki. There have been problems with Dai's healing. Coffee?"

I slumped against the wall in the corridor. I needed to pull my damn self together. Yes, it had been stressful, but as I understood it, the worst part hadn't even started yet.

Once back in the private and much warmer bathroom, I tried to stop shaking. I'd never screamed so loudly in my life. What was this stupid job turning me into?

"Yes, please, Dola, a black one. That was stressful. Is there a brownie? What's the problem with Dai? Will he be OK?"

"I am sorry, but I have no further information yet. There must be a problem because they both intended to attend today's justice."

I reached out to Rollo. It was a weird sensation, having him in my head. But in his defence, he'd stayed out of the way while I dealt with things. At least he didn't do that annoying man thing of always thinking they knew best.

The inside of my head bubbled, like my brain was laughing, and I heard, *I'm right here, you know?*

So? I was admiring your good qualities not being rude.

While I ate my brownie and tried to calm myself, I wondered how to work out what had caused this connection. I should have asked Glais'Nee, shouldn't I? But Jamie being marched out against Mabon's instructions had thrown everything else out of my head. Was the guard an idiot or a traitor? I owed Glais'Nee big time. No, I didn't. Mabon did. I should tell him. And I should—Gods and Goddesses, I was sick and tired of all the shoulds and shouldn'ts in my life.

I'd like a lot more wants and far fewer shoulds.

Hey, Rollo, trying to work out what caused this link. Did you have any unusual gifts or talents, before the yellow power download, I mean?

I sensed uncertainty, as if he wasn't sure how much he wanted to tell me. The link was an odd thing. It seemed to mostly keep private information private, but thoughts or words about or to the other person got through clearly. It wasn't like the usual purposeful Fae mind link, more like an open phone line. Sometimes you could feel the other person's emotions without any words. Other times you needed to ask. It was odd.

Yeah, some things have always been different. I've always assumed it came from my mother.

Dola interrupted, "Niki, Finn's stream shows they are bringing John out."

It was time to learn what they did to oathbreakers. I'd disliked John, and I'd had enormous contempt for him by the time we realised what a lazy, useless lump he'd been, but I was a modern woman. This business of putting people into stocks, outside of a theme park, was so antiquated. But it wasn't under my authority. This was the royals' show.

Back in my box, the excitement was palpable, and everyone was preparing to leave, gathering coats and the basket Mrs G had carried since we left the Gateway. Was it full of rotten tomatoes?

An awful thought struck me. It wasn't for the damn head, was it?

"Are you all going?"

Mrs Glendinning hooked the basket over her forearm and turned to me with a surprised expression. "The ceremony begins, my lady. Are you not coming down?"

I couldn't imagine anything worse than being in the middle of the enormous crowd of people with their angry auras and bloodthirsty energy. The ceremony was surely going to make it worse, not better. "I'll come later. Go on without me."

In my ear, Dola said, "I have the audio feed from Finn's camera, Niki. I shall send it to your earbud until your presence is required."

From my spot by the fire, I had a clear view through the window. Finn was making his way through the crowd towards the centre by the stocks. His camera cleared a path more quickly than the palace guards had earlier. For all his assertions he didn't want to do the prince thing, he could walk with purpose when he chose to. Perhaps my Knight Adjutant was finding his own authority where it concerned his beloved tech and his right to use it without anyone blocking his shot.

I caught mumbles in the crowd through the audio feed. "Livestream... News Portal ...let the TEK pass ...Knight coming through ... watch it back on the portal thing ...Jonesie, move your stupid arse." Finn's TEK title had really caught on in the realms, perhaps because it sounded more like a nickname?

Then a wave of sound so huge, I felt it in my bones crashed over the square. John Fergusson was led out by two men in red robes. He looked quite different to the portly, pompous man who'd chided me as if I were an ill-mannered child for holding up my own ascension ceremony when he arrived late to it.

John had lost weight but didn't seem to have been ill-treated. He was tracking the proceedings, and he glared at all the people who now formed an orderly line around the edge of the clear centre area. Fi and the group from my own box were close to the front, and several other women had joined them.

Four more men in brown robes carried a table covered in a red cloth, which ... what the hell?

The table contained a selection of knives, skewers, and implements. Honestly, I didn't want to think too hard about what those implements might be. But it looked like a torturer's table—a very clean torturer's table full of shiny, sharp things, from one of those movies I refused to watch because they gave me nightmares.

A man in a long red and gold robe, his head and face covered by a large hood, walked across to John, who was now secured in the stocks. It was only when I recognised the body language and saw the red and silver sparks from his feet, I realised Mabon was back. Whoa, he really looked godlike today.

He threw back his hood, surveyed John, and shook his head. With a few words of Welsh, he had men rushing towards him carrying a different kind of wooden thing. Actually, I knew this, didn't I? This was a pillory rather than the stocks. It had a taller wooden stand with holes for the offender's hands and head.

Mabon turned to the crowd, and, without shouting, his low, authoritative voice carried effortlessly to every corner of the square. "He will hear his transgressions on his feet, as a man should."

John looked unhappy at this, but I didn't know why.

"I will remind you all I will tolerate no diversions from or interruptions to the most important part of this ritual. Until everyone who has cause to do so has shared their words with the supplicant. Only in this way can he avoid making the same bluddy awful, cocked-up mess of his next life."

There was general laughter, and many heads nodded at Mabon. I mostly worried about the fact that he was speaking clear English instead of his usual Yoda speak. He was angry about something, but I didn't think it was John. I hoped Dai was doing OK with the Fae. But I still hadn't seen Ad'Rian arrive.

Mabon continued, "My daughter is in charge of the correct order of things today. If any of you think to steal souvenirs before everyone has had their rightful chance to speak, I will tell you all she informed me she's had a bitch of a week and is suffering from PFT."

A wave of laughter at that, but I didn't get the joke. In my head, I heard *Pre-Flame Tension* from Rollo. Crap, I just kept forgetting he was there, didn't I?

Are you watching it through my eyes or something?

No, Dola is streaming Finn's feed onto the large screen in the kitchen for me.

Oh. Is Tilly OK? Are you OK?

She is asleep, and I'm fine. Niki, you understand how this ceremony will go, don't you?

Not really, no. Fi said everyone has their chance to tell him what he did wrong so he can do better in his next life, and then they execute him.

There was a tense silence outside the window. I looked down at the table full of shiny things in the square and swallowed hard. I wouldn't be able to watch torture, if that was what they were planning. I couldn't even watch gruesome scenes in a movie. It was years before I'd realised you never actually saw the guy lose his ear in the famous scene in *Reservoir Dogs*. My squeamishness used to amuse the hell out of Nick.

But it was OK. So far anyway.

Mabon had pulled Finn forward to make sure he got good quality footage, which meant I had clear audio through my earbud and a good view from my window.

I leaned out a little to sense the mood of the crowd. They were angry, but outwardly patient. They were all here with a joint purpose. Now it was time to complete their task, the crowd's energy had lightened and was less unpleasant.

The line shuffled along, and the next woman moved to stand in front of John. So far, there had been a variety of civilised complaints. One of the dominant themes was John hadn't listened to anyone about anything. At least if the number of people saying it was any indication.

Another strand covered how lazy and unwilling to take any action he'd always been. Even though the issues fell under the duties of the Knight Adjutant, and he should have made sure he informed the Recorder of this or that.

Caitlin leaned out of the window of the adjoining box, so close I could see the clouds her breath made in the freezing air. "You doin' alright, my lady?"

"Fine, thanks. Why are you not down there?"

"Mabon will call us down when he's ready for us. We speak last and cut first."

"Pardon?"

Caitlin focused on me, her gaze sharp. "You checked with the Book, didn't you? You know how this goes, don't you?" Rollo had just asked me the exact same thing, hadn't he? Did everyone think I was stupid?

Wait, was I being stupid?

I told her what I'd told Rollo. "Not really, no. Fi said everyone tells him what he did wrong so he can do better in his next life, and then they execute him."

Breanna's head appeared next to Caitlin. In a low voice to her daughter, she murmured, "Her KAIT has a duty to inform the Recorder of those things she needs to understand and to advise her on her options."

Breanna offered me a hip flask. "Uisge, Recorder?"

Oh shit.

There was a tap on the door of my box, and it opened to reveal Caitlin. "So, Teacher-Mode activated."

I remembered when I'd first broken it to Caitlin that I planned for her to be the teacher and Finn and Dola to be the warriors. She'd been outraged. But she'd begun to take the concept on board in some interesting ways since then.

"OK. What am I missing?"

She looked around the box. "No Dolina?"

I gestured at my earbud. Caitlin leaned into it and said, "Send the Recorder a brandy please, Dola."

It appeared in a brandy glass on the bench, and Caitlin passed it to me. I sipped. I'd no idea why I was sipping, but Caitlin looked serious and worried about me. It was unsettling.

"Right, the bit you should have looked up. If you've harmed, or tried to harm, a ton of people, and they all hate you... Druids believe you should take some time between reincarnations to fully process your sins, errors and slagging stupidities."

I nodded. "I got that bit. Do better next time. Not a bad idea, really."

"Yeah, so back when they dreamt this stuff up,"

she paused, looked at the adjoining wall between my box and Breanna's, winced and lowered her voice, "and I'm sure I should be able to tell you exactly when that was, but ya know." She wafted a hand to indicate the past. "They used to quarter people and spread the pieces about."

At my uncomprehending look, she added, "Ya know, four people each took a quarter of the body in the direction of the compass points—north, south, east and west—and they couldn't leave the pieces until they'd crossed running water."

Light was dawning in my brain. In Britain, people had been hung, drawn and quartered for high treason until recently. Well, if a couple of hundred years was recent. That was what the knives were for? Yuck, messy.

"So, they behead him and then chop him into pieces and send them where?"

But Caitlin was shaking her head. Her voice almost soothing now. "Ya can't have people breaking oaths, Niki. We categorise oathbreaking with treason and regicide. It's one of those things everyone needs to be really clear not to do. So," she pointed out the window, "an object lesson from a much scarier teacher than me will be taking place out there in," she stood, peered out of the window and finished, "about an hour. Juna wants his middle finger. She says she wanted to give him the middle finger so often while he was alive, it's appropriate for her to have his."

I laughed because her sister Juna was a sweet, soft-spoken, nurturing woman. Almost the complete opposite of Caitlin, and with all the social skills Finn always said he didn't have.

My laughter died when she gave me her serious heir-apparent stare. "Glynis wants his balls to dedicate to all the women whose rapes she holds him responsible for. If John had listened and taken the action he should have when she first made the formal reports to him, about a dozen of Troels' early rapes, things could have been different. Instead, he told her she was being a silly girl repeating pure hearsay."

I couldn't imagine it. I just couldn't. You could ignore one accusation. You shouldn't. But you could. But a dozen women saying the same? Surely he must have—

Caitlin cut across my thoughts. "Glynis thinks it might have saved more than a hundred and fifty women. She was in talking to Ma about it last week, asking about you, and were you like your gran, and would you be another one who'd turn a blind eye?"

Caitlin shoved the brandy towards my lips. "Ma said you wouldn't. Drink up."

CHAPTER

TWENTY-ONE

I t was horrific.

The thing that made it worse was this wasn't an unruly mob. The crowd kept complete control over their anger. They followed the ceremony to the letter. They told John over and over again what a worthless piece of shit he'd been in their eyes. And, yes, the occasional person tried to create some drama, but the crowd just politely moved them on.

Then they returned to their endless repetitions. How every single time they'd asked him for assistance, action, advice or access to my gran, he'd failed them.

The small group of women who'd waited in the Red sector for their friends this morning had swelled now, but I recognised them as they reached John.

Glynis, no longer in her dragon form, shepherded them forward. Almost all held photographs.

Glynis let out a distinctive three-note whistle, and about another thirty women moved out of the line and headed towards her. Fi released Corby's supportive hand and moved to stand with the group in front of John. Other women disentangled themselves from husbands and wives and headed towards the group in front of John.

Rollo sent, *You're so angry. What's disturbing you about that group?*

Not certain. But I wouldn't want to be John right now. I think a lot of "foolish, silly, not-so-young anymore women" are about to make him face up to how determinedly blind he was.

Finn was brilliant with his livestream camera. He didn't close in on the women or crowd them, but from my vantage point above him, I saw he'd zoomed in on the photos the women held. They showed handsome young men interspersed with an occasional attractive young woman. Every damn one of them had the unmistakable look of Troels. The women thrust them under John's nose. One of the Red Celt women said, "See now, can you, Fergusson? See who his father is? Or call me a liar again, will you?"

A lot of the photos looked like Jamie, and some of them, the blonder ones, might have been Rollo's brothers and sisters, which confused me. If Troels was ... but ... Rollo's father hadn't looked like Troels ... Well, they were both blond, but ... My thoughts trailed off into confusion.

My grandfather had very dominant genes.

Crap. I'm so sorry. I forgot you were there again, didn't I?

Rollo felt weary and unhappy in my mind as he sent, *It's OK. This is why you were asking Glais'Nee to identify the father of the children privately? To help the women who don't want to come forward and file petitions to establish paternity?*

Yes.

When I cautiously risked using my Gift on John Fergusson, his initial disbelief had given way to a bone-weary, soul-deep acceptance. He wasn't accepting responsibility yet, but he had finally realised he'd been wrong to doubt the women.

Rollo sent, *That's an intriguing talent. I always wondered if these ceremonies worked. Maybe they do.*

I sent back, *Try it yourself, with the yellow power, although I'm almost certain this is the McKnight Gift, rather than the Gateway power. The power can help me see what's in people's hearts and sometimes their realm of origin, but anything connected to emotion-sensing is McKnight all the way.*

I didn't know what to do. Caitlin had explained Mabon would call the royals down soon. Technically,

I was the most senior because I ran the Gateway, so I'd probably have to go first to tell John what I thought of him, and then the monarchs would follow in rainbow order. After Ad'Rian, who still hadn't arrived, had spoken last, because violet completed the rainbow, I'd go first again, and I was supposed to ask for a piece of John.

Seriously. A piece of him!

I couldn't quite grasp the concept of that, and the scene from *Reservoir Dogs* ran on a loop in my mind. Several people said they'd take his ears, as he'd never bluddy used them. At the current rate, they'd have to chop his ears into about twenty pieces.

A warm, mellow voice sang "Stuck in the Middle with You." Huh, Rollo had a good voice, lower than Gerry Rafferty's tenor. Funny though, he had the same movie reference as me for this ceremony. Oh, no, wait. He was getting it out of my mind, wasn't he? This was weird.

Now I finally understood what Rhiannon meant when she'd said she was saving the head for me. I couldn't imagine anything worse than having to dispose of John's head.

OK, actually, I could imagine worse things—but seriously—a head? An ugly, mostly bald head with his smug face on it. I shuddered, glad Mrs Glendinning had a plan for it, however eccentric that plan was.

Why would the man have allowed Mrs G's mother to die away from her family? What would one elderly woman coming for a final visit to her daughter, granddaughter and great grandson have cost him?

I just didn't understand his attitude.

The bubbling sensation in my brain when Rollo laughed was followed by, *John reminded me of the perfect incarnation of a Jobsworth. It was always more than his job was worth to do whatever simple thing you were asking for. A five-minute meeting with the Recorder, perhaps? Stop the trade in the herbs they made the drug from. Use his brain, ever. Find his spine and stand up for something. Whatever anyone asked for, he always said it "didn't fall within the parameters of his role, and it would be more than his job was worth to ... whatever."*

I laughed loudly. It was the perfect description. I'd thought the same myself about Jamie. Immediately, in my ear, Dola asked, "Are you alright, Niki?"

"I'm fine, thanks, why?"

In a gentle tone, she said, "You appear to be cackling in an empty room. Nothing amusing is happening. Women are crying, and a young woman has just spat at John." There was a short pause before she layered concern into her tone and asked, "Is the event too stressful for you? Do you need support?"

"Sorry, Dola, I was just talking to Rollo."

Silence. Then, through my earbud, I heard Dola

and Rollo talking in low voices. Then she laughed too.

I wasn't even angry with John for myself. I mean, sure, he'd ignored my request for help. He told Aysha, when she'd written to him as my solicitor, that her client was a disturbed young woman, as though I were a fourteen-year-old having a tantrum. He didn't know she was my best mate. What if she hadn't been? What if she'd believed him?

He refused a request from a partner in a legal firm to check on his son's possible misconduct. All because he believed Jamie had "one of the finest legal minds in the country." So, yeah, he was deluded too. But how would I have felt without Aysha to support me? Like all these poor women, I supposed. My heart sank.

But the real fire fuelling my building anger was all on behalf of my gran. She'd had many faults, and no one knew them better than me, but she would have taken action on many things if John had ever let her find out about them.

The combination of her one-in, one-out rule, her refusal to embrace email, snapping at people so they didn't think they could come to her with their concerns, and allowing John far too much authority all had a place in what I saw as the Recorder's failure in these matters. I couldn't hold him totally responsible, but he was culpable.

I knew my gran would have helped Mrs Glendinning's mother through the damn Gateway and probably wheeled her around to Fi's. Gran was no saint, but she wasn't cruel to old ladies.

Rollo sent me a soothing sensation, but his mental voice was firm. *Niki, say all that to John. People need to hear you give voice to it. To understand you're not your grandmother. Things are already changing in the Recorder's Office. He wouldn't be here today if you hadn't seen through what was going on. The rumours about you being the one who found him out have spread. Validate them publicly. Finn is recording. Why not think of it as a training session for John? You seem to be comfortable with that concept.*

Then Mabon called, "Any Deities, the Recorder, Queens, Kings, and heirs having business with the oathbreaker John Fergusson, come forward and speak now."

I swallowed and made my way swiftly down the stairs.

We had a short queue and I didn't have to go first. HRH was at the front. "Recorder, you will lift me up. I won't waste energy on lifting myself when I will need it to serve justice to him."

I did as I was told. When we stood in front of John, I crooked my arm to make her a perch, as I often did for Tilly. The small cat stared into his face, and I could sense energy being used, but even using my other eyes, as Ad'Rian called them, I couldn't see what she was doing.

"Fergusson, your soul is filthy! You knew he wasn't your genetic son, and you still didn't test him before you risked all the realms and the very Gateway itself. Remember the day I warned you about him, when, as a child, he tried to tie a firework to my tail? You said, 'Show me the proof, and, anyway, cats can't talk.' Well, in a few moments, you should listen closely, and you may observe this one having the last word.

"I'm finished with this mouse dropping for now, Recorder. Your turn."

Quiet gasps ran through the group of royals behind me, and I could hear the gossip spreading through the crowd. "Not his genetic son," and "Well? Who was it?" Finally, from Glynis, who sounded all out of patience: "Who the hell do you think? Have you never looked at the son?"

A stab of pain from Rollo shot through me, and, without thinking, I sent soothing waves back to him as I addressed John. "You let my grandmother down repeatedly with your weak, narrow-minded, ignorantly arrogant ways. I don't think it was laziness, as many here seem to. I believe it was your overwhelming cowardice."

As I said this, my right shoulder twanged. I told the truth. Yeah, I kind of knew that. "In your next life, try to remember a coward dies many times, but a brave man only once."

I turned, still holding HRH, who appeared to be perfectly happy perched on my arm, and walked to the back of the line of royals. Ad'Rian still wasn't here. I whispered to the cat, "Do you know if Dai is OK? And is Ad'Rian coming?"

"Glais'Nee is holding the space for him. The king has been detained. Dai still struggles, but he is strong, if currently stupid. He will survive. Whether he will find his own courage is another matter. An apposite quote, Recorder, you made me almost proud."

Colour me amazed.

Mabon, who began the rainbow order as the Red Celt king, laid into John about the ill-treatment of his children at Fergusson's hands.

I caught the end. "As busy as you always were ignoring Jamie's failings, never failed, did you, to pick at the offspring of others? Help, you never offered. Only criticism of everyone. About everything. Fortunate, it is, for you, the woman you always called an uncivilised hoyden had more self-control in one of her smallest spines than you have in your entire yellow-streaked body. Rhiannon will have the last laugh. And as for the daughter of my heart, well, she brought about your overdue downfall and that of your useless adopted son, didn't she now?"

With an angry huff, he moved to the end of the line and stood behind me. Fury and worry emanated from him.

Gradually, we progressed. Emperor Alphonse bitched about how John had never understood the importance of trade and the freedom of movement between the realms. He held him responsible for not making Gran step up to do her job. His last comment about how John's apathy had been contagious, made me think I must organise a meeting between him and Fi, the Gateway's new director of trade. Perhaps she could right some of those wrongs.

But my biggest worry kept pushing to the front of my brain. How the hell could I get out of having to choose a piece of John?

Rollo gave a discreet cough in my mind. I tuned into our link and nearly laughed out loud. *Good plan. Oh, yeah, I could do that.*

Breanna was mid-rant in front of John when I concentrated back on the drama in the square. Her long, spun-copper hair, the colour of new pennies, swung wildly around her head as she put her whole body into telling him how spineless, unhelpful and annoying he'd always been.

"But it wasn't the worst part, Fergusson. Your worst failing was how often you were so slagging wrong about everything. You told me women couldn't be the Knight Adjutant. Ignorant man. And, on that note, my daughter, the current Knight Adjutant, has some words for you. My son, the current Knight Adjutant for Electronics, will follow her. You worthless heap of rusted slag."

Tossing her hair one last time and leaving John open-mouthed, she moved back, and Caitlin stepped up. "Oh, close your jaw, Fergusson, my queen is correct. You were wrong about everything for thirty years, if the evidence is anything to go by. We gotta hell of a job in front of us to clean up the dungheaps you left behind. And I've no shits left to give to explain all the ways you were wrong. Because *we're* all too busy righting those wrongs."

The spontaneous burst of applause from the crowd surprised her. She gave the assembled people one startled look and a wave before making her way to the back.

Finn stepped up, and, typically, Finn made no speeches. "Craven oathbreaker, your deity will judge you. I already have." He stepped back to gesture the next person forward and then realised it was me and HRH.

We looked around for Ad'Rian, but Glais'Nee approached. "I stand in my liege lord's shoes. He is saving a life, something you never did in the whole of your wasted one. He has no time or words to spare for you."

And then HRH was at the front, and Mabon held up a hand.

"I think we'd all rather just take his head and be done with this. But duty calls us all this day for the sake of this man's soul in his next life." Oh dear, Mabon was speaking English again. He must be very stressed.

"I am needed elsewhere. My true daughter, Rhiannon, will lead these proceedings now. But I remind you all, do not be responsible for his death with what you take. Or you may join him there. If you do not yourself have the skill, the magic, or a talented ally, to claim your piece of him now and leave him alive, then you must wait until the end when Rhiannon will give it to you. Let me hear your understanding and consent to this."

I watched, amazed, as the Welsh half of the crowd went to one knee. There were calls of "Your Majesty," "My Liege," and "ap Modron."

The royals all bowed their heads. Mabon looked at me. I nodded solemnly at him. HRH didn't move a muscle.

CHAPTER
TWENTY-TWO

An enormous, glossy full-dragon glided in to hover over the market square. Rhiannon was nowhere in evidence now. This was all dragon, and it was even bigger than it had been this morning. There was intelligence in its eyes, and I was certain it was her, thanks to the black markings down the dragon's glossy red side. If you squinted, it looked like they said, *Bite Me. Go on. Try it.*

I really wanted to know how the dragon stuff worked. Would she tell me if I asked her? Probably not. Breanna had said Rhiannon didn't play well with others.

The crowd had judged the space to avoid her wingspan perfectly. No wonder they didn't need barriers to keep them at a safe distance. She was terrifying. I glanced at Finn, but he'd obviously had time to prepare himself. He was totally engrossed with his cameras and appeared calm.

HRH said, "Brace yourself, please, Recorder."

Unsure what she meant, I planted my feet and straightened my spine. Then a wave of sound came out of the small cat. She roared like a lion in the jungle. Thank goodness she'd warned me to brace myself.

The noise was terrifying, and it inspired a true flight response in me. Some part of my hindbrain understood that noise meant dinner was about to be eaten, and it would be a great idea to get far, far away, so you weren't on the menu.

John strained back against the wooden surround of the pillory, abject fear and complete astonishment warring on his face as he considered the furry bundle now standing almost upright on my crossed arms. At a more normal volume, she addressed him, "I will take one of those things you never used. You were blind to injustice, blind to your duty, blind to your son's perfidy."

Her paw shot out, and when she pulled it back, John was screaming, and on her claws, like a pickled onion on one of those special three-pronged forks, was John's eye. Before I could even stop myself, my eyes were drawn to the empty socket, but there was no blood. Just a cavity where the eye had been.

The cat dug one of her back claws into my arm. "Recorder, you are next; gather yourself."

Yes, she was right. I could find out what the hell had just happened later. "John Fergusson, we always make a choice with our actions. I won't lose what you tried to take from so many others. I choose to keep my dignity and not participate in this."

I paused; I breathed; I glared at him.

I could do this.

I found my new librarian-style Recorder voice.

"But I don't solely represent myself today. I stand here as current head of the almost-thousand-year-strong line of McKnight women. You were so proud that several of your forefathers also served as the Knight Adjutant, and yet you gave no respect to the millennia of McKnight women or the sentient house who cared for them."

Somewhere in my walk down here, I'd finally realised, if Jamie had sent the bulldozers in, he would have murdered Dola too.

"My ancestors are all angry you didn't serve one of their own with honour. They're disgusted you allowed your son to endanger the Gateway they gave their service and their lives to. Under your influence and lack of duty, your weak, feckless son would have sent the bulldozers through it, murdered a wise 1400-year-old entity and stranded millions of good people in their own realms."

I had to stop as an enormous roar of approval came from the crowd.

It surprised me, but I took a leaf out of Caitlin's book. She understood the kingdoms better than I did. I smiled, waved and breathed again until they quietened.

It took longer than I expected.

Rollo had been right. They needed to hear me say this.

"If my grandmother were still alive, I know she would say you gave her pitifully little honesty or support in life, and she would want nothing from you now. So instead, I give you something from her and all the other McKnight women whose sacrifices you dishonoured." I swung my arm back, intending to slap him lightly across the face for Gran. But my arm was suddenly bionic.

I've heard the saying "with the strength of a thousand men," but this was like the righteous anger of over a thousand years of McKnight women. When it connected, John's head rocked on his neck. Whoa, had I concussed him?

In my mind, several sentences in a foreign language were followed by, *Sorry, Niki, I'm tired of everything the little toady stood for, or rather didn't.*

I acted as if I'd meant to do it and looked at Rhiannon. "I cede his head to..." Shit, did I even know Mrs Glendinning's first name? Er, nope. "The Glendinning women. The prior claim is theirs."

Rhiannon gave me a look that, if it wasn't on a dragon's face, might have been approval. As it was, it could mean anything, but she didn't breathe fire at me, so I guessed it was OK.

I walked back down the line of royals towards my box. I had to sit down. Almost at the doorway to my refuge, the cat, whom I'd forgotten I was carrying, said, "Recorder, are you quite well?"

I ignored her until I entered the box and slumped onto the damn throne. "Dola, please, may I have a large brandy? Although, what I really want is one of Mabon's cigarettes. I'm starting to understand why he resorts to them. I might burst into flames with anger."

Instead of the requested brandy, a tub of ice cream with a spoon stuck in it arrived.

Dola said, "This will be better for you, Niki."

She was right. Ice cream was underrated. Dola continued, "You may want to stand by the window and listen to the audio feed. Alphonse is hilarious."

I looked around, but the cat had disappeared, so I ate my ice cream and watched as Alphonse bowed to Rhiannon. "In inadequate recompense, I claim your thumb. The one you always had stuck so far up your arse, you could get nothing useful done for the kingdoms you were sworn to protect."

The crowd laughed, and Dragon Rhiannon's head nodded in what appeared to be assent. Then she looked across at the table of knives. Alphonse strolled over, selected a butcher's knife, and I closed my eyes.

John's howl and the crowd's approval drifted upwards through the window. As I opened my eyes again, Alphonse walked back towards his box, triumphantly clutching a bloody thumb.

Gods and Goddesses, this was insane. The Alphonse I'd met at his daughter's bonding had seemed such a nice man.

Everyone will take the pieces back to their home realms. They believe it will delay his reincarnation. I can't see how. I've never understood why a dead body in bits would delay a soul's return. It's not my belief structure. But Alphonse's people suffered a lot from John and your gran's views on trade not being an essential. His crops tend to be perishable.

Rollo was quite handy—a bit like a cultural guide in my head. He laughed, and I felt a warm mental hug. *You're doing well, Niki. There's no need to watch, but you are expected to stay until all the royals leave.*

I stayed. Empress Sabella was up next. She bowed to Rhiannon and spoke English with her attractive Galician accent. "By your leave, I would request *you* to remove his tongue at the appropriate time. A priest will preserve it using special techniques on behalf of my children and the lies he told about them. We will display it publicly so the many other parents who suffered from his spiteful and inaccurate words about their own offspring may visit it if they wish. Perhaps if there is justice in his next life, he will be mute."

She got the largest round of applause so far and cheers from many of the women, and bowed to the crowd. Alejandro escorted her back to what I was now calling the royal enclosure, making no request of his own.

Rollo, what would you have requested, and what do you think Troels might have asked for?

Troels wouldn't be here. He avoids the other royals. I would. I'd have claimed his spine.

Okaaay? Because?

Because it's so lightly used. He never displayed any. Spine, I mean. He ignored all my requests to ask your grandmother to ban the trade in threecease.

I'd never heard that word. *Threecease?*

You call it droit de seigneur. *If she had, it would have changed the position of all the women in my realm and the others for the better.*

Then I caught a thought not aimed at me but which instead felt more internal. *Perhaps I need to work on finding my own spine and fixing this abuse finally.*

I was about to ask more, but Breanna walked up

to John like a warrior queen, all her bright liveliness hidden now. This was a woman who could and had lopped the heads off criminals and terrorists with her own sword held firmly in her own hands. She looked terrifyingly controlled. I'd never seen this side of her. Through John Fergusson's single remaining eye, it must have looked as though Karma herself had come calling.

Then, as Breanna looked up and caught the dragon's eye, she said the most unexpected thing. "I claim his nose, in one piece, undamaged. The nose he so often stuck into everyone else's business without ever noticing the mess in his own home. The nose he looked down at everyone with. The nose I've so often wanted to break." She paused, waiting for a nod from the huge dragon's head. When she got it, she continued, "Please don't allow anyone to punch it. I intend to decorate the front of flower pots with a cast of it. Perhaps I'll grow stinkweed in them. I will definitely encourage my dogs to piss on them."

Laughter erupted in the crowd, and a plume of smoke escaped the dragon's nostrils. It looked like she was amused too. The dragon's eye focused on the men in robes, and one scuttled over with a marker pen and placed a red cross on John's nose. He looked horrified.

Breanna bowed and ceded her place to Caitlin.

Caitlin spoke directly to John. "I don't want any

274

part of you. I didn't want you interfering in my life when you were alive, and I refuse to give slag like you any space in it once you're dead. However," she bowed to Rhiannon, "my sister Juna claims your middle finger."

I was tremendously proud of her. Then she astonished me when she reached, took the livestream camera from Finn and stepped back with the cam still focused on John's face.

Finn walked over to the table of shiny, scary things and came back carrying an old-fashioned straight-edge razor. He stopped in front of John and bowed to Rhiannon. "I want his eyebrows. I'd like to remove them now."

Rhiannon inclined her dragon head. My quiet, peaceful Finn, with no fuss and considerable expertise, shaved the former Knight's bushy eyebrows off. He blew them to the four winds and stated, "Now, he can't wiggle those caterpillars intending to demean anyone else for not being his 'so wonderful' lying, thieving son." There was only one tiny scratch with a single drop of blood on John's face. Did I underestimate Finn?

Caitlin filmed it while the crowd hooted with laughter, applauded and called support to a red-faced Finn. She returned his camera and walked back to the box and her mother.

Glais'Nee was up next again for the Fae. He

bowed to Rhiannon. "My liege lord expressed a desire to grow calla lilies in this lily-livered coward's liver. After sixty years inside him, he says it's perfectly suited to them. They symbolise rebirth and purity, so he feels they will assist the oathbreaker in making the necessary changes before his next incarnation. I have the skill to remove it now, but by your leave, I would prefer to collect it later. I would not wish to curtail his opportunity to learn."

Rhiannon inclined her dragon head again, and I watched as the last of the royals walked back towards their boxes.

Could I go home now? I didn't want to be here anymore.

TWENTY-THREE

A s I sighed in relief that I was free to leave, there was a tap on the door of my box, and Mabon stuck his head in. Still wearing his formal red and gold robes, he looked powerful but frayed at the edges. His aura was dull, and his many scars stood out on his face in stark contrast to his skin.

"Nik-a-lula, wanted to check you're well? Good, you did. Made me proud. Pleased your gran would be. Most of it wasn't her fault. Fergusson, now had he been a man of honour, they'd have held their own, even with her lower power level. But he wasn't so…" He sighed, and the expression of weariness deepened on his face.

"No, I suppose it wasn't all Gran's fault, but it's still embarrassing, Boney. How's Dai?"

"Not good. Come around, he will. Ad'Rian says so. But you look tired too."

No point denying it. He was right. I was exhausted. I gave him the fifteen-second overview of yesterday and the drama with the toxic yellow power.

"Do you truly understand the power's actions?" Huh? Suddenly we had less Yoda speak? It must be important. Did I understand? Nope, I didn't.

"Not really, no. I'd never heard of regnal power. I didn't know it even existed until yesterday. The Book says you all have it. But you and Ad'Rian have some other kind too?"

Mabon settled himself unselfconsciously on one of the enormous golden thrones and gestured me to sit on the other one. I perched on it. I wasn't accustomed to a throne being my right, and I wasn't sure I ever would be.

He focused his lapis lazuli eyes on me. "So who has the power given Viking's regnal power to?"

"Rollo."

He relaxed against the throne. "Well now, the right choice, that is. So why are you showing me such a long face?"

"Because he doesn't want it."

He gave me an assessing look for a long moment before he tapped his earbud. "Dola, the Recorder and

I will need some refreshments, please." There was a pause. "Yes, we're in her box. Yes, sounds lovely, it does. My thanks."

Mabon was still considering me. "Learn much history at that posh boarding school, did you, *bach*?"

"Some? Any particular period?"

He retrieved glasses and bottles from the ledge inside the window embrasure. "The kings and queens of ... well, anywhere. But in your type of school, England, I expect."

"Sure, what about them?" I accepted my glass of wine, and he clinked his beer bottle against it.

"Ever notice, did you, how many times the younger brother or the cousin made a better king than the one who was supposed to inherit?"

"No, I've never noticed it. But now you say it, I can think of a couple of examples. But I'm not sure I'm getting your point. Rollo doesn't have any siblings?"

"Live as long as I have, notice you do, the best rulers never wanted to rule. Those are the ones who understand the true burden of the crown. And it's not the weight of the bluddy gold they make the circlets from. The ones who grab the power at the first opportunity rarely do the best by their people. They only consider what's in it for them."

"How old *are* you, Boney?" I'd pondered this a

few times since I became the Recorder. He'd admitted to knowing Arthur Pendragon and having fought the Romans. I couldn't let this opportunity to get an answer pass me by.

His warm, contagious laugh rolled out and made me smile before he even spoke. "Let's just say I'm old enough to know better and young enough to still break the rules, shall we?"

That was no damn help. I sipped my wine and watched as he helped himself to a whisky from the bottle of Girvan Sovereign Dola had sent him along with his beer.

Mabon wriggled his shoulders. "Tell me if the Book already told you this. But Rollo doesn't have to accept the yellow power for himself. No force in the universe can make him become the King of Viking."

"OK. No, I didn't realise. He says he doesn't want it. He only agreed to keep it safe—whatever that means."

Mabon spoke slowly, carefully, "But when the Gateway power makes clear its wishes, listen hard, we should. Knows bluddy well, it does, Troels stole the regnal power from Jonvar. And they weren't brothers, or half-brothers, or whatever *cachu* Troels is spouting these days. Jonvar was the full-blooded legitimate king from the House of Odin's Horse, and Rollo is his heir."

Cachu was Welsh for "crap," and it showed me Mabon felt passionately about this.

He swigged from his beer bottle and, at my raised eyebrows, added, "Troels was a by-blow with a taste for power. He seized it as Jonvar was dying. Ad'Rian had the account from Rollo's mother. There's a letter somewhere tells the tale. But the babe was still in her belly, so she couldn't do anything about it for all her Fae power. Her dying request was her family pledge to keep watch for the lad—because accidents can happen to children. Troels would have favoured his own idiot sons."

"It sounds like the plot of a movie, Boney."

"Have to get their ideas from somewhere, don't they? Nothing new under the sun if you've been around for a while. But when Troels wouldn't pass the throne on to the boy when he reached twenty-one as any regent should, told Ad'Rian he'd never been the child's regent, he did. Said he was his half-brother's preferred heir. Said he'd had the words from Jonvar's own lips as he died. There were only five people in the room. Troels and his wife, Rollo's parents, who are both dead, and the child still inside his mother. So who will the people believe?"

I nodded.

Mabon continued, "In fact, if the account I had is true, he made the lad's life so unbearable, Ad'Rian was forced to give Troels a choice. Treat Rollo better.

Allow the lad to go off and study in Caledonia as he wanted to, or Ad'Rian ..." he paused.

He sipped his beer, his eyes searching the walls of the box as though to retrieve the memory. He nodded approvingly at one of the gorier hangings and, in a fair approximation of Ad'Rian's beautifully articulated, dulcet tones, he said, "Ad'Rian told Troels he wouldn't be able to hold back the three witches any longer."

Rollo's attention sharpened in my mind, and I wondered if I should let Mabon know he was listening in. Something stopped me. The yearning for more information to help him make the right decision that came from Rollo, perhaps.

Mabon glanced at another hanging, frowned at it, and, as if he'd now retrieved the correct memory, said, "Ask Ad'Rian yourself, you could. The Recorder has the right. But the story I had was he told Troels something like, 'They're very cross with you. And, Gunnar, you know those three. Their curses tend towards shrinking important parts of the male anatomy until it drops off, turns black or pops while you're using it. Of course, daaarling, if you feel you must take the risk, and your little pecker isn't important to you, well, I respect your choice and your courage. But if it is, you have one week to send Rollo to Caledonia, healthy and happy. Otherwise, I will loosen my control over the sisters and release the bitches of war on you and your realm.'"

I laughed. "Trust Ad'Rian to cut to the core."

Mabon nodded at me. "Quite right. Threaten his manhood, only thing he cared about, wasn't it? Did the job. Ad'Rian should have done it sooner, but it wasn't until he made Rollo tell him what had been happening. Then realised, he did, Troels never planned to relinquish the throne. But it gave the lad a chance at his own life, and he always looked better for it."

He finished his beer and looked about ready to go, but I still felt guilty. "You didn't tell me anything about Dai? What's wrong with him? I'd hate it to be anything I did. But was it?"

He sipped his whisky, and I asked Dola for another beer for him. I was nursing my wine. I was so tired, if I drank it, I might curl up on this stupid throne and sleep.

"Do you know what PTSD is?" He pronounced the acronym carefully, as if he'd only recently learnt it.

I nodded.

He smiled at me. "Oh, thank the Goddess. Explain it to me, *bach*. Is it just a new word for an old thing?"

Oh, bless him. It couldn't be easy when people changed the vocabulary on you so many times during a long life. "I think they used to call it shell shock, but it's not only for people who've been in wars. Aysha had several clients, victims of domestic abuse, who were diagnosed with it. From what Aysha said, it's a lot to do with being stuck in a situation where you don't feel safe, and you can't, or at least you don't think you can get out of it. It's when you feel under threat all the time. Then afterwards, even when the threat has passed, some part of you doesn't trust or believe it, so you're still badly affected by it."

Mabon stiffened. His stillness had an "oh shit" quality to it.

Slowly, he asked, "So if someone thinks something is going to happen to them, and they don't want it to, that could drive them crazy?"

I debated challenging his word choices and then thought, given his age, I'd allow him a pass this time. "Yes, I think so. But surely Ad'Rian would know better than me?"

"Almost exactly the same, you said, as he did earlier. Just didn't want to believe him, did I? Well, that, and he uses such long words even though a short one would do."

At my confused expression, he added, "Suicidal ideation, I ask you? Turns out, it only means Dai doesn't want to live. I mean, we've all had those days, for the Goddesses' sake!"

I shook my head, but he barrelled on, "It's the root of his problem right now. Dai is fighting the healers."

"Do they know what's caused it? Caused it to come to a head now, I mean?" I wouldn't fall into the trap of saying Dai always seemed fine. Because he hadn't, had he? He'd been unhappy, frustrated and pretty short-tempered at least over the few weeks I'd known him as an adult.

"Me, probably." Mabon's normal grin was absent, and his tone despondent. "I haven't taken his problems or the things he's said seriously enough."

He sipped his whisky. "We've no dragon queens, and we have to have them. People don't realise this; the Book would tell you: half of the Red regnal power is all for the dragons. Those dragons, little arsonists they can be as hatchlings, but they're the backbone of the Red Celt realm. Well, without them, we'd just be Celts, wouldn't we?"

I tried to process his words. What did this have to do with Dai's obviously deep depression?

"But I thought Rhiannon was the dragon queen?" Why did I think that? Had the Book told me, or was I assuming based on her bearing and attitude?

"She is a sort of queen. But she can't do it alone. I shared the dragon's portion of Red's regnal power with both the kids when they were old enough.

Rhiannon took to it straight away. She's a true daughter, that one."

Yes, he always called her his true daughter.

Did I not understand the significance of the term? And what did it have to do with Dai? He'd often seemed annoyed or bored by the dragons and having to schlep up and down the mountain, but he wasn't afraid of them. Wasn't fear a key part of PTSD? I'd need to look it up.

"But what's it got to do with Dai?"

"It's complicated. I have half of the Red regnal power; it's for the realm. For ruling. Then the kids get a quarter each to control the dragons. We've had a single dragon king or queen in the past. But I've two kids. Have to treat them fairly, I do. But a few hundred years without new queens being hatched are making it more urgent now. More need breeding."

"What's stopping them? Sorry, Boney, I don't think I'm getting this."

"Rhiannon and Dafydd, they won't—" He interlocked all his fingers, pushing them in and out. "They're not together on it. Have to be together, they do."

"But why?" I wasn't quite getting this. Maybe the Book would help. I was wondering how half-siblings could be joint rulers. Perhaps my middle-class mores were getting in my way, but I couldn't get past incest to any intelligent questions.

Yeah, no, I really couldn't. "But if they're half brother and sister, I mean, they can't ... well, they couldn't ..."

I trailed off.

"Can't what?" Mabon's confused frown didn't help. He looked so tired.

I forced my question out, "Wouldn't it be incest?"

His fabulous infectious laugh rang out loud and long. "Oh, funny that is. Needed a laugh, I did. Thank you, *bach*. The king and queen don't have sex for the eggs." He shook his head at himself. "Well, of course they could with other people, but not with each other." His laugh rang out again. "Others have the eggs, and the king and queen use the regnal power to make them part of the pack." He shook his head as if he understood he hadn't conveyed his meaning clearly.

"Dragons, like humans, it isn't." He waved a hand as if to erase his words and started in a different place. "The king and queen aren't in a, what do they call it these days? A personal relationship? Theirs is a power relationship. To attach and then rule the dragons. When you put the quarter powers together, it's—"

He gave up and lapsed into Welsh, and I heard Dola's name.

Dola's voice through my earbud said, "Mabon is trying to explain the dragons' half of the regnal power is an entire power too, equal to his own Red regnal power. Or it should be. But split in two between Rhiannon and Dai, as Mabon did, it is too weak to do its job. Because Dai won't work as part of the dragons' ruling team."

Mabon nodded and added, "What is it Ad'Rian said? Oh, yes, if the kids join, it will be far more than the sum of its parts." Then he laughed again, his entire face looking smoother and happier. "Wait until I tell Rhiannon. She'd love to bite Dai's bluddy head off. Might even consider it worth it. Sorry, *bach*." He dissolved into more laughter.

Well, I'd unwittingly perked him right up. I hoped I wasn't blushing. "No, I'm sorry. Not sure how I misunderstood."

He waved a hand at me, looking relaxed now thanks to the hilarity I'd inadvertently provided. "Dai has to step up. I don't know how he's held off the change to dragon. Their twenties is the usual time for them to embrace their dragon side. He's been fighting and resisting the change for a hundred years. The boy will make a powerful king if he doesn't drive himself datt first."

He let out a long sigh that tugged at my heart-strings.

Before he burst out, "PTSD, by the Goddess! Everyone is so free with their labels and categorisations these days. It can't be a good thing, can it? This person is a narcissist, and that one is a sociopath. But if you live a long enough life—and Dai will—well, you might have all their labels attached to you at one point or another."

He gestured with his beer bottle, obviously feeling better. "Bit of a screw-up right now, he is. That's for sure. But more serious than that? I don't think so. When I was younger, there was the time I drew Bloodletter and left more than a hundred slain Vikings who'd pissed me off in my wake. Berserker rage, we called it then. Did it make me a psychopath? Well, it would by today's standards because I didn't lose a moment's sleep over it."

At my frown, he said, "Oh, I gave the wives and kids some gold, let many of them move to my realm. I still keep an eye on their descendants as I come across them. Blondie, remember? The nasty *ast*, the one who struck you—she was one of their descendants. But can I blame the drop of Viking blood that might be left in her? I don't think so. Woman was just a wrong 'un. That can happen."

I sipped my wine. He was probably right because I'd got pretty good at knowing which realm a person felt they owed their allegiance to. Yes, she'd been an unpleasant woman. My face throbbed even thinking about her, but she had considered Mabon to be her king.

Mabon said, "Dai hasn't killed anyone, has he? Not that I know of, anyway. Boy's just struggling to find his way to the right path. My deity power, from my mother, allows me to see if someone is irredeemable or if they've just not grown up yet. I'm putting Dai into the latter camp. Am I right? I don't know, he's my son. Biased I might be."

He finished both his drinks and stood up. This time there was a certainty to the set of his shoulders that he hadn't had earlier.

"Must have needed to get that off my chest, Nik-a-lula. Thank you."

He gathered me to my feet and into a hug and held on longer than he usually would. But when I checked his energy, the sparks were coming back into it.

"Give Rollo a message from me?"

"Sure." I was intrigued.

"Tell him it's his life. If find a way, he can, to face himself in the looking glass, he'll do better than ninety percent of people. The decision isn't important. Making a bluddy decision, that's the important bit. Leaving a realm without a ruler, it's not good. Decide within the month he should."

Everyone wanted to give Rollo deadlines, didn't they?

With that, Mabon kissed my cheek and marched to the door before he stopped. "Remembered what I came in for. I owe you a debt for saving Jamie. I'd have been forsworn. That boy Hughes is deaf. You thought that, didn't you? Folk said they saw you signing and mouthing no at him. Why I have a deaf soldier in a position where he can't take orders is a problem for the boyos. But I checked him myself, and Glais'Nee agreed. He's no traitor, just not suited to being a guard. I've sent him off to herd the coos. He can keep them down by the river where they should be as a bit of a punishment. He can be Hughes the Coos for a year or two. At least, being deaf, he won't be disturbed by their lowing and mooing. I'm in your debt, Recorder."

He did the formal bow the realms always accompanied these words with. I was collecting debts from all over the realms this month, wasn't I?

Once he'd gone, I asked Rollo, *Did you get your message from Mabon?*

I did. Thank you. I'll think on it.

Can I go home now?

Yes. The image he sent me of his open arms was awfully appealing. I'd wanted a hug throughout this horrid day.

This had been an odd ceremony, but apart from John Fergusson's eye and his thumb, they hadn't cut him to pieces as I'd feared. I suspected they would after the dignitaries had left. But maybe the chance for everyone to say their piece with the added entertainment value and all the laughter and applause were a way to clean Fergusson's pernicious influence out of the realms.

Although I was incredibly grateful they didn't expect me to stay and watch Rhiannon and those druids work on John.

PART FOUR
SATURDAY

This journey must always begin with *you*.

Face your demons. How can you defeat them until you acknowledge them?

The mirror is a good place to begin. Our inner self shows clearly on our face and through our posture.

What do *you* see when you look deeply into your own eyes in the mirror in your private quarters?

If you can appreciate what you see—revel in it. Celebrate yourself.

If you don't—take courage—change needn't be hard. But it should begin now.

Finding your Inner Fire: How to Claim your True Self by Peggy Hwybon

CHAPTER
TWENTY-FOUR

S aturday, 27th February—Gateway Cottage—Refreshed O'clock

I slept late on Saturday morning. The stress of the week had caught up with me and mugged me in a dark mental alley, and my brain had shut down. But a reset had occurred while dreaming, and I'd woken refreshed and focused.

I had a to-do list.

Currently, it had three top-level items on it.

Coffee. Shower. Fix shit.

After my shower, I dictated items onto my Fix Shit sub-list while I drank my coffee. Two out of three ain't bad.

I reached for the face moisturiser I'd been allowed to buy from Morven, the Beauty Alchemist. I hadn't noticed any magical effects this week, but they were great products and my skin was glowing and my lips were soft. Let's be honest—we never believed the claims that any skin creams made, did we? But if they smelt good and Morven's were truly divine and made us feel good, that was all we could ask for, wasn't it?

Having finished with the Holding Out for a Hero face cream, I applied the Kiss me Senseless lip balm and giggled to myself. At forty-one, I was pretty sure I'd never actually been kissed senseless—which was a rather sad statement about my life thus far.

Today I planned to stay home, walk Tilly, and relax. I'd take time to breathe and devise strategies to deal with all the things on my Fix Shit list over the next few days, including rapists, dragons, and Aysha. I sent Autumn a unicorn meme and giggled at the Aunticorn one she sent back to me. "Like a normal aunt, but magical." I missed her. Maybe I should go down and have lunch with them? Except I really didn't want to explain the whole Dai mess to Aysha. Not until I had some more information about why it had all happened.

I wore my favourite, stretchy, fit-like-a-second-skin jeans, with one of my new thermal tanks with the built-in bra. This one was a sunny yellow, and it might have been my favourite. I threw on an old soft grey sweatshirt that might send Aysha looking for the nearest flagpole if I ever let her anywhere near it.

Only when I headed through to the kitchen did I remember a whole new section of my Fix Shit list that was going to need a lot more items.

He bent over my worktop, facing away from me to bring his head down to HRH's level. The previous evening, I'd offered him the guest room for another night while he adjusted to the yellow power. He and Finn had disappeared into Finn's Foxhole to play a new game they were both excited about.

Watching him now as he spoke to HRH in a low voice, I resolutely refused to entertain any thoughts about how well he filled out those leather trousers. I'd always been a sucker for long thighs and a well-shaped butt. And the width of those shoulders. Oh wow. I could picture myself holding on to those shoulders while he ... I drifted into a happy daydream.

Damn it! I was doing it again. At forty-one, was I truly unable to control my own thoughts? This was ridiculous and beyond embarrassing. I had to get Rollo out of my head literally so I could properly appreciate him privately—oh, Gods and Goddesses, how much deeper could I dig this hole for myself?

I plopped myself at the table and buried my glowing cheeks in my hands. This wasn't me. During my entire marriage to Nick, the worst thing I'd done was appreciate, briefly, as I conducted a wedding, a handsome best man in a well-cut suit. Or occasionally noticed someone in the supermarket had a cute smile. Rollo was breaking my patterns. I'd never, ever wanted so badly to see what was under…

I told myself to concentrate on my to-do list and *only* that.

"Dola, can you see if Glynis has any time for me tomorrow, please? I know you said the Recorder usually announces her impending presence, and everyone fits in with me. But Glynis is a busy woman too, and the St. David's Day thing must increase her workload. I only need fifteen minutes, and I can work around her."

"Yes, Niki. I did it yesterday. It is on your calendar. And Dai is now recovering."

Oh, thank goodness, I'd reassured myself constantly that Ad'Rian was the best. But when his patient had needed Ad'Rian to work on him for so long, I'd worried. It hadn't boded well for Dai.

"Is Mabon OK?"

"He is well. You have a message from him."

I took my phone out. Completely accidentally, and I would swear so until my dying day, however much it made my left shoulder hurt, I opened the camera and snapped a quick shot of my view of Rollo as he leaned over chatting to the cat. I paged determinedly over to the messages app. Mabon said Ad'Rian and his team had healed Dai. All was well.

Rollo stood up and smiled. "Good morning, Niki, sleep well?"

Oh, thank the Goddess, he didn't seem to have heard anything in my head. Now there was an idea: was there a Goddess who accepted the prayers of women who repeatedly embarrassed themselves? The Goddess Mortificatia perhaps? I needed to find out and light a candle to her. A large candle.

"I did, thank you, very well." He hadn't heard all my inappropriate thoughts, had he? But the creases around and the twinkle in his eyes and those adorable dimples on either side of his slightly smug grin said he had.

Kill me now.

I found my manners. "We should ask the Book if it has any good ideas about why you can't use the yellow power. Did HRH offer any advice to help us out?" I looked around, but the cat had gone.

Before breakfast had been served?

I didn't freaking think so.

I got cross.

I'd asked her to stop doing that.

I pulled power, forgetting, as I did it, we were trying to keep the people who knew I could use the power outside the Gateway to the minimum.

Rollo picked up my thought because he said, "My word on it, Recorder. I'll hold anything I've learned in your home in trust." That was nice. At least he wouldn't tell people I fancied the pants off him, would he?

Oh, FFS, just bury me now.

I took my disgust at myself out on HRH. I swirled power around the kitchen, crooning, "Here, kitty, kitty. Come along, poppet, I know you're here. Where's the cutest little kitty-cat in all of Gretna Green hiding herself today?"

"Recorder! *Really!* Consider my dignity. Or, at the very least, your own."

The cat appeared, sitting on a chair at the table. "We discussed the use of baby talk and nonsense names when you were eight. Do I need to review the material for you?"

"No, you don't. However, apparently I need to review my instructions to you to stop hiding in my kitchen. I have a right to privacy in my home. If you're here, I want to know about it. I'll put a bell on you if you don't stop it."

The cat stretched and blew herself up to twice her usual size. Every hair stood on end. Outrage personified.

"Tuna, Recorder."

I dumped tuna into one of her dishes but didn't drain it properly. She could take a number and get to the back of the ever-lengthening complaint queue. I was pissed off with her. I had limits, and peace and privacy in my home were those limits. She could probably read my mind, which didn't normally bother me. But then I wasn't usually thinking about whether, if I bent over the counter, Rollo might— Nope. Not. Going. There.

I placed the tuna on the table and turned her own too-frequent injunction against her. "Unless you need to speak to me, don't let me detain you."

She twitched her tail, and the dish of tuna followed her out, leaving Rollo and me looking at each other.

Rollo said, "Recorder, we need to talk. Do you believe we are private now?"

"Why 'Recorder'? But no, not a damn chance. She'll be back through the wall in invisible mode the second I stop thinking about her. And," I checked the clock, "Finn will be through for a bacon sandwich any moment."

He sighed. "I thought I had problems getting any privacy. And, Recorder, because you're right, I'm not making progress on using the yellow power, and I need the Recorder's advice."

"I know a place where Dola and my shields can trump other people's nosiness. Follow me."

We'd settled in my gran's former office, which I'd turned into my den. Dola had made me a public office in the annex, and I didn't like the lounge with its negative vibes of confronting Jamie, and, anyway, it just wasn't a very nice room. So I'd converted Gran's office into a cheerful private sitting room. Dola and I had overhauled it several times. It was my little haven now.

"Dola, please keep the cat out of here until Rollo and I have finished talking."

"Gladly, I shall erect a shield around the doorway too. She has no shame and lurks in the flower bed if you ban her from the house."

I suppressed my giggle and considered Rollo.

He sat on the other end of the small sofa, with his feet up on the footrest, and looked, for the first time since I'd met him, relaxed. I wafted a little power, and the garden doors opened, letting in a warm breeze and the spring scents from the cherry blossom. Tilly moved from her favourite chair to the patch of sunlight that always shone on the eternally flowering cherry tree about this time in the morning. She often had to fight HRH for it. Well, she'd won today.

Rollo sighed happily. "This is a lovely room. Even the dog's relaxed." He gestured at the tree. "How is that flowering in February?"

"Magic. Did you have breakfast?" He nodded. "Do you like Krispy Kreme?"

His eyes opened wide. He grinned and pushed up to a seated position, extricating himself from the couch's embrace. "There's one near here? When I lived in Edinburgh, I often had them on the last Saturday of the month. Isn't that strange?"

"Well, yeah, I think restricting yourself to KK once a month is extremely strange, but what makes you say it is?"

"Because I was thinking about them five minutes ago when you were watching me in the—I mean, before you fell out with the Great One."

I did not blush. OK, I did, and you all knew that already, right?

I tapped my head, and before I could go any redder, said, "We might be picking random stuff up from each other. Or maybe we both like KK?"

Two identical black coffees arrived in two identical wildly colourful mugs. I smiled at mine, a reproduction of Edvard Munch's *The Scream*. The text said, *When someone says they don't like coffee.*

We both looked at our mugs, clinked them, smiled at each other and sipped in perfect companionable silence.

"Did I tell you the healers have released Dai?"

He nodded. "I heard rumours you and Dai were ..." He trailed off, but I picked up curiosity and something else from his head.

There was nothing private about it, so I answered his unasked question. "I had a crush on him when I was a kid. We used to play backgammon in the

Gateway together. But since I came back a month ago, he's been peculiar. He's alternated between being kind, understanding and helpful, and strange and bullying. I'd never wish him any harm. And I'm delighted he's recovering, but ..." Now I trailed off, shaking my head. I realised I'd settled into a new normal.

I hoped Dai recovered fully, but even if he did, his actions had disturbed me too much. His lack of honesty, too-swift temper, trying to lock me in, and my Gift nagging at me—all these things meant I was putting him firmly into the might-be-a-friend-if-he-shapes-up column.

A large plate of mixed doughnuts arrived. I swigged my coffee and picked up a plain glazed as Rollo reached for the same kind before he drank his own coffee.

In unison, we said, "You've got to start here and know it only gets better."

The laughter removed any remaining tension from my shoulders, and I clinked my mug to his again. "I said *exactly* the same to Mabon when I first introduced him to the delights of perfect doughnuts, and he asked me where to start. Here's to Saturdays with KK."

A sad look crossed his face briefly, and, unconsciously, I accessed our mental link. I got a clear picture of a view out across a city and his hand in front of his face holding a filled doughnut, about to take a bite. The sun was just coming up. I recognised the view! It had been a beautiful memory for Tilly and me before Nick spoiled it.

"Would you like to do something crazy?"

He gave me a slow, sexy grin. "Anytime."

"Cool. You'll need a coat," I glanced at his socked feet, "and shoes."

His expression said the crazy he'd had in mind didn't involve a coat or shoes, but when a leather jacket and pair of boots arrived, he put them on and politely thanked Dola.

"My waterproof jacket and hiking boots, and those doughnuts to go please, Dola. Oh, and Tilly's lead."

A couple of minutes later, I picked up Tilly and took Rollo's hand. "Empty your mind, please. I'd prefer not to go via Viking."

My world turned rainbow-coloured. Then I opened my eyes in the dark.

CHAPTER
TWENTY-FIVE

Arthur's Seat—Edinburgh—Sunrise

I set Tilly down and turned around. "Ha! We're even here first."

I looked out at the full snow moon setting over the waters of the Firth of Forth. It was a heart-warming and magical sight. The lights of Edinburgh twinkled beneath our feet, and the outline of the castle was barely visible in the distance. It was almost silent up here at Arthur's Seat, high above the town, except for the wind whistling around the back of the rocks. But I'd landed us in the sheltered hollow with a splendid view of the city and the water.

Rollo gave me a startled glance. "How did you— sorry, I'm being slow, aren't I?" He took in a lungful of the brisk Scottish morning air. "Too dark still for anyone but idiots to try to get up here. We were often

309

those idiots, though generally not in February. Your transporting thing is like being in a computer game. I need data. I should experiment and ascertain if the yellow power will take me anywhere except Viking."

He looked around, and his brow creased. The light of the setting moon cast a shadow on his face. "But why's it still dark here? There's no time difference; we were only what? A hundred miles south? Wasn't it after ten when we left?"

He stilled. *Streth mik, that would be phenomenal. Did we seriously just time travel? We did! Yesterday, when she was so specific about the time we should arrive at the Gateway... Streth, sci-fi geek's dream come true. Real time travel, I wonder ...*

I interrupted that train of thought. *Remember all those things you might learn in my home? Well, whether we did or didn't, I can't answer right now because the cost of the wrong people knowing is too high.*

He gave me a serious nod of understanding. Why on earth did I trust this man? Was it because my Gift trusted him?

He stated rather than asked, "You got the memory of here out of my mind."

"No, only a quick flash, but I recognised the location. And you felt sad and homesick. And ..." I trailed off. Then I thought, sod it, and shared my plan. "The sun will come up over there in less than an hour. At least Google said it would. I wanted to do something silly."

I didn't know a way to explain the truth to someone I didn't yet know well enough. I'd wanted to reclaim a younger, sillier me. It sounded too ridiculous to say aloud. I'd wanted to let the world know I wasn't always a boring wife with all the joy, laughter and spontaneity nit-picked out of me. I could feel like a silly student again for an hour and eat my doughnut with one of the best views I'd ever seen, and one Rollo obviously loved as well. There wasn't a time of day when this place didn't give you an incredible view. But at moonset and at sunrise, it was superlative. It was a frequent entrant on those "the twenty views you should see before you die" lists.

He took my hand. "You're right. This is home for me; Viking never was. And I understand all the rest much better than you might guess, Boo."

Boo? Did he just call me Boo? Who the hell calls anyone Boo? What does it even mean?

His laughter rang out, deep, rich and joyous. He was almost doubled over now with amusement.

"What?"

"Perhaps for different reasons, but that's exactly, and I do mean *exactly*, what shot through my mind the first time a child at university unselfconsciously called someone 'Boo.' Well, she seemed like a child to me. You're aware I enrolled late? Didn't Finn say he'd told you about all the trouble with my guardian?"

"No, the only thing Finn told me about you was you had a brain, a fistful of degrees, and I should stop falling for your eye candy persona."

I heard his smile in his voice. "That persona has served me well. Being Troels' heir has necessitated a masterclass in misdirection."

"But you're not his heir, are you? At least the Book and HRH don't seem to think so."

"It's complicated." I waited for him to brush me off the way Dai had when I'd asked anything about him, but he surprised me. "I know he stole the throne from me. And, at worst, he should have handed it over when I came of age, but I'd hate to be the Viking King. Can you imagine anything more appalling? Troels loves it. His people love him."

"No, they don't. The Rightful King of Viking is a master of self-delusion. Over eighty-seven percent of them want rid of him." Whoops! I'd spoken before I thought and answered him on auto-pilot. I hoped Dola didn't mind me sharing her data.

His head spun round. Suddenly I was more interesting than the view?

Cautiously, he asked, "Might I inquire how you're so sure? Is it a Recorder thing? I'll understand if you can't answer me."

"No, it's a perfectly normal data thing. But it's not mine to share. One moment."

I tapped my earbud. "Dola, sorry we left our coffees behind. Can we have fresh? And do you mind if I share the Viking part of your data with Rollo?"

I switched on the camera and did the usual 360 for her. I focused on a moonlit flat rock which might serve as a table. Rollo watched all this with fascination.

Coffee arrived on the rock along with a ... what was that? "Huh. Thanks, Dola, brilliant plan." I picked up the waterproof blanket and threw it to Rollo. "It seems we're having a picnic."

Quietly, through my earbud, Dola said, "The decision is yours, Niki. I can tell you, from the help he gave us when we set up the streaming on the Rainbow Network and from my monitoring of his Dolina, Rollo keeps information to himself."

I wondered if I could use Port 22, our private mental link, the way the fae used mind-to-mind connection to speed things up.

I reached out and was about to ask his permission to try it. I'd never instigated this before, although I'd been on the receiving end a few times. But before I had chance to ask, Rollo said, "I've done it too with my mother's fae family. I consent—let's see if we can do it."

I'd always suspected the finger to the third eye

was merely a focus for both parties. Rollo and I were already connected, so I tapped on his mind, and it opened for me. I sent him everything I remembered from the Viking's responses to the questions we'd asked the realms on the extensive questionnaire we'd set up for the boring moments between the bondings on the livestream. Finn had called them adverts, but Dola had obtained some useful feedback for her PR courses from her polls and quizzes.

He let out a low whistle. "You can tell you did computer science too. That explains a megaton about why you're so different to my lady Elsie. So how did you come up with the idea—"

He shook his head. "Sorry, none of my business."

But it wasn't private information. We planned to share it with most of the royals once we'd extracted and formatted the useful data. "It wasn't me. It was mostly Dola. She needed some data to play with for a course she's doing."

I picked up my coffee before it got cold in the freezing air. Aww, Dola had put it in a thermal mug. She really was the best. I chose a doughnut, feeling I'd earned it.

Rollo asked, "Did you know we have the same birthday?"

I'd been watching the February moon, the one they called the snow moon, set as the sun rose and was lost in a world of my own. When I looked back at him to say "pardon," he had a doughnut too and was doing something very interesting to it. The words died on my lips.

Mabon had done almost the same thing, and it had embarrassed him when I asked what he'd said in Welsh. Then Dola refused to translate it and let him off the hook. But Mabon had made me giggle. The look in Rollo's eyes was light years away from my lovely friend Mabon having fun.

Rollo's look said he meant me to watch him.

So I did. And I melted faster than the icing he was now licking slowly off his fingers before he returned his attentions to the soggy-looking doughnut.

Lucky bloody doughnut.

I chewed my bottom lip. For the life of me, I couldn't have looked away. Had I even blinked? Thankfully, he put the last piece out of its misery and, after scraping surplus icing off his plump bottom lip with his teeth, gave me a megawatt grin, dimples and all.

Gently, he asked, "Please would you explain why you were beating yourself up so soundly at breakfast yesterday and this morning? Why is it so inappropriate? I guessed it was a status thing, but it isn't, is it? You don't even think like that, do you?"

"Huh? Status? What?" Gods and Goddesses, I couldn't even draw a full breath. What had he just said?

I swallowed coffee. Think, Niki. Think.

What the hell did he say?

You can do this. The blood will return to your brain any minute.

Say, "pardon," Niki.

Say any damn thing!

Along with his chuckle, he sent, *I'm still doing it, you know.*

The first rays of the rising sun fell on his face, and his hazel eyes sparkled with good-natured humour.

This is the sort of amusement that says we can trust each other, can't we? We're both in a strange and vulnerable position, but one of us has to push it. And you weren't going to. But you did share data with me, and that's virtually a dowry between computer geeks, and you know it. Don't we deserve some fun and maybe a lot more?

Whoa! I wasn't thinking this!

He was thinking this!

He wasn't wrong though, was he?

Were we both thinking this?

I stood up. I'd shivered for an hour waiting for the perfect timing. I'd wanted to see the moon set and then the sun rise over Edinburgh because this week had felt like the beginning of a watershed in my life. I wanted to capture one beautiful visual to attach to what I might, in years to come, look back at as the real beginning of my new life.

I hadn't imagined Rollo being here with me for

my moment. I'd simply wanted to mark my personal achievement. I'd survived one of the kingdoms' more barbaric rituals with my dignity intact. I wanted a new beginning, perhaps finally accepting I'd been born to this job. And I could do it. Maybe not perfectly, but I'd do it.

Now the moon and the old Niki had gone, and I deserved some sunlight in my life. I would watch the damn sunrise and breathe and think and try to work out what my brain was saying.

But, strangely, I had no urge to close him out of my mind.

I walked towards the edge to see the full sweep of the town below and the sun's rays hitting the water where so recently the moon had been. Rollo walked up beside me. We inhaled a deep breath of the cold, fresh Scottish morning air, listened to the birds' morning calls, and he held out his hand to me. I took it, tucked it around my shoulder, and snuggled into his amazing torso. We breathed out together and enjoyed the sunrise.

Edinburgh is a stunning city, and he was a stunning man, and not only on the outside. They both stole my breath.

Some time later, it was shaping up to be a beautiful morning, cold, clear and bright, when I asked, "Did you say something about birthdays?"

Rollo asked, "Is your dog OK?"

I looked, and the little beast was rolling merrily in the grass. Even ten yards away, her full body expression of complete bliss was apparent. "No, the little shit probably found some to roll in. Don't worry, Dola installed an automated dog cleaning shower a couple of weeks ago. But don't let her near you until we check her; she'll stink."

Rollo looked searchingly into my eyes. "Are you OK? Did I push too hard? Are you uncomfortable?"

Pushed? Me? What was he talking about? He hadn't pushed. He'd teased me remorselessly until I could hardly breathe, couldn't think and felt like a puddle of need. None of that was a damn crime. He hadn't even touched me, but then something tickled my intuition, and I turned my Gift on him. With him in my head, I'd barely used my Gift on him since our first meeting. I hadn't needed to. This time, I dug a little deeper.

But when I did. Oh shit. Well, yeah, that would explain a lot, wouldn't it?

"What did you do?" He sounded unhappy. "That felt different to our normal connection?"

"You sensed it?" People usually had no clue I'd read them. Hmm.

"Yeah, it was like a virus." He shook his head. "That's not right." He gestured to the air between us. "This feels like a permitted connection. What you did was like an intruder, someone or something uninvited."

"I'm so sorry. I used the McKnight Gift on you." At his querying expression, I added, "I wanted to know why you thought you might have pushed too hard. You didn't push me at all. You definitely enticed, but I'm pretty sure that's no crime. Well, if it is, every bakery in the world would be guilty."

"Enticed, nice word for it." He gave me his warm, sexy smile again. I swallowed, but, honestly, I loved, after all these years, I was feeling something again. And thanks to our connection, I was pretty sure it was mutual.

"Sorry, Rollo, I probably should have asked you, but you didn't seem to want to talk about it."

I ground to a halt, wondering if I'd overstepped, as Dola would say. But last time I'd wondered how a guy who looked like him, who was smart and funny, could be frustrated and lonely, he'd bitten my head off and muttered about consent in Viking and how could one trust it. Then he told me he could read my mind, so I never got to understand what his problem might be.

I tried to run my thought process through my head the way I did when I was explaining something to the power, so he'd get it through our connection. I wanted to share why I'd been reluctant to ask him to put into words everything I'd picked up with my Gift.

He nodded sadly. "Well, yeah, you got straight to the bottom of my fears and hang-ups. How many cases are there against him now?"

I shrugged. "Over seventy and maybe another two hundred who won't file."

The look of horror that spread across his face and the wave of repulsion that came with it was like a stomach punch.

"And I never want a Single. One. Against. Me." He bit off each word. I saw a picture in his head. A horrible picture. When he was younger, a girl had brushed off his hopeful advances. He'd laughed and moved on like any normal guy. But later the same night, she'd arrived at his longhouse in tears, half naked and drugged, and informed him he must do whatever he wanted to her.

He'd wrapped her in a blanket and sent her home. He'd told Troels to keep his nose out of his private life and received a black eye for his impertinence. That was when his determination to study in England and Caledonia and to never risk noticing another Viking woman again solidified.

He'd intentionally shared the memory with me. It was too bright and complete. Now I sensed his shame at his realm and his misery—and wanted to change the atmosphere.

We'd been strolling hand in hand aimlessly around the top of the grass-covered, inactive volcano of Arthur's Seat to stop ourselves freezing. The view was magnificent, but I was cold now. "You said you used to live here. Do you know why it's called Arthur's Seat? Is it after King Arthur, some legend?"

"I asked King Mabon once. I thought, as he was acquainted with Pendragon, he might have the answer." He laughed. "He said, 'Noooo, now a few taverns down in the town, they should surely be named after him. But him sit up there on a bluddy damp, miserable hill when there was ale being served by smiling brew women by the fire? No, *bachgen*, that I can't see.'"

I looked at my phone. We'd been here about three hours. If I went home now, I'd arrive back shortly after we'd left. I would have stolen myself a morning with Rollo. Oh my goodness, Great Granny Florrie would be proud of me. I mean, it wasn't a fisherman's bothy, but I had plenty of time to work up to her level of sneaking in some healthy exercise, didn't I?

I giggled, and Rollo asked, "Who's Florrie?"

We were still connected. We'd need to address that too.

I told him the stories about Florrie and her time-travelling bonks. He got a far-away expression in his eyes. "How far can you go? Or how long, rather?"

Crap. The Book had said not to tell people about this, hadn't it?

"I'm sorry, Rollo, I shouldn't have said anything. I'll have to ask the Book some questions before I can answer. I don't want to distrust you, but there are Recorder rules. Ugh, I sound like Breanna with her damn Strictures, don't I? Sorry."

But he only smirked. "Slagging Strictures, I think you mean."

I laughed. He was right.

Then he said, "I don't break my word. Ask anyone."

"Actually, everyone told me you didn't when we were all talking about you proposing to Caitlin." The moment I said it, I clamped my mouth shut. Fear sent bitter bile rushing up my throat, and I swallowed convulsively.

But Rollo laughed. "Oh, what a twisted blade of a mess that all was. Troels is such a—" He cut himself off and looked down at me with concern. "Hey, are you OK? Did I do something?"

I sensed him reaching through our connection, and I felt so out of control, I let him see. I showed him a day when I'd innocently told Nick that Aysha and I had talked about him when he wasn't there. I can't even remember what it was all about now.

Something and nothing, his new car, or was it his new golf clubs? I no longer remembered, but Nick had gone ballistic. The atmosphere in the house had been horrific for weeks, and he'd made digs about "his wife" not respecting his privacy for years.

"It's such a damn shame he's dead."

What? That was what Dai always said, and as it had with Dai, my right shoulder pinged. Truth.

Why the hell does EVERYONE keep saying that?

Rollo looked baffled. "It's a saying, isn't it?"

"Not where I come from, no."

"Well, if you lose someone you love, people say 'condolences on your loss,' or the Fae do the Summerlands blessing." He paused and looked at me. I nodded. "And if some complete tosser dies swiftly or painlessly, we say 'such a shame he's dead,' the inference being it's a shame because now we can't kill him slowly as he deserved. So people won't say it about John Fergusson, for example, because he died slowly, and people are glad he's dead. Make sense?"

It was the damn brownies and the Smiths all over again, wasn't it? I hadn't understood the context. Why hadn't I just asked Dai? But I hadn't asked Rollo, had I? I'd only thought it. I had to get better at communicating. I couldn't have a mind-to-mind link with everyone.

"Niki, I'd be happy to spend all day with you, but

you're cold, and I think you had an adrenaline spike, and we both need caffeine. I can't help thinking I'm keeping you from important stuff."

"You're not. One of the first things I put my foot down about was the attitude everyone had that the Recorder is always on duty. I have things to do over the next few days, but you were the only urgent thing on my Fix Shit list today. We need to work out what the power wants with you so you can get your life back."

A harsh laugh suggested it wasn't high on his agenda. "Fix Shit, hey? Would you like to see my flat?"

"Where you used to live, you mean?" I surveyed the steep descent, which would be slippery in February. *No thank you, not if I have to walk down there.*

And of course he picked up my thought. "Do you know Princes Street?"

"Yeah, I do, why?"

"There's an alley behind it." Into my mind, he sent a crystal-clear picture of a brick alcove in an attractive, modernised alleyway. But along with it, I got more information.

"Hang on, d'you mean you still have the flat?" I remembered Caitlin showing me the photos when the room Dola created for Rollo freaked her out. But those had been old photos. She'd scrolled a long way back to find them.

"Yes. I own it."

"And it's empty? Of people I mean."

He nodded, looking confused.

"Then why don't you simply transport us to your flat?"

"Me?"

"Well, you took us to Viking the other day. If it goes wrong, I'll whip us straight back to the cottage. But why not practice while I'm with you?"

A grin spread across his face. He looked as gleeful as a six-year-old with a hot glue gun. And—just as you would with the imaginary child some complete idiot may have given a hot glue gun to—Aysha might never let me live that one down, I ran through the safety checks. "Focus on the time, get a clear picture in your mind, hold firmly to anything or anyone you want to take with you. Check all those things before you form a clear intent and say GO."

From novice Recorder to transporting teacher in barely a month. How my life had changed!

And my pupil was quite the teacher's pet.

We all arrived safely, and I asked for the bathroom to wash my revolting stinky dog before she touched anything in this lovely apartment.

CHAPTER
TWENTY-SIX

W hen I came out with an angry, still-damp dog, who would never understand why humans didn't appreciate the multi-layered delicious scent of several different kinds of shit squished into a Bichon's Velcro-like fur, I smelt coffee and smiled.

This was a lovely apartment in an old building but sensitively and tastefully modernised. We'd arrived in a spacious, well-proportioned hall. I'd washed Tilly in the spotlessly clean white bathroom en suite to the guest room.

The guest room had high ceilings with original plasterwork around the light fitting and beautiful coving. The sage-green wallpaper behind the bed and the lighter tones on the other three walls gave it a restful vibe. A citrusy perfume lingered in the air, and a woman's red jacket peeped out of the wardrobe. He wasn't a complete monk then.

He gently kicked open the door and came in, carrying a mug in each hand. I put Tilly on the floor and said, "No rug rolling," in my firmest voice. It wouldn't work, but in someone else's home, I felt obliged to try.

"This is a lovely room." Why was I making small talk? I was suddenly nervous.

"It's Kari's."

Kari's? The name rang a bell. Ah, yes. "The same Kari who didn't have a bond but claimed sanctuary from the Recorder?"

"Yeah, I think you and Fi named her Princess Entitled, thanks to her impolite email."

I laughed. "She was great once she relaxed a bit. We had a message from her last week about the first Rainbow Council meeting and a request to book her real bonding check. She sounded so happy and relaxed. We're doing the bond check before I unseal the yellow gate so her father can't mess it up for them."

He winced. "Ben's a great guy, but she's right to be cautious. Halvor and his Dirty Dozen gang of warlords will use anyone and anything to push their own agenda. People consider Troels to be the problem, but Halvor's group are the brains behind a lot of the worst crimes."

He handed me the mug. I breathed in. The coffee smelt amazing, almost as good as Dola's and better than mine. I was about to ask more about these warlords, but Rollo was still speaking. "Now you understand why I was so surprised when you showed me the email she'd sent to your grandmother. 'Our match has been approved by the Gods.' How did she even come up with such garbage?"

He held the door open for me, and we walked back into the wide hallway with its highly polished but obviously original wooden floor.

"While Troels had me restricted to Viking, Kari's kept an eye on the flat … and some other things … for me. There's a cleaning service, and Kari and Ben used the flat a lot while they were trying to get their ducks in a row. She couldn't afford to be seen too often in Gretna Green. Troels has spies all over it, you know."

I wondered how you could restrict an adult to a realm and tried to find a polite way to ask. He picked up my question from my mind. "Troels never threatens me anymore. I only realised why yesterday when King Mabon was talking to you about Ad'Rian threatening Troels if he didn't treat me better. So he threatened to 'withdraw his protection' from people I care about if I didn't come home and play the dutiful heir."

I had no idea what to say to this. It was all so

Middle Ages. Sometimes with the realms, I felt like I was stuck in a historical costume drama and not modern-day Britain. Why were they all so stuck in the past?

Rollo smiled at me. "Well, that's the question, isn't it? But it's not because the people want to live in the Dark Ages. But in Viking, at least it suits the senior warlords and the king to block any changes."

I followed him into a bright sunny kitchen and smiled involuntarily. A lovely wooden kitchen table held sunflowers interspersed with some dark blue berries and small white flowers. They graced a clear vase with a heavy base. They looked real but must have been exceptional fakes because there was no water in the vase, only some beautiful tumbled crystals.

The amber and tiger's eye stones drew me to the vase. Their multiple shades of gold and brown, with tiny inclusions of deep blue, red, and gold, matched Rollo's irises. The larger chunks of some stones I didn't know secured the arrangement.

Still smiling, I turned my attention back to Rollo. "We discovered one spy in the Gateway, and Fi's put a stop to that, and then a Fae woman told me there are many more. But, honestly, I thought she was paranoid."

"She probably isn't."

Tilly put her entire small body into her roll on the

colourful rug under the table. She was, as always, desperate to clean the smell of shampoo out of her nose and fur. I sighed.

Rollo looked out of the window and then leaned forward to the sink to fill a ceramic bowl with water.

I watched the show. Those leather pants were … words failed me, but they really were. Amazingly, I didn't feel bad about it. What was it about him? I had been lonely long before Nick's death, but the strength of this attraction wasn't like me.

"Rollo, how old *are* you?" I might as well find out what level of inappropriate behaviour I was almost certainly about to commit. Because I rather thought I was going to do things that had felt impossible just yesterday.

The bigger decision wasn't yes or no. The bigger decision was becoming now or later, after I'd helped him to control his yellow power. Recorder or woman? Which took priority? It was an interesting question. But it was my day off, so …

He turned around, bowl in hand, and bent to place it carefully and excruciatingly slowly on the floor. He stood and watched me. "I wondered if it would work. It seemed to have quite an effect on you this morning."

I looked for something to throw at him. This damn kitchen was too tidy. He grinned. "I told you earlier, but I don't think you were listening then either. We share a birthdate."

"WHAT? No. You said birth*day*. And I wondered how you knew even that much?"

I tried to find words but couldn't. Didn't anyone in my new life look their age? I shook my head helplessly. I couldn't do this. He looked like that. I looked like, well, like me. We couldn't be the same age. He was half-Fae, though; maybe that contributed to him looking mid-twenties and so hot? But he didn't have the other Fae characteristics. His skin was golden not lilac. I gave up. No one was ever what they seemed in the realms, were they?

I drank my coffee and noticed a motto—no, not a motto, some runes on the mug. It looked vaguely familiar. "What does this say?"

"*Drengr*. Niki, look at me. No, even better, bring your coffee." He took my hand and pulled me gently to my feet. "This way. May I show you something, please?"

We walked into the bedroom I'd seen in Caitlin's photos. She was right. Other than the bed, I'd come close to duplicating this room.

"Wow, those photos didn't do it justice."

"Photos?"

It was a gorgeous room with huge, white-framed, floor-to-ceiling windows. The room had a semi-circular tower in the corner, as many of the older

Scottish buildings did. In the tower section was the enormous white wrought-iron bedstead. It couldn't be. He was a Viking and Fae. I walked over and touched the metal. No, it wasn't iron. It was some kind of reproduction.

Rollo was waiting with an expectant tilt to his head. What had he asked? Oh yeah. "Caitlin was surprised when she saw the bedroom Dola and I created for you. She thought I'd been here."

"I thought I *was* here when I first woke. But the bed wasn't right. It was confusing. How did you know?"

The pattern in the head and foot sections of the bed was the Viking's Yggdrasil tree motif. It was beautiful. But I didn't know how I'd pictured this room, or why I'd wanted to recreate it for him. So I shook my head helplessly at Rollo. "Power downloads are stressful. I asked myself what kind of room would make you feel safe when you awoke."

The admiration in his gaze warmed something deep in my belly. And I glanced away before I blushed again.

The room was almost identical to the one we'd made for him. Yellow and white with a blond wood floor, warm sand-coloured walls and a lot of creamy, soft rugs. I wanted to take my boots off and stand on them. Actually, I wanted to roll naked on them. I was worse than Tilly.

CHAPTER
TWENTY-SEVEN

W hen I turned around, Rollo stood by a full-length mirror wearing only his leather trousers. My mouth went dry as he took my hand again cautiously. I didn't feel at all like a shopping trolley as he gently stood me in front of the mirror.

May I take your sweatshirt off? The request in my mind came with a sense of, *Relax. Trust me. Let me show you this.*

I lifted my arms and squashed the fleeting thought that my tank matched the room. I'd had yellow on the brain this morning too, even if it was subconsciously.

He put my ratty sweatshirt on a chair behind him as carefully as if it were cashmere. Then he turned back to the mirror, wrapping his arms around me from behind and linking them below mine at waist-level so I felt safe but not trapped.

"Look at us. We were born on the same day. After sharing this connection with you for the last few days, I've learnt, in many ways, we've dealt with the world similarly. Let's see if we can take the armour off, let the shields down and see who we really are, shall we?"

It was such an astonishing request.

It was what I'd tried to get Dai to do. Show me who he'd grown up to be. But he'd made me feel intrusive for asking even the simplest questions.

Now Rollo was just offering me unvarnished honesty.

How could I say no?

I considered the two of us in the mirror. In my eyes, we were so different. He looked taller than usual. My head barely reached his upper chest. Tall, blond and gorgeously ripped meet short, still-too-skinny and bland. Well, apart from my hair—I loved my new choppy-cut, rainbow-coloured hair.

I was about to pull away when Rollo sent, *Niki, you're beautiful. Relax. Meet me halfway on this. It's about what we show the world. And neither of us shows the world the person we'd like to grow up to be—the person we'd rather be. Or perhaps I mean that, when we do, it's unintentional —we don't even realise we did it.*

He pointed at the mirror. "In Viking, a man needs

to look strong enough so everyone decides there are weaker fish to catch." He tensed his muscles in a parody of a bodybuilder pose. "And be powerful and well-connected enough that the price for causing offence is too high."

He lifted me into the air with barely any pressure on my body, using only his linked arms under mine. Wow! OK.

Returning me gently to the floor, he continued, "But one can never seem to be too clever. And, ideally, one would appear to be a young playboy warrior still sowing his wild oats—such an inane phrase, don't you think? But importantly, a play *boy*. Not a man. Not yet old enough to pose any threat to the existing order."

There was the subtlest shift and a slight change of body language, and the delicious eye candy I'd met at my ascension stood behind me.

OK, that was just freaky!

In the mirror, he now looked shorter.

But he wasn't, because his arms were still wrapped around me in the same place. In the mirror, his muscles looked larger and glossy with oil. But they weren't because his arms left no grease smears on me.

I was so fascinated, I forgot to be nervous. "You're a smart guy, aren't you? I wondered how you did that. You put this on after he tried to kill Tilly. One minute you were sitting at the conference table being yourself, then you gave me a hug, and the next minute, you were all oiled muscles. It's a damn Fae glamour, isn't it?"

I twisted my head to use my peripheral vision. Yes, I could just, but only just, see it. And only because I knew it was there. I used the Fae sight Ad'Rian had taught me in childhood. He'd told me then using my other eyes would show me who a person truly was.

I blew out a breath. "And it's a very complex, immensely clever glamour. You can even adjust the age. It's no wonder I thought you were an unusually mature twenty-something. That's Ad'Rian-level work." I pulled a twist of power as I had with Ti'Anna in my kitchen, enough to curl in my hand, and swivelled in his arms to view him properly.

"No," I said, surprised, "not Ad'Rian. It's L'eon's work. I had no idea he was so skilled yet. But why would he make this complex a glamour for anyone outside of Fae? You guys must be close."

Rollo's mouth formed an O of surprise. He tilted his head down and kissed me. Gently at first, and then, as we melted into each other, much more thoroughly.

Quite some time later, when I realised I was trying to climb him like a tree, my sanity returned, along with embarrassment.

No, sod it! Why should I feel bad about it? We were both single, and we weren't making each other false promises. Shit, he *was* single, wasn't he?

I'm still doing it, remember? Because we haven't yet worked out how to turn it off. But, yes, of course I am. My last relationship ended several years ago, about three months before my uncle summoned me back to Viking.

He turned me back to face the mirror. "Niki, it's your turn now."

"Huh?"

The real, and in my eyes, at least, much more handsome Rollo without his Fae glamour was back again. I pulled power and checked.

Yes, this was all him. The real him. He still looked younger than he was but now appeared to be mid-thirties. And he was still drop-dead gorgeous. The true Rollo was even taller, his hair was about six inches shorter, only coming to his shoulders, and he had more attractive, longer muscles.

I didn't miss fake Thor's "I spend so much time working out, I don't have time for a life" gym bunny, bulked-up persona.

I met his eyes in the mirror. "I prefer the real you."

He grinned. "Oh, so do I, but Troels got more vicious and bloodthirsty as I got older, so I stayed young. Showed him a younger, slightly stupid warrior. He understands them. Much less of a threat to him, you see?"

I did see, but I was sad for him.

"I showed you my armour and the what, why, and who it's for. Take yours off for me, Boo."

"OK, but first, what the hell is with this Boo business?"

"Show me your armour and your real self, and maybe you can have the answer as your reward."

"I hate that you know my curiosity will always drive me where I shouldn't go. Hell, I wouldn't even be the Recorder if I hadn't been too curious. Curiosity might not kill cats, but it definitely traps Recorders. This *is* the real me."

He tightened his arms slightly until I looked in the mirror again, and then he released me, and I relaxed back against the width of his chest. It was a safe place to be. His cheekbones were high and quite sharp. Why had I never noticed them before?

Because even at its lowest setting the glamour is also designed to make me look more Viking and less Fae.

But even without the glamour, he had none of the Fae's violet tinge to his skin?

He answered my thought, "I told you yesterday, my grandfather, Jonvar's father, had very dominant genes. Troels' children don't particularly resemble him, you know. We just all look like my grandfather.

My inheritance from my Fae mother seems to be more internal."

I gazed at us both in the mirror. I didn't have an armour or a glamour. And this was difficult.

She has amazing cheekbones herself, a luscious mouth, not only to kiss, but also to watch while she's talking, and several terrific voices. Is she ever going to focus on herself because ...

"OK, point taken. But what do you mean, several voices?"

"Do yourself first, Boo, and then we'll talk about what I think." He sounded firm. It was sexy.

His arms tightened fractionally until I finally studied myself in the mirror. What I saw surprised me. With Rollo's much larger body acting as a literal frame for me, I saw myself differently.

When I put lipstick on, I only focused on my mouth, not on my whole face. When was the last time I had truly viewed my entire body other than to check whether my clothing hung properly?

It had been a while. Since before Nick's death probably. And I'd changed. Huh!

I tried to play fair and give Rollo the quick overview he'd given me. "If by armour, you mean what I show the world?" I paused until he nodded at me in the mirror.

"OK, when you marry regular people, you need to dress smartly, but not be too eye-catching or noticeable. The bride, in fact the entire wedding party, are the stars of the day. Also, my boss was a Class-A bitch, and it was much easier to smooth the way than ever stand out. So I blended."

I changed my own body language as he had changed his, but mine had to fold in on itself.

In my memory, I heard Mabon telling me off during my first week in the Gateway as he'd pushed my shoulders backwards and down. What had he said? I couldn't remember. But I must have taken it to heart because I was surprised to discover I had to hunch them quite a long way forward and up now to fake being a registrar again.

It wasn't a good look.

I shook it off and looked into Rollo's eyes in the mirror. He watched with interest and understanding.

"My late, unlamented husband had a thing for Kate Moss. He thought I had a look of her."

Rollo nodded. "You do, actually, but her more conventional side. Which is a shame because I bet you'd suit those cut-off denim shorts she used to wear."

"Hmm, her Daisy Duke Glastonbury vibe. I wouldn't have minded that. But Nick wanted me to emulate her red carpet waif look, skinny with all her bones showing. Being underweight brought out *my* amazing cheekbones, apparently. But I didn't have her confidence or charisma, so I never pulled it off."

I sighed. I liked Kate too, and I might have been able to get close to her appearance, if respectability hadn't been so high on Nick's list.

What did he mean by respectability?

I considered his question. "I couldn't have a trendy hairstyle. Well, I could, but I'd get twenty-four-seven whining from him about how boho chic isn't suitable for the wife of a successful businessman."

But you're gorgeous. What did he get out of squashing you into a box?

I think he thought if I was more confident, he'd lose me.

A great gust of laughter came from Rollo. He was so amused, he let me go. As he had earlier up on Arthur's Seat, he gave in to his amusement, bent over with his hands on his knees, laughing uproariously.

I connected to his head to find out what was so damn amusing. But I only got a jumble of a language I didn't speak.

I turned back to the mirror. I actually looked OK now.

Nick would absolutely hate everything he saw if he could look in this mirror. From the top of my multi-coloured head through my relaxed shoulders and skin-tight jeans to my bare feet snuggled into Rollo's fur rug. It made me incredibly happy to discover I'd turned into someone Nick wouldn't have liked. Now that *was* bloody progress!

Rollo got his amusement under control and appeared behind me again. "Sorry. The shield maidens have a saying they quote often: 'Treat your wife like a goddess, or you'd better remember karma is a goddess too, and we'll all help you to meet her.'"

I grinned. "I like it."

He paused. "The original references a Viking Goddess called Hel, but that's the closest I can get to the meaning without a lot of mansplaining."

I snuggled back into him. "You know telling someone something they want to learn isn't mansplaining. Explaining something incorrectly to a person who, sometimes literally, wrote the book on it is mansplaining. Or even womansplaining, it isn't just men that do it. My ex-boss was the mistress of it."

"OK, noted. I'd missed the distinction. But at the risk of repeating myself, it's such a shame he's dead."

"It so isn't. I've never been happier than when the police came to tell me. I wallowed in guilt about it for months."

Then the fury at all the spy cameras I'd found in my house two weeks ago washed over me again. Goddess, was it really only two weeks ago? It was a miracle I hadn't just had a meltdown and taken to my bed. I nodded at myself in the mirror. Maybe I wasn't doing so badly after all.

Rollo swore softly and viciously. It was one of the

Scandinavian languages, and while I didn't understand a word of it, his disgust came through our link
clearly.

"What language *is* that?"

"That's a complicated question. Well, no, it's not,
but the answer is. In brief, it's ours. It grew out of the
old Norse we spoke when we founded the realm. For
now, back to the mirror, please. I want to understand
you. Show me Nick's wife?"

I gazed into the mirror and tried to picture myself
several years ago. A wave of panic rushed over me. I
didn't want to show her to Rollo. No, that wasn't
right. *I* didn't want to see the poor, sad, trapped,
stupid woman. She hadn't been trapped at all,
though, had she?

I'd just believed I was.

I went up to my tiptoes in the imaginary too-high
heels Nick had loved to see me in. Wriggled my
shoulders, trying to hunch them far more than they
wanted to. Put my chin down, and looked up at the
world through my lashes and the floppy fringe I no
longer had. Heaven forbid I should challenge anyone
with a straight-on stare.

Tilly stopped rolling on the fluffy rug and came to
nose at my leg. She whined, *Now, Mum, we don't do
that anymore, remember?*

I squatted to soothe her. "No, pupsicle. We don't
do it anymore, do we? And isn't it a fantastic and

amazing thing?" I laughed, she sneezed, and all was right in the world again.

"That wasn't good to watch. I'm so sorry I asked —because you sure as hell aren't whoever she was anymore. You're gorgeous, intelligent and fun. Before our connection, I thought the so-powerful Recorder was the real you. But once we," he gestured between our heads, "connected, I realised I'd been wrong. You have no idea what an interesting combination of welcoming, authoritative and competent you appear to be to the royals, your staff and even the Gateway visitors."

I didn't think I was gorgeous or authoritative. Welcoming, I could believe. But through our link, I knew he was sincere. He believed what he'd said. And my lie-detecting shoulders weren't arguing.

He tightened his arms around me and bent his head. His breath on my neck was electric. No, really, like static electricity. "What is that? It's not just when we shake hands, is it?"

He kissed my neck, and the skin buzzed under his mouth.

That could be a very interesting sensation in … other places. He moved back and kissed my spine above the back of my tank. He worked up vertebra by vertebra, kissing and biting softly until he reached my hairline, when he sighed. "Your brain is very busy. And mine is overwhelmed with how soft your skin is. I'm sensing an incompatible mood here."

Hmm.

I delved into our mind link. *Are you there?*

I felt the smile as I got, *Yes, sorry, still doing it.*

I sent him as clear a picture of me as I could create. Me, on his bed, hanging on to the wonderful white bedframe with my eyes half-closed, looking blissed out.

At least it was how I hoped I'd look. I wasn't sure I'd ever been blissed out in bed. But I'd seen movies where women seemed to get better treatment than I'd ever had. Bearing in mind his understandable Troels-related hang-ups, I said, "I think you'll find that's what unequivocal consent looks like to me."

He picked me up as though I weighed less than Tilly and placed me gently on his bed, and then he got a lot less gentle in all the right ways. All the ways I could have dreamed of.

And if that sounds corny … trust me when I tell you, I mean it literally: all the ways I'd dreamed of or ever hoped for. I'd need to set some new goals.

CHAPTER
TWENTY-EIGHT

We'd both napped. When we woke, Rollo had brought us the rest of the coffee from earlier and gone back to make more. I swallowed deeply. It was still excellent coffee.

Suddenly, I was ridiculously grateful to Dai. I'd need to see him when Ad'Rian cleared him for visitors. But if it hadn't been for his stale instant coffee and his bullying, I might not be here now. And I'd never felt better in my entire life.

Tilly was asleep on the end of the bed. I'd thought Rollo wasn't keen on dogs, but he hadn't minded when she jumped up and settled down behind me as I snuggled into his chest afterwards for our nap with a huge satisfied smile on my face. Our connection told me he was just as relaxed.

You couldn't fake an orgasm when the guy was in your head. Although I'd never bothered with Nick; he hadn't cared. But the mental connection Rollo and I temporarily shared had made the last few hours a very different experience from what I'd been used to. Who knew sex could be like that? I was starting to understand the lyrics to some songs that had always confused me.

I sipped my coffee and drifted, gazing at the mug. Then my brain came online. I sat bolt upright. *Drengr* on the mug. I studied the runes carefully and pictured Rollo's back and the part of his tattoo under his left shoulder blade. I'd licked it and bitten gently on the rune that looked like an upside-down trident, until Rollo moaned and said *harder* in my head. Yeah, turned out I could only remember the one rune. Where *was* the man? I needed to see his back.

I checked the mug. Yep, the upside-down trident was right there. The loading screen of *Drengr— Conquer with the real Vikings* ran in my mind. I'd played that game a lot. It wasn't about Vikings exactly. It was a strategy game where you built a realm or civilisation of your own and then picked one of the other rulers to be your principal opponent and others to be your allies.

There had even been a Recorder-type figure called the umpire who controlled certain tasks and whined about snarky or rude player-to-player comments. No, not the umpire. What had they called the old battle-ax? I couldn't retrieve it.

I hadn't played it since before Nick's death. But when it was first released, he was working overseas. I'd been alone. After I got home from work and walked Tilly, about five nights a week, I did little except take over the imaginary worlds around mine. It was clever, addictive, and successful.

A very sheepish-looking Rollo came back into the bedroom with a fresh pot of coffee. "Fill you up, Boo?"

I saved the sight of him into my memory. The long golden length of him, hair tousled, eyes sparkling, smiling down at me and carrying coffee. A memory which would brighten any miserably grey Scottish day that might dare to lurk in my future.

I reached out with my empty mug and smirked at him. "I'm pretty sure you did precisely that already. But more coffee'd be great. We need to talk."

"The four words no man wants to hear from a woman in his bed." But his eyes were happy, if cautious. "Just so you know, there doesn't seem to be a distance limit on this," he gestured at his head, "connection. I heard your thoughts."

"Didn't we work that out yesterday when I was in Pant y Wern?"

He sat on the side of the bed and slipped his robe off his left shoulder. My brain turned to mush again. Goddess, he *was* gorgeous. Mug, back. Back, mug. Yep, we have a match.

He smiled tentatively at me over his shoulder. "It was the Moderator, the name for the Recorder-type role. Sorry. Oddly, it never occurred to any of us her granddaughter might play it. Can't imagine why we didn't consider the possibility."

I shook my head. It had been quite an accurate depiction of Gran in a certain mood and not unkind.

"Before I forget, what's that tattoo by your," I struggled for the right word. It was ridiculous I could have mind-blowing sex with him and still not know what to call his … I settled on "lower belly?"

He rolled back on the bed, ditched his robe, and pointed to the spot inside his left hip bone with a querying expression.

"Yes, that one. I wanted to ask before, but then you distracted me. Is it a game token?"

He laughed. "No, it's an old coin."

I raised an eyebrow, and he sighed. "I didn't quite have the nerve to oppose the seer. I was still young, and you know what Viking seers are like, so it seemed wiser to just go along. Actually, I've become fond of it."

It couldn't be, could it?

Whoops, he was still talking. "Oddest thing,

really. He called it something foreign—I'll retrieve the name in a minute. He gave me two options for the design and instructed me to have it tattooed close to my heart."

I was going cold as I considered the tattoo. The design had a man on a horse holding a coin. That design came from the low value coins. We might call them pennies today. Several thousand years ago, they placed them on the eyes of the dead so they could pay the ferryman who took their souls to the afterlife. What was that damn ferryman's name? It would come to me.

I thought about my mother and sighed. "Was the other design a gorgon?"

He frowned at me, so I added, "A head with snakes for hair?"

"I know what a gorgon is, but how in the nine realms did you know?"

I felt him reach down through our connection, but I wasn't ready to let him see the whole damn horrible mess. So I closed it all away behind my shields.

He must have felt me shut him out, but he didn't say a single word. Bless the man. He stroked my shoulder and waited.

I could manage words, couldn't I? Yes, I was a damn grown-up now, or at least I'd like to be. I offered, "It's like me."

"Like yours? I didn't see any tatts on you. It's a

refreshing change actually, between the Vikings and the Picts and their endless paint. You can't move for tattoos usually."

I started shivering. When had my life become so completely insane? Well, dur, Niki, when the damn power landed on you, of course.

He gathered me into his arms, wrapped the duvet around us, and when Tilly stood up and whined, he told her, "It's OK, dog, I've got this."

She subsided with one eye on me. Why did he always call her "the dog," or "your dog" and never her name? But it was interesting that she still trusted him, as I did. But did either of us know why?

"Why did the guy tell you to get it? I know nothing about Viking seers, only the Fae ones."

"Oh, it came with the usual prophecy. He said I needed the coin to remember and open the way. I had to survive to adulthood, but if I didn't get the coin, I would never be free to reach my full potential or destiny or some such. I wrote it down somewhere. But their reasons are always a bit vague. Except when you look at their prophecies with hindsight. They sometimes turn out to have been literal and incredibly accurate."

The tattoo didn't look old enough for him to have got it as a teenager. "So why didn't you have it done near your heart?"

Through our link, I felt him considering how

much to tell me. But without invading his privacy, I couldn't tell what he was thinking about. He hadn't tried to invade mine, so fair was fair.

Eventually, he said, "Two reasons. That particular seer is famously crackers. I mean, clinically insane—a lot of them are. Augury is a hard gift, I think." At my understanding nod, he said, "But his accuracy can be uncanny. It's the same one who told Kari if you called her through, it would all be OK."

I nodded again. Kari had told me that herself.

"The second reason is … it was just before I decided to blackmail Troels into letting me go to university. I only found out yesterday when you were talking to King Mabon my blackmail probably only worked because Ad'Rian had already threatened him. But at that point, I didn't know if I could get out, and I was thinking about the Viking dress code."

I had no clue what the Viking dress code had to do with anything. I hadn't seen much of it except none of them seemed fond of clothes. Which I was beginning to appreciate. Oh!

He put his hand in the centre of his chest over his heart. Where his leather waistcoats always swung open, revealing his bare torso.

"It would be on show most of the time—people would ask about it. Vikings keep this spot free for the name or insignia of their spouse, usually with their heirs and children's names around it in a circular design. I didn't want to have to answer questions about the seer all the time. Oh, and Caitlin always looks at any new paint I get and usually criticises whoever did it. And she'd never see one there." He pointed downwards.

I started laughing.

Then I couldn't stop, even though I could hear the hysteria in my own laughter.

Tilly got up, gave Rollo a filthy look, as though to say, *You said you had it, but you didn't, did you, pretty boy? Look at the state of her.*

She planted her paws on my chest and barked just once, right in my face. It had been her OK-Mum-I'm-done-with-your-drama-it's-food-time bark from the months after Nick died when I'd cried and laughed hysterically far too often for her happiness.

It stopped me dead. "Yes, you're right, Tilly-flop, sorry. Let's eat. You hungry, Rollo?"

But he hung on to me. "I'm sorry if I upset you." He felt so confused in our mind link. I sent him a wave of reassurance and even attempted a smile.

"Hey, I'm fine. Life's just completely crazy sometimes, isn't it?" I filled my head with thoughts of food and grabbed my jeans and vest. I'd shower when I got home. To distract him, I asked, "So how did it end up there?" and pointed at the spot now hidden beneath his leather trousers.

"I'd say I wanted it somewhere private, but you could say I put it close to my second heart." And he smirked at me.

I winced at the cheesy line but then couldn't help laughing at the smug expression on his face.

CHAPTER
TWENTY-NINE

I 'd planned to go straight home, but Rollo easily dissuaded me by offering food from what he swore was an exceptional Indian restaurant who delivered quickly. I missed authentic Indian food so much in my new life. I'd been spoilt in Manchester with the curry mile on our doorstep.

We'd ended up back at his kitchen table. I'd relaxed—mostly because Rollo was fun company. Tilly was in seventh heaven because we'd taken a quick walk before the food came, and she adored Indian food as much as I did.

Rollo's jar of mango chutney was welded closed. I enjoyed watching his real, but still impressive muscles flex for slightly too long before I reluctantly showed him the run the lid under hot water trick, which he said he'd never seen.

"It's not all about strength. It's being smart enough to combine it with other knowledge. In this case, physics."

I'd expected a snarky response from him, but he only looked thoughtful.

The atmosphere was warm and safe, and a happy post-sex cloud floated around us as I topped up our wine and he made us more coffee.

"I'm amazed Dola hasn't interrupted us. I can't remember ever having ten hours' peace since I took the role, unless I was asleep."

Rollo gave a guilty wince. "Ah, when you went to the bathroom, and I put our earbuds to charge, I asked her to give us some private time unless anything was urgent. Was that OK?"

I leaned across and kissed him. "It was brilliant. Go you!"

I'd over-reacted—hadn't I? So he had a coin tattoo, and the way his seer had described it coincidentally made it sound far too much like my birth name for my peace of mind. Whatever. Possibly coin tattoos had become a thing while I was becoming boring and wifely. But then an unanswered question struck me.

"How did you know my birthdate?"

An enormous grin split his face. "Finn worked it out. We both thought the other must have changed the password. Dola wasn't involved with the

Rainbow Network before you. She helped with ordering the connection and did the cottage end of everything, but mostly Finn, L'eon and I just got on with it."

I thought about the day in the Gateway when I'd installed the very first video device for Dola just before I summoned Mabon. I'd been so angry, frightened and lost that day, desperately trying to work out how to use the power and make sense of the Recorder's role. Without my memories or even any idea how to summon anyone, and armed only with the limited information the Book had given me.

Rollo brought me back to the present. "Once we worked out it hadn't been either of us, we emailed Dola, and she said the new Recorder had changed it, and it would be up to Niki McKnight to communicate with us. Finn put two and two together: the old password was your name and your birthday 0610— sixth October, right? I mean, you wouldn't do the numbers the American way? So Finn found you.

"He realised you'd done comp sci at uni, the password hadn't changed in decades, and we wondered if you'd set it up originally for your gran. He tried a few things for a password that might go with someone who was in the mood to use a ByteMe username. He didn't think you were trying to make a proper password—more like you were trying to piss someone off. New Recorder, angry about something and with a tech background. But I'd always liked the old password because it was my birthday too. When I googled you and saw your uni dates, I thought you must be a year younger than me. But then on the ProfLink site, it showed you'd taken a gap year."

"So we're the same age."

He'd only done what I would have done. He'd thoroughly researched someone he might need to know about.

"Niki, are you OK?"

He must have caught my thought. He looked so young when he felt worried.

He grinned and shook himself. "Sorry, old habits die hard—always ask those questions tentatively, appear smaller, use the glamour to look younger, and never appear to be capable of deposing the king." He must have immediately discarded his glamour because he instantly became ten years older and about six inches taller.

I mused, "You know, when you hugged me after Troels tried to hurt Tilly, it was the first time I realised how tall you were."

"He wasn't trying to hurt her. He would have killed her—never doubt it."

His statement allowed no space for disbelief. And damn it, I'd put bitterness back into his tone.

But then he shook it off. "Are you really OK?"

"I am. Surely you know." I pointed at our heads

and grinned. Then I sobered. "Did you want to depose the current ruler?"

"No! I mean he's bad for the realm; he's horrific for the women, and I think replacing him is a wonderful idea. But I thought I was the only man in Viking who thought so. What people will say publicly and what Dola's data says don't match. I'd trust the data, but I still don't want to be the sacrificial lamb who takes his place. Especially when people might not stand behind what they said in Dola's poll. The warlords will assassinate whoever takes over. Even if it's one of Troels' sons."

"I saw you do this earlier." He pulled a little of the yellow regnal power until it curled in his hand. "Do you think this is supposed to help me work out how to help Viking? What can it do?"

"Well, it helped me see through your glamour. But that's a skill I'd already learnt from Ad'Rian. So it's probably more accurate to say it helps you be better at things you're good at or have studied. But, because you only have the yellow, it might focus more on the Viking realm. You'll have to test it and find out."

He nodded.

I thought about it for a minute. "You could try pulling a tiny bit before you throw a knife. Although, having seen what you did to save Tilly, you may not need to improve that skill much. It was very cool."

We'd obliterated the food. We'd both built up an appetite with what Great-Granny Florrie would have called healthy exercise, and we cleared away in perfect sync as though we'd shared a kitchen for many years.

I thought about his question while I was loading the empty containers back into the takeaway bag for recycling. I hadn't yet experimented with splitting the power for use in the different realms, had I? But the thing the blue power did for Breanna during the arbitration when it showed her the history of her realm for the last millennia was amazing.

"Seriously?" Rollo looked like all his ships had come in. He must have got the picture out of my head. I reached into our connection to see what about the idea had pleased him, but his brain was a muddle of hopes, dreams and fears.

"Yeah, why?" As I'd done earlier, I tapped his mind and showed him quickly what happened when we'd asked the power about the Smiths' agreement with House Albidosi. And I thought Caitlin had been there at the time; I needed to ask him about her. I really had believed they had a thing.

But he answered my unspoken thought.

"We didn't. Cait did have the hots for someone. That's not even fair—she had real feelings for someone, but it wasn't me. I've always been more like a big brother to her and Finn. Not so much Juna; our interests have never overlapped. Cait, well, it's her story to tell, not mine."

But from his mind, I saw *he* had been the one to take her to the Fae for healing when she'd realised something. What had she realised?

I told him, "I know something about that. She had to let me scan her before I offered her the Knight Adjutancy contract. But it was Fae work and none of my business."

He smiled sadly.

I wanted to cheer him up. "You're techy; the power was eager to help me with all kinds of electronic things. Try it on your computer." An expression of horror greeted my suggestion. "OK, start with your monitor then. All those curved widescreen ones I heard you admiring in the Gateway were created by the power."

Now his horror morphed into delight. "There's one here; no, two of the ones here are almost four years old because I got called back to Viking. They're overdue for an upgrade."

"Cool, can we play with them?"

He said yes, but he felt like a chef who didn't want anyone else to use his knives. Even as I thought it, he gestured me back into the bedroom and to the mirror again. I glanced in it. Whoa! I'd thought I'd changed when I looked at myself earlier. But now I saw a whole different woman.

Great sex and a bit of an ego boost were better than a face lift.

Rollo pushed the mirror, and it sprang open to reveal a hidden doorway into his office. Like the one I had into my bathroom.

It led into a large bright room with several skylights and a long, low window with a view over to Edinburgh Castle. There were lots of shelves and a long, curved desk with a PC at one end and a Mac at the other. A bank of monitors filled the gap between them. He was a geek, but as Finn said, he had social skills too. Interesting man.

"Thank you. Coming from an interesting woman, I take it as a real compliment."

I blushed.

I surveyed the shelving with curiosity—some rows of books, mostly sci-fi and non-fiction. The other two walls were full of boxes from older games; PC, Xbox and PlayStation games; manuals and paraphernalia.

I grinned at a shelf with the various *Drengr* games. And then I paused. That row of games followed seamlessly from a row of far more famous games I'd also enjoyed. The original manufacturer's logo on the first three games, before the company was bought out by the big boys in Silicon Valley, looked a lot like one of Rollo's other tattoos. Maybe he'd worked for several companies?

There was eye-catching artwork in beautiful hand-crafted frames on the walls, including several large photos. One was a group of people in their twenties in an office or maybe lecture room, all raising glasses to the camera. It was covered in signatures and doodles.

The other wall held two box frames. One had a disassembled early iPhone, maybe the 3G? It was dismantled, the pieces blown out and the components mounted to look like artwork. The other held an old lock with several beautifully intricate keys below it.

Just as I was going to inquire about it, he asked, "Remember this?"

I glanced over in time to see the loading screen for Drengr on his monitor and laughed, happiness bubbling. I'd loved that game. It had been pure escapism. I couldn't prevent Janet saying "Ah, Niki, you're finally here," at 8.45 a.m. every damn morning, but when I got home, I could rule this world any way I wanted to. My own little piece of paradise waiting for me every evening.

"Is it true? *Drengr* is some old Norse word for 'badass'?"

Rollo had obviously worked on it. I refused to fangirl over a game developer. But I was intrigued. That *Drengr* meant "badass" had been the rumour at the time, but I didn't know if it was only a good PR story.

"Sure is. Well, strictly speaking, it means a few things, but badass is one of them. Do you remember your username?" With quick clicks, he opened the developer access to the game server.

Huh, check out my stats, would you, Rollo? They might just surprise you.

When I gave him my game name, he shot me a quick baffled glance and muttered, "I bet you made tons of eager teenage male game friends."

I watched as he typed it in incorrectly. "No D."

He looked at his screen and then at me. His forehead creased.

"No D. Not NakedGirl. NakeGirl," I elaborated.

"Hey, I know that name; didn't you take top player one year?" He changed screens, searched, then grinned at the screen and at me, and held up his hand to high-five me.

"We all assumed that username was just a typo. Why did you choose it? You're not the kind of game bunny who'd choose a name like that."

"It's my real name. Well, part of it, anyway." I waited for the penny to drop for him.

"Niki, hmn? Nicola? Nicole? Nicolette? Nikita? Nicolina? No, not getting it, sorry."

I didn't want to do this; it had been such a fun

day. But I supposed I had to. Even though I suspected it might change things between us forever.

"My birth name was Danake. I changed it to Niki when I went to Uni." I spelt it for him.

"Oh, cool. Nice to have an old mystery solved. Not a typo." Then he went very still.

I walked towards the door and turned around just in time to see the Danake drop in his head.

PART FIVE
SUNDAY

Do not allow the fear of what *could* happen block everything good from happening.

Sometimes our desire to be proven right attracts the very disaster we were trying to avoid.

Better to be wrong and happy, I believe.

But we all fail ourselves sometimes. Never judge yourself for spiralling down into those dark places. Only judge yourself if you stay there. Let the light in, rebuild your flame and set something on fire. That's always cathartic.

Finding your Inner Fire: How to Claim your True Self by Peggy Hwybon

THIRTY

S unday, 28th February, Gateway Cottage—
Gretna Green

Rollo had opted to stay in Edinburgh. He planned to transport himself back to Viking to test out the yellow power once he'd had time to mull over his options. So I was back at my kitchen table. Alone and confused.

I gazed at the source of my confusion. The tarot cards in front of me. They felt wrong.

The Seven of Cups, the Lovers, and the Wheel of Fortune.

Sure, those cards were a perfect fit for what had occurred over the last few days. I stroked the Lovers gently and swirled my finger around the Wheel. It was certainly turning, and if I'd asked, "What the hell just happened to me?" Then, Seven of Cups, you made an unexpected choice. The Lovers, you had an incredible, and, yes, a loving experience with a man who confused you. And the Wheel of Fortune would tell me Rollo had astonished me and also say, "But now you're not sure where it's going and feel like things moved, but you had no control over them. Just go with it—it'll be fine." Then this would be the perfect answer.

But these cards weren't right because that wasn't what I'd asked.

My tarot cards were a part of me—almost an extension of my psyche. I understood them intimately. They'd been mine for many years and I loved them. But the cards on my kitchen table didn't answer the question I'd actually *asked*, which was, "What does Dai need, and what can I do to help him and Mabon?"

Did Dai need to make a choice? Had he hoped for a relationship with me? Maybe. But I was less certain as every day passed that he'd ever wanted Niki. My Gift suggested he wanted the Recorder and her power on his side.

The decision I'd made yesterday about Dai at Rollo's had solidified into certainty now. Aysha and I had made a solemn promise to each other many years ago. We renewed it frequently when she found someone to have fun with and still be a responsible mum. We didn't bonk crazy. Or as Rachel, Aysha's fun friend always said, "We don't let cray-cray in our va-jay-jays."

With the best will in the world right now, Dai wasn't rational. So I wouldn't allow him to appear in a personal space for me.

I wasn't sure I'd ever wanted him to. I'd had a crush on him when I was a child, and I'd been drawn to what I'd thought was his smell, sure. And I was attracted to the idea that eventually I might have someone special in my life again.

But what else could this spread mean? Well, it might mean all kinds of things, but the cards simply felt wrong.

I wouldn't hold Dai's behaviour the other day against him. Not when I considered what Mabon had told me after the sentencing. Now, Ad'Rian had told Mabon that they'd released Dai. According to Dai, he'd been told to take it easy and stay away from stress for the next week while his healing settled in.

Ad'Rian was confused. His normal practice was to put a thirty-year limit on *any* blocks. Dai's block should have evaporated on its own even if no one asked Ad'Rian to remove it. Ad'Rian hadn't done anything different when he installed Dai's block. He was at a loss to explain how it might still prevent Dai from speaking about certain things. Ad'Rian could see no proof that it was. And yet, I'd seen Dai fighting against the block to give me information. So either he was a hell of an actor, or he was telling the truth.

Surely the head of the Fae healers was too skilled to make such a mistake. So, yeah, I was confused.

But quiet and calm was the prescription until Ad'Rian could assess Dai again next week. I'd picked up a subtext that suggested Ad'Rian wasn't telling Mabon something. But then do doctors ever tell family the whole truth—it's not necessarily their business, is it? Especially if the patient requests otherwise.

But now Mabon said Dai wanted to apologise and explain everything to me himself, and no one had bothered asking me if I wanted to listen. Mabon had said, "Right and proper, that would be, I thought. So would you pop along to Pencoed at your first opportunity, please, *bach*, for me? And then come and see me so you can report, and I can return her locket to you."

I'd agreed, somewhat reluctantly, to it all. The problem was I'd no clue what to do for the best. So I was casting about for guidance, which the cards weren't giving me. I didn't *need* to go until tomorrow, but I'd rather get it out of the way than have it hanging over me.

I gathered the cards, and, as I put them back in

the drawer, I spotted the letter my gran wrote to my mother that was to be given to me if I didn't have her address. Yeah, I wasn't ready to face that. But next to it, I saw the tarot deck Breanna had gifted me after her arbitration.

Perhaps a deck that didn't know me so intimately would give me more clarity. I took them out and shuffled, admiring them. They were old, beautiful, and the illustrations were different to the ones on my own deck.

I moved back to the table to try a quick spread with them as Finn strolled through from his apartment. It must be bacon sandwich time, but he shouldn't be going to work on a Sunday. I would put my foot down if necessary.

"Whatchya got there?" Finn gave the cards I'd put on the table a long stare. "Look familiar."

"Your mother gave them to me for getting you back safely, I think. Remember, you brought me the package when you came back from the Broch to move in here?"

But he shook his head. "Nah. You got a life debt for my rescue. But she asked us all if we were OK if she gave those to you. A personal gift, family things, ya know. But we didn't care. Ma said they should be used. Great..." his eyes slid around in their sockets as though he were counting, "... Great-Great-Great-Granny Bronwyn would want them to be used. Ma has her own. Can *you* use them?"

Finn was unusually chatty today. I looked at him as I answered, "Uh-huh." I focused, shuffled and then laid three cards face down. "I've asked the question, and these cards are the answer."

"What was the question?"

"It's private. You don't have to tell anyone your question. You ask the cards and focus your mind on the question while you shuffle. Sometimes I can guess what the question was from the cards that answer it. But Aysha, for example, never tells me what her questions are."

I turned the cards over.

Seven of Cups, The Lovers, Wheel of Fortune.

Oh, Gods and Goddesses. When you get the same cards twice, especially from different decks, the universe is sending you a clear message whether you want to hear it or not.

Finn shuddered. Because I'd had half a thought about whether he was OK after his too long speech, I noticed the wave of repulsion coming from him. I looked at the cards. These weren't scary cards. There was nothing in them to repel anyone.

"You OK, Finn?"

"Slagging dragons, every card."

"What?" There was only one dragon in the tarot deck. It *was* on the Seven of Cups, but the other cards didn't have dragons on them. At least they didn't in my set. People created entire decks with beautiful artwork based around dragons, but this was a standard pack. It seemed to be based on some precursor to the classic Rider-Waite deck to me. But when I looked where he was pointing ...yep, he was right, dragons everywhere.

On the Seven of Cups, the usual baby dragon peeped out of its chalice. But on The Lovers, wrapped around the apple tree on the left of the card in the Garden of Eden scene, in place of the serpent, was a dragon's tail. The spiked end pointed at the woman. The dragon's body made the traditional phallic mountain that appeared behind and between the couple.

The Wheel of Fortune was even more dragon-themed in this deck. The serpent was still there, but Anubis had been replaced with a red dragon.

Serpents in tarot usually represented deception, temptation, and people who made false promises or offers. I wondered what dragons meant?

I'd need to think about this, but the universe was definitely saying, *would you pay attention, woman*? I snapped a quick photo.

"Can I have a go?"

"Sure," I gave Finn the deck, "concentrate on your question while you shuffle. Then put down however many cards you sense you should."

"However many I *sense* I should?" The horror on Finn's face at this airy-fairy, unscientific system gave me a much-needed smile.

I shrugged. "You'll know when you feel as if you shouldn't bother putting the next card down."

He gave me a disbelieving look and shuffled with complete seriousness and focus. His eyes followed the movement of the cards closely, and his lips moved, repeating his question to himself.

I tapped my Gift lightly. Finn was in good shape, and doing well contrary to my attempt to use his well-being as an excuse when I didn't want to visit Dai. But I had been right not to want to go, hadn't I? In fact, my instinct to avoid being stuck up a mountain with a man on the verge of a meltdown had been extremely sound.

Finn was good. He loved his new apartment and was enjoying his work. What more could any young guy ask? Well, if the intensity with which he was shuffling was anything to go by, I could hazard a guess.

He laid his cards down face up and looked at them with confusion. "Well, no dragons. Good. What do they mean?"

The Fool, Six of Swords, The Magician and the Princess of Wands. I turned the McKnight Gift on those cards and barely stopped myself laughing out loud. Oh, this was going to be such fun to watch. I snapped a quick photo on my phone and sent it to him. "I think you should research them, Finn, and then let's talk about any ideas you have."

He nodded, always happy at the idea of research.

"I have to pop and see Glynis later. Does she have a younger sister or even a daughter? Do you know?"

Oh, yeah, it looked like I'd nailed it. The tips of his ears turned pink as he nodded.

"She has a daughter, Tegan. We're all meeting up at the St. David's thing tonight. D'you need her?"

"Nope, I'm good. I'll speak to Glynis, and we'll see." Well, that wasn't a lie, was it? But I was intrigued by how this might play out. I remembered Finn saying something about he wanted a real girl-friend, not an online one. Well, tick one. But the second part had been someone who didn't care he was a prince and never, ever called him Your High-ness. Surely Glynis's daughter must be aware of exactly who Finn was?

I'd watch this with interest. Now I didn't have time to watch soap operas and reality TV, I had to take my entertainment where I could find it. It would stop me mother hen-ing him.

"Hey, you're taking a full day off, aren't you?"

Finn looked torn and then nodded. "Yeah, going through for the Dewi Sant eve. The food's always good. Dilys excels herself."

I must have frowned because he added, "Mabon's

cook. Makes those *Crempogau* you were raving about? Made me put them on the News Portal?"

"Oh, yeah, the cheesy ham crumpet things. They were delish. OK, well, have fun. Might see you there later."

He wandered off with his bacon sandwich once he'd given Tilly her tithe and told her she had to stay here because he wasn't going to work today. I smiled at their antics.

Once he'd gone, I turned the fifth card over. Most tarot spreads are odd numbers, and I wanted to know what the next card would have been. I giggled at the Two of Cups and took a photo of the full five-card spread. At some point, Finn would realise he'd stopped one card too soon. Oh, yeah, this would be great fun to watch. I'd better check out this Tegan and make sure she wouldn't hurt my Knight.

From the Dolina, I heard, "Niki, might I enquire what you would take Finn's cards to mean?"

I considered it. "That depends. Do you promise not to tell Finn? He needs to work this out for himself. I think he's almost there anyway."

"Understood."

"Interpreting tarot is a very personal thing. But to me, the Fool and the Six of Swords are Finn growing into fresh adventures. Finding a new home and a calmer, happier place to be. These days, the Magician often represents someone with tech skills. It can also mean it's time to take chances with love. The Princess of Wands—" I broke off, unable to speak over my giggles. Then I started coughing and laughing, picturing how this might go down when Finn worked it out. Then I got the hiccups. I was a wicked woman.

A glass of water arrived on the table. "Niki?"

I got myself under control. "Sorry, Dola. In a modern Thoth deck, the Princess of Wands is fiery and would mean passion, sexual attraction. Someone extroverted who loves life and exhibits bravery, beauty, power. But this is an unusual antique deck. My Gift suspects it means a young dragon or even a dragon's daughter. Which is why I asked about Glynis. The Two of Cups would bear that out. Everyone believes that card means a perfect partnership, but you have to take the other cards into account. I'd say it means there is some growing up to do and a few cultural challenges to overcome before the Two of Cups can come into play."

"OH!"

"Yeah, exactly: Oh."

Then I looked back at my own cards and frowned at their multiple, possibly deceitful, dragon-serpents and thought unhappily about Dai.

If I was going to the freezing Red Celt realm later, I planned to use everything I'd ever learned from reading women's magazines, especially those How to Use Layering Intelligently lists.

I missed Rollo. I wanted to ask him for his advice, especially since he'd been so helpful during the bizarre ceremony of John's sentencing. The moment I thought it, I heard, *Still doing it, Boo* in my head. And I melted.

Hey, what's the Boo thing? You said you'd tell me!

There was a pause.

Might we defer it until we're together and have time? There's a story behind it. I'd much prefer to be with you and have some time to discuss it when I tell you. I could pop through later or tomorrow? I still have some things to do here before I head back to Viking.

Any excuse to see him again worked for me. At least it would once I'd discharged the responsibilities on my currently crappy-looking plate.

Sure, let's do that. I assume there will be a reward for the deferred gratification?

The mental image he sent me definitely looked gratifying.

THIRTY-ONE

"Thanks so much for fitting me in."

Glynis's small office was still crowded, warm and cosy. Every surface had files, trays of paperwork and items obviously on their way to somewhere else.

"Recorder," Glynis stood and bowed, "thank you for being so understanding."

Weren't we both being polite? I thought about the fierce dragon I'd watched defending her brother. She'd also been prepared to fight for Troels' victims when it seemed to me no one else had lifted a finger to stop him or help his victims. She must be far more than a well-mannered woman, and I needed to get beneath her professional façade.

I put my coffee down on the only empty surface in the entire room. It barely fitted into the space next to her teapot on the small table, and she shuffled a milk jug so I had a little more space. The fire was a welcome sight, and the flickering was relaxing. Tilly agreed and settled in front of it.

I gazed at Glynis until she said, "I'm sorry, Recorder; please sit."

As we settled ourselves in the only two chairs in the room, I checked my brain's privacy settings and filed everything I didn't want her to have access to behind solid shields. I smiled at her. "I'm happy to share my thoughts about Troels, my plans for his arbitration, and what I'd like to do about the victims. Would it be quicker for us to link as we planned to before Boney so rudely interrupted us the other day?"

She giggled. Actually giggled. Of all the things I'd ever wondered if I might one day experience, a woman I knew to be a dragon giggling at me wasn't even on the Cold Day in Hell section of my list.

My face obviously gave away my astonishment.

"I'm so sorry, my lady, forgive me. It's hearing you call him Boney. He's been storming about the castle like a bear for days, and everyone is creeping around cautiously on their eyelashes here. Why do you call him Boney, if I may ask?"

I debated, but I needed her to relax. I could share something personal.

"It's not particularly interesting, I'm afraid. I had

speech problems as a kid. Apparently, my grammar was dreadful, and some combinations of letters confused my tongue. I simply couldn't say Mabon. It came out as Bone Man or Boney. Fi's mother was actually a big help when I was about six or seven."

At her confused expression, I added, "Mrs Glendinning? She was a teacher's helper at our school. I went to school with Fi; didn't she tell you?"

"No, she didn't." There was an edge to her voice, but I'd no idea what had caused it.

"We've known each other since we were five, minus thirty-some years in the middle. Shall we take a shortcut?" I waggled my fingers on the table, but Glynis was transfixed by her narrow window. There was a Highland coo peeping in, and she hadn't noticed, so she obviously wasn't focused on the actual view.

"Give me a child until they are seven, and I will show you the adult. Which is probably why Fi said I should trust you. I wish she'd explained it. It would have saved so much time. Yes, let's take the shortcut."

But I had questions now and moved my hand back to my lap. "Sorry, but why would it have been different if Fi had told you we were at school together?"

She shoved her small, capable hand vigorously through her unruly mop of reddish-brown hair, scrubbing at her scalp as though she wanted to pull it out by the roots. "It would have saved so much time."

She'd already said that, and she was an empath. It would be rude to use my Gift on her again now I was aware of it. So I sat quietly and willed her to use her words.

She poured more tea, even though her cup was half full. She added a dash of milk and such a tiny amount of sugar, it couldn't possibly affect the taste. Then she stirred it slowly, the spoon tinkling against the cup. I resisted the urge to tap my foot.

Finally, she sipped the tea and made an unhappy face. "I didn't believe her. She'd only worked with you for a week when she said it. My Lady Elsie gave me hope the first time I met her. But after she spoke to Fergusson," just like Breanna, Glynnis almost spat the former Knight's name, "she told me all the girls were too young for their stories to have credibility."

I wondered why the hell my gran hadn't checked the girls with the McKnight Gift? On my previous visit, I'd wanted to defend my gran against Glynis's suggestion that the Recorder had let the women down. But everything I'd overheard at the sentencing and the thoughts I'd gathered from Rollo led me to change my mind about my gran's actions. Despite not having intentionally done harm, it was clear she'd done pitifully little good.

In her letter to me, she'd told me my job was to keep the realms in line. Well, she'd managed that much, but these people had needed her help, not just her authority.

I considered Glynis and wondered what kind of person you'd need to be to fight for justice for others so relentlessly and with so little support. I tried to lighten the mood. "Yes, how old did he think a woman had to be exactly to know she'd been raped? But then, did you hear he informed my solicitor I was a disturbed young woman after I told him his son wasn't doing the Knight Adjutant's job? And I'm forty-one."

Glynis laughed warmly now, but I wasn't quite finished. "I'm not prepared to hold Troels accountable because he attacked my dog, as you said at our last meeting. But I do believe the way a person treats animals is a shortcut to predicting how they will treat people."

Glynis's shoulders relaxed. She sounded stronger and felt more like the dragon with the total control and pinpoint accuracy of her flame I'd seen at the sentencing, and less like the mouse who'd greeted me on Thursday. "I was astonished when you spoke to him the way you did at the sentencing. Everyone needed to hear you make that statement, my lady."

I grinned. Thank the Goddess I'd taken Rollo's

advice. "I had a wise advisor who told me to say what I've been thinking for a month."

"And the way you held the Lady of the Flame so steadily while she dealt her own justice. Her roar made me want to cower under the bed. And I'm a bluddy dragon."

The Lady of the Flame? The Great One? How many names did the cat have? Did every realm give her a different title?

Glynis continued, "And, of course, the dragons are mired in guilt."

At my raised eyebrow, she added, "In the old days, one of the queens would've decapitated Troels, laid flame to his holdings and 'suggested' the Vikings move on in a better direction. But with no queens hatching, we're powerless."

"Mabon mentioned the problem, but there was no time to get into why they're not breeding?"

"We don't know for sure. Rhiannon says one of the older Recorders had an idea about why it might be and how to fix it. But she died before she could implement it. The problem with dragons is most of our records go up in smoke when someone loses their temper."

"Hmm, should I suggest a fireproof safe to Rhiannon?"

She gave a laugh comprised of half amusement

and half nervous titter. Was she frightened of Rhiannon?

Then suddenly, all business, she stretched out her hand and clasped mine firmly. "Let's take the shortcut you suggested."

The link was instant, but it lacked the clarity of my connection with Rollo. This was a wash of emotions. Confusion, anger and unhappiness all fought for supremacy. But, under it all, there was a determined conviction that if she was stubborn enough, justice was possible.

I saw some of her time working in modern-day Scotland with rape victims. The problems she'd experienced keeping her dragon side under control when her anger at the injustice of many of the verdicts overwhelmed her. Then her happy return home, and a reunion with—oh … well, that was obviously private. She probably had no idea how much she was sharing.

In return, I pushed clear information at her: the petitions, the options, the plans. My confusion about how this had even happened, never mind been allowed to continue unchecked. Boney wouldn't tolerate rape; it wasn't in his nature at all. From her, I got a picture of glasses, cups, tankards and even wooden drinking vessels, along with a feeling of repulsion. Was Troels using something like Rohypnol? Spiking drinks?

We sat holding each other's hand, and Glynis said, "My Gift isn't like yours. I can mostly sense truth or lies as you can, but I can't send information as clearly as you did. It's the *droit de seigneur.* That's how they do it. And it isn't only Troels, although we are focusing on him at the moment. But Warlord Halvor may even be worse. He's certainly more intelligent and completely ruthless."

Halvor... I'd heard the name but I couldn't retrieve it? *Droit de seigneur* though, I had the vaguest idea about this from books. A lord could demand to sleep with a maiden who was about to leave his lands to marry. The cover of a historical novel danced in my mind. But hadn't someone else said it recently? Breanna? No, it had been Fi, hadn't it—at the sentencing? Maybe? Or was it even Rollo? I tucked it away to think about later when I wasn't being read by Glynis.

Rollo sent, *I mentioned it at John's sentencing, and when Kari, she's Halvor's daughter—*

Shush, Boo. She's an empath; we'll talk later.

Too late. Glynis's eyes widened. Shit.

In my firmest Recorder tone, I said, "Glynis, I offer you my word. I shan't mention any of the *extremely* private things I picked up from you, ever." I sent her the clear picture of herself half-clad in leather, and not Caitlin's kind, that she'd inadvertently shared with me. "And you will forget what you just sensed and never even think of it again. If you truly want justice for these women, then I need *everyone's* help."

She swallowed hard, her eyes taking in my face. Then she nodded. "Unexpected help, but, yes, I agree. I have nothing against the prince, my lady. In fact, a lot of women I have faith in tell me he can be trusted. And, yes, I think we do both want justice for the women and their kids."

But I shook my head. "Not the kids. Not me, anyway. If you ask me, the kids got a great deal out of this horrible mess. That complete slimeball seems to have picked awesome women, who have gone on to be amazing mothers. The kids aren't part of this for the Recordership. Other than the mothers, who definitely deserve paternity payments, which was clever of you."

She gave me a long look, then nodded and released my hand. "This Fae you kept sending me thoughts of—have I met him?"

"Have you seen a handsome, seven-and-a-half-, maybe eight-foot-tall, deep purple warrior wandering about? He was at the sentencing the other day, in Ad'Rian's box and carrying a spear about my height."

"Oh, yessss," her comment came out on a sigh, "he was one fine specimen of manhood." She looked dreamy for a moment. Why did short women like tall men so much? Well, I could hardly talk, could I?

"He certainly is, but he can also identify people's DNA without subjecting them to any intrusive or expensive tests. He can identify whether Troels or someone else is the children's father. I'm going to need you to throw some kind of event, a coffee morning or a party. If you can put as many of the mothers and kids together in a room for him as possible, he'll give us evidence so the women won't have to testify unless they wish to. Don't forget the adult children. Perhaps especially the adult ones, to prove how long this has been going on. No one will argue with Glais'Nee's evidence, except perhaps Troels. He seems to have an unreliable relationship with the truth."

There was a tap at the door, and a stunning young woman stuck her head in. She had multi-toned brown hair, skin the colour of clotted cream, and a mouth as naturally deep pink as the strawberry jam we so often ate with that cream. But her eyes—wow! They were the colour of the Aegean Sea and sat below impeccably groomed, perfectly arched brows. She was stunning. Go, Finn! I had no idea he had such good taste.

In jeans, a black T-shirt and a cosy-looking bright pink fleece hoodie, she looked relaxed as she thrust a plate through the gap in the door. "Dilys says they need you in ten. You're to *eat.*"

She opened the door wider and finally looked into the room properly. Her vivacious face dropped in mock horror. "Oops, sorry, I didn't realise you had someone in here. Gotta go, Mum, meeting the DM in," she consulted her watch, "ten. Need anything before I go?" She delivered the plate to the table, tapping Glynis's shoulder. "Seriously, eat."

She felt the teapot, shuddered, poured the rest into the cup for Glynis, threw a casual, "You wouldn't want it; it's horribly stewed," in my direction. "She's the only one who can drink it like this. Can I get you anything?" Then she looked at me properly for the first time. All her confidence disappeared; she started to curtsy, stopped herself, bowed and said, "I'm so sorry, my lady, I didn't ..."

"Tegan, I assume?" At her hesitant nod, I gave her my warmest smile. "No, thank you, I have coffee, and I'll see your mother eats before she leaves this room, my word on it. Have fun."

In my mind, Rollo and I literally rolled on the floor laughing. *She calls him the DM, awww, cuteness overload.*

Rollo sent back, *He is an excellent Dungeon Master, I'll have you know. Mages quake before him, and gaming beginners sing his praises for years.*

Glynis waited until the door closed. "It's not *that* kind of DM."

I smiled, shoved the plate at her and said, "Yeah, a gaming DM. Role-playing, Dungeons and Dragons-style, right?"

She looked relieved, took a *crempogau* and gestured I should take one myself.

There were six, so she could spare one. I was hungry, and Dilys was a superb cook.

"Thanks. We seem to have agreed in principle, anyway. Liaise with Fi, because you two have a relationship, but include Dola, my equerry, please. She keeps the Recorder's calendar now Fi's in charge of the trade desk. I'm going to accept the petitions. It will give me time to set a date to hear them. But I think I need to call Troels through and get an idea of what he intends to answer."

She gave me an uncertain look, but at the same time, a wave of fury came off her.

"Glynis, what are you so furious about? I mean, of course you're angry for the women—but what specifically made you mad just now?"

"I'm annoyed with myself. Part of me still thinks I should have taken Rhiannon's advice and saved everyone this trouble."

I considered what I was pretty sure Rhiannon's advice would have been, and, honestly, I could see both sides of the argument. But if we did it through the Gateway, at least the Vikings wouldn't be searching for their missing king for the next few years.

I wandered the castle halls in search of Mabon before someone told me he was conducting a ceremony for Dewi Sant. I'd read up on St. David, and apart from the food, his festival just didn't sound very interesting. No wonder I had no clear childhood memories of this event.

Everyone I met in the corridor bowed, wished me happy and encouraged me to "do the little things." *Do the little things*, WTH? Was it somehow more meaningful in Welsh?

I decided I was going to bite the bullet and go up the mountain to see what Dai needed to tell me.

I thought about Glynis sensing Rollo in my mind. *Rollo, do you think Glynis only heard you because my shields were down to connect with her? I'm going to have to keep them closed at Dai's. I have no idea of his capabilities. Until we know what we're doing, I don't want anyone I don't trust knowing about us.*

Rollo queried, *You don't trust Dai?*

I sent him the scene where Dai had known Tilly wanted ice cream and said, *Dai talks to Tilly; I mean, it's simple stuff, but I don't want him in my head.*

Rollo immediately repeated, *You don't trust him,
do you?*

*I don't right now. No. He's going to hear about us if
the gossip-mill gets hold of it. But it hasn't yet. And if
there even turns out to be anything to hear about. I mean,
we haven't decided anything beyond we both deserve some
fun, have we? But none of it is Dai's business.*

Rollo sent me a warm mental hug. *I've decided,
Boo. I'm simply waiting for you to catch up.*

I swallowed hard and wished it had been a real
hug. Part of me was doing a happy dance, and of
course he felt it. The other part was having trust
issues. Nope, that wasn't true at all. The other part
thought it *should* be having trust issues and couldn't
work out why the hell it wasn't.

*OK, we'll talk. But now, when Dai's fresh from the
healers, isn't the time. It feels wrong to me. I think his
needs have to come first while he's healing.*

I filled him in on the whole no access to wi-fi or
the power up at Pencoed. He muttered *Tree Tops* in
my mind.

What?

*His house, it's called Tree Tops. It's what Pencoed
means. It won awards. It's viciously modern and minimal-
ist. I went to a party there once.*

"Viciously modern" was a pretty accurate
description of what I'd assumed was a house Dai was
still in the process of moving into. If what I'd seen

was the finished version, then he certainly wasn't a man who liked comfort.

OK, I'll let you know once I'm out of there.

I felt his grin, and it came with a kiss as he sent, *Take care of my nakegirl.*

The man made me laugh.

THIRTY-TWO

I landed about a hundred yards from Dai's house. I wanted to see if there was any signal outside. There was, and I drew power. As I did, the same rainbow I'd been unable to focus on clearly in the driving snow the other day curved away. Maybe it wasn't a rainbow, because it was still in the same spot. Was it some kind of sparkling prism effect from all the ice up here?

Because, of course, the day was freezing again, but with clear grey-blue skies. A weak wintry sun sparkled off the snow and cast the dark grey-black mountains into sharp relief. My eyes followed the rainbow as I thought about pots of gold at rainbows' end. The end of this one was near a tumble of rocks. It looked like a partially collapsed archway.

I love rainbows. My gran always told me to make a wish on them. The memory made me smile. And the broken rock arch reminded me of the beaches in Portugal where Aysha and I had swum and paddled through similar but intact archways. Admittedly, this one, with three feet of snow surrounding and half burying it, was less appealing. But my thermals were holding up. I had clumpy but waterproof boots on, and Tilly was wearing her coat. We were prepared.

I poked my phone to see where I was getting a signal from. "Dola, can you see where my phone is on the network?"

"No, I am searching, but you are not connected in any recognisable way. How were you certain you would have a signal outside?"

"Because you said Mabon usually does outside and sometimes even inside too. Can you send the cartons to the doorway there, please?" I pointed my phone's camera at the door in the squat, unimpressive front of Dai's house. If I hadn't seen it for myself, I wouldn't have believed the vastly more impressive back of the house existed from this angle.

My phone buzzed with an incoming message from Dola and a screenshot. It showed my phone using a network called *Eiddof Fi*. Well, that looked Welsh, but I was no wiser.

"Niki, there is something unusual about this. It is

partially connected to the Rainbow Network, but it should not be able to."

Well, I'd known something odd was going on, hadn't I? "Can you ask Finn to take a—no, strike that —don't contact Finn. I forgot he's having a well-deserved day off, and he has plans with Tegan. I can't imagine I'll be here for long. I don't think Dai will be well enough for more than a brief visit." I'd look myself when I got home. Then I had a brainwave.

"Could you ask Rollo if he might have any ideas?" He'd said he wasn't busy today. I hadn't adjusted to having people in my life who would intu-itively know what to look for on the network. Did Rollo and I have more in common than a sense of humour, mind-blowing sex, and a birthday? Yep, I was pretty sure we both liked mysteries too.

I had a good idea what was going on. But I couldn't prove it yet.

I surveyed the surrounding area. The views were breathtaking now the driving snow had stopped, and if Pencoed did mean Tree Tops, I could see how it had been named. The house was above the treeline, and as I looked down, I saw … tree tops. Behind the house, there was an almost vertical slope. That explained the jaw-dropping view. I probably hadn't given it the appreciation it deserved in my caffeine-deprived state the other morning.

I had to do this, however much I didn't want to.

As I had the thought, the front door opened, and Dai's head popped out. A wide smile split his face. "Hey, I thought I could feel you. Strangest thing. Come in."

He frowned down at the boxes piled in front of his door. "Are these yours?"

"Nope, they're yours. Happy housewarming."

He looked confused. "I've lived here for several years?"

"But I didn't get to come to the housewarming. If I had, I'd have brought these. So … happy housewarming."

He hugged me and then sniffed. "You smell different."

And I was thinking exactly the same about him. The pheromone I'd thought was his, the one which had always made me melt and want to sniff him more wasn't there. All I could discern now was the faint aroma of coal smoke and a body that had needed a shower for several days. His smile didn't disguise the pallor of his skin. His shirt was crumpled, and there were smears of something down the front of his jeans.

Rhiannon appeared behind him. "Recorder."

I wasn't in the mood for her today. Aysha's advice to take no shit and make difficult women work for what they wanted had turned out OK last time. I'd try it again. I picked up the box I wanted, closed my shields and replied, "Princess ap Modron."

She growled at me.

"What would you prefer? I obviously can't call you Rhiannon, as you won't call me Niki, even if we are both visiting the sick. What would make you happy? Chairman? Chairperson? Just Chair?"

"Chairman?" The glare she gave me was worthy of Aysha after she'd been up all night caring for a child with projectile vomiting.

"You're going to be chairing the Rainbow Council. Pick any damn name or title you choose, I don't care, but if you don't let me through to the kitchen with this, I'm going to get short-tempered again."

I walked. She moved. Dai had picked up Tilly. His body language looked protective. I checked, but she was fine. Couldn't Rhiannon be trusted around dogs? No, I didn't yet trust the woman, but she wasn't cruel to animals. I knew that for sure, so what was Dai's problem? Oh, shit, he was fresh from the healers, and Rhiannon and I were bickering like ill-mannered teenagers. Grow up, Niki.

I plonked the carton on the shiny glass table and looked for a knife to slit it open. A large one appeared very close to my nose. Thanks to Rollo introducing me to his blade, Nanok, which was much larger and scarier, I took it from Rhiannon with a calm, "Thanks. Vanilla latte again for you?"

As I unpacked the coffee maker and used her knife to open the other box, which had a pod holder and an extensive selection of coffee pods, she started laughing. "I heard about the stale instant coffee. Did anyone tell you why that was?"

I shook my head as I filled the machine with water, found two mugs, and slotted the first pod in, a vanilla one for her.

"Because my baby brother wants to discourage me from visiting him. He's entitled to his privacy, and I disturb him."

Her sweatshirt today had writing on it as usual. And, yes, a deep red sweatshirt and pants made from some kind of animal skin, not quite leather, maybe suede or even ostrich, was all she wore in this freezing wilderness. The sweatshirt said, *Some days contain far too much shit and too few shovellers.* Aysha would love one of those too. It made me think about friends and whether Rhiannon had any. Everyone seemed to be, if not actively terrified of her, at least extremely cautious around her. That was no way to live, was it?

I gave her a level stare. "You know I read the Book for fun? Agnes said you were a wonderful woman, a great friend and a complete hooligan— well, she used some other older word I can't remember, but Dola said it meant a hooligan. She also stressed your strong sense of justice. I look forward to meeting that woman one day. But for now, I think your baby brother needs to sit down before he falls down. And I need coffee."

I turned to Dai. "Come on, you're wiped out. Where do you want to sit?"

"Under the skylight."

I followed him into the room he'd shouted at me in the other day, but then there had been a snowstorm. Today the room took my breath away. What had appeared to be white panels between the polished wooden planks of the ceiling were actually windows. They must have been covered in snow. Now they were glass sheets almost three feet wide. They followed the slant of the roof and then came straight down the wall. By sitting under them, you could see the sky, the mountains and even the drop into the valley. Wow!

He sat heavily on a sofa by the window and below the arching, full-height skylight.

"What would you like to drink, Dai?"

"A beer'd be great." He noticed my enquiring glance. "I'm to dose myself with some potion for the next week and take it easy. But I can eat and drink anything I like."

I wandered through to the utility fridge where I'd seen beers the other day. Rhiannon followed me. "A word, Recorder."

"Princess?"

"Oh, for Iris's sake, fine, you win this unimportant battle, *Niki*. A quiet word, please." She led me towards the terrace where the hot tub was.

I held up a finger. "Your brother is convalescing, remember? I'll take him his beer and meet you there." She looked baffled. This wasn't a woman who knew how to tend to anyone, including herself.

Back in the lounge, I said, "I'll see Rhiannon out and be back. Are you OK with Tilly?"

Dai frowned, but at what, I didn't know, and I wasn't sure I cared. The sofa looked hard, and Dai looked uncomfortable. I looked around for cushions, a throw, anything. But there was nothing.

Nothing soft. Not even anything living, no plants or flowers in this room, only clean, modern lines.

Now I understood why Rollo, with his fluffy rugs, amazingly cosy duvet, squishy cushions, comfy chairs even in his bedroom, and vibrant flowers, had described the house as viciously modern.

Another ap Modron who didn't know how to care for themselves. And yet their father loved soft, fluffy things. He'd wrapped me in a blanket the other day when his damn son sent me down the mountain in tears.

That would not be happening today.

When I got back to the kitchen, Rhiannon was drinking her own coffee and had even put a pod of Columbian in for mine. Wonders would never cease.

"Hoyden, Agnes used to call us hoydens." She actually smiled. "My brother has been avoiding his responsibilities for far too long. He needs to step up. I'm running out of time. If you can help, please do. Agnes always told me I should give people at least a chance and not make everyone fight me like she had to before I listened to her. I miss her."

I wondered how a woman could be gone for hundreds of years and still generate such fresh grief in the eyes of the people who had cared about her. The Book told me Agnes died in the 1600s. Wasn't that long enough for people to move on and make new friends?

Then I re-ran what she'd said. "Why are you running out of time?"

"Because the dragonets will start hatching soon."

"OK, and what does that mean?"

She gave me a tired look. "Which word didn't you understand?"

I sighed. "I don't understand the significance of the hatching, the relevance of the time factor, or what the dragonets need to make this suddenly urgent?"

She looked surprised, as though people didn't usually simply explain what had confused them. What did they normally do, I wondered?

"Oh, OK." She gazed out at the mountain, then twisted slightly and pointed. "Over there are several hundred eggs."

I nodded.

"When they hatch, they're feral," she paused, as though I might not know what feral meant.

But I did, so I nodded again. "Wild? Uncontrollable? Not part of a group or pack?"

Now she nodded cautiously. "Feral dragons are a danger to everyone and everything. They're stupid, hungry flame-throwers with wings. They have teeth and talons as sharp as knives and turnips for brains and kill people and livestock accidentally."

I rolled my hand in a *carry on, I'm with you so far* gesture.

"We have several hours after they hatch to bond them to the pack. If we can bond them, some of them stay in dragon form. Others change immediately to human babies. Those ones usually make the strongest dragons when they change in later life."

At my wide-eyed confusion, she added, "Dragons are magical. You can't apply human logic to them. They're the soul of our realm."

I saw she was losing patience for teaching the ignorant Recorder, so I parroted what Mabon had told me the other day, hoping to get more information from her. Something I would actually comprehend. "And without them, you'd just be Celts, not Red Celts?"

A huge smile split her serious face. "Exactly."

That seemed to be it, as far as she was concerned.

So I offered her my biggest confusion. "But I'm still not sure exactly what you need Dai to do?"

"Step the flaming hell up and combine his regnal power with mine, so we can bond them all. If we do, we can control them. Fewer accidents and deaths, more functioning new members of dragon society. More power for the realm."

I couldn't use my Gift on her; she'd made that clear when she visited the Gateway to tell me about Gwyneth. So I looked at her steadily with what I hoped was an expectant expression.

It worked. In an unutterably weary tone, she finished, "It's hard enough without any true dragon queens to help. But the future Dragon King is too busy selling coal to the Vikings to save lives. So I'm handing dead babies over to their parents and having to kill feral dragonets."

Crap!

Oh boy, I really hadn't understood this at all, had I?

"Rhiannon, pretend I'm stupid. Because I'm missing some part of this. Neither you nor Mabon have explained what I could do to help. I need to fill in the blank patches in my understanding."

She sipped her coffee, and her expression softened slightly. "Agnes used to say pretend I'm a numbskull. What don't you understand?"

"What happens if Dai doesn't step up?"

Oh shit, wrong question. Her face froze over as quickly as if I were watching a cartoon and someone had poured icy water on her. In a glacial tone, she spat, "The regnal authority has to be exerted soon after they hatch. If it isn't, the ones who reverted to human die in the cold. The dragonets go fully feral, and we have to hunt them down and kill them."

She drew in a long slow breath. "And by we, I mean me. And I simply won't do it again because he won't get his fire together."

I knew I still hadn't fully understood, but Rhiannon was turning away now. She wiped away a tear, and every instinct I possessed said if I asked any more questions, she would bite my head off to prove she didn't own a softer side. Perhaps Dai could explain.

"I will see what I can do, I promise. However..." I held up a hand when she glared at me, "according to Ad'Rian, they nearly lost him on Friday, and the McKnight Gift..." I paused. She nodded. Obviously, Agnes had explained the difference between the McKnight women's own abilities and the Recorder's. "...*Really* wants me to ask you what would you have done to solve the problem if he had died? And, bearing in mind what it would take to almost kill the son of a god, how hard do you want me to push him today?"

Her shoulders slumped. "Agnes could sometimes tell when …?"

"Tomorrow or perhaps Tuesday I can push."

She turned back, gave me a nod and a long considering stare and, still carrying her mug, walked out onto the covered hot tub terrace and through the glass doors to the outside area.

I watched as she stood and took several long breaths of the fresh icy air and gazed up at the sky. Then she drank a deep draught of her coffee, put the mug carefully on the table and jumped off the edge!

My stomach lurched unhappily. I dashed outside, looked down—nothing.

But circling above the house was a deep, glossy red dragon with black stripes on one side. Rhiannon appeared to be riding it, but as I'd discovered in the Gateway, that wasn't the case at all, was it?

I drank my own coffee on the calm, silent mountainside, waved as she circled back and watched as she headed down to Pant y Wern.

I'd love to ride a dragon. I wondered if … no, probably not. But she looked amazing. The wings were so glorious. The whole thing was so damn elegant, not cumbersome, as I'd always thought a dragon would be when I'd read books about them. Rhiannon looked lithe, sinuous and … oh shit, I'd been quite slow, hadn't I? She looked quite serpentine. Snakelike even. What the hell had those cards been again?

I went back in to Dai, and, on the way, I checked the photo of the tarot cards I'd snapped earlier. Yep. Dragons and serpents.

And, as I'd known it would, the phone signal, and therefore my connection to the Gateway power, had gone with Rhiannon. How was she creating that network?

THIRTY-THREE

D ai semi-reclined on the sofa in his lounge, with Tilly asleep by his side. I settled on the floor nearby. There wasn't a chair I could pull over; they were all fixed to the floor in their positions as though it wasn't permitted to disturb their perfect arrangement. But the perfect arrangement was too far apart to converse at a comfortable volume in this huge room. I didn't want to share the couch with him. It was too close, and I needed to see his face.

"How are you?"

In answer, he handed me the order blank from the restaurant in Galicia. I'd written my questions on it so he'd stop forgetting them. "I owe you some answers."

"Dai, they can wait a day or two if you're not up to it."

But he shook his head. "Think I'd feel better for doing it."

I took a long look at him with my Gift. His shields were *still* like smooth rock walls, and his aura was murky. Something weird—actually I was pretty sure I meant *wyrd*, if it meant uncanny and non-human as I thought it might—glimmered in his eyes.

I stopped my instinctive shiver with sheer will. Well, and by sitting on my hands.

I was the only one who was uncomfortable with this because he took a relaxed pull on his beer bottle. "I was born to be the King of the Dragons, and I don't want to be. I didn't ask for it. Don't see how they can force me to do it."

I'd worked that much out. Mabon and Rhiannon had filled the rest in. Not the actual born-to-be-king thing. But the realms were lousy with royals. As Gran had said, kings and queens were ten to the penny here. It didn't tell me what it meant from his perspective though. "What specifically does it involve that you don't want to do?"

"Dragons are a bit like dogs." He stroked Tilly. "In dragon form, they're pack animals. They need to know who's in charge. Right now, no one is, and their behaviour is reflecting the lack of an ultimate authority."

Interesting. He'd avoided answering my question,

but he hadn't lied. I considered what Rhiannon had just told me and the number of complaints the Recorder's Office received about dragons burning crops and how many times Mabon had grumbled about them. "But they listen to Dru and your dad and Rhiannon, don't they?"

"Rhiannon has the power, but without any true queens to lead her, she's just not up to the job. It's different for me. They challenge my authority every time. If I were the king, they'd still challenge it. But once I proved it, it would stick for a long time, probably forever, or at least until another king was born."

"So is this what Rhiannon's had to do while you're thinking about it? Fight them every time? Is it why she's losing dragonets?"

His scowl at my words frightened me a little. It told me I'd gone off his preferred script. Nick had done this to me. This, it appeared, was about Dai, not anyone else.

I tried a different tack. "So why don't you want to be king?"

"Because it's so flaming boring and annoying, and the female dragons are ... lumpy and dumb. They aren't ... I don't ..." He paused, seemed finally to weigh his words. "Because I prefer to use my brain, not animal instinct. I enjoy running the trade side and making agreements that favour the Red

Celts, and I'm naturally very good at it." He nodded as if to emphasise the truth of his statement. But my left shoulder pinged. He was lying, but mostly to himself it seemed?

"If I accepted my dragon side, the instincts would be overwhelming for decades. I don't want my entire life run by out-of-control dragon hormones. I'd end up as crazy as Rhiannon. Perhaps I should have given in and changed years ago, when I was younger, but I didn't." Well, that was all true.

"And it's my Da's fault." And that wasn't.

Maybe I should humour him? "Parents don't have the right to decide a child's life path, do they?"

He nodded fervently. "Exactly. Knew you'd understand after what your mum and gran did to you."

But I didn't understand. The solution was simple, wasn't it? "So give Rhiannon the dragon power you have and aren't using so she can save her dragonets, and then you'll be able to do whatever you want with your own life. Be whoever you want to be."

It didn't seem too complicated to me. Rhiannon was good at it but lacked power. He didn't want to do it, so the power was wasted on him.

His shoulders hunched. He scowled again, and the look in his eyes was a little scary now. "That power is *mine*."

The image of a child holding all its toys and saying "Mine" that the Gateway had sent me when it retrieved the yellow regnal power on Thursday flashed in my mind.

But the Gateway had passed the yellow power on to Rollo for safekeeping. Why wouldn't Dai do the same? "Well, yeah, but only if you're the dragon king. It's for the dragons, isn't it? Didn't you say you'd rather run the trade side? Didn't you just say it's your strength?" I didn't think mentioning my shoulder thought he was lying about being naturally good at it would help anything.

His hand fisted on his thigh.

I reminded myself he was fresh from the healers. Perhaps I was missing something.

He blew out a breath and smoothed his angry facial lines into an unconvincing facsimile of a smile. My shoulder started causing me pain before he even spoke. "I should have started this with an apology. I treated you badly. And none of it was your fault."

Well, dur! But it didn't seem as if it would help anything if I said so.

And he *still* hadn't apologised, had he? He'd only talked about what he should have done. He was all *let's keep saying the word apology*, but without ever giving one.

He'd done this to me once before when he'd

emailed the Recorder's Office and then complained because Dola read it. I'd pointed out Dola was my equerry. It was her job to read the Recorder's email. If he wanted privacy, then he should have used my personal email address. But he hadn't apologised. It was as though *he* hadn't made the mistake—*we* had.

Nick had done this all the time, too. After his death, I'd done some reading and discovered it was a common trait in people with narcissism. Dai reminded me entirely too much of Nick. I'd talked myself into believing only my unfortunate marital history had caused me to imagine similar traits in Dai. Now I wasn't so sure.

I'd read an article that talked about how we're drawn to people who are just like our ex. Even if they'd been toxic for us.

It had scared me. Would I pick the wrong ones repeatedly, mistrust all men for the rest of my life, or keep falling for assholes?

I knew there were lots of lovely people out there, but feared I was a magnet for the others. Then, yesterday, I'd compared how amazingly different it was to spend time with Rollo. How open, transparent and generous he was in his behaviour and communication. His heart, his aura, even his head, were open to me. Which was probably a one-off caused by the power, but even so ... Aargh, I couldn't think about

Rollo now. But I already missed his bright, fun energy.

I settled for, "Uh-huh."

He sighed. "It doesn't sound as though you're accepting my apology?"

I stopped myself from gaping at him. Seriously? He was behaving exactly like Nick. This was *not* my imagination.

Slowly, I said, "Well, I will. When you give me one. But you haven't yet, have you?"

An expression of poorly hidden anger crossed his face. "I'm not sure I understand." And my left shoulder throbbed again. It was painful now.

I couldn't let him get away with this. Some part of me, the Recorder, my McKnight Gift, or even just freaking common sense, knew he was well aware he hadn't said those three simple but essential words: *I am sorry.*

I drew in a steadying breath and prepared to make my questions clear. "I need to know why you thought locking the Recorder, well, any woman in your house was reasonable?"

I waited. Nothing. His eyes sparkled with something strange. It made me uncomfortable.

OK then. "Why didn't you listen when I told you I had responsibilities and appointments? Some of them on Thursday were important to hundreds of women."

I paused, looked at him.

Nothing.

My chest tightened, and breathing got more difficult.

"What did you think gave you the right to ignore everything I said?"

It was as though he was just waiting for me to run down. It was creepy now. My chest hurt. My heartbeat pounded too fast and too loud in my own ears. I didn't want to be here anymore.

Was this like the other day when the power had needed me? Or was I just panicking at the silent treatment from Dai?

I couldn't contact Dola from here. But there was someone I could ask whom I didn't need wi-fi to reach.

Rollo, would you ask Dola if everything is OK in the Gateway for me?

There was a pause, where Dai still said nothing. He wasn't even looking at me. He was gazing around his lounge with a pleased smile on his face.

All good here. He's not healed, though, is he? Please don't let him get to you. Imagine you have a glamour, put a smile on the outside and go home soon.

Sensible. Should I go home? I could come back tomorrow with Mabon? Or Ad'Rian? Or both of them.

Dai was outwardly calm and unresponsive, but my Gift told me inside he was a ball of boiling anger. It was as though he was waiting me out. Waiting for something—but what?

Rather than a fake smile on the outside, I decided to try one more time to get at the truth before I visited Mabon to report. "Why would you think an avalanche would stop the Recorder descending the mountain safely? What did you think gave you the right to even have an opinion on my necessities or my role?"

Dai buried his face in his hands, breathing carefully. Then he stood up, left the room, and returned with a bottle I recognised as holding a Fae healing potion and a fresh bottle of beer. He poured the remainder of the potion into the remnants of the first beer and swallowed it down. The little pantomime finished with a comical grimace from him.

He'd literally stepped over my empty coffee cup to get his beer, but he didn't offer me anything. Strike One. There's no excuse for poor manners.

OK, he's still healing. Chill out, Niki. Breathe.

I picked up the order blank and surveyed the questions. Perhaps if we started somewhere else, we might circle back to whatever had inspired his stiffness on Wednesday and his downright crazy behaviour on Thursday.

The first question was pretty impersonal. "Do you know what's up with your shields now?"

He nodded.

I waited. "And what is it?"

He shrugged.

I looked at him. Was it me, or was this just rude? No, it damn well wasn't me. "Dai, if you want to rebuild my trust, then not answering everything I ask won't cut it. Why are your shields so tight *all* the time?"

He shrugged again. "I need my privacy."

"But there are times we should allow people to help us, aren't there?"

Nothing.

Strike Two.

I looked down at the list. What could I ask that he might answer? Actually, if he wasn't going to talk, why was I even still here? *He'd* asked to see me.

"Dai, *you* asked to see *me*. Your father told me you had things you wanted to explain. What exactly ARE those things?"

"Just to see you and to redeem my word to answer these questions."

"OK. Great, so when do you plan to start?"

He gave me a surprised look.

I drew in a careful breath and, in a pleasant tone, said, "You haven't answered a single question yet. I'll come back in a few days when you're feeling better. Can I get you anything before I go?"

He sat up looking quite panicky. "No, Niki. Really, I'm trying."

"Okaay, but you've just been healed. Ad'Rian says the block isn't there anymore. And we're in your home, which is where you said you'd be able to speak freely. So which question would you like to start with?"

I looked at the list again. "Who was your mother if she wasn't Fae?" That wasn't my business, was it?

"Why did you lie about *Home de lume*?" Well, he'd explained it meant a man of fire. I guess the whole dragon thing explained it, but did the waiter know that? How?

Why had I frightened him so much when I asked about riding a dragon? Perhaps not the one to start with. Oh, sod it. I wanted to know.

"Sorry, Dai, but if you're not apologising, and you're not answering my questions, which is exactly what you told your father you wanted to do, then why the hell am I here? Why did you freak out when I said I'd like to ride a dragon?"

It had taken me ages, and I'd listened several times to Dola's replay of our strange after-dinner conversation, when he'd just upped and left my kitchen table, to work out that my happy question about riding a dragon had been the final straw for him.

"Dragons are not unicorns, Niki. They can and do throw anyone who tries to ride them off in mid-air. What would you do then?" He shifted uncomfortably in his seat as though he'd tried it himself and could still feel the pain of the landing.

Well, unicorns weren't tame as he seemed to think, but following up on that question wouldn't get me anywhere.

Next.

Why didn't he like me being calm about things, like when he told me his age? He'd said I was too confident, and it had triggered me.

This was a swamp of quicksand. There must be somewhere I could start?

Why Dola spied on him? Well, I already knew the answer, thanks to Mabon's muddled explanation about his mother, the Goddess Modron, having to find Dai, didn't I? The question didn't feel like a big deal. I could start there.

"Why were you so paranoid about Dola?" *Whoops, probably could have phrased it better, Niki.*

But he surprised me with a laugh. "It's not paranoia if they *are* out to get you."

"And were they?"

"Yes, Da says I was a tiresome child. Boastful, he

called it. Apparently, I said too much to the wrong people about being the son of a god and the future king of dragons. He was all 'loose lips sink ships' about it. I think the war must have been on at the time."

Well, at least he was talking, but "the war"?

The loose lips thing was from World War II, wasn't it? I did some quick mental arithmetic. "But wouldn't you have been in your forties back then? My age. Isn't it a bit old for childish boasting?"

"Flaming hells, Niki, you sound just like him! He had everyone on the lookout for me, reporting all my movements to him. He got Ad'Rian to install a tongue block so I couldn't give anyone any private family information."

"But those kinds of blocks are safe. We were considering one for Autumn. I discussed it with Ad'Rian."

"Sure they are. If your father doesn't get himself concussed, forget half the stuff he did and not bother asking anyone to remove it."

He'd told me before Mabon had a concussion, but Dola had described it as a grave injury, including a shattered skull that took him some time to recover from, hadn't she?

But my real question was why any forty-something couldn't at least try and address their own problem. "But *you* hadn't forgotten. You knew you still had the problem. Why didn't you just go directly to Ad'Rian?"

"Ad'Rian doesn't like me. He would have involved my Da."

"So?"

I felt like a terrier digging relentlessly away at the problem, but I'd waited weeks for any sensible explanation of his behaviour. And although I'd tried to be calm about him locking me in his house on Thursday, the idea he might have done it to a woman who couldn't just transport out haunted me. What if I'd sent Fi up here to talk about trade opportunities with him? Or was it only me he was weird with?

I looked at Dai, waiting for an answer. It didn't seem like one was coming, so I repeated the question. "Why didn't you just go to Ad'Rian and take charge of your own brain? You were an adult; why would Ad'Rian have involved your father?"

"He doesn't like me."

"Oh, rubbish! He just expended more energy than he had to save your life. He pulled in energy from half the healers in Fae and worked on you without ceasing, or caring for himself for almost twenty-four straight hours."

"He did it for Da. Not for me. You don't know him like I do, and, anyway, everyone says he adores you."

Wow! Just wow.

He'd said the same thing to me before when we talked about Autumn riding Diamant. Now, he made it sound like an accusation. *You wouldn't understand. He likes you. Poor me.*

FFS.

He'd been acquainted with Ad'Rian for eighty years longer than I had. But he didn't know him at all, did he? The generosity of Ad'Rian's spirit was legendary. Yes, he could be shouty occasionally, but only because he cared deeply. He hadn't been angry when I left Diamant's paddock unlocked and he injured himself. But perhaps my abject, sincere devastation and my grovelling apology, along with my childish tears and my promise to learn from and never repeat my mistake, had something to do with it? Or was it simply because I'd been nine at the time?

I'd assumed my nerves about coming here were just my stupid programming after Nick. I was simply distrustful of men right now. But I wasn't. I trusted lots of the men I'd met up here. I started to list them in my head, got to thirteen and stopped.

I considered it the other way around. I'd only distrusted two men since I arrived at the cottage: Jamie and Ross. And I'd often had an odd, niggling feeling about Dai. I truly hadn't wanted to come here on Wednesday—it hadn't just been nerves.

I needed to go home, think this through and speak to the kings.

I stood up and collected Tilly. Dai tried to hang on to her, but as soon as her eyes focused on me, she disentangled herself from him and settled on my arm. Was that why he'd been so protective of her? Because he knew I wouldn't leave without her? Well, he'd done her no harm, or she wouldn't have stayed next to him. Would she?

"I'm going to let you get some much-needed rest and heal, Dai. I'll pop back tomorrow, and we can try to resolve this."

"You don't believe me?"

"All I hear is you blaming other people, me, your father and Ad'Rian. But what I don't hear you saying is, 'I was a young idiot, and I should have asked my father what was wrong with me fifty years ago. Instead of putting my entire life on hold, choosing to look fourteen and playing backgammon with the Recorder's granddaughter.'"

He started to speak, but I was on a roll, and I'd only plucked up enough courage to do this once. He still wasn't at his best, but his behaviour had been dangerous, abusive, and coercive. Maybe I'd never get an apology, but I needed to give him something important to think about while he rested.

I remembered the fear and panic the Gateway had greeted me with when I got back. I hadn't even known the power could be so frightened. "If you'd succeeded in detaining me here against my will on Thursday, the Gateway might have fallen. You could have trapped millions of people in their realms *forever*, with no way out, all because you were having a bad day and couldn't control your own emotions. Does that sound reasonable to you? Does not having wi-fi or any coffee for guests so your sister can't keep asking you to step up and do your job sound reasonable?"

He laughed. But it wasn't a happy sound.

In a patient tone, he said, "Niki, I understand it's an important job you have. But millions of people trapped because I asked you to wait somewhere and be safe for a few hours? Self-important exaggeration much?"

Strike Three. Well, I didn't feel bad leaving now.

There was a smirk behind his pleasant, amused expression, and it troubled me. Well, I could wipe it off his face, and would he then consider the possible consequences of his over-controlling actions?

"Do you even understand what the Recorder's primary job is?"

"You bond people."

"No, Dai, I said the primary job. It's keeping the Gateway open and the power functioning and happy. Dozens of Gateways have been lost off the grid over the last millennium. You might ask your father about them."

I wasn't getting through to him. He still had a patient, patronising smile on his face.

"If the Gateway falls, you're all stuck in your own realms. Some of those realms have no land access to the others, do they?"

He nodded, but as though he was confirming a fact, not as if he understood my point.

"The Gateway was under attack. The power was calling me. Our Gateway is one of the few remaining because the McKnight women have held it open, sometimes at the cost of their own lives. The Recorders have one important job: it's keeping the Gateway stable and operating. If you'd held me long enough, those lumberjacks would have chopped through the yellow gate. And you might have been stuck in Red forever."

I paused for breath.

"You're new. You don't understand the role, Niki. Let me explain."

Was he serious? Let him explain my own damn role to me? When he hadn't even realised I could transport? Oh, this should be good. "Go ahead."

"You're under the impression your role is important. All the bowing and scraping from everyone cements your belief. But we wouldn't have been trapped. Consider Troels—he was tired of being locked in. It's not as though he did anything except hack at a door as I understand it. Someone would have opened the Gateway again. One of the Gods or Goddesses might. Not that I wish you any harm, but you're hardly indispensable. You need to relax."

My face must have turned to stone, because why the hell would he think that? I'd studied with the Book. Once a Gate fell, it couldn't be re-opened other than by the correct line of Recorders. It was why there were so few Gateways left. Or so the Book had told me.

And then something even scarier stood up and waved in my brain. He'd had his breakdown on Thursday and been with the healers until Saturday. When had he had time to find out what was going on? He had no access to the network up here. Had Rhiannon told him? No, because, according to the Book, he was wrong, so someone had given him misinformation. That didn't feel like Rhiannon's style. And if the Gate had fallen during the attack, it would have fallen over my dead body. What part of that didn't he understand?

"Someone has given you incorrect information. You would have been public enemy number one to everyone in the six realms. You'd have made John Fergusson look like a saint. The Red Celt prince who allowed the Gateway to fall because he was having a bad day and could only use his mouth but not his ears, and wanted to rant at the Recorder. Being the King of the Dragons might be light relief compared to that option. Why don't you think about it while you're deciding whether to grow up or not?"

He still didn't look even vaguely apologetic. He looked as if he thought I was the one behaving childishly and having a tantrum over nothing. Something was wrong here. This man was not healed. Not anywhere close to healed. Why on earth had Ad'Rian released him? I needed to speak to the Fae king. Now.

CHAPTER
THIRTY-FOUR

I arrived back in my bedroom seething and put a wriggling Tilly down. She chased away before I could even remove her coat, and I heard her drinking water furiously from her dish in the bathroom. She'd been at Dai's with no water and her coat on in a warm house.

I'd been so confused and upset by Dai's continued rudeness, I hadn't even noticed, and she'd not chivvied me. I felt like the worst dog mum in the world, but it was also extremely unusual. She was a little fiend if her needs weren't met, and yet, obviously hot and thirsty, she'd still slept quietly with Dai.

Considering he'd told Mabon he wanted to speak to me, he hadn't been at all welcoming. He'd not offered any kind of hospitality. It must have been intentional. He could communicate with Tilly. He'd proved that when he knew she wanted ice cream in Galicia. So he'd have known she was thirsty.

And I hadn't been offered a seat or a beer. Nothing other than the single small coffee from the machine I'd brought with me as his housewarming gift. And Rhiannon had made it for me.

I was being petty. The man was recovering, but it wouldn't have prevented him saying "help yourself," would it? Two things jingled loudly in my head. I'd promised myself several times I wouldn't ignore my Gift, so why was I doing it now? Those tarot cards swirled around my brain. Serpents. They represented deception, misdirection, temptation, and perhaps someone who made false statements or promises.

"Dola, can you connect me to Ad'Rian if he's not busy?"

She didn't even answer me, but moments later: "Nik-a-lula, are you well? I'm devastated I missed the justice meted out to John. But I couldn't refuse Mabon. However, Glais'Nee reports everything went well, and you surprised him."

Rule number one with Ad'Rian: don't fall for his encouragement to volunteer gossip unless you have an hour to spare.

"He's such a nice man. I don't want to keep you from your book, but I have a quick query."

"Of course, daaarling, what do you need?"

"When will Dai's convalescence end? I mean, when will he be totally fit?"

"But, daaarling, he is. He's not healed, of course. All his mental chakras are a mess, and there are ... other issues. But those will take longer to heal, and Dai will need to do some of the work himself. But if we are speaking purely physically, he is back to normal now, otherwise he would still be here with us."

"Yes, that just struck me. So why would he still be taking a potion? And why is Mabon under the impression he needs another week off and calm and quiet during that week?"

There was a brief silence, and then, cautiously, Ad'Rian said, "A clarification please. It is not always quite clear with you as yet. Are you calling as the Recorder? Or as my little Nik-a-lula?"

I paused. This was my lesson of the month, wasn't it? I found my Recorder voice, even if I still secretly thought of it as a librarian—why were librarians the ultimate authority in my world? I should work that out sometime, shouldn't I?

I tried again. "Your Majesty, my apologies for disturbing the Head of the Fae Healers at this hour on a Sunday evening, but I'm afraid the Recorder needs some information."

Would that do it?

It seemed it would.

"Oh, well done, my lady. Then skirting around patient confidentiality, as it's official, and you must have an excellent reason to ask. Speaking hypothetically, that's what lawyers and such say when they're simply going to tell you the truth, isn't it, daaarling?"

"Mmm hmm."

"If someone had several psychological and personality issues and needed a good sturdy kick in the direction of aligning with their higher purpose, then they might be sent home with several bottles of potions and advised to take four drops twice a day for the next few months."

"So they wouldn't be advised to tip a third of the bottle into a beer and glug it like unpleasant-tasting medicine?"

"No, they would not. As I know you must already be aware. Do I need more information here?"

"Well, equally hypothetically, if someone was behaving as strangely after you released them as they were before you treated them, would you want to know about it?"

"But of course—tell me more."

I thought about it, but I'd feel like a tattle-tale. The longer I spoke, the greater the likelihood I'd stop talking out of sheer embarrassment or burst into tears as I had with Mabon. I trusted Ad'Rian with … well, with everything.

"Can you do a mind link over a Dolina?"

"Only with someone whose skills are far greater than your current level. I mean no offence. But I have time now if you want to pop in."

"If you're sure. Something is nagging at me, and I can't isolate what it is. Dai feels … wrong. And I need you to check Tilly for me."

The moment I said it, it clarified the problem for me. Dai felt the kind of strange that meant something bad was about to happen. Like when your steering doesn't feel quite right, and five miles farther down the road, the tyre pressure alert pings on. It's almost a relief you weren't simply imagining something was wrong.

Dai had seemed unaware of how fragile the gateways were. He'd grimaced too obviously after he poured the last of his potion bottle into his beer and finished it. But somewhere in the back of my mind was the thought I'd never had an unpleasant-tasting medicine from Fae.

Ever.

It usually tasted like your favourite thing. When I was a kid, mine had always been pineapple-fizzy flavoured.

"If you truly don't mind, I'll be there in two minutes."

Ad'Rian welcomed me as I landed in his book-lined study. He moved a pile of papers off the chair next to him and gestured me to sit down. But I didn't. He surveyed me carefully.

I held Tilly out to him. "I know you're not a veterinarian, but is she OK?"

Ad'Rian's usually immobile face focused intently on me. He tucked his long, bright silver hair behind his ears and focused on Tilly. His forehead gave the slightest of twitches.

"Come to Uncle Ad'Rian, little one; let me see how beautiful you are." He took her carefully and put her on the chair he'd obviously been using and knelt next to her. His eyes turned white. Tilly gazed at him, and I could almost see the energies moving between them.

He moved his hands over her body about two inches above her fluffy white coat, from nose to tail. Crooning to her, he made gathering gestures and threw into the air whatever he'd just collected. I couldn't see a thing. But Tilly felt lighter now.

Ad'Rian blinked, and his eyes changed back to their usual silvery-blue. "She is fine, Niki. She tells me she was only thirsty and sleepy, and Dai was deeply unhappy and wanted her to stay. Was he keeping her there so you wouldn't leave? Perhaps. Or maybe he didn't even do it consciously. But because she is your soul dog and protected from this kind of influence, it only partly worked. I think you'd better give me a full briefing in case I can help, or worse, in case I bear any responsibility for this."

Tilly jumped down from his chair. Her tail wagged happily, and she looked much more like herself.

Ad'Rian gestured me to a chair. "We may as well be comfortable, daaarling. You might be bringing me a problem, but you look wonderful; you're glowing. Your aura is blossoming wonderfully. What *have* you been up to?" His eyes gleamed with interest.

Oh hell, I'd forgotten Rollo, hadn't I? Ad'Rian would spot him in a millisecond. He reached his finger out and waited for my consent. I recalled Glais'Nee's comment the other day.

"Before you do that, please know I am aware of the connection. Glais'Nee called it a soul link or something."

"Oooohhhh, yes, he mentioned that." He almost purred the words.

Well, of course he bloody did! Because the King of the Violet Fae and one of the most ancient and powerful Fae warriors in his realm had absolutely nothing better to do with their time than talk about my private life, did they? Goddess save me from men who called it a briefing, a sitrep, or intelligence, and not what it damn well was—gossip.

"I consent." And we were connected. It was definitely getting easier.

Practice helps, Niki. Ah, nephew, our greetings. Your aunt mentioned only last week she hoped you'd be able to get out of Viking for Kaiden and L'eon's wedding celebration. It's almost arranged.

Ad'Rian said, "If you would think where you wish to begin, Niki, and then allow it to unfold for me …"

I'd decided to run all of my interactions with Dai since my return, like a mini movie in my mind. I was worried I might have missed something important. I didn't mind sharing the whole of it with Ad'Rian. He needed to know to advise me. And absolutely nothing private happened between Dai and me. We'd never even kissed, and the moment I realised it wasn't *his* smell I liked, I didn't want to be close to him. But he'd seemed friendly at first. When had he begun to make me so twitchy?

I'd wanted the high-speed mind link, because I needed a fresh perspective. I couldn't tell if I was judging Dai unfairly because he'd tried to hold me prisoner and pissed me off with stale instant coffee. Ad'Rian's renowned impartiality would be helpful.

I began in the Gateway when I first realised the Knight Adjutant candidate whom Mabon introduced as Dafydd had been my childhood playmate Dai. The high-speed movie in my mind played. It progressed from the help Dai had given me to understand, finally, who the Quack Pack and the Smiths were, to our encounter at the Broch with Hugh McAlpin.

Surprise came through the link from Ad'Rian as he watched me coat myself in power in my sitting room to persuade Mabon to stop keeping his promise to my gran and nannying me. At the time, my conscious attention had been completely focused on Mabon to see if my message to him had hit home. But running it back for Ad'Rian, I'd noticed, subconsciously at least, how Dai's interest sharpened when he realised I could pull power outside the Gateway.

Ad'Rian's mental laughter cheered me up as he viewed the scene in my sitting room and the garden. When Mabon got his new phone and danced around my garden doing his best rock god impersonation, Ad'Rian laughed aloud.

"Delightfully creative way to achieve our goals on his phone. I wondered how you intended to manage it when you so confidently gave me your promise. All he would say when I asked him was, 'Move with the changing times, we must.'" Ad'Rian could be an accurate mimic, and I grinned at him.

I ran the memory of Dola alerting me to Dai's invitation email having arrived and my swift response. Then we moved forward to Valentine's week, when Dai really didn't want to join us in the centre of the Rainbow during the bonding checks. I'd assumed, like so many of the other royals I'd dealt with during that week, he simply wasn't coping well with any of the changes. We watched him as he kept a constant eye on me with his excellent peripheral vision and then saw how sweet he was with Autumn.

I'd actually forgotten most of this until Ad'Rian paused my sending and rewound it to study Dai's resistance to joining his father in the centre. After another viewing of it, we moved forward to later that evening when, in the middle of a conversation about riding unicorns and dragons, Dai rudely stood up and left.

Ad'Rian let out a low melodic whistle. I showed him the Saturday night when I'd been in my pyjamas trying to get an early night before my first Valentines Day in the Gateway. A grumpy Mabon requested I summon him and Dai as a favour, to save them walking down the mountain.

Dai had expected me to get dressed and go eat with him, and then refused my counter-offer that he come to the cottage because he thought Dola was spying on him.

We moved on to the Sunday and all the bondings where Dai pushed me to join "everyone" at *Carnaval*.

But when we arrived, it was only the two of us and Tilly in the trattoria.

We watched through the ridiculous meal where he fed Tilly so caringly but couldn't remember any of the questions I'd asked for more than a few seconds. Through our mind link, I could feel Ad'Rian nodding along, and he sped it up until Dai started talking about Fi's appointment as Director of Trade in the Gateway and his own role with the Red Celt's commerce.

The events of the last few days unspooled smoothly in my mind, without a murmur from Ad'Rian until we reached today, and my conversations with Rhiannon and Dai.

Finally, we got to the point when I'd realised Tilly had slept in a warm coat in Dai's hot home without a drink. She was too sleepy, and I was suddenly angry and worried. It triggered some "mum" part of my brain unconnected to my job, the power or anything other than my love for my dog. And so here we were.

"I have questions, please, Niki. Is this link troubling you at all, any headache?"

"No. I'm good, thank you." Actually, I felt fine now. Was he healing me, too?

"Only a little, daaarling, just smoothing your ruffled edges. At some level, you're aware you both had a lucky escape. My nephew may have helped there. Your link is grounding you both. I suspect

Dai's power couldn't find a way into your mind, which is why I think he tried your adorable puppy. I'm clearing your stress hormones a little. But I'm still unsure what Dai wanted, and I have questions. Show me the clips where he requested you to magically connect his phone to the Gateway's network, please."

I ran those again. He mm-hmmed.

"You never wanted to add his phone to the Rainbow Network. That signals distrust from you, Niki. Your technology is one of the key ways you connect to the people you care about. And you didn't want Dai connected in with them, did you?"

"When you put it like that—no." I hadn't wanted to zap Dai's phone, had I? But I didn't know why.

"It's interesting, don't you think?"

"Honestly, I'm not sure I understand?"

"He was obviously using his power on you to attract you. But you kept brushing it away. Do you know why?"

I shook my head helplessly.

I wasn't sure I'd grasped what Ad'Rian was asking. Did he mean attract, attract? Because, no, Dai had never done anything like that. A flash of Rollo sucking his doughnut into submission flashed through my mind.

Whoops. I tucked the memory firmly away and turned my attention back to Dai. I had felt some mild, if very nervous attraction to him in Aberglas in the Iron Pig bar. But Dai had never connected with any part of my true self. He hadn't been interested in being honest with the real me, had he? Only with my Recorder aspect—now I thought it through, it was pretty clear.

Our easiest conversations were the ones about what a great job I was doing in the Gateway, how pleased he was I'd appointed Fi to the new trade desk. He'd helped me with background information on the Smiths. He'd been interested in the bond Autumn had shown him. Recorder-ish things held his attention. But had I personally ever held his attention? And yet today he'd made it sound as though Recorders were unimportant.

"Just clarify one point for me. What *is* this about his scent?"

Oh yeah, that.

I ran my memories for him of how amazing Dai smelt every time I hugged him. How I kept wanting to sniff him.

Ad'Rian must have got the scent through our connection because he said, "I adore Palo Santo. There's a reason they call it the holy tree, you know. We have a grove of them in the foothills of our mountains. It's an incredible place to cleanse your aura. The trees aren't particularly attractive except in blossom season, but when the sun hits them at noon, the fragrance, oh my. You should visit, Nik-a-lula; it's a wonderfully healing place. So how did you work out the fragrance wasn't coming from Dai?"

I ran the next part of using my Palo Santo to cleanse the yellow energy for Rollo.

"Ah, *that's* why you're shielding my nephew." He sent me approval.

We focused on when I realised the box containing my Palo Santo had been living in my lingerie drawer since I'd moved to Scotland. In Manchester, it had always sat on a shelf in my kitchen. I'd brought it with me on my first trip assuming, before I knew Dola existed, my gran's cottage might need some energy cleansing. But when Dola unpacked all my things as she created my bedroom, she'd put it into my top drawer with my underwear.

Dai's incredible body heat had made the Palo Santo scent drift up from *me*. From my bras, tanks, camisoles, even some T-shirts whenever he hugged me. I'd tested it by buying new thermal camisoles that hadn't yet been stored in my dresser, and, sure enough, when he'd hugged me, I'd smelt nothing nice or woody.

Ad'Rian nodded in understanding. "Let me show you what you'd see if you'd used your other eyes." He called seeing the higher energies "using my other eyes." He'd taught me how to do it when I was a child. But it was a difficult skill for non-Fae to master, and I had to exercise the skill consciously. It took real concentration, and I wasn't sure it would ever be second nature to me the way it was for any competent Fae. For the Fae king, it was like breathing, and, wow, did it open my eyes to what had really been going on.

THIRTY-FIVE

A d'Rian took control of our link now and ran my own memories back for me, but this time he showed me what his talents saw, and I hadn't.

Gosh, it must be confusing to be Ad'Rian!

Instead of clear air between Dai and me, when I looked with Ad'Rian's Fae-sight, there were eddies and vortices in the currents of power between us. Dai's power was deep, gloomy red; the Recorder power was rainbow-coloured, of course; and the McKnight Gift was green.

In the bar in Aberglas, when Dai turned my stomach upside down, there was a trail of red power reaching to the door as Mabon and I entered. It had pulled me towards Dai. He wrapped more around me at the table while Mabon was at the bar.

He'd used the same red power on Enid, the

young Red Celt saleswoman in the Smiths jewellery shop when I'd bought presents for Aysha and Autumn.

The next night in my cottage I declined to zap his phone, and he almost immediately asked me on a date. Far more red energy had surrounded me as I'd hesitated because I didn't want a relationship.

Although I took a step back from his offer of a dinner date and changed it to dinner with a friend, I *had* agreed to it. So some of the power had reached me.

I saw it all through Ad'Rian's eyes.

The other thing I noticed was how often Dai used his vape along with the red power. The vapour floated in the air and was frequently accompanied by his red power.

Ad'Rian murmured, "Yes, a literal smoke screen. Although he may be unaware of how much he is using the power. Perhaps he believes his vape calms him, and then he is more able to get his own way. I shall look into it."

At my kitchen table, when Dai didn't want to explain why he thought Ad'Rian wouldn't have taken Autumn, a sassy child, on Diamant—Ad'Rian snorted at this. "The boy is far too concerned by everyone's rank and some ill-perceived notion of relative importance, isn't he? She is a delightful child;

we had fun. Sometimes that's the most important thing."

When we'd discussed me riding Dusha, my soul-bonded unicorn, the air was vibrant with dark red energy strands until it surrounded me. It looked as though he'd been trying to pull me towards him.

It hadn't worked. Probably because Aysha and I had strict rules about what it meant for me to be in surrogate mum mode for Autumn. Those rules, engraved on my heart for almost eight years, would have overridden anything Dai was trying to persuade me into. No wonder he'd given up and gone home when he couldn't distract me from my enquiries.

"Yes, he was attempting to divert you from your line of questioning. I do not believe he couldn't answer your question. He merely didn't want to."

When I wouldn't go to Galicia with him wearing my pyjamas the night before my first Valentine's Day in the Gateway, he'd pushed a tidal wave of red power towards me. I hadn't even been aware of it because the Gateway's power had immediately deflected it back at him.

In every case, a deep red energy came from Dai and surrounded me. Ad'Rian showed me, when we were in the Gateway, the power stood between me and Dai's attempts to manipulate. It was always with me these days, thanks to the Rainbow Network, and it was blocking his red power. The Gateway protected the Recorder. Even if the oblivious Recorder didn't even know she needed protection.

A cold lump formed in my stomach. Why had Dai really wanted me to stay in his house? The house where there was no Dola, no wi-fi, no connection to the outside world. And no rainbow power.

I hoped he wasn't just that kind of asshole – it would be so ... sleazy. But I hadn't ever had the lecherous vibe from him. Whatever he'd wanted from me, I didn't think it was that.

Ad'Rian ended his little blooper reel with Dai in his lounge on Thursday before his mind snapped. The air had been full of his vape, and he'd shouted furiously at me, telling me I wasn't going anywhere. He'd surrounded me in a web of dense red power, which knitted tighter with his every angry word.

I finally had the opportunity to laugh at the look of astonishment and fury on his face. He'd gaped as I simply disappeared in a cloud of green McKnight power and transported home. He had known Recorders could transport. But he'd been sure, without access to the rainbow power, he could keep me there. What had he planned to do if he'd held me?

The cold lump in my stomach grew. "I didn't even see that, Ad'Rian. How are you able to show it to me?"

"You saw it, Niki, but didn't remember it consciously because you were frightened and angry. I merely calmed you a little. One needs only a little help to retrieve it. It is one of my skills. Everything we perceive is stored in our brains, daaarling. One simply needs to access it. Hypnosis can work well. Or, in this instance, my power."

I'd read stuff about hidden memories—but weren't they supposed to be unreliable? Ad'Rian shook his head at me almost imperceptibly.

"No, Niki. Even as a child, you knew not to take Dai seriously, and it seems you still don't trust him. These memories aren't hidden, or you couldn't share them with me. You were focused on other things while Dai was attempting to manipulate you. You were not using your other eyes."

Now he sounded like the teacher he'd always been to my younger self as he continued, "He was blocking you with those shields. So much stone is in extremely poor taste. But why didn't you simply use the power to overcome his shields?"

Why hadn't I? Because it felt rude and invasive. "Because it would have been abusive. People have a right to some privacy in their own minds, don't they?"

Ad'Rian looked me over carefully. "I'm wondering if this is one of those generational things? All these rights you young people are determined everyone is entitled to? Yes, as an individual, of course they have rights. But not if they're holding things back from the Recorder."

I sighed. "I'm still struggling with the role thing. You're right. If I consider the Recorder as a kind of librarian, it's easier."

"Well, daaarling, of course. Librarians are not an authority to trifle with."

"I was so dumb. He nearly hurt Tilly, and I didn't even sense it!"

Ad'Rian corrected me immediately, "He was not attempting to hurt her, simply keeping her docile so he could focus on you. You wouldn't transport away without her. Accept my word on this. The little one took no harm from it. Perhaps fleeting thirst, but no harm, especially now I've removed the remnants of the power he used. See for yourself."

But tears sprang to my eyes anyway. Tilly was my weak spot, and Dai knew it. Rollo and Ad'Rian both began soothing me. They met in the middle of my mind. It was a most peculiar sensation.

Ad'Rian sent *Apologies, nephew, I didn't realise. I thought it must be more of a business arrangement. A Recorder matter. Where are you right now? Ah, Edinburgh. Well, it could be worse. Your mother would have encouraged you to come to me if you have need or wish counsel.*

Smoothly, Ad'Rian moved his focus back to me.

"Don't take on the guilt. Dai was not trying to hurt your little one, only to control her. And I think control you through her. But before you flagellate yourself, please consider I was so occupied trying to heal him without losing him that even I didn't observe subtle signs I should have noticed. We did almost lose him, you know? And he was trying to go. Only the volume of power I was able to pull from all my other healers saved him. I was so focused on saving a life, I didn't check the rest of him thoroughly enough."

For once, I raised an eyebrow at Ad'Rian. In answer to my unspoken question, he said, "I'm only sharing with you part of the lesson I'm giving myself. He's one of my oldest friend's children, but it shouldn't have prevented me from checking him much more thoroughly. I may have erred both in releasing him and in not realising the danger he might pose to others."

At my astonished look at the idea of Ad'Rian making a mistake, he paused, laughed and said, "Daaarling, great age and experience do not preclude errors. But Dai simply didn't want to stay here any longer. Only in rare and specific circumstances can we hold a patient against their will. We had to let him leave."

Dai had always reminded me of his father, and yet it seemed he was nothing like him. How had I, with the power and the McKnight Gift, been so easily confused and fooled?

In an effort to make sense of it, I asked, "What *is* the red power he was using? Dai always felt a lot like Mabon to me. I trust Boney implicitly. Is that a part of how Dai fooled me?"

"Nik-a-lula, I fear I must decline to answer you right now until we can include Mabon in our conversation. He made a mutton-headed decision, and I should give him the opportunity to tell you about it himself."

Between Mabon thinking Dai should tell me things himself, and now Ad'Rian saying Mabon should, this seemed to be the week when everyone thought everyone else had the right to own their own mistakes. I'd only wanted some answers.

But I could wait now he'd reassured me Tilly was unharmed. Except ... "Are you talking about how he divided the dragon power between Rhiannon and Dai? Because Boney already told me about it."

Ad'Rian's eyebrow actually rose in surprise. "He did? Well then, there is indeed hope he will finally do the right thing, Nik-a-lula."

THIRTY-SIX

Home again, in my still-wonderful and comforting bedroom, I put my jammies on. I needed a hug, but my softest pyjamas would have to do instead. The fact they were my Just Be You ones and made me feel closer to Rollo was completely coincidental. But, oh, what a luscious sight he'd been yesterday holding me in front of the mirror so ver—

Still doing it. You must be home from Ad'Rian's, if you're sending the nice thoughts my way again.

I giggled. Gods and Goddesses, don't let me become a woman who giggles. I'd be squealing next.

Don't see the problem myself, in the right circumstances, obviously. If I transported to you, would I end up in Viking by mistake again? If not, we might gather empirical evidence on whether squealing would really be so bad.

459

The visual that accompanied his light tone was distracting.

I wish you could. I'm pretty sure it would be safe as long as you remember to focus on exactly where you're going and only there. But, sadly, my evening is going to be a lot less fun. I need to do some research, and tomorrow I'm almost sure I'll need to go and lasso Rhiannon once we've processed the data and I've consulted the Book.

Part of my head knew everything I'd said was sensible, responsible, and true. But there was another part of me that very much wanted to sleep in Rollo's arms.

I sighed. Ours wasn't that kind of relationship. We were just … what the hell were we?

Rollo sent, *Rather you than me. I sent you an email about your bandwidth thief on the network. I might know how she's doing it. It might fix two problems with one sword. Shall we speak later? Why don't I transport down? We both need to sleep. Why not do it together?*

It turned out kissing someone in your head didn't quite work. But we gave it our best shot.

"Hey, Dola, is the kitchen empty? I'm in a foul mood, and I don't want to meet Finn and upset him."

"We are alone. Finn is still out. He messaged me earlier to say he will be late. He knows I worry."

I frowned. "Why does he think you worry?" She

could track his movements to about a square foot. She knew exactly where he was at all times, as she did with me and anyone else on her network.

"That is psychology, Niki."

"It is?"

"Yes."

"Explain please."

I swear she sighed. "If Finn messages to report in to me, he has an illusion of privacy. So he doesn't have to consider I am always aware of his movements and what he is doing at any moment. And currently he is not running a role-playing game. He is in Tegan's quarters but we do not have to acknowledge it. The psychology text books inform me young men of his age need their independence and privacy. Or at least the illusion of it."

A laugh burst out of me. She was a better parent to Finn than Mabon had been to Dai, wasn't she?

"Do we have anything urgent on the schedule tonight or tomorrow morning?"

"No. At lunchtime tomorrow, the Red Celts have invited the Recorder to the official St. David's Day ceremony. We are free until then."

"As I've had a tough day, can I have a portion of chicken for Tilly, a glass of wine for me and an hour of your time?"

Confusion filled her electronic voice. "Niki, you have all of my time. I am your Equerry."

"Well, I'd like you to be my friend for an hour, please."

"OK. Shall I call Aysha?"

"NO!"

I sighed and tried to unearth the thinking part of my brain from the depths of my muddled emotions.

I missed Aysha, but like any pair of close friends, I knew her too well. She was an Aries, and the best part of that was she always had an opinion, and she was almost always fun. If the question was "Who's up for doing shots and dancing until we drop?" Even in our forties, the answer would be, "Line them up, and let's move those hips."

But if the question was, "Hey, Shay, have you noticed I've changed a lot? I have new priorities and a whole new sense of self-worth?"

Her answer would be, "I'm glad for you. But it's only been a few weeks, let's not jump to premature conclusions. You were depressed for a long time. Shall we see how you feel in another few months?"

We hadn't seen each other enough since I moved up to Scotland. It would take her at least a week of my almost undiluted company to fully grasp how much I already knew I'd changed. I'd need to find that week because I couldn't afford to lose Aysha. She was one of my rocks, possibly my actual foundation. But right now, I didn't have a week to show her the changes in me. So Dola might be able to stand in for her.

"I mean no, thank you. She's part of the problem. I'd like to talk stuff through with *you*. I'd like you to do what you do best, which is listen to and evaluate the evidence and tell me if I'm going crazy or simply being paranoid. But if what I think is happening, *is* happening, I need to know how the hell am I the only one working it out? The kings have had decades to see Dai was behaving oddly. Why didn't they?"

"I have some ideas. Why not tell me the rest of it, and we will plan?"

"Yes, please. Listen, apply your psychology and PR studies, your life experience and everything you learned while tracking Dai for Mabon. I'm not asking you to break confidentiality, or trespass on Mabon's connection with you, but factor in your own knowledge and tell the Recorder what you come up with."

I paused and tried to find words to describe the feeling my Gift had been giving me since I first landed at Dai's before he even opened the door. "He keeps saying he has no say in his future, but Ad'Rian showed me Dai's using this red power to control people. I'm not certain whether it didn't work on me because I'm the Recorder and the power protected me, because I have the McKnight Gift, or simply because he isn't using it for the right thing."

I stopped talking and tried to find a better way to

explain my feeling. Did you ever have an inner certainty, but the more you attempted to explain it, the crazier you sounded?

"Sorry, Dola, I'm probably not making any sense. Serpents are deceit. I'm considering whether Dai might have been fooling everyone. Is that why no one noticed his odd behaviour? Is it some kind of PR strategy? All I have is intuition, so I'm looking for facts or proof. Do you remember at the Knight's lunch when we showed them your message to the Vikings about the MMA match?"

"Yes, they laughed."

"I don't suppose you made recordings back then, but can you recall what Dai said? Wasn't it something about he needed to improve his image?"

"One moment. I am bringing the file back from offsite storage."

Offsite storage? What the heck? Nope, I had too much on my mind to investigate this right now. I probably didn't pay her enough, though.

I waited.

Dola said, "Here are the reactions to the announcement of the restrictions I placed on the Viking's network access."

Through the Dolina, I heard Mabon say, "Oh, *bach,* that's priceless. Priceless it is."

Dai's voice broke in, "Niki, could she fit me in as

a side hustle, d'you think? I could use some Dola-style PR."

Finn, sounding much younger, even though it was barely a month ago, said, "I'm gonna learn so much from you, Dola. I know how I coulda done it. But I wouldn't have dared."

Caitlin, the humour obvious in her voice, was next. "Dola, I love it. But for future reference, I prefer the term 'the Albidosi heir apparent.' It makes me sound less girly. Princess makes me think of Disney movies, and I don't have the waistline for that."

Dola broke in, "That is all, Niki. The conversation moved to other matters after Caitlin's comment."

"And did Dai ever approach you about doing some PR for him?"

"No. He never speaks to me and does not trust me. However, his internet access shows he has been researching it. I flagged it because of my own studies. He focuses on areas around brand, reputation and changing consumer perceptions of your image. His computer skills are extremely limited." The contempt in her voice made me smile. "He does not understand nothing on the Rainbow Network can be hidden from us. He signed the agreement without reading it. But he was still in his teenager persona at that time, so I didn't challenge him."

She was probably right about his lack of tech skills. I

kept recalling how he'd emailed me via the Recorder's Office and been angry when Dola read it. Suddenly, what she'd just said stopped me mid-thought.

So Dai had spent more than a hundred years of his life appearing to be the teenage boy I'd played backgammon with in the Gateway. It was a bizarre choice, wasn't it? Did it explain the distance I'd always sensed between him and the other men at the table? During the meal with the potential Knight Adjutants, I'd thought it was an age thing, but, in reality, he was much closer to L'eon's age than to Caitlin's, and yet he'd seemed more relaxed with her than with any of the men.

It was freaking peculiar, and I should look into why Dai made the choice to appear as a child for so long. But right now, I had other decisions to make.

Then I remembered Rollo and his use of a glamour so Troels wouldn't consider him mature enough to pose any threat to the Viking throne. Had Dai done the same? But with the far greater ap Modron power, he'd been able to choose his own age. Had he chosen an age where people wouldn't expect him to embrace his dragon side, so he bought himself time?

Then I finally processed what Dola had said. "Dola, can you play it again please?"

She did, and, as I listened, I heard she was right. Unlike the rest of us, Dai never addressed Dola directly. Mabon chatted to her all the time, and Ad'Rian loved his Dolina. But Dai had asked *me* if Dola could fit him in, as though she wasn't an individual with her own self-determination and power.

I wasn't sure what it meant though, so I tucked it away to think about another time.

I refocused on my own problems.

"Aysha can't help me tonight. I messaged and told her I was fine, but she won't be able to get past who I used to be with Nick. But I'm not the same woman anymore."

Rollo and I standing in front of the mirror in his bedroom flashed into my mind.

Until he'd asked me to show him who I used to be, I'd been unaware how huge and all-encompassing the changes had been. I'd thought the circumstances of my life had changed. But, yesterday, Rollo's mirror hit me around the head with a metaphorical brick and forced me to see how much *I'd* changed in the last month.

I summed this up for Dola and concluded, "At least Aysha won't be able to do it quickly enough, and my Gift keeps telling me I'm running out of time here. I bought us until tomorrow, and I don't think Dai will do anything drastic before then. So let's get to work."

THIRTY-SEVEN

An hour later, I'd given Dola all the information I could think of about everything that had happened since Aysha threatened me on Wednesday when I didn't want to visit Dai. Well, at least everything that wasn't private, adult time and none of her business. She'd missed quite a few things she needed to know between my time travelling and being out of reach.

When I got to the end, I asked, "What do you think?"

Dola said, "I think you should consult the Book, and I'll consult the data. We should regroup in thirty minutes. Niki, you fed Tilly, but you haven't eaten. What may I get for you?"

"I'm stressed right now, Dola. Maybe later, thanks."

I collected the Book from the worktop and wondered if I could take a shortcut. "What do I need to know to help Rhiannon ap Modron?"

A page appeared. I scanned it swiftly. "Under what exact circumstances did Agnes allow you to show this page?"

The Book flicked one page, and I read, **Anyone asking about Rhiannon with the sole intention of helping her.**

"OK, and how many times have you shown this page to other Recorders?"

Nothing happened.

I tried, "Have you shown it to anyone?"

The Book remained quiescent.

"And would it be because my ancestors weren't trying to help her, or because they never asked?"

It flicked one page, and I read, **Since the 7th Recorder's demise, your ancestors have either been terrified of the Queen of the Red Dragons or disliked her intensely.**

Yes, I knew it!

"If she's already the Queen of the Dragons, why do they need a Dragon King as well?"

History. Habit. False beliefs. Mabon ap Modron and his overwhelming commitment to being fair and dividing things equally. His prior error in dividing the dragons' regnal power.

Well, that was almost what Mabon had told me. I

snapped a photo. "If I ask you later, will you be able to show Rhiannon these pages? How about Mabon?"

If you restrict yourself to these questions only, yes.

"Then, before I round them up tomorrow, I have a question about Agnes."

This had been niggling at me since my dream about it last week. I kept intending to ask the Book and then forgetting. Watching HRH in the Gateway cleaning Rollo's yellow power had reminded me again.

Quite how I expected the Book to be able to answer this, I wasn't sure. But I saw no harm in asking it. "I had a dream. Does the cat who accompanied Agnes in the Gateway have any relation to or connection with HRH?"

It opened to a page with only two lines. **Prove you know her. Reveal my contents with one of her lesser-known names. You have two chances.**

Goddess, Agnes had been paranoid too. I suppose it didn't mean they weren't out to get her though, did it? I mean, they got to her in the end, with a load of rocks, if the stories were true, hadn't they?

She meant the cat, right? Lesser-known names? So not Great One or HRH. Lots of people seemed to call her that. Not kitty cat. Both Autumn and I had called her that. Dola knew her real name, but I doubted she'd say it if I just asked her. Why *did* she hate HRH so much? Someone losing their shit once in hundreds of years, even if it created the need for building work, didn't feel like enough of a reason for a centuries-long feud. Although, thinking about the Hobs and my ancestors' refusal to bond any of them for centuries, maybe a good reason wasn't required?

I focused back on the Book. There was one name I'd only ever heard Gran use. "Cuddles."

That is a partially correct but incomplete title. You still have two chances.

OK. Well, I didn't know any more of it. Cuddles was all I had.

Oh!

The other day when HRH had been muttering about Troels while fighting to purify the toxic yellow power, she'd said, 'Or my name's not ...'

I offered the Book, "The Mistress of Dread."'

A page appeared. Well, hell, who knew?

If you are her friend, feed her all the spare power you can, whenever you can. When you have proved yourself, she will give you the answer to the next question.

Well, I'd been doing that for weeks. I'd done it even as a child when I used to brush her with my hand coated in power.

I waited.

Nothing happened.

"What's the next question?"

Excruciatingly slowly, as though the Book was extruding the letters with care, the words appeared. **"What is her favourite food?"**

Hang on, it couldn't be so easy, surely? It said HRH would give me the answer.

She didn't give me the answer. I'd known it my whole life. I'd fed her that breakfast when I was a child too and even in my first week living here. We'd discussed it only the other day.

Were the Book, the cat and some long-dead Recorder all ganging up together to set me up? Was her favourite something different centuries ago? But what did I have to lose? Only a blank page, I guessed.

"Smashed eggs and far too much salmon." Shit, should I have said scrambled eggs—I mean I wasn't a child anymore, was I? And did they even eat salmon back then? Wasn't it all mutton and pearl barley and soup?

Danake?

My head swam. Why would the Book call me Danake? It usually called me Recorder. In fact, wait a damn minute. Hadn't *I* had to tell *it* my full name was Danake when it had refused to tell me more about the coin and key prophecy?

"Erm, yeah, sort of, sometimes."

I waited. Nothing happened.

I tried again, "Well, I was once, I suppose. I might

be again in the right company." I didn't mind being Rollo's *nakegirl*. Oh, Niki, get a grip on yourself.

About damn time. Help Rhiannon; come back. We will talk.

I gazed blindly at the Book and closed my open mouth with a snap.

This couldn't actually be Agnes. She must have pre-programmed it because this was definitely one of her secret pages. What had Mabon prodded me to do on Thursday? I'd been a bit off my game and still shaken after I'd finally decided I wouldn't allow Dai to lock me in his house. Mabon had said something about *have you asked the Book if Agnes left any messages for you?* I'd laughed it off, hadn't I? I'd thought the woman's been dead for almost four hundred years. How could she possibly have left a message for me? But could he be right? He'd told me to think about it, hadn't he?

Before I could panic any more, I swallowed hard, cleared my suddenly nervous throat and offered the Book the problem I had with its advice. "Rhiannon doesn't like me."

Rhiannon doesn't like anyone, but she does love deeply and never breaks a promise. NOT her word. Her word is like pottery, friable and easily broken.

But a promise, you may trust.

I was completely unconvinced. I couldn't think of any way I could get Rhiannon to even listen to me, never mind offer me any promises. I suggested all this to the Book. More words appeared.

Only after you've tried everything you know, and everything you can think of, if you fail:

Tell her, "Dragons can fly because they take themselves lightly. The angels just stole all the best lines."

TRY not to use it unwisely because I only have two of these pass phrases, and it would be much better to build your own friendship with her.

But you must help her before it's too late. The Red Celt realm may fall without the power of the dragon queens. Mabon is ofttimes a dodipoll.

I snapped a photo just in time before the whole page cleared, as if it had never been there. I checked the photo. Yes, I had it. Phew.

I started shaking, whether from nerves or excitement, I wasn't sure.

That had been surreal.

It looked as though the book had updated most of the language for me, but it didn't have an equivalent word. I could guess from the context, but— "Dola, are you familiar with the word 'dodipoll'?"

A chuckle came from the Dolina, then she said, "It was a good word. I should reintroduce the internet to it."

"But what does it mean?"

"My apologies, Niki. It was replaced by 'nincompoop,' but in the current times, 'dickhead' would be a reasonable substitute. Where did you come across it?"

"In the Book."

My laptop landed gently on the kitchen table. Once I'd stopped shaking, I opened it, and Dola sent a beautiful rainbow-coloured chart and some circles to my screen. She'd extracted the data about the Red Celts from the poll she'd conducted on the livestream during the gaps between the bondings. Now she'd added the results of her larger survey.

I analysed it. OK, Mabon's subjects almost universally loved and respected their king—only to be expected. Rhiannon's numbers were on the floor. Seriously, they were almost into the negative. I clicked the "more info: link. Ah, the question had been, "Do you like her?"

Yeah, no one liked her. But the next question gave the highest positive of all the Red Celt questions at ninety-nine percent. I clicked it and laughed.

"Does she do what she says she will?" There were dozens of notes in the "Would you like to add a further comment?" window.

I tapped, scrolled and laughed, tapped some more, scrolled and almost choked at one respondent's report.

Rhiannon ap Modron ALWAYS did what she promised she would. Whether you wanted her to or not.

In fact, even if you *begged* her on your knees not to.

Even if you'd believed she couldn't pull your tongue out and force you to write, "I will learn to hold my vicious, lying, gossiping tongue" fifty times with it.

If Rhiannon said it would happen, it did. She made no idle threats and no false promises. It just happened. As the Book had told me, her promise could be trusted.

Dai's data was almost the reverse. He was popular enough, but under, "Does he do what he says he will?" the numbers were in the low thirties. Sometimes he did. Often he didn't. Huh! The comments suggested forgetfulness and an urge to please without being able to deliver on his ideas. Some of it might have been my gran restricting the flow of trade with her one-in, one-out rule. Dai had bitched about that, hadn't he?

A few minutes later, I said, "I'm up to speed. Do you have any thoughts about everything I told you, along with everything else you know?"

"I think I have something better than thoughts, Niki. I have data."

I thought about Rollo's words about data being

better than a dowry between geeks. He was right, wasn't he? We loved the proof.

Still doing it, Boo. Also, more seriously, I emailed you to your private email. I didn't think you'd want the staff to see it—but you may need to share it with Dola. I think she's looking at the same things I am.

Of course, his background in informatics could be invaluable here. I opened my email, read his, whistled in surprise, and forwarded it to Dola's private email with a note that said *For Your Eyes Only.* I waited, expecting a snarky comment about the eyes she didn't have, but nothing happened.

Even the beginning of it sent shivers down my back.

It began, "The times Dai ap Modron has lied to me, my realm or my friends. Caitlin may have more examples, but I'm not sure if she'll recall them."

The list was pretty extensive. It included simple things like trade deals that never went through, broken promises and lies Dai had told and Rollo only discovered the truth later. None of them had been important enough to make a fuss over. Rollo had simply tagged Dai as mostly unreliable and moved on.

But there were two things that disturbed me. Or, rather, two parts of the same thing worried me.

Dai had promised Rollo's countryman and friend Kaiden sanctuary with the Red Celts if he needed it.

This had been when the Vikings were in the process of judging him for being in love with L'eon. But when the time came, Dai said it would endanger Red's trade deals with Viking. He'd backed out of it, and that was how Ad'Rian had come to offer Kaiden sanctuary in Fae.

Afterwards, L'eon had told Rollo, when he'd asked Mabon, the king said he knew nothing about it. Dai hadn't ever discussed it with his father.

Which was odd because Mabon's consent would have been necessary for the offer of sanctuary to be valid. I'd learned that much when I'd researched the sanctuary rules when Kari Halvor claimed it from the Recorder. Otherwise, any random citizen could extend an offer, which might create a war between realms.

So, Dai had not only lied; he hadn't even asked his father before he made the offer to Kaiden. Given the options the Vikings had on the table for Kaiden were excommunication or execution, that was dangerously negligent of Dai.

The last example in Rollo's email was confusing and involved my own Knight. I started to read it, shook my head, and when I got to the part that said, "I'll explain it properly when you don't feel so busy, but I think this is another instance of Dai being dishonest."

I gave up trying to disentangle all his comments

about, "I'm bound by confidentiality, and I can't break a promise, but you seem to know some of this, and I think I should at least give you enough of a clue to speak to Cait again."

It would be easier to talk to him about it. It didn't sound urgent right now, and I needed to make a decision about Dai.

"Dola, can you summarise where we're up to?"

"In summary, I can validate Dai often behaves stupidly. Regrettably, he does not think before he offers promises he cannot later keep, and he is unreliable. I might even say some of his actions make him appear weak, but I cannot find any evidence Dai is a bad person. Although there is considerable evidence he has done some bad or at the very least ill-thought-out things."

I thought, yes, like trying to hold the Recorder hostage. Was it simply bad luck Dai was being a controlling little shit while Troels was planning to send lumberjacks to chop the yellow gate down?

I was probably being paranoid. Coincidences did happen. That was what made them coincidences, right?

Dola continued, "I have enough data to suggest he requires further consultation with and healing from the Fae. Through Ad'Rian's Dolina, I overheard some confidential conversations between him and his healers. We should inform the king of the extent of the problem we suspect, Niki."

"I've already done that. If everything I showed him wasn't enough, I don't know what would be."

Silence from Dola, then, "I did not hear you share information with Ad'Rian during your visit?"

Of course we'd done a mind link. She wouldn't have heard most of it. I filled in the gaps for her.

"Ah, it may explain why he has summoned his current visitors. Then I think you have done everything you need to for now."

"So, in conclusion, Dola, are we agreed Dai needs to go back to the Fae healers?"

"Yes, and Ad'Rian and his senior healers are about to let Mabon know that."

I'd better go to bed. I needed to make an early start tomorrow if I was to speak to Mabon and Rhiannon before I dealt with Dai and attended whatever this St. David's Day ceremony that required the Recorder was.

A final thought struck me. "Dola, you speak Welsh. What does *Eiddof Fi* mean?"

"You may not be pronouncing that correctly. Please write it down."

Instead, I sent her back the same screenshot she'd

sent to me of the working network I'd found at Dai's before Rhiannon left and it disappeared with her.

"Ah, yes, in that context, I would say it means, 'This Belongs to Me.' There is a more elegant way to say it, but I think she is playing with the Fi and wi-fi."

I'd wondered if it was something along those lines. "Do you think there is any way Rhiannon could use her dragon's own power the same way I use the Gateway power to create a sort of mobile hotspot for herself?"

But Dola disagreed. "If it could be done, surely all the Dragonkin could do it. And none of the others have."

"Oh well, it was worth a thought, thanks."

I went to bed and snuggled up in the dark with my dog snoring softly in my arms. She was showing no ill effects from whatever kind of hoodoo Dai had tried to use on her, and I chatted with Rollo. We talked about the game *Drengr*.

He'd obviously been checking out my game stats and strategy more thoroughly now he knew who I was. He told me he'd worked on the negotiation and hostage sections of the game, the areas I'd often done well in. I asked about the research he'd done for them.

After a while, he said, *You're not seriously thinking she might ...*

But my Gift and some of the answers in the Book were telling me Rhiannon really might try it. If I'd thought it would work, I might have let her. But I was certain it wouldn't, so I needed a better plan.

There was a burst of yellow power, followed by, "Streth, it's dark!"

"Dola, lights on ten percent please."

"Niki, I allowed Rollo through my shields because he was our guest until yesterday, and you were missing him. However, we will need a clear protocol for this in the future if it is likely to reoccur. There would have been an unfortunate splat if I hadn't been alert."

Rollo and I looked at each other and tried not to laugh.

Feeling like a teenager who'd just been caught with a boy climbing up the trellis to her bedroom, I offered, "I am sorry, Dola. Rollo and I will discuss it and get back to you with a policy."

Rollo said, "A splat, hey? I didn't think this romantic gesture through at all, did I? I only came because you really wanted a hug earlier, and I could use one myself."

We snuggled into bed together, and I instantly felt better. Which disturbed the *I'm an independent woman* view of myself I'd been trying to cultivate since I arrived up here.

Rollo hugged me. "I'll find a particularly tricky jar for you to open tomorrow to restore your superiority."

I laughed, but now I felt safe and warm, I couldn't prevent myself falling asleep. Although if I'd known how early my day would start, I might have stayed awake and made better plans.

PART SIX
MONDAY

We all have moments of epic failure when our wings tangle or are damaged by an enemy.

Rise from any embarrassment and pain like the magnificent beast you are, and set the world ablaze with your splendour.

Never forget we always fly higher after a tumble.

Finding your Inner Fire: How to Claim your True Self by Peggy Hwybon

THIRTY-EIGHT

M onday, *1st March, St. David's Day—Abominable O'clock*

"Niki, I apologise for waking you, but Rhiannon is at the red gate and requesting the Recorder with some urgency."

"What time is it? Coffee, please."

Coffee arrived in a bright orange mug with a sunrise graphic. It said, *The hour before dawn is only the darkest if you are awake to see it. Why not sleep through it?*

"Damn fine splendid idea," I muttered.

As I sipped my coffee, my brain came online. "Is Mabon alright?"

"Rhiannon did not suggest otherwise."

"What *did* she say?"

"She shouted into the Gateway and requested the Recorder's urgent appearance. She said please."

"Please, hey? Wow." My insane idea last night that she planned to kidnap me might not be so mad after all.

I staggered through to the bathroom, and on my way past the mirror, I glanced at the Gateway feed. A dragon's head poked through the red gate again. There was smoke. It looked nervous. "Shit."

I checked my watch and took a leisurely thirty minutes to make myself look respectable. Drank another cup of coffee and dressed in my warmest thermals—I was going to need them if I was right. Tilly snored softly on my bed, cuddled into Rollo's warmth. He gave me a devastating sleepy smile. "Am I in the way? I can go home."

"Home?"

"Back to Edinburgh, I meant. It's always been home in my mind."

"No, you're not in the way. It's lovely to have you here. I'll be back before you know it. I need to deal with a dragon who thinks she's cunning, but I think she's simply desperate."

I bent and nuzzled his neck, needing his fresh seashore scent in my nostrils to help me get through the shitshow I was now certain Rhiannon had planned. I had to talk her out of her stupid plan before Mabon found out about it.

I gave Rollo a chaste peck on his stubble. I couldn't allow him to distract me, but his sleepy, murmured, "Miss you already," did just that.

Let's find out what ridiculous story Rhiannon had dreamt up to tell me.

I gave Dola a bunch of instructions and concluded, "I'm going to transport from here. Hopefully Tilly will sleep through it and think I'm just showering. She didn't like the dragon the other day, and I don't need one more thing to worry about while I try to negotiate with Rhiannon."

I checked the photo of the page in the Book one last time. Then, holding two travel cups of coffee—one of them contained a vanilla latte, and Dola had etched it with the phrase I'd requested—I time-travelled and transported straight to the red gateway five minutes after Rhiannon's original request for the Recorder.

I strolled straight through the red gate and out past the dragon's neck into the lane in Pant y Wern.

Still creepy.

"Good morning, Rhiannon, vanilla latte? I've no idea how I'm supposed to get it all the way up there, though."

Rhiannon sat in her half dragon form again a long way above my head. Unusually, there were no coos around at this end of the town. Maybe it was too early for them, or perhaps they knew better than to hassle a dragon.

"Good morning, Recorder, you were quick. I didn't know you were an early riser. Hold the coffee steady, please." A tail with spikes on the end wrapped itself around my waist and suspended me far too high in the air behind Rhiannon, just above the dragon's back. This damn job seemed to find new ways to have me in mid-air on a daily basis.

The tail lowered me gently onto a spot near the shoulders free of spines. It looked and felt like Dusha's back. I stopped panicking and reminded myself I'd wanted to ride a dragon—I could do this.

I reached forward to wave Rhiannon's coffee under her nose. She took it from me, and we were in the air before I could draw breath. The flight was so smooth, much smoother than the pegacorn's. With them, you felt the movement of the wings and the rippling of their muscles. This was more like being in a glider or a microlight. Only the air current caused any disturbance.

The area in front of me where the woman's hips met the dragon's lower neck was strange. The connection was seamless, as though her torso simply grew out of the dragon. I had so many questions, but I didn't think she'd answer them yet, so I drank my coffee.

"Thank you. I really wanted to ride with a dragon. It's quite different from the pegacorns."

She stiffened. The muscles under the sweatshirt tensed, and she sighed. "It only seems fair. I can't believe you played so perfectly onto my wings. I'd say I'm sorry, but I don't have a choice."

"It's fine. How's your coffee?" I drank my own.

She sipped it. "As excellent as the one the other day, much better than the pod thing at Dai's. You're very calm, Recorder."

Now, I sighed audibly. "Really, Your Majesty, we're back to that, are we? And I thought we'd made such progress the other day. Do I need to go back to insulting you by calling you Princess to get you to use my name? It only feels polite you should if you're kidnapping me."

The mountains below me stole my breath. The snow glistened in the last of the sparkling moonlight. In the distance, a rainbow curved by the rock arch. How the hell could there be a rainbow in the dark? My idea about that might be correct too. My coffee cooled quickly in the frigid air. I drank it down.

As I pondered the rainbow, Rhiannon twisted her coffee mug against the dwindling moonlight and frowned at the words on it. "What does this say?"

I was pretty sure she could read it. Dai's peripheral vision and night-sight were excellent. Of course, at the time I'd noticed that I didn't know why, because I was unaware of the dragon side of his heritage.

I ignored her question. "I'll work with you, Rhiannon. What Dai's doing is wrong. But your plan won't work because you've based it on a false premise. Well, on dozens of lies, deceits, and a metric ton of misinformation."

I drank my coffee. She'd catch up eventually. No one had ever suggested she was stupid, just difficult and anti-social. The fresh icy air blew the last of the sleep from my brain, and I revelled in the flight. This was glorious. I'd never felt such freedom before.

She swivelled around to look at my face.

Oh, it was most peculiar. I swallowed hard and tried to focus on her face. "Sorry, but that's bizarre."

She looked down at herself. "What?"

When she'd turned, she'd actually swivelled her entire torso so her front now faced me. It messed with my perception, like one of those images where you were supposed to see two things. I felt bilious. I focused instead on her sweatshirt. In large black letters, it said, *Everyone has me, but no one can lose me. What am I?*

Underneath, in tiny print, was, *Stop staring at my boobs and answer it.*

I smirked.

She said, "Well?"

"Oh, come on, what are you, the sphinx posing

riddles now? At least let's try a more interesting one. Anyway, it's not even true. It's easy to lose a shadow —at least it is if you live in Scotland. If there's no light, there's no damn shadow, is there?"

Rhiannon laughed. "You remind me of her. She adored flying too, and she could always make me laugh."

"You described her once as hell on wings, and I still didn't work it out. I'm catching up, but I'm no Agnes, not yet. The problem is, if you threaten to throw me off to make Dai change to save me—it's what you're thinking, isn't it?"

She nodded cautiously.

"He still won't change. Two reasons. One, your negotiation technique is flawed. You're thinking he cares about me. He doesn't. I think he just wanted the Recorder's power at his back."

"It's worth a try." But even she didn't look convinced about her own plan.

She must know her half-brother? Why would she believe he'd suddenly want to play the hero? He'd made it clear. He didn't like the dragons and didn't want to be one. "Has Dai ever done *anything* to make you think he gives two shits about other people's well-being?"

She tilted her head. The words on her sweatshirt had changed. They now said, *Dragons can fly because* …

495

OMG. She had read her coffee mug. It couldn't be coincidence. Coincidences like that were just for the worst kind of stupid movies.

I risked playing my ace or, more accurately, my best tarot card.

"I have a far superior plan to save your dragonets. One which will actually work. And it doesn't depend on your half-brother having any honour or any generosity of spirit."

She looked intrigued, but she wasn't biting. I considered those three tarot cards and laid my best one. People forget The Lovers can be a mutually beneficial business arrangement too. I considered her sweatshirt and went with my gut.

"I'm offering you a partnership to fix this problem. Agnes told you this day would come, didn't she? One of her prophecies, I expect?"

A tiny involuntary nod before she pokered up. "You'd say anything so I wouldn't throw you off a dragon, wouldn't you?"

"Rhi-Rhi, you're making me sad now. I thought you were brighter than Dai. I'm here by choice, and you know it. What the hell did Agnes see in you?"

She let out a peal of sincere belly laughter. I didn't know she had it in her. It gave me hope. I drank the last of my coffee and looked around the awe-inspiring mountains, a happy Recorder. There were worse ways to start a day.

"Rhiannon, you must realise I'm determinedly refusing to understand you're even considering dumping me off a dragon in midair? I can't allow you to threaten a Recorder. You know the penalty for that? Wasn't it you who had to find somewhere to dump the body of the last one who tried it? How the hell would poor Boney feel when he had to kill you? He's probably the only one who could. I have a better solution. Let's go somewhere quiet and, ideally, warm and talk about my far superior plan. I'm not built for this cold."

She nodded thoughtfully. "And if I agree?"

I smiled at her. "We'll fix this. I'll meet you in the Gateway."

And I transported back to the cottage. Her face as I left was a picture. The ap Modrons really needed to learn you can't hold a McKnight woman hostage, especially once her coffee has run out.

Back at my cottage, things moved swiftly. I used the thirty minutes I'd bought for myself. My Gift wanted me to ask Rollo to stay, but I had no idea why. Was I doing that stupid female thing? Oh, he's so pretty, he should stay. I'll be finished in a couple of hours, and we could have more private fun.

Grow up, Niki, you have a job to do.

I breathed and asked my Gift, did it want Rollo to stay? Oh hell yes, it did.

OK, but why?

I got a strange sense of the Albidosi family. All of them—Breanna, Caitlin, Finn and even Juna, the youngest sister, whom I'd only met a couple of times.

"Rollo, if you want to stay while I do this, you might help."

I sent him the pictures my Gift had given me, and he nodded. "Was that a breakfast buffet I picked up from your mind?"

"Yep, first thing I discovered in this role. Feed people, and they tend to be more amenable to whatever the power and I need."

He swung out of bed and wrapped me in a warm embrace. "Breakfast is the decider. Count me in. I've no appointments until this afternoon. Then I need to pick up some paperwork from Viking and spend a couple of hours in Edinburgh at the lawyers'. I plan to get as much use as I can from this yellow power while I have it."

"Lawyers, hey? Anything I need to know or just personal stuff? And don't forget you can retrieve things with the yellow power if you don't want to go there."

But he shook his head. "Not this. It's not in my home; it's at Inge's." I was about to tell him it shouldn't matter where the item was located. Provided it was his, the yellow power should be able to retrieve it, but he continued, "I need to see her anyway, and I have a theory I want to check past the lawyer. If it works out, I'll need to speak with the Recorder."

"OK. Is this Inge as in Troels' first wife? Import/export Inge who Fi likes?"

He nodded. "She was a kind of step-mum to me until I was almost eleven. She's still a friend."

He swatted me gently on the butt and kissed me. "I'll grab a shower and see you over there. I've missed the realms while Viking's been locked down. It'd be good to see everyone."

I'd asked Dola to wake Mabon and Caitlin and tell them both to get up and dressed because I'd be summoning them in twenty minutes. Dola was organising the small breakfast buffet for the conference table, and she was going to get Finn to work from his Foxhole this morning. I didn't need him stressed by Rhiannon's presence.

Tilly and I strolled through the lightening pre-dawn darkness to the Gateway so I could think and she could water things. She seemed normal. Ad'Rian said she was fine, but it had shaken me I hadn't noticed Dai trying to control her. What use was all this power if it couldn't protect the ones you loved?

The air smelt different today, damp and green.

Well, the damp seemed to be normal for Scotland, but the fresh green smell was new. Spring was on the way. There were snowdrops and some crocuses. Their colourful heads peeped cheerfully at me from the side of the path. They gave me confidence I'd get through this the same way as the earth got through winter every year. Because I didn't have a choice, did I?

As I entered the Gateway, Dola said, "Please summon Juniper. When I contacted her, she was making breakfast items to take through for St. David's Day for Mabon's cook, Dilys. She has enough extra for you and your guests. She won't even charge us if you don't mind summoning her staff too so she can get her food through to Pant y Wern in good time."

"Wow, you're a star, brilliant idea. If her food doesn't improve the atmosphere and calm everyone down, I don't know what will."

I dropped my shields, connected to the power, and shared my thoughts with it. It was showing me pictures of Rollo now. I checked our link. He was showering. The power was insistent. I told it he was coming.

"I summon Caitlin Albidosi, Juniper Hobb and her staff, Mabon and Rhiannon ap Modron." The gates at the end of the Red, Green and Blue sectors swung open, and three grumpy people and a happy dog arrived. Dru bounded over to Tilly and sniffed her carefully. He gave her several licks, and they settled under my desk in their usual spot. Something inside me finally relaxed. If there had been any remaining problem from Dai's actions last night, Dru wouldn't be so normal now.

Finally free to concentrate only on the events in front of me, I spoke before any of them could start whining, "I know, OK? But we all have a busy day, and the Recorder is certain we are running out of time to fix this before something goes horribly wrong. If you could keep the grumbling to the minimum so we can get on with it—that would be wonderful."

They all looked surprised, perhaps because, except for Rhiannon, I sounded more awake than they looked. They made their way quietly to the centre. Rhiannon glared at me the entire way down the Red sector, and as she reached the top, she muttered, "This is not a quiet chat in a warm environment. This is a flaming meeting. I was conned."

I ignored her and gestured everyone to the conference table.

Juniper arrived in the Green sector with one of her hostess trolleys, followed by an unusually long line of ducklings—Hobs laden, as always, to their noses with boxes.

"Thank you, milady. This is a great help." Juniper

handed over the hostess trolley and a small pile of green plates decorated with leeks and daffodils. Wishing everyone at the conference table, "*Dydd Gŵyl Dewi Hapus*," and throwing, "Do the little things," over her shoulder, she headed towards the Red sector. She was followed there by the same greeting from Mabon and Rhiannon, who'd both responded on autopilot. And a somewhat belated, "Happy St. David's Day to you too, Juniper," from Caitlin.

Dru and Tilly emerged from under my desk with their food-seeking noses in the air. Tilly shot straight under the conference table, ready to keep the floor clean if anyone dropped anything. Dru crawled in on his belly, but when I looked underneath, I could have sworn he'd got smaller. Huh.

Mabon and Rhiannon were deep into a private conversation as everyone loaded their plates. Mabon's had grown to the size of a tea tray to accommodate all the food he'd dumped on it.

By the time we'd all settled around the table the atmosphere had changed for the better.

"Boney, did you speak to Ad'Rian?"

He gestured his mouth was full and tapped at my mind. We connected, and he sent me a stream of information, including the angry bollocking his old friend had given him. Ad'Rian had been cross. In return, I sent him an update on my meeting with Dai yesterday and Ad'Rian's insights on how he was using the red power along with exactly what I thought might be going on with Dai.

While Mabon and I swapped information, Caitlin and Rhiannon were actually chatting away. I caught, "Oh, no, it's a whole new order in here," from Caitlin as they exchanged a furtive glance, the kind the kids in the back row sometimes shared behind the teacher's back. Oh well, whatever worked. Rhiannon was going to need allies, and Caitlin could be a strong one for her. I couldn't get past my intuition, which had been borne out by the data from Dola, that Rhiannon was lonely.

From Mabon, I got a strong feeling his guilt was impeding him from taking the right actions. He knew he should. He just couldn't bring himself to do it. His sense of fairness got him into this mess, and his innate sense of equality hindered him horribly from fixing it.

Rhiannon put down her cutlery. "Thank you, Recorder. I needed food. But as delicious as it was, I still have the problem of the dragonets."

I stared at Mabon. He nodded. "Fix this, the Recorder will. A fair woman, she is. Even as a child, never greedy or selfish was she. A bluddy nuisance, yes, often, and a little hellion sometimes, but not unfair."

They all laughed.

Then he stood and bowed to me. "Niki, we need to be quick. Back I must be in Pant y Wern for the joyless bastard's day."

I raised a brow. "Was he a joyless bastard?" I'd read up on St. David in the Book, and he certainly sounded a bit dour and humourless, but it was unlike Mabon to be rude about a man his people venerated.

"The man drank only bluddy water! And ate bread without butter or salt and lived on watery leek soup. Which is why Dilys makes watery leek soup every time she's cross with me. Lucky we were, an intelligent comrade of ours was there at his death and carried his 'verified' last words around the valleys. Could have been a lot worse than 'Do the little things,' don't you think?" He gave me a huge stage wink.

"Anyway, the little things in question today are a lady who's reached her century, hale hearty and fond of a beer at lunchtime, and a couple married for sixty-five years. Never a cross word, so they report, if you do the little things."

The disbelieving expression on his face was hilarious. "And they need their king to do the necessary this morning. Special we'll make them feel. So, if need me you do, then best to be quick. Be there for nine o'clock, I must."

I nodded. "I will need you, Boney. But we're in

the Gateway, so it doesn't matter if we take our time, does it?" The fact I needed to remind the man who'd first educated me about time moving more slowly in the Gateway worried me. He wasn't himself this morning.

I gave him a smile. "The Book says I can't do it without your authority. The power could do it, but it won't because it trusts your judgement. So let's get on with it. You OK if we bring Caitlin up to speed on all this?"

He nodded.

"KAIT, you asked about dragons the other day. Here's your quick overview. Rhiannon will help if I go astray." I paused and raised an eyebrow. She glared back at me. I wasn't forgiven yet.

I walked around the table and bent to her ear. "Dragons can fly because they take themselves lightly. I need you to get on board with this and stop fighting me, Rhi-Rhi. Your one chance to get my help is now. Right now."

She murmured, "If you know the rest of it, I'll get on the Recorder Train."

"I do. I need your promise on it."

"You have my word."

"Yeah, that won't do. I need your promise." Now, she glared into my eyes, her face stony. "Are you doubting my word, Recorder?"

"I am. It's friable apparently. Which I had to look up, by the way."

Because our gazes were locked, I saw not shock in her eyes but hope. Oh hell. I'd have to explain, the information was just from the Book.

In a quiet, hoarse voice, she said, "I promise, if you have a solution, ideally a fair one, but at least one that allows us to bond all the dragonets, I won't fight it."

"Oh, my solution isn't fair at all. It's much better than fair." She'd almost finished her coffee. Any moment, she'd be able to read the next part of the pass phrase I'd asked Dola to put at the bottom of her mug. "Finish your coffee, Rhi-Rhi."

One ap Modron down, two to go.

"Rhiannon, would you explain to Caitlin and me what the issue is, please?" I was almost certain I knew the whole of it, but if I was about to take such a drastic step, I wanted to be damn sure.

But Rhiannon was busy. She gaped into her now-empty coffee mug as it refilled itself. Then she shook herself, nodded at me and then turned out to be an almost Finn-quality summariser.

"Mabon," she nodded at him, "prides himself on being fair. You can't give to one without the other. I was born Queen of the Dragons, but while we waited for the King of Dragons to arrive, I got a quarter of the ap Modron regnal power. Our regnal power doesn't only rule people; it rules dragons too. When they're born, the dragonets need to be bonded to their future pack. It requires a ruler with regnal power, lots of it. I don't have enough to bond them all."

She shrugged, but her eyes were still haunted as they had been at Dai's house. "The unbonded ones go feral. Crazy. They attack and burn everything. They can't change into humans and usually can't even become a semi-dragon."

At Caitlin's confused look, she added, "Like I was this morning?" I nodded. Caitlin still looked unsure.

But Rhiannon was on a roll and pressed on. "We have to hunt them down and kill them. Just before death, they realise what happened and what they lost, and they cry while they die."

She shot her father a look of such fury, it took my breath away. Her eyes were almost black now, and his skin turned the colour of milk. "He can't do it. So guess who has to?"

Mabon gave her a sad, tired smile. "Can't it is, daughter, not won't. Try to remember that, hey? Without any dragon regnal power of my own, I can't do it. Help you, I would if I could."

With the bite of frustration still in her voice, she asked, "And what's Dai's excuse? He's draining the regnal power, and you know it."

At my raised hand she said, "What?"

"How is he draining it?" I asked.

She glared at me but answered, "When it's used correctly on the dragonets to bind them, they can grow up as a full member of the pack. They retain the power while they grow. But as they grow and mature, so does the power. And, at their maturity, it comes back much increased to the pack and the queen. It gives me yet more power to help the next clutches. It's alive; it grows once you use the whole of it. Dai is preventing that from happening."

She paused, took a sip of her fresh coffee, and swallowed harder than the sip warranted. Glaring at Mabon again, she said, "Dai won't use his half for the dragons. He uses it to make people like him and to get his own way."

Mabon opened his mouth, but now Rhiannon was like a train hurtling down a hill with an amateur on the brake. "Even when he uses it for the good of the realm, smoothing a trade deal doesn't return the power to the dragons; neither does making people like you. He's frittering it away. He's using the dragon part of the regnal power instead of getting Mabon to use the king part. The monarch's power is supposed to be for the benefit of the realm. But Dai wants everyone to think he's just naturally a great salesperson. So he won't ask Mabon for the help he should have in case the king makes him do something he doesn't want to in return."

She paused and seemed to run everything she'd said back through her mind before she added, "And he can't negotiate for shit. Making people promises you can't keep isn't negotiating."

Rhiannon snapped her mouth closed, then thought better of it and stuffed the last *crempogau* in.

I glanced at a still-pale, unhappy Mabon. "How long have you been considering taking it off him before he irretrievably reduces your own power too?"

"It's not so simple. Need my mother's help, I would. Use the power, Dai would, to stop us taking it from him. Rhi and I can't do it alone." He shook his head and nodded at Rhiannon.

She continued her earlier explanation, "The regnal power in our realm is designed to be half for the dragons. They're the backbone of the realm. Without the dragons, we would only be some celts, not the Red Celts." She nodded at me, obviously recalling our conversation yesterday. "They're our link to the goddess, to our heritage, to everything we were and are. And they're important for reasons we won't share with outsiders."

She gave her father a quick glance and received a firm head shake back. Huh? I wondered if the Book might know.

She continued more slowly, "The ruler of the dragons and the ruler of the realm should be a strong and equal partnership. Half the regnal power for us and half for the crown." She nodded at Mabon.

Looking directly at me, she said, "The only reason the king hasn't been overthrown is he has part of the ap Modron deity power in addition—well, and everyone likes him too."

Our own data bore that out, so I nodded at her.

"But I don't have other power, and I'm losing half of every clutch. It's a flaming mess. Dai doesn't have to step up. No one can or should make him. But if he won't, he can't have the power. It's to keep the dragons alive, not to close deals or sell coal scuttles."

She looked shocked she'd been so candid. But it was pretty much verbatim what I'd told Dai yesterday. He couldn't have his cake and eat it.

"Why am I telling you this? This is private realm business. How did you make me tell you?" She looked worried now, rather than angry.

I waved a soothing hand at her. "The power urges people to speak and share things that pertain to the problem unless they're truly private. I use it better than some of my predecessors because I like people, and I'm interested in what they have to say. Apparently, it was originally to assist the Recorder during arbitrations by encouraging people to be open with each other. Quite a few people have noticed it. Rollo mentioned it recently, so I asked the Book. It's a feature, not a bug."

Caitlin and Mabon looked confused, but Rhiannon laughed. Her understanding of a geek joke reminded me what I'd meant to offer. "What you're doing with the power to create a network isn't helping your power level, is it? I might be able to fix it for you if you'll let me on your back again."

"Well, Recooorder," she drawled the title, "there's a game you can play with dragons. It's called IF-you-can-land-on-my-back-I'll-take-you-wherever-you-need-to-go. One of your ancestors loved it."

Mabon laughed and was just saying, "Oh, she did. Won more than she lost too. Remember the time when—" as Rollo strolled in through the green door.

He brought the table to an abrupt silence.

THIRTY-NINE

Rollo helped himself to breakfast, settled at the conference table, grinned at Caitlin and gave Rhiannon an assessing but pleasant smile. "What did I miss?"

While Caitlin filled him in, I watched Mabon.

He was twitchy and glanced at his phone constantly. I sighed. He wasn't on board yet. Why not? The Book had told me I could just do this without him. But steamrolling over my friend and mentor felt wrong. He checked his phone yet again. So I messaged him.

> Niki: Boney, you're in the Gateway. It's not even dawn in Pant Y Wern yet. What's up with you? Relax and pay attention, please. We need you here.

> Mabon, King of the Red Realm:
> Sorry, bach. Feeling bad I am. You're
> right. It isn't fair on Rhi or the
> hatchlings the way it is.

> Niki: Or Dai. He needs healing.
> Ad'Rian can't heal him until he stops
> fighting him. Dai's using the dragon
> power to block Ad'Rian. He already
> told you this, didn't he?

> Mabon the Inadequate Father: He
> did. But I …

The bouncing dots continued, suggesting he was typing another message, but his hands were still. He gazed helplessly at his screen.

> Niki: What am I missing, Boney?
> How I can help?

Mabon put his phone down and looked straight at me. "You can't. In the old days, if a man was struggling, we had a few beers, a good meal, and sometimes a lady of his acquaintance volunteered to help send his blues on their way." He gave a small smile. "By morning, it looked brighter—usually. These modern mental health things confuse me. Feeling my age today, I am."

I leant over, gave him a hug and whispered, "Let's just get it done, and you can go and eat too much yummy food and have a few beers. Tomorrow, the joyless bastard's day will be over. Why don't we have a watch party with Ad'Rian later this week? I know a movie you'll love. It's got a frozen mountain, a woman with a goal, a cute snowman and some great songs."

He gave me his crooked grin, and things felt better. But I was wondering about all the crazy identifiers that showed up in his messages. I must speak to Dola about them. I'd thought she was doing it to help him learn how to use his phone. Now, I wasn't so sure.

I summarised my plan for everyone around the table.

Rhiannon was sceptical it would work. Caitlin nodded, and Mabon looked sad and tired. "Better than disturbing my mother. She's sleeping. Wake up for her cake on Mothering Sunday, she will. Best to manage without her until then if we can."

It was mostly up to the power and me then. Well, I was getting used to that.

"I summon Dai ap Modron to the centre of the Rainbow."

The power and I had agreed and thought we could do this. In the Red sector, we'd created a small area surrounded by a force-field. We used the template for the glass cages, but we'd constructed this one from pure power. We couldn't use one of the glass cages, which had worked so well in other situations, because we needed to strip the red dragon power from Dai. A glass cage would prevent us from drawing the power out.

If you squinted really hard, you could *just* see a faint outline of the power cage. But I was pretty confident Dai would be paying too much attention to his father in the centre as he sauntered into the cage.

Ad'Rian had made it clear the dragon regnal power must be removed, even if only temporarily, so Dai could be healed properly.

I wasn't totally happy about conning Dai. But Rhiannon needed the power. Dai didn't want to be a dragon, so he shouldn't have the dragon power. Most of all, he needed to be healed before he harmed himself or someone else. On that clichéd thought, I pinned a smile on my face and waited.

The gate opened, and Dai strolled through.

He looked better. At least his jeans and shirt were clean today, and his hair was still damp. He'd made it to the shower then. Perhaps Ad'Rian's healing was taking hold after all. But my Gift disagreed. It thought Dai was just putting a better face on things so his family wouldn't push him any further. But he had a smile on his face and started talking as he moved through the door, the same way Mabon often did.

"This is a pleasant surprise, Niki. Thank you. You've forgiven me, then?"

Then he saw his father behind me, and his face darkened. "Ah, no, it's work again, I see. I thought I was on the sick list, Da? One day off I had." He sounded very hard done by, and his voice didn't have its usual strength.

I pasted a sympathetic look on my face. Just walk another few feet, Dai.

I checked his shields. Yup, still like a rock wall.

Mabon said, "Sorry, *bachgen*, need something urgently I do, and you're the only one who can help."

Now Dai looked pleased and intrigued. I sealed the box of power behind him and held up a hand. "Just stand there, please, Dai."

He stood still.

Caitlin and Rhiannon came over from the conference table. As they rounded the new living willow screen, Dai noticed them and turned to me. "Is this the Rainbow group thing you kept talking about?"

I ground my teeth. Kept talking about? Wow, there was a Nick-ism. *The little woman goes on and on about something that will probably never happen, and I can't even be bothered to remember its name.*

As though he sensed he'd pissed me off, and because I watched closely with my other eyes, I saw the red power as he sent it towards me. Not a muscle twitched on Mabon's face, only his eyes slid to catch mine, and I knew he'd seen it too.

"Sorry, Nik, I've been with the healers, remember. My memory's not what it should be. The Rainbow Committee, was it?"

I said, "Council, the Rainbow Council." I felt petty but then saw he wasn't listening anyway. The whole time he talked, more red power streamed in my direction. But for now, the box was collecting and holding it. Caitlin walked over ahead of Rhiannon.

"Hey, Dai. Ya look rough." He gave her an amused half bow.

Now I thought back. He often did that around Caitlin, didn't he? There had been the time when he realised she'd amputated Svein's finger. He'd had the exact same half-smile on his face. I'd thought it was amused respect, but now I was using all my Gift and the power on him, I wasn't so sure.

I pulled more power. Dai watched it coat my left hand and walked towards me. Did I raise my hand too slowly, or was he just ignoring me?

I winced as his foot connected with the front of the box. It was half full with the red power. He gave his foot a confused look, reached out with his hand, frowned and faced his father. "Really, Da, more bluddy games? Don't I even get the chance to heal?"

He didn't seem to notice the red power. Did he even know he was using it?

The moment I thought it, Mabon leaned into me and, in a low voice, said, "Summon Ad'Rian? Still missing something, we are."

I didn't know why, but I wanted Glais'Nee too. "Mabon, you know who his mother is, even if he doesn't, right?"

"No. Not important, is it?"

At my look of astonishment, he said, "How would I? We talked about this. You don't have sex to make dragonkin. They can, but I can't. Supply the magic end of it is all I do. The magic chooses the best…" he paused before he sent me a picture of a circle containing dozens of dragonkin females and a single word, "candidate."

He added, "Then after the eggs are laid, everyone takes care of them. Males and females. A group thing, it is. Some sit on eggs; others leave to feed. Different, it is."

OK, I was both wiser and more confused. "So we don't know if his mother's genes might have caused these problems?"

I crossed to the anvil and placed the star on it. "I summon Ad'Rian, King of the Violet Fae, and Glais'Nee, honoured warrior, to the centre of the Rainbow."

Mabon nodded at me. "Not a part of his upbringing, his mother. Many helped though."

I wondered if the peculiar arrangement had

contributed to Dai's developmental problems.

In an undertone, I shared my concern, "Thing is, Boney, the force-field cage should be able to contain the regnal power until we're ready to remove it. But he's still strong enough to make us think he's innocent of any ill intent, and he's doing it all by accident. He's getting power through it towards us somehow. It worries me. I can make it a glass cage, but if I do, we won't be able to take the regnal power from him, and that's why we're here."

As the violet gate swung open, Mabon nodded at me and walked swiftly over to Ad'Rian. Their facial twitches told me they were mind-linked, and I guessed he was bringing Ad'Rian up to speed.

I headed to Glais'Nee. "I'm sorry to summon you so rudely, but we have a situation."

He bowed and gave me his beautiful smile. "I am always happy to assist the Recorder." His gaze raked around the Gateway, taking in the entire situation in one fast sweep of his eyes.

"Could you use your skill on Dafydd ap Modron please? His father can't help, and something unusual is happening. We'd like to know more about the ..." What had he called the female line when he gave me my own genetic history? Spear? No, I remembered the mnemonic I'd created for myself. The spear was pokey energy, so it was male. Oh yeah, that was it. "... distaff side of his heritage."

He moved towards the Red sector, and I watched his eyes turn the pure white of a Fae Master using his magic. Then he shook his head, as if trying to dislodge water from his ear, and covered the ground to Ad'Rian and Mabon with long, swift strides.

I decided to address my other concern while the senior kings conferred. They'd fill me in. I no longer thought they'd leave me out of decisions. Neither of them had broken their assurances to include me.

Caitlin stood at the end of the Red sector, her head on one side as she surveyed Dai. Could she see the red power? I'd ask her later, but she looked fine right now.

I crossed to the conference table, where Rhiannon and Rollo were finishing what must have been their second plates of food. I smiled to myself, not so much fiddling while Rome burnt as breakfasting while chaos ensued.

Rollo knew quite a bit about how the McKnight Gift worked. We'd talked about it several times. So to Rhiannon, I said, "Did Agnes ever share information about the McKnight Gift with you?"

She nodded.

"Well, mine is very unhappy right now about Caitlin. For some reason, I keep seeing her collapsed on the floor. It might not be now. Sometimes these things are in the future, and it's just a warning, but will you both keep an eye on her while I deal with him?" I gestured towards the cage of power and Dai.

Rollo nodded. Rhiannon raised an eyebrow. "Any more to work on, so I know what to keep my eye focused on?"

I breathed. Did I trust her? Not exactly, but she didn't mean Caitlin any harm. And if my nagging intuition and my unhappy stomach were right, Caitlin might need her assistance. I considered exactly what I'd given Caitlin my word on when I found her box. Yeah, I was in the clear. This was not an Albidosi secret, and it was now directly relevant to the Recorder's Office.

In barely more than a whisper, I told them both, "This is her private business, understood?" Rhiannon nodded. "But my Gift thinks it's connected somehow to this." I gestured at the Gateway and her half-brother.

"I do not gossip, Recorder." My right shoulder only half agreed with her until she added, "Well, only about certain TV shows with one colleague." Then my shoulder was fully onboard, and I hid my smile. Who would have thought Rhiannon liked trashy reality shows too? We might have more in common than I'd thought.

"Caitlin went to the Fae for healing." I brushed away the querying expression on her face. "I don't know what it was, something emotional and none of the Recorder's business. She pictures it as an iron-wrapped wooden casket. It's inside her aura and bound to two of her chakras." I rubbed my roiling stomach. "It feels unstable, like it might split wide open. Get ready to catch her?"

Rhiannon looked thoughtful. "You believe it's connected to this?"

I nodded unhappily. "Not for sure. But my Gift has been nagging about it for weeks. Now it's really whining." I rubbed my stomach again reflexively.

Rhiannon's gaze tightened on my hand as I rubbed my belly. "Flaming hells, whenever Agnes did that, havoc usually came to play. Yes, I'll watch her."

In my mind, Rollo said, *This is why you needed me to stay, right? You know I know about it?*

I guessed you were the one who took her to Fae.

I was. I hold the code phrase to release it. But she has to ask for it. Otherwise, I would be breaking my word.

He said the last in such a firm mental tone, I widened my eyes at him. *What if she's unconscious and dying? Because that's one of the options my Gift is showing me if this goes wrong.*

He stood up swiftly and crossed to Caitlin, drawing her away from the Red sector and spoke in a low voice.

Rhiannon drawled, "I'll just sit here in ignorance and catch her; don't mind me."

"Thanks for understanding, Rhiannon. I truly appreciate your help."

Her T-shirt changed to *Just call me a mushroom.*

I laughed. "But on the bright side, I'm only keeping you in the dark; I'm not feeding you shit. In fact, wait. Didn't I just deliberately *not* do that?"

She bit her lip to keep from laughing, but as I walked away, I heard one tiny snort of amusement follow me.

Mabon and the two Fae were still deep in a mind-link as I reached them. "Gentlemen, I'm ready for my briefing."

Ad'Rian scooped me into the link, and information flew at me. Dai was getting power through the box to us. Through Ad'Rian's eyes, it was perfectly clear. I gave them a precis of the McKnight Gift's worries about Caitlin. I had no idea what the connection was, but it niggled at me.

Mabon sent me a stream of pictures of Dai disappearing to the Pict realm repeatedly on "trade missions" for several months a couple of years ago. He didn't know any more about it.

When Glais'Nee shared what he'd learnt, I thought, well, I've freaking heard it all now!

Mabon was mostly Dai's father. How the hell could anyone be mostly someone's father? Fatherhood was a binary concept, wasn't it? You were or you weren't. Wasn't it like you couldn't be a little bit pregnant?

Apparently, the realms defied logic. Dai had two distinct spear energies. Two fathers? WTAF?

The majority came from Mabon, but there was another contributor too. According to Glais'Nee, those other genes also came from someone with deity powers!

Mabon was calm about it. Apparently with dragons, illogical and bizarre things were the norm.

I gave up.

On an easier-to-understand note, Dai's mother had simply been an average Red Celt dragon. He sent us all a mental picture of her. Glais'Nee told us he sensed the mother had hatched other dragonkin children before Dai but she'd since died. Mabon remembered several of them and said they hadn't been noticeably crazier than any other dragonkin. Which left only the mysterious other father or spear energy that might be contributing to the problem in front of us.

I asked what felt like the obvious question, "Do you know of anyone who carries dragon god energy?"

But Glais'Nee brushed my question aside. The other father wasn't a dragon god. In fact, his genes might explain how Dai had so successfully resisted the genetic and hormonal imperative to change into his dragon form. Glais'Nee wondered if the other energy might be one of the Sun Gods. There were Sun Gods? I mean, I'm not a complete idiot, I'd heard of Apollo and the Egyptian chap; Ra, was it? But the way Glais'Nee said "one of" made it sound as though there were dozens of them.

I gave up—I'd exceeded my limit of craziness for one day. I'd have to come back to this once we had the urgent stuff out of the way.

I sent the group my own feelings that, as fascinating as this all was, we needed to deal with the problem in front of us. Dai's dragon regnal energy needed removing until we were all sure he was truly healed and ready to step into his responsibilities. Once we had it out of him, Mabon should decide whether to take it back and hold it for Dai. Or he could give it to or even loan it to Rhiannon.

Ad'Rian sent me approval.

Glais'Nee simply nodded.

Mabon said, "And this is why we need the Recorder to keep us focused on today's problem. I have to be back in Pant y Wern soon."

I laid my plan out quickly to the mind-linked group. Everyone nodded. We broke the link.

Ad'Rian took out his phone and sent a message. He must have picked up my stray thought about why a man with such vast mental powers was using technology instead, because he said, "Unlike my old friend Mabon, I do not believe in using a Liverpool Hammer for all problems."

"For the sake of the Goddess Addie, it's a Birmingham Screwdriver. Never do you get these things right."

Ad'Rian just smiled. "People understand me, daaarling. Isn't understanding the goal rather than accuracy? My brain is always overflowing, as you well know."

I ignored them both and repeated, "Are we ready?"

It seemed, finally, that we were.

CHAPTER

FORTY

The plan was elegant in its simplicity. Mabon would give the Gateway his consent to remove the red dragon power from Dai. We would gather it back into the Gateway, send Dai off to the healers again to get the job done this time, and Mabon would make a decision about what to do with the dragon power.

Simple.

I felt pretty confident. Only days ago, we'd done a similar but much larger scale operation with Rollo. Dai only had a quarter of the regnal power. With Rollo, we'd had to gather *all* the regnal power from Viking and all the other realms, and we'd cleaned it, which had taken hours. Surely that must have been the bigger job?

I dropped my shields, held Mabon's hand and connected to the power to give it his consent. The minute my shields were down, the red power moved in on me. *Poor Dai, poor lonely, misunderstood Dai. Lovely Dai, who'd always been such a good friend to Niki.*

"Stop it, Dai. If you told me you were on fire, I wouldn't believe you until I saw the flames. Stale instant coffee, remember? The Gateway was under attack without the Recorder because you were too busy playing self-centred games, and don't get me started on what you tried to do to my dog." I realised I was being very unprofessional and stopped ranting, pulled power and batted away his nonsense.

Mabon offered his consent to the Gateway. I'd never noticed before what an easy connection he had to the power. It responded to his permission instantly, and soon there was a swirling red vortex forming above the centre. Dai shouted now, but, as most of it was in Welsh and aimed at his father, it was easy for me to tune him out.

Glais'Nee walked over to Rhiannon and Caitlin, and I glanced their way, but it all looked fine. The two women were just talking.

Rollo had one eye on Caitlin and one eye on the red power. As there had been with Rollo's power, there were some streams of dark red power coming in from the other realms and joining the small ball in the centre. But these were mere trickles compared to the large amounts of yellow power Troels had dispersed around the kingdoms on his sexual raids.

Mabon watched the streams too. "Not been wasteful with it, the boy. Rhiannon suspected he had. And good and bad it is. Have to spread it about, you do, but he was always a child who didn't like to share his toys. Never did he grasp the idea of getting back more than you give." He sighed.

But I was focused on the power. It looked odd. "Why is his power so dark? I always see yours as scarlet and white shot through with silver lightning?"

"It's the ap Modron power you usually see. From the Goddess my mother, it comes. A happy power it is, or at least a passionate one. A lot of laughter it's been a part of. The dragon power is the colour of, what do they call it now? The blood that's got no oxygen in it? Grubby purply-red colour?"

He gave me a look of complete confidence that I would work out what he was talking about. But I had no clue. His phone buzzed, and he glanced at his screen. "Yes, thank you, Dola."

Turning to me, he added, "She always did understand me. The ap Modron power is the colour of arterial blood: bright red. The dragon power is rarely happy. It's the colour of venous blood. Power adapts, *bach*. The colour shows you how it's been treated."

He gave the power a gloomy look. "Don't

remember it being so dark though. Work on that, I should. A bit more supportive to Rhiannon I might be."

I thought about how Troels' toxicity had leeched into the yellow power and how much power he seemed to have stolen from others. I scrutinised the dark red power and ran a colour wheel in my head.

Oh shit.

I requested the power to stop retrieving the regnal energy for a few minutes while we regrouped and checked stuff. It did. Then I sighed, when, as I'd half expected, I rose into the air.

As I hung in mid-air, I tried to explain to the power what I thought.

I'd been so big on everyone's right to privacy, but as Ad'Rian had told me firmly last night, sometimes the Recorder needed to trample on people's rights to ensure everyone else's safety and well-being. If I'd done that with Dai—we might not be in this damn mess.

The power and I sensed the dark red power together. Unlike the yellow power, it didn't feel tainted. But it didn't feel right either. It only partly felt like Mabon. It surrounded me, and instead of batting it away as I had with the toxic yellow power, I sank into it. Who or what else did it feel like?

Caitlin—which was weird but might explain my unhappy stomach. But there was more in there. I

tasted sweet, spicy bread. Whirly? Not him personally, but a similar energy perhaps? One that felt like
his and Twirly's had. Changeable, mutable, not fixed.
I'd have to ask someone.

This was waaaay beyond my experience. But we
needed to pause because I might be playing into
Dai's plans, or if I was misjudging him, we might
hurt him. My stress level rose. My heart beat too fast.
I hated how constantly I was out of my depth in this
role. I swallowed and tried to remind myself I'd got
through worse since I moved to Gretna Green.

Admittedly, right at this moment, I couldn't think
what, but there'd probably been worse. At least
today had started with coffee.

Then Fi arrived at work. Whoops, I'd forgotten all
about her, or I would have suggested she take the
morning off. I worried for some reason what this
amount of dragon power might do to normal people
in the Gateway, but she looked exactly as usual and
smiled up at me, unperturbed.

"Good morning, Niki. My mum sent these for
you." She carried one of Mrs Glendinning's special
cupcake-transporting plastic boxes.

Cupcakes to say thank you for allowing her to
have John's head.

Gods and Goddesses, I used to have such a
normal life.

I started laughing. It was probably only a way to

relieve my stress at yet again being in mid-air, but I obviously sounded hysterical because my uncontrolled laughter upset everyone except Dru and Tilly, who both put their heads out from under the table. Tilly gave one unamused woof, and then they both went back to sleep, which calmed Mabon but not Ad'Rian or Glais'Nee.

The comments, "Recorder, are you quite well?" and "Daaarling, really, the joke wasn't that funny," reached me at the same time.

What joke? I hadn't heard a joke.

The tone behind both of their comments suggested I wasn't behaving appropriately. Well, sod that and them.

I hadn't made any of this mess. Not one bit of it. But no one was apologising for a hundred and twenty years of Dai's poor decisions landing on my head, were they?

I didn't want to explain the macabre humour of sunny yellow black-eyed Susans growing out of a blue skull as a memorial for Mrs Glendinning's mother or the lemon-curd cupcakes she'd sent me exactly as she promised.

Honestly, I was sick of explaining myself. What had Dola said? Embrace my weirdness, wasn't it something like that? Oh, yeah, cease conforming to people's expectations.

I rode the power above the anvil and glared down

at them. "Glais'Nee, please ignore everything I'm about to say. None of it is aimed at you."

He nodded solemnly at me and gave a small bow.

"Ad'Rian, you released him," I pointed at Dai, "in that state. I understand your ethics mostly prevent you from healing people who don't want to be healed. But shouldn't you have warned someone he'd been released in such an unstable state? And that he was possibly or even probably still a danger to others?"

I checked Caitlin, but she was still fine. Rhiannon and Rollo were right next to her. But my insides were so unsteady, I could no longer tell whether my unhappy feeling was about her or about Dai. I just wanted this finished and my feet on solid ground again.

I paused. I breathed. Ad'Rian gave me a half-bow acknowledging my accusation.

"What's worrying me now is what will happen if we remove all Dai's dragon power. I'd like a plan instead of trying to stuff a serpent no one seems to fully understand back into a bottle."

I surveyed the power in Dai's box and the ball of it next to me. "We'll have the last of it out of him in two or three minutes, by my best guess. Does this power truly feel like dragon regnal power to you, Boney? Rhiannon? Because it doesn't to me."

Mabon glanced at the time on his phone. "And as

for you, Your Majesty." His gaze shot upwards to me, surprised to be given his title. "How many times have you led the St. David's Day celebrations?"

With confusion in his tone, he responded slowly, "Well, dead he'd been for a long time before we started celebrating him, but around eight or maybe nine hundred years?"

"Then isn't it time you gave someone else a chance to shine? Don't you have anyone in your entire realm who could stand in for you? You have one son, one daughter and one problem with them both right here. You've already done the other thing hundreds of times, and you didn't even like the guy. Focus on doing the right thing, right here, right now, will you, Boney?"

His scarred face actually looked chagrined as he mouthed "sorry" at me.

But then he straightened his shoulders and strolled over. He called up, "Come down, can you?"

"Sorry, no. The power doesn't seem to think so until we deal with this." I gestured at the dragon power. "I'm helping to hold it in some way I don't understand."

"At least move away from the bluddy pain-making anvil, can you?"

I asked the power. Yes, it was fine with that, and I slid sideways. Then, with his feet sparking red, Mabon met me in mid-air. Wow!

"I didn't know you could do that?"

Mabon fixed me with an intense stare. "A lot you don't know yet. Now, listen. Should have explained this when you were a child. Seems I didn't. Sorry for that, I am."

He looked serious. Some part of my brain recognised this tone from my childhood, so I nodded solemnly at him.

"The little things. They're important. Their king bothering to do the little things. Important that is too. Not someone else—*me*. Right you are. Look after my kids first, I must. But no one else can be me. See?"

I felt his sincerity. "What am I missing, Boney?"

"*Gwnewch y pethau bychain mewn bywyd*—it means, 'Do the little things in life.' Think about what life is like when no one bothers to do them. If no one cares to make anyone else smile. What if everyone is too busy being a king or a Recorder, so no one says good morning or offers anyone a coffee, a hug or a smile? Sometimes a smile is a little thing, isn't it?"

Shit, he was speaking English. I ran everything he'd said back through my mind. "Okay?"

He huffed at me. "How many people have you told that Dai had only stale instant coffee? He wouldn't give his own sister or you a decent cup of coffee because it's unimportant to him. It's a little thing, and Dai—well now, *bach*, Dai doesn't do the little things, does he?"

I shook my head, but Mabon was on a roll.

"But you do. Little things bluddy matter. And my people want their king to do the little things today. Very well, you're doing. Working hard at being the Recorder. But remember to make time for the little things. And thank Pendragon annually by raising a glass to him in gratitude."

At my confused frown, he added, "Told you I did. One of our own edited the joyless bastard's last words into something useful, didn't I? I mean, it might have been 'salt is the devil's work; avoid it. Leeks and water will give you all you need.'" He guffawed. "Pendragon might have repeated that much, but once Dewi said ale must be avoided, all bets were off. Good man, Arthur was."

I tried to process whether he'd really just said what I thought he had, but then he was on the ground again and called up, "Happy St. David's Day, let's get on, hey?"

Rhiannon sauntered over and stuck her hand into the red power. Her hand changed into a dragon's talon. "Yes, there's something else in it too, Recorder." She gave her half-brother a sharp look. "What did you do to it?"

Dai ignored her as though she hadn't spoken. She glanced up at me and shrugged.

I said, "He does that a lot, doesn't he? Silently

ignores anything he doesn't want to answer. It's ill-mannered and annoying, and I'm getting really freaking tired of it."

Caitlin called, "Niki, ya doing OK?"

Oh dear, was I looking or sounding as sharp as I felt? Embracing my own strangeness didn't mean I should become a snappy bitch, did it? Do the little things, Niki.

"I'm going to be doing just fine when you throw me one of those cupcakes up here."

Caitlin looked around in confusion.

Fi immediately snapped the box open. "Niki, I'm on my way to see the Quack Pack. They have some trade ideas to talk about. Do you need me to stay? I can delay them."

No, I'd prefer she wasn't here, but I didn't know why. "No, that's good, Fi; send them my regards."

She nodded and threw a cupcake up to me. The only person in the Gateway with her priorities straight. Feed the Recorder some sugar while she calms down. Perhaps my gran's unusual training of Fi to provide tea and biscuits at difficult times had been more important than I'd realised. I was really starting to like her.

I caught the cupcake one-handed without squashing it, and that stupidly small victory gave me confidence. I peeled the paper case open slowly and wallowed in the fragrance. It was so fresh and still slightly warm. Mrs G must have got up early this morning to make them. I bit into it and moaned as the tart lemony top notes washed the sour taste of this whole debacle out of my mouth and left a lingering sweetness behind.

"Fi, those cakes are well worth a skull's ransom. Please give your mum my sincere thanks."

She giggled.

I caught a stray thought from Rollo, *By Freyja, she looks like a Goddess herself. Flying above them and so righteously angry with them all. So beautiful, fierce and in command.*

Huh. Did I really? Wow!

His admiration grounded me even though I wasn't sure I deserved it. But maybe I wasn't making a complete pig's ear of this after all.

Glaring at them all again for good measure and ignoring the hopeful looks on Ad'Rian and Mabon's faces, I said, "I'll pass the cupcakes around as soon as you've all concentrated on the problem and offered me solutions. Mabon needs to leave shortly, and this is a long way outside my current circle of knowledge. I've paused it, but we need intelligent decisions and a workable plan and soon."

Rhiannon wandered over. "No rude advice for me, Recorder?"

"Sometimes, Rhiannon, you catch more flies with cake than vinegar. You kept trying to make your father listen to sense. He doesn't do that. Try bribing or guilt-tripping him instead. It works better."

I heard her mutter, "Engrave his flaming phone, you mean."

"Whatever works. Want a cupcake?"

She spun around so quickly, she was almost a blur. "They smell great."

"I rest my case. Bribe them into it—it must run in the family. But you can have one for never actually intending to drop me off a dragon's back." I nodded to Fi.

Mabon gave Rhiannon a horrified look. But as our gazes met, she actually smiled. "I read the flaming coffee mug, you know!"

I smirked. "...but the angels stole all the best lines."

Unexpectedly, Rhiannon flapped her arms like an imaginary snow angel's wings and grinned at me. While I hung up here and waited for the royals to decide what was safe to do, I amused myself and used the power to make wing shapes for me. Like a snow angel but with the rainbow power instead of nasty cold white stuff.

Ad'Rian looked up at me and gasped.

"What, darling? You guys had a brainwave?"

But he shook his head and said, "We will speak later."

And then HRH arrived.

Oh good. We were obviously reaching the interesting bit.

FORTY-ONE

Mabon, Ad'Rian and Glais'Nee went into a huddle. Rhiannon ate her cupcake. She moaned softly too. Baking was definitely Mrs G's superpower. Rollo and Caitlin chatted quietly, and then I heard her say, "Oh, yes, I trust her. She's slagging odd, but even Ma trusts her. If she tells you she needs my codeword, just do it, Rols."

It was build Niki's confidence all around today, wasn't it? So why was my stomach still roiling with an unhappy presentiment?

The violet gate swung open, and two of the tall warrior Fae and two shorter ones, healers I assumed, walked through carrying a long violet stretcher.

For all I'd just kicked Boney for fretting about getting to his ceremony, I was conscious of the time myself. The Gateway needed to open to normal traffic shortly. People needed access to the red gate for the Dewi Sant ceremony. And I needed most of this mess either dealt with or at least out of sight pretty soon.

Surveying the force-field around Dai, I considered changing it to an opaque glass cage and hiding it behind the new living willow screen. It might work, but felt cruel. Could I use Indigo for storage? I must pop through there and see if there was any storage space. It was obviously inactive at the moment. I should have done that before, shouldn't I?

But I always seemed to be so damn busy.

Indigo had turned into the laundry hamper of dog towels you keep meaning to wash, but there always seems to be a more urgent load to process first. At least until they start to smell. I added an investigative foray into Indigo to my mental list.

HRH arrived on the anvil's throne. "A most fetching look on you, Recorder."

"Huh?"

"Your wings. Amusing yourself, I see." But her green eyes bored into me as if seeking something.

Before I could answer her, Caitlin walked purposefully across the centre and jumped effortlessly onto the anvil's throne. She gave the cat a confused look as she stood up next to her plinth. "Need a word."

I was about to use the power to lift her up to me

when I remembered her tendency to vomit during a simple transport. I squashed the amusing thought of the elegant cat covered in Caitlin's regurgitated breakfast, thinking better of it. I asked the power to drop me down even a little, please, and it did.

In a low voice, Caitlin said, "There's Pictish power in that ball. Should there be?"

HRH's mouth was open. She licked the air. "You are correct, KAIT. But it is not the Picts who trouble me. Recorder, observe."

The cat drew a small amount of the power to her and split it into its component parts. About eighty percent dragon power, maybe two or three percent blue Pictish power, and the rest was Indigo energy.

I went cold.

I'd just this minute considered storing Dai in Indigo. Had it been a random thought, or had he sent it to me? The indigo power couldn't hurt me in the Gateway, and if Dai was *still* trying to coerce me into doing what he wanted, surely it was all the more reason to get this finished.

I suggested to the power we remove the Pict energy first. It liked the idea and did exactly what it had with Rollo last week: split it out into a small blue ball next to the larger ball of indigo energy now forming overhead next to the red one.

Then, instead of coating the blue gate with the

Pictish power as I expected, it sent it straight to Caitlin.

She gave me a querying look, and I nodded. "The power seems to think it's yours, or maybe just that you can take it safely home?"

She set her feet and breathed in. The blue power disappeared into her as we all watched. I didn't take my eyes off her in case this was what my bad feeling was related to.

But nothing happened.

Mabon looked up at the dragon power and then watched as more blue power headed towards Caitlin. He didn't seem to notice the ball of growing indigo power.

"Gentlemen, were we expecting that?" I asked.

Mabon glanced upwards at the balls of red and blue of power floating above him. "Always good when the gates of hell don't open, *bach*."

Ad'Rian shot him an amused look and gestured at his healers. "We are prepared and ready to take Prince ap Modron, Recorder. Perhaps you simply need to continue with what you were doing?"

Such a polite way to say, "Hey, you're keeping my guys waiting." But he was right. I was delaying, and I didn't know why. I told the power it could resume collecting the dragon's regnal power from Dai.

Then it hit me. Barely above a whisper, I asked

HRH, "Is it my imagination or has *no one* else noticed that indigo power?"

She put one paw to her mouth in a silencing gesture.

I glared at her but quietly asked, "Did you want it?"

Equally quietly, she answered, "It is not mine to take. But it should go back, Recorder. It was doing the job its owner intended it to do."

I thought about that. I hated it when I had to take lessons from a cat. Not because she was a cat, but because she was always so mysterious about it. A cat goddess who still reminded me of my headmistress when she was in full-on "I do not know how I could have erred so much in my youth to be sentenced to educate you gels" mode. The memory of her terribly proper upper-class English accent still made me smile. She'd been a real character even if I hadn't appreciated it at seventeen.

I glared at her. "And who *is* its owner?"

"I'm not able to say. But it has no connection to this Gateway; send it back to the boy."

No damn help there then, what a surprise. But it wasn't my imagination. The royals and the healers were all focused on the red power. Glais'Nee watched Dai, and Caitlin's gaze was fixed on the blue power. No one paid any attention to the indigo ball.

I called to it. A single strand came to my hand.

The cat was right again, no surprise there. The curl of power, now in my palm, clearly but politely told me *I am not yours or any part of your Gateway.* Well, crap. Just when I thought I was starting to get better at this job, something else I didn't understand arrived.

The Gateway had completed the split of the red regnal energy now, and two balls floated in the air next to me: moderately-sized red one and a smaller but still growing indigo one. The blue power funnelled directly to Caitlin. She absorbed it with no apparent problems.

I met Glais'Nee's eyes briefly as he smiled at me, and then went back to observing Dai carefully. Even the powerful Fae didn't seem to see the indigo power.

Then Dai stood up. Was he trying to call the red power back to him?

I thought about what Ad'Rian had said yesterday. People don't have a right to privacy if the Recorder truly feels she needs to know something for the good of the realms. Given I had no idea what was happening—this might be that time.

I gathered power and did something I never thought I would. But we all needed to know for sure if he'd been in cahoots with Troels.

I simply asked the power to help me get through those rock walls Dai called shields. That was when he resumed shouting about his rights and the abuse of his privacy.

I felt bad for about a millisecond, then I thought about how he'd abused *my* rights and how great my need to protect the Gateway was as the Recorder.

Gently but firmly, I sent the thought to him, *I won't hurt you, Dai. But I need to know. The easy way or the other way. Your choice.*

No response from Dai. It was as though he hadn't heard my mental communication.

I had to know if he'd planned to hold me away from the Gateway in a place with no access to the power so Troels could attack. The timing was awfully coincidental. Yesterday in his lounge he'd sounded sympathetic about Troels being locked in, and he'd been dismissive of my warnings about the danger to the Gateway.

Perhaps everyone who'd told me Troels had spies everywhere sparked this. It wasn't from my Gift. It was me, the woman who wanted clarification. But "self-important exaggeration much" when I'd told him truthfully the Gateway could have fallen was either a line worthy of Nick, or surely he was a spy.

Niki and the Recorder both needed to know which.

I pressed on. Rhiannon came to stand beside me, out of the healers' way. "I've never been able to get through. He learnt too well from me."

"We reap what we sow, you know."

She nodded grimly.

Then the screaming began. I stopped instantly. I hadn't done anything to cause him pain. But Rhiannon laughed with apparently sincere humour.

"What?"

"Have you heard the thing Glynis quotes all the time about 'Give me a child until he is seven, and I will show you the man'?"

"Yeah, she said it the other day. Didn't make much sense to me in the context she said it, but, yeah."

"He screamed like that from birth until he was about twenty," she said at my surprised expression. "Truly twenty or maybe even twenty-five. He was a late developer. Whenever the slightest thing didn't go his way, he wailed like a banshee. Mo-Mo actually sealed his mouth shut for twenty-four hours once as a lesson. You're causing him no pain. Trust me."

"Mo-Mo?"

"Our grandmother. Press on, Recorder. We need to help him, even if he doesn't want us to. And Caitlin isn't annoying. Let's make sure it's not going to backfire on her, shall we?"

I resolutely cast aside any amusement at Modron, the mother goddess of the Red Celts and Mabon's progenitor, ever being known as Granny Mo-Mo, took Rhiannon's advice and pressed on.

Once I told the power I needed in, Dai's shields simply weren't there anymore. And I went digging.

When I came back to myself, I was stiff and aching. I wanted to cry, and my head hurt. A lot.

But I'd learnt some important things. I wished I'd done this after the night two weeks ago in Galicia when Dai had confused me so much. It could have saved us all a lot of trouble.

Because now I understood why Dai's shields were like rock. He wasn't a traitor. He was just utterly and completely messed up.

I shook my head to try to clear some of Dai's misery, pain, and powerlessness out of it and thought longingly of coffee.

Rollo sent, *Don't judge him too harshly. Something I've discovered by sharing this link with you is you have no idea what it's like for the heirs in the realms. Certainly Dai's had the rough end of it, but none of us are much better balanced. And Dai's had to put up with it all for longer than Cait or me.*

But maybe Rollo hadn't seen enough in my mind because I sure as hell wasn't judging Dai.

For the first time, I sympathised with him.

Not because he'd used the red power on me but because he needed help. He wasn't a bully or a traitor. He was hanging on to the end of his rope by his fraying fingernails in a world where his fate had been decided before he'd even been born. Poor bastard.

Well, I could do one thing for him because the part of Dai's memories that shocked me was where the indigo power had come from.

Dai had met his other father. And that indigo power had helped him stave off the change to dragon. I'd need to talk to him about it, but he was in no condition to make any decisions for himself at the moment. So for now, until I fully understood it, I'd maintain his status quo.

In the future, after Dai's healing was complete, he could decide for himself. But he *really* didn't want to be a dragon, and without this indigo power, his ap Modron genes would have forced him into the change. It wasn't a decision I had the right to make for him.

And it wasn't one I was prepared to let Mabon make for his son either. Because he'd had one hundred and twenty years to be a good father to him, and if what I'd seen in Dai's mind was true, and my right shoulder thought it was, the kindest thing I could say about Mabon was he might have meant well. But he'd mostly been more of a hindrance than a help to Dai.

I gave HRH a long look and said one word: "How?"

She twitched her tail, and the indigo power moved back towards Dai. It stopped at the energy barrier, and she glared at me. *Instruct the power to give it access* echoed in my already painful head.

So I did. The power allowed the indigo energy through to Dai. He reached out to it like a drowning man, and as it entered him, he collapsed.

I removed the energy barrier. "Ad'Rian, your men can take him now."

The two healers and Ad'Rian moved swiftly over to Dai, who lay on the floor of the Red sector.

I waited, hoping I'd done the right thing. Ad'Rian announced, "He is physically well. We will care for the rest of him."

Dai was loaded onto the stretcher and on his way to Fae in two shakes of a lamb's tail, as my gran always used to say. The Fae healers and guards left with Dai on their stretcher. It followed them through the violet gate unaided. Magic was extremely cool.

I surveyed the now much brighter red ball of power, watched as the last of the blue power disappeared into Caitlin and thought about the noxious yellow ball we'd cleansed a few days ago for Rollo.

I mentally dubbed this week Goodness Gracious, Great Balls of Power! I started humming the tune in my mind. Now that was an earworm.

CHAPTER
FORTY-TWO

The clean-up went smoothly and surprisingly swiftly.

Rollo formally asked the Recorder's permission to leave. He privately sent me an intimate and amusing cartoon-style graphic of him completing his errands in Viking and Edinburgh, and rushing back, if I didn't mind. I didn't mind at all. He was fun, and he made me feel better about myself.

That stopped me in my tracks for a moment as he headed towards the green gate and I admired his departing rear view. I realised he was the first man I'd ever had a relationship with who'd made me feel great about myself.

I felt his hug in my mind as he sent, *Such a shame he's dead.*

HRH finally spoke and drew my attention back to

her. "A nice job, Recorder. Once you have finished here, we should speak about," she gazed around the Gateway at the busy people and the red power floating overhead and concluded, "other matters, dear to us both."

Remembering what the Book had said about feeding her any spare power, I took a small amount and directed it towards her.

She preened as she always did in the power flow. And I stroked her fur with my left hand, coated in power, exactly as I used to when I was a child. When she looked suitably stoned on the power, I said, "Do you remember when Dai placed a bet with you, and you said, 'My man had placed a large wager on Mabon's phone surviving?'"

She purred, "Hmmn?"

"Why did you describe him that way?"

She pulled herself together enough to glare at me. "I did not, Recorder. I am no fool. I presumed you would wish to know *he* had described himself in that way to his father and to me."

Damn. I had to get smarter and listen harder. She'd given me a clue about all this weeks ago, and I'd missed it. Because Dai hadn't intended to abuse me. Use me, yes. Because he'd thought—correctly, as it turned out—I might be the one person who could get Ad'Rian and even Mabon to finally grasp Dai had never wanted to be the King of the Dragons. He was frightened they'd bully him into it, and he truly would rather die.

He'd thought I could help him. Not because I was the Recorder but because "everyone likes Niki." I'd have to think about it properly later. I'd had no idea that sometimes I could make changes just because people thought I was likeable.

I walked over to Ad'Rian and Mabon in time to hear, "We will not rush it this time. I shall send you reports."

I pulled Ad'Rian to one side. Even though he hadn't seemed to notice the indigo energy, I wasn't taking any chances. "Sire, if you should find any unusual power as you heal Dai, the Recorder requires you to call her before you take any action or make any clinical decisions about it. I also require you to pass the same message on to any healers who may work on him. It is important."

His inexpressive face almost managed to form a small line between his eyes. "Can you share any more information?"

"Sorry, no. It's probably nothing, but contact me if it happens."

He nodded. "Now, Nik-a-lula, I assured you if I remembered any further additions to the old prophecy, I would advise you."

My attention sharpened on him. "And you have?"

He nodded. "... 'The anvil will be found sitting in state on a living throne of its own creation with royalty at its feet, a goddess by its side and a champion at its back. Once the angel watches over it, the ripples of small changes will become larger waves until ...something, something.'"

I sighed.

"I did not think you were an angel either, daaarling, but today you had the appearance of one. It may mean nothing, but I gave you my word to share any recollections. The next part is escaping me. I have some threads, but I believe they're in the wrong order as yet. A pair of twins with unusual powers, a throne falling, an old realm rising again, or was it the dead rising? Something rising anyway. It will not come to me. I told you it was an old and gloomy prophecy, didn't I? Perhaps the Book?"

I nodded, but I didn't hold out much hope. Then an awful thought struck me. The only twins I knew were Lis and Mags Hobs. Just freaking great.

Rhiannon, Glais'Nee, Ad'Rian, Mabon and I settled at the conference table beneath the ball of gently swirling red dragon energy. The moment the indigo power had gone back into Dai, the Gateway power had put me back on the floor. The explanation from the power was it had needed the Recorder's help to deal with something I struggled to put words to. Perhaps an alien energy was the closest I could get to the feeling it had sent me. I remembered the wyrd, alien presence in Dai's eyes when I'd visited him at his house and hoped we could get to the bottom of it and I hadn't just made a horrible mistake returning the strange indigo power to Dai.

But for now, I finally got my coffee and some painkillers.

Dola sent refreshments, including an enormous tray of doughnuts that almost filled the Magic Box. Everyone stood by the box, passed things out and claimed their choices. Once everyone was supplied, I realised Glais'Nee was empty-handed. "What may I get you, Glais'Nee?"

"You wouldn't have my drink of choice, Recorder. Please don't trouble yourself."

I tapped my earbud to get Dola's attention. "What would your choice be if I had it?" I could barely imagine what phenomenally strong alcoholic thing such an enormous specimen of an ancient Fae might want to drink, but Dola had surprised me with both the things she could and the things she couldn't supply—we would find out for sure.

Glais'Nee had been a big help today. I owed him a drink surely?

He blushed. Fae men blushed very prettily. With the silver violet blush lightening his dark purple skin, he smiled bashfully. "I'm partial to Vimto. And I know Dola doesn't—"

He broke off as I opened the cupboard with a broad grin to see my own deep purple bottle of totally non-alcoholic fruity Vimto cordial. It had moved up here from my kitchen cupboard in Manchester.

"They invented it in my hometown, you know."

Autumn had gone through a stage of demanding warm Vimto after her swimming lessons, and I'd kept a bottle in for her.

Glais'Nee reached to take it from me with delight. "The complex mix of fruits, herbs and the special acid are very similar to a drink we stole from the Romans. The label is correct. Refreshingly different is exactly what it is." He held the bottle up to Ad'Rian, who smiled back at him.

As we reached the table, Ad'Rian glanced at me. "You've made a friend for life now." Then Glais'Nee regaled Ad'Rian with the information about how this modern version of his old favourite had been invented in Manchester.

I considered Mabon. Ah, hell, how could I fix this?

I pushed the doughnuts towards him, along with the whisky. "Drown your sorrows, Boney. Better to find out sooner, don't you think?"

Wow, Niki, got any more platitudes you want to spout? I berated myself.

Mabon huffed, "What is it the kids say now? Oh, yes, I'll eat my feelings." He reached for a creme-filled. Rhiannon watched him with interest.

Looking at me, she said, "Mabon told me about these. I don't know why I haven't had them before. I should spend more time out of the realm. Which would you recommend?"

In perfect unison, Mabon and I pointed at the plain glazed and spouted, "Start with that one and know it will only get better."

Her mouth dropped open. But she took it.

I checked Caitlin. Her treasure chest, as I'd begun to call it, was still inside her aura, still securely iron-wrapped and appeared no different to the way it had been when I'd last checked it. Had we avoided a disaster? How? Was it because I'd allowed the indigo power to return to Dai? The things I didn't know drove me crazy. What I did know was my unhappy stomach had settled down. Maybe I should just be grateful?

Mabon was doing obscene things to his creme-filled as usual.

Rhiannon said, "It's disturbing to watch my father doing that—you know it, too, don't you?"

Mabon was unfussed. "Keep his skills honed, a man must. Wait until you try one of those caramel ones Niki likes. Not so prim will you look then." He sat back with a loving but terribly smug expression on his face as I passed one of the Biscoff doughnuts to Rhiannon.

"Now she's busy, what about this? Better it looks." He pointed at the dragon regnal power turning lazily above our heads. It was a much healthier colour without the indigo and blue components.

"You once told me there was no job a woman with brains and balls couldn't do." I gestured at the woman he always described as his true daughter. She looked on the verge of a great deal of pleasure as she stuffed the last of the doughnut into her already overfull mouth and reached for another. "She's got both. What's your problem?"

"Always try to be fair, I do. Don't give to one without the other and so forth."

"What if they weren't your kids? Imagine instead they were in your army in the old days. Would you reward two soldiers equally if one had volunteered and worked their guts out for you and the other had been conscripted, didn't want to be there and always seemed to be AWOL when there was any grunt work or clean-up to be done?"

I paused and drank my coffee. I had one chance to make this man listen.

"Boney, you've bullied your son, lovingly perhaps. But you haven't listened to him, have you? He's been telling you for a hundred years he doesn't want to be the dragon king. He'd rather die. Literally. Ad'Rian informed you of that, didn't he?"

Across the table, Ad'Rian gently said, "Old friend, our children are not ours to direct once they attain adulthood. He does not want this." He gestured upwards at the dragon power. "The Recorder is correct; he would rather go to the Summerlands now than be forced to live the life you've chosen for him for hundreds of years. He wants to serve your realm, but he does not like the dragons."

I added, "You can wait until he's truly healed and make him say it again. But how is it fair to lose dragonets because Dai was playing games with the regnal power? He did that because you wouldn't listen and insisted on giving it to him. He told you he didn't want it, didn't he? After you forced him to take it, he started to abuse it."

Mabon grunted. He looked guilty now but not yet convinced.

"As you said about me, I've always known you to

be fair, Boney. Where did I learn to be fair, do you think?" I grinned at him. We both knew he was the one who'd hammered the concept of fairness into my seven-year-old head. "Annoying but fair. Can you explain, for the Recorder's understanding, how you think punishing one child for the other's actions and sentencing half the clutch to death is fair?"

I heard, *Nice job, Nik-a-lula. Now press that point in until he bleeds,* inside my head from Ad'Rian.

But I didn't. I gazed at Mabon in silence and waited. He needed processing time, and he didn't like to be nagged. He *was* a fair man. He'd just lost touch with his own beliefs.

But he'd get there. I passed him the Girvan, his coffee and another doughnut as if I had all the time in the world. I'd learnt when I was a child you only had one chance to make your case with Boney. After that, all the *please, please, pretty pleases* in the world wouldn't change his answer if your first point hadn't been good enough. It had cost me a lot of missed ice creams to learn this lesson.

But, good heavens, that doughnut must be whimpering in surrender.

Mabon stood up, pushed the remains of the revoltingly soggy doughnut into his mouth and mumbled something incomprehensible. He swallowed then poured himself a small measure of the Girvan and tossed it back.

I waited.

"Mistakes were made. Many of them by me. Right. Right you are. No denying it, is there? Stupid to try. Ready, Rhiannon?"

Rhiannon shot me a genuinely startled look, and as she passed me, she muttered in an undertone, "That wasn't a bribe, a guilt-trip or a debt repayment."

"No, Rhi-rhi — it was lessons learnt not licking on an ice cream."

She growled at me. Actually growled. "I need to take you to dinner and listen hard."

I called after her, "Fine by me. Do you like Indian food? I offered to take your brother once if he told me all the things he wasn't able to explain. He never did, but maybe you'd like to go instead? How's a week on Friday for you?"

I wanted another ride on her dragon badly. I'd swap her info for flights. The Book said I needed to build my own relationship with her. Well, someone had said it in the Book. I couldn't think about it now. I needed to give her this power.

But I didn't.

As I strolled over, I heard, "Stand or sit, Rhiannon? You took the first half easily, but the last of it hits hard sometimes at the end."

I added the advice I'd given Rollo, "And open your shields. It helps minimise the headache."

Her head spun around. "Truly, or do you just want a chance to dig about?"

"Truly. You'll have a hell of a headache if you keep them closed."

"Then I want your promise you won't dig in my head even though I'm in the Gateway."

Ha! She'd remembered what I'd told her when we first met. And I recalled Aysha's advice that I needed to stop giving people what they wanted too easily. "I can offer a negotiation?"

She growled again. Was she nervous about taking this power?

"What do you offer? And what do you want?"

"I offer a promise of mental privacy to you until you've assimilated the power, or tomorrow, whichever comes sooner. In exchange, I need your dragon to take me somewhere important and for you to wait ten minutes while I try something."

"Fine, ten minutes. I'm not a flaming air taxi though."

Mabon had lost all patience now. "Sit or—"

She interrupted him, "On my feet, of course!" Mabon smiled at her warmly.

She stood as Rollo had. Except, quite unlike Rollo, she wanted this. She grabbed the dragon power and pulled it towards her. She devoured it until her aura glowed red and vibrated with the energy.

A true queen of the dragons, standing solidly the entire time.

The moment the last of the power entered her, she bowed to the anvil, kissed her father warmly on the cheek and turned to me. "I have shit to do—a flight and ten minutes, Recorder. I prefer to settle my debts quickly. Let's go."

CHAPTER
FORTY-THREE

During the flight, I learnt a lot from Rhiannon. She was probably drunk on the power and didn't realise how forthcoming she'd been. If HRH fell for it, I couldn't blame Rhiannon for doing the same.

She'd chattered away in a manner quite unlike the angry woman I'd previously met. The Red Celt mountains were the only place where the dragons were truly safe and comfortable, she'd explained. They hated buildings; they frightened them, as I'd seen the other day.

Then she gave me a quick historical overview. In the past, what records hadn't gone up in flames—always a challenge with dragons around—told them the dragons and the Gateway had a symbiotic relationship. They protected it, and it supplied the magic needed to breed true queens.

But there hadn't been a true dragon queen born in the realm in centuries.

As Rhiannon was only confirming everything I'd suspected and some things the Book had told me, I let her talk. Then I asked her the thing I was still confused about. "How would I know a real queen? I thought you were the queen now you have the regnal power?"

"I am *the* queen. But not a *true* queen. Mabon always told me I'd be the one to bring the queens back. It's why he calls me his true daughter." She sighed.

I risked a "But?"

And it worked. "But although the regnal power gives me dominion over all the dragons to prevent the hatchlings from turning feral and dying, a true queen is dramatically different..." she trailed off.

Her shields must still have been down because I saw a picture so clear, it might have been a painting in her mind of an enormous magnificent rose-gold dragon with a baby queen flying by each wing. Shit, it looked more than twice the size of Rhiannon, and her dragon was big enough. "We call them the golden ones, but truly, they were a pinkish gold, like the Red Celt rose gold we manufacturer for the

Smiths. They were glorious. There's one painting which …"

I thought I might push her for more, although I was pretty sure she was referring to the painting I got from her mind. But she was looking dreamily around the mountains as though she was in the past.

"If you don't want to explain, I'll ask the Book, but I try to go to the source when I can. How else would a true queen differ? I mean, why are they important?"

"They were immensely powerful with very different abilities. But they're gone."

"Do you know why? Or where they went?"

"They died out, and no new ones were born. Splitting the regnal power caused some of the problems, but I can't blame Mabon for all of it. The changes were already in process even before he split the power. It might be why he wanted to split the dragon power to try something different.

"Agnes said she had an idea to fix it … but she never told me what it was, then she was gone. Too suddenly. You could ask the Book what her idea was?" There was a note of faint hope in her voice and then anger as she added, "She told your flaming Book a lot of things she shouldn't have."

"Did she?"

"Well, yes. Where else did you get the pass phrase from? Only she knew it. I gave it to her in payment of a debt; it was supposed to be …" she trailed off again. Not a woman who trusted easily, Rhiannon ap Modron.

"It was supposed to be for her to use to help you?"

"YES! Not for her to tell some bluddy new Recorder."

"And did I?" At her quick glance over her shoulder, I elaborated, "Help you get what you needed?"

"Well, yes, but it's not the point, is it? She couldn't know that, could she? She's dead."

I opened my phone to the photo of the page in the Book and passed it forward to her. "Agnes secured this with a sort of spell, so only a McKnight descendant who was sincerely trying to help you stood any chance of getting access to it."

About damn time. Help Rhiannon; come back. We will talk.

Rhiannon doesn't like anyone, but she does love deeply and never breaks a promise. NOT her word. Her word is like pottery, friable and easily disposed of.

But a promise, you may trust.

ONLY after you've tried everything you know, and everything you can think of. If you fail:

Tell her dragons can fly because they take themselves lightly. Angels just stole all the good lines.

Do TRY not to use it unwisely because I only have two of these pass phrases, and it would be much better if you can build your own friendship with her.

But you MUST help her before it's too late. The Red Celt realm may fall without the power of the dragon queens. Mabon is ofttimes a dodipoll.

Rhiannon laughed and muttered, "Dodipoll, now there's an accurate description. She knew him so well, and I'd flaming forgotten it. Dodipoll. Ha!"

Then her shoulders went so rigid, I thought she might be weeping. I kept very still and quiet. If she realised I was aware of her turmoil, she might breathe fire at me.

We soared over the peaks. Watching as Pant y Wern disappeared behind us, I realised this must be the route I'd walked with Dai and Tilly.

Dragon flight for the win. No question. It all looked lovely from up here. Although it might not have been as much fun in a snowstorm.

I gazed around at the glory of the mountains and down into the valleys. Wonder bubbled up at the sheer scale and beauty of the landscape. The silence was almost palpable, broken only by the gentle susurration of the dragon's wings and the occasional cry of a bird soaring on the thermals. It was a flight I knew would stay with me forever, a moment I wanted to freeze in time and treasure.

The roof of Dai's house came up below us and off to the left. We must be nearly there. "They're awe-inspiring," I murmured. It was a phrase people overused, but the mountains inspired true awe in me. Nature at its finest.

As Rhiannon banked towards the house, I got a new vista and gasped. "Wow! Flying over these whenever you want, what a gift."

Rhiannon almost spat at me, "Women could learn a lesson from these mountains. It is our right to take up space and look flaming majestic doing it."

I couldn't argue with that. Maybe I should set it as my next goal?

CHAPTER
FORTY-FOUR

When we reached the damaged archway, I asked, "Can you fly around it for me?"

"Not a taxi driver. I mentioned that, yes?"

But she circled. And I saw it. The prism effect that caused the rainbows I'd repeatedly seen up here. It wasn't the sun reflecting off ice. It was power. Gateway power. This close, it called to me. It came out of a narrow gap in the top of the rock arch.

For the second time this week, I saw something that looked like the cover of *Dark Side of the Moon*, but instead of HRH's spine, this came from the top of the broken rock archway. All the colours of the rainbow were there instead of only some of them.

"Hover here, please." My tone must have struck the right note because, astonishingly, Rhiannon did as I'd asked.

I reached out to it as I would in the Gateway because this *was* Gateway power.

My Gateway's power, and it wanted to come to me.

I tried to pull power even though I wasn't sure that enough could get through the small crevice. But because I was with Rhiannon and connected to her network, there was some.

But not enough.

Nowhere near enough.

This was why I'd needed her to bring me here instead of me simply transporting. I'd known there would be no connection to the Rainbow Network up here, but I hadn't factored in Rhiannon's personal network might not have enough bandwidth.

Damn it.

I messaged Dola.

> Niki: Are you throttling Rhiannon's Eiddof Fi network connection?

> Dola: Yes. Prince Rollo said she was stealing bandwidth.

> Niki: Can you stop?

> Dola: Yes. But why?

> Niki: I need a lot more capacity for ten or fifteen minutes. It's an experiment.

Dola: OK

I gave her a minute and then tried again.
It was better but still not enough.

Niki: I need more. Give her
everything we have for the next
fifteen minutes.

Dola: Everything?

Damn, I should have talked this through with
Dola, but I hadn't expected Rhiannon to bring me
here today. Now she was getting antsy while I
messaged Dola.

Niki: Shut everyone else down for a
few minutes if you have to. Send
everything we have to Rhiannon's
Eiddof Fi network.

Rhiannon held the dragon almost motionless over
the prism. Her gaze fixed on it.

She made a curving gesture in the air with her left
hand. At my querying look, she said, "Iris. She's the
goddess of rainbows. Draw her curve, thank her for
their beauty, make a wish. Don't you do it?"

"My gran used to make a wish on rainbows, but
not the rest of it."

"Times change. Rituals are lost. But sometimes wishes do come true. Iris is still a power."

At my confused look, she pointed down. "It hasn't been there in years. I've wished for it many times."

Dola would need a minute or two to divert the network, so I answered Rhiannon's unspoken question. "It's me. The power is drawn to Recorders."

"But why now? I saw this when I was very young, but I haven't seen it in centuries."

"Have you had a Recorder on your back in centuries?"

She went rigid before she collapsed into laughter. "You may not want to use that particular phrase around dragons, Niki."

Aww, she called me Niki. We were making progress. "Why not?"

"Have you seen dogs mate?"

"Er, yeah."

"Think bigger. Someone on your back is a euphemism for dragon sex."

I had absolutely no idea what to say to that, but I was going to need her help, so I tried small talk. "Are you a dog person, Rhiannon? Or a cat person?"

"No. I'm not even a flaming people person. Although flaming people is always tempting…"

I'd been pulling a tiny amount of power while we talked. It didn't even cover my left hand, then I felt it shift. The power shot up to cover my arm. I breathed. The power was usually unstable when it did that, and I couldn't afford an unbalanced energy source for this task.

Rhiannon had done the swivelling thing again and now faced me. She gave my rainbow-covered arm a wide-eyed stare. "Was that supposed to happen?"

"Not exactly." I hid my smile. "I don't know if I can do this, but I want to try."

"I transported and landed next to the broken rocks that might once have been an intact archway. Rhiannon's shadow hovered over me. Both the woman's and the dragon's eyes were glued to the remains of the rock archway.

There used to be a Dragon Gate, the Book had informed me. It gave the mountains access to the Rainbow power, which allowed what it called the Golden Ones to be created. Those dragons possessed abilities far beyond the ordinary ones. I couldn't believe I was describing any dragons as ordinary, but that was what the Book said. It also told me the Gateway missed its dragon protectors, which was the only reason I thought this might work.

Bits of information I'd gathered from the Book during my nightly reading sessions had sparked suspicions. Those fragments of ideas led me to believe there might be a connection between HRH going on a rampage, Mabon's injuries, the fall of the dragon gate, and something odd that happened to the Recorder before Agnes. When I'd asked about the sixth Recorder, the Book wouldn't tell me a damn thing except she hadn't held the role for long.

I hadn't been able to confirm any of my ideas. Of course, it might simply be I read too many mystery novels and saw clues everywhere.

But if I could re-open this Gate, I'd have one more piece of evidence, and it might help more than just the dragons.

I walked around the pile of rocks while I ran my plan through in my mind, looking for the weak points in it. Something had broken the Gate hundreds of years ago. The oldest of the last Golden queens had died, and all the recorders since Agnes had either been terrified of the dragons or disinterested in them.

My plan was to pull power through Rhiannon's *Eiddof Fi* network and see if I could use it to resurrect the Gate. The rainbows of power I'd seen told me there was still some access. But not enough power. Nowhere near enough to repair a broken Gate.

I pulled power. I'd need a metric ton of it, and it was coming to me now—but it felt wrong. I pulled harder.

"Stop!"

The shout from Rhiannon drew my attention. The

upper half of her body was slumped on her dragon's neck. Even from down here I saw how pale she was. Crap.

Was Rhiannon's private connection really a part of her in some way? Was I draining her to pull the Gateway power? Blast.

"You OK?"

She sat upright again, and in a voice much softer than her usual firm tone, she said, "Don't do that again. It was …unpleasant. Thought I was going to pass out."

"Sorry, you should have told me *you* were fuelling the network."

Then I had a brainwave, poked my phone and used her network as a hotspot to connect to the Rainbow Network. But even though Dola had supplied the capacity, Rhiannon's limited connection still caused a bottleneck in the power I could pull.

"Rhiannon, can you safely increase the bandwidth on your connection? Even temporarily would make a big difference."

At her frown, I explained, "I'm using it as a hotspot so I don't drain you again, but it's too slow. It's blocking me from connecting properly and getting enough power."

Thank the Goddess for a woman who also liked tech. She immediately sat up straighter, and glowing red power surrounded her.

Oh yeah. Now I was cooking with gas. I rose into the air and hovered next to Rhiannon. I'd felt far safer with a dragon beneath me.

But oh no, because now the power was here. So, obviously, I was in mid-air *again*. Those dark, snow-dusted rocks below me looked much sharper than the Gateway floor.

I swallowed convulsively, closed my eyes and tried to focus only on the job. I pulled and pulled, and nothing happened.

The power itself felt reluctant.

I tried to let it see what I saw. I showed it what I thought must have happened when a previous avalanche, or maybe even a rockfall, had blocked its access and broken its gate.

I showed it what a nice mountain this was. No nasty lumberjacks up here.

Wouldn't the power like to stretch its legs a bit? I was pretty sure it used to like it up here with dragons to help protect it.

The power was nervous. I coaxed. I pulled, and then I pulled some more. Then I sent the power the picture of the rose-gold dragon queen I got from Rhiannon's mind. *We could help her to make these?*

Oh, yes. It liked the queens.

I felt it shift. Power flowed fast and free.

Then it all stopped.

Rhiannon's face appeared in my mind. I sent back, *Yes, she's right here.*

My brief glance at Rhiannon showed a woman who'd surrendered hope. The drooping shoulders and the flickers of fury and disappointment in her eyes revealed her anger at herself for daring to think this might work.

The power sent me a mental snapshot of a mobile phone and an old document.

I hung in the icy air, momentarily confused. Then it clicked.

The power liked consent. It wanted to be sure the Dragon Queen would honour her side of the old bargain.

I transported to Rhiannon's back. She did the swivelling thing yet again, so she faced me. I wondered if I'd ever get used to it? Probably. We did that, didn't we? Become accustomed to even truly bizarre things.

She wasn't happy. "What? You can't do it, can you? Flaming hells, I should've known better than to get my hopes up."

I considered her. The past few days had been difficult for her too. And she was probably still trying to assimilate her new dragon power. I noticed when the royals were tired, sometimes centuries of habit could shift them into the right headspace.

I found my authoritative voice. "Rhiannon,

Queen of the Red Celt Dragons, the Recorder needs your consent on behalf of the Rainbow Gateway."

I'd expected her spine to stiffen and the queen to emerge from the disappointed woman. Instead, she started laughing.

"By the Goddess, Niki, sometimes you could be her sister. She always did that when I was missing something important. She called it her Imperial Voice, or maybe her Imperious Voice. Who knows anymore? It was a long time ago."

I grinned. "I call it my librarian voice."

Rhiannon actually smiled back at me. "Sorry, what did I miss?"

"The power wants your consent. It needs to know if we open this gate again, you'll abide by the agreement." At her quick frown, I added, "I don't know. It sent a mental image of an old agreement. Thought it might make sense to you?"

Now she nodded. "It does. It used to share power with us. The Golden Ones swore to defend when necessary. I can do that."

Then, slowly, as if she wasn't sure whether to mention it, she asked, "Do you think Troels attacking the Gateway might have precipitated all this?" She gestured between us and then down at the broken rock arch below us.

"Agnes said something once about the next time a monarch attacked a Gateway, everything would change. Something about trees and devils, I think. Or angels and devils." Then she shook her head. "Maybe it was keys and Goddesses. Who knows? It was some nonsense that only made sense to her. But there was one thing she said I must remember. If I was still alive, I'd need to pray hard to whichever God or Goddess was in vogue in the future. Because the Recorder of that era would need a brain and the spine to use it."

She looked me up and down slowly. "We could have done worse, I suppose. What do you need me to do?"

Honestly, I didn't know. But I knew how to get someone to give me their consent to upgrade their phone. Maybe the same principle would work here?

I held out my hand. "Take my hand. Give the power and me permission to do this, and then you should send it an assurance. One you're prepared to swear over the anvil, to defend it in whatever way this document requires."

She nodded competently at me and grasped my hand in her strong and much warmer one. She focused on the prism of power below us and addressed it, "I'll give you any help you need if you can help me breed queens again. My word as ap Modron."

At my head shake, she sighed. "OK, OK, then. I promise."

Something shifted. I transported, intending to land on the ground by the rocks, but the power held me in mid-air again.

I was going to demand danger pay.

I pulled like a madwoman, or more precisely, like a Recorder on a mission. Now the power flowed. Like a river in full flood, the torrent of power raised me higher and higher.

Rhiannon had flown higher alongside me – if I didn't know better, I'd have thought she was getting ready to catch me.

I felt like I was hovering above a geyser. I shouted, "Move over there," and pointed across the space, trying to tell her to move two hundred yards away.

Of course, she ignored me. I thought about Aysha. One of her sayings was, "I give them one chance. The second time, they don't argue with me."

I pulled more power, panting now like a woman in labour. There didn't seem to be enough oxygen up here.

The problem was I didn't have Aysha's courage, and I'd no idea what would happen when I got enough power. "Last chance—you'd be much safer over there." I pointed again.

She ignored me. I couldn't wait to introduce Aysha to Rhiannon.

Then a rush of power moved me out of the way,

and, with a cyclone of rainbow light, the rock arch reformed itself.

I got a perfect view of Rhiannon spiralling arse over wingtip as the Gate reopened below us. Served her right. Maybe she'd listen to me next time.

I checked she'd stopped spiralling towards the ground and hid a relieved smile as she headed back towards me.

I looked at her back, the nice bit there between the spines, and thought, GO.

I landed in front of her, facing her.

Her T-shirt now said, *I'm well aware I'm not everyone's cup of tea… I'd rather be the right person's shot of tequila.*

She pointed at her chest. "As you're not a complete idiot, you get this pass phrase for free." She swallowed. "But if you just did what I think you did, I'll owe you something else."

Damn it, I liked the woman, er, the dragon, erm, nope, Niki. She's the queen now, remember?

I snapped a photo of her T-shirt. "Thank the power. But I'll take it to replace the one Agnes gave me in the Book."

The new door in the rock archway looked utterly bizarre on the top of the mountain. But wonderful. The fresh new wood gleamed in the sunlight. Unlike the main Red Celt access in the Market Square, which led to the Rainbow Gateway, on this Mountain Gate, the Red Celts' dragon symbol curled sinuously upside down. Its head at the bottom and the tail was now at the top of the door. If you squinted the tail made an infinity symbol. It still looked scary, though.

"Will it work?" Rhiannon sounded both doubtful and desperately hopeful.

"As long as you told it the truth when you gave it your consent to the old agreement, it will."

Now the tears flowed. I needed to get down and out of her way. She was not a woman who wanted anyone to say "there, there."

I landed by the new gate. She circled back around to check it from all sides. I called up to her, "Breed those glorious queens, Your Majesty."

Then I walked back through the new Gate to check it came out into the Gateway.

But it didn't.

It came out right next to the original Red Celt Gate inside the castle walls by Mabon's home. A lot of people and far too many Highland coos were milling about, staring at the new Gate. They gave me startled looks as I walked out of it and next door to the usual red gate with its dragon the correct way up.

I dragged my tired body home. I'd had to deal with far too much power for one day. But my heart yearned to see one of the beautiful rose-gold queens in the sky over those majestic mountains.

PART SEVEN
TUESDAY

CHAPTER
FORTY-FIVE

T*uesday, 2nd March—Gateway Cottage—Gretna Green—6 a.m*

After opening the new dragon gate, I'd popped to bed for what I intended to be a brief nap and had awakened the next morning. As I staggered through to the kitchen in the dark, dragging my robe on, still mostly asleep, I was astounded I'd slept for over fourteen hours.

Dola said, "Good morning, Niki. I didn't want to disturb you. I fed Tilly last night, but the fractious feline has been prowling around me, waiting for you."

I slumped at the kitchen table and retrieved my phone, which I'd abandoned on charge when exhaustion had overwhelmed me yesterday.

I thought the icy, refreshing mountain air had

deceived me about exactly how much power it took to re-open the dragon gate. I'd come home, eaten an enormous late lunch, and the moment my stomach was full, my brain shut down.

I scrolled through messages and emails. Nothing from Rollo. I calculated in my head that I'd seen him less than eighteen hours ago. I chided myself not to begin our relationship by being needy. I hoped his meeting with the lawyer had gone well. He seemed tense about it.

My connection with Rollo was still there. I could feel it. But it reminded me of when a friend puts a phone down to do something: the line is open, but no one's talking. Was that what someone being asleep was like if you were mentally connected? I tried, *Hey, are you still there?* And got no response. But it was still stupidly early. I wouldn't wake him.

HRH appeared through the door from the annex. Not through the doorway, but through the actual door. She stalked across the kitchen, leapt easily onto the tabletop in one agile movement and sat in front of me. "Recorder, I am concerned about Viking."

"Yeah, snap. But I'm not sure what to do about it. I'm thinking about it."

"Really, Recorder, as that American gangster once said, 'When I require your opinion, I shall give it to *you*.' Your thoughts do not interest me. Action is required on these petitions."

As annoying as she was, she wasn't wrong.

Somewhere in my blissfully long night of sleep, I'd made my decision. "I'm going to hear the petitions. But I need to let Troels know. The Book told me it's normal practice to inform the royals if they're involved. I did it with Breanna. Is he going to contest them or, as Aysha would say, settle on the court steps?"

"I am not familiar with the phrase, but I can extrapolate. So you plan to summon him?"

"I guess I'll have to. But I don't want him doing the emperor's trick and being away so his representative must come in his stead. We don't need another idiot like Leif arriving, do we? Rollo said Troels tries to avoid the centre of the Gateway. I wouldn't put it past him to have some sort of avoidance plan set up for when I summon him."

"Your political acumen improves. I may offer you a pearl of pertinent wisdom in return for the requisite morsel of a new variety of fish. One tires of tuna."

I smiled because I'd gone shopping last week for exactly this eventuality. I settled in to haggle with her. For a woman who'd never argued about anything, I seemed to spend half my life in my new role negotiating.

"Razor clams?" I offered.

Her head twisted around rapidly to stare at me. Her expression was one I hadn't seen before. It was a picture. I only wished I'd thought to have my phone ready to take a photo. Her green eyes were enormous in a face that normally showed only contempt. "You have such a thing? Here? Now?"

"If you can guarantee to give me advice to get around any problems and allow me to deal with Troels, yes."

Actually, I had a can and a jar of everything fishy an exclusive deli in the nearest town offered. I wasn't telling her about the caviar yet because I dreaded to imagine what I might need to use that for, but my Gift was insistent. So I bought it all and mentally thanked Gran for my inheritance money.

"We have a deal, Recorder. I'm rarely surprised. But razor clams are surprising. You must summon him today."

"Hmm, maybe, but I want to speak with Ti'Anna first. She wasn't honest with me the other day. Well, that's probably not true—she is Fae. So she probably was honest, but within such stupidly tight limits, I'm not sure it didn't border on a lie. Even Ad'Rian suggested she'd sliced the truth too finely about Jamie. If he said as much, I could probably call it lying. She withheld a lot of information, and I've only pieced some of it together."

I opened the cupboard and removed the jar of razor clams. But HRH wasn't finished with me.

Cautiously, she said, "You know I have certain … talents?"

"Uh huh?" I didn't know anywhere near enough about her talents, but it seemed razor clams had opened up her communications, and I didn't want to get in their way.

"I could offer advice about the correct wording and timing."

"OK. I'm all ears?"

"Use the title he gave himself and is so attached to. Summon The Rightful King of the Vikings. It is possible using any of his given names may trigger the escape plan or transfer the summons to his appointed representative. As for timing, soon, Recorder, very soon. Not later than luncheon today. I fear we and many others will regret it profoundly if you wait past luncheon."

I'd never summoned anyone before. Well, obviously, I had with the star on the anvil, but not just as myself without using magic. However, I couldn't think of another way to describe the message I sent to Ti'Anna.

> Niki: The Recorder would be pleased to receive you for morning coffee today at 10.30 a.m. to convey news about Fergusson, McPherson and MacDonald. Please confirm.

> Tina: How kind. I shall come through the woods to avoid the spies. Please inform Dola. She will release the back gate so I may avoid the iron.

> Niki: No problem.

I had no idea what she was talking about, but when I told Dola, she said, "OK."

As I headed towards the shower, Dola said, "Niki, Mabon asked if you'd had time to do the book quote for him? The author's publisher has contacted him."

Shit. Yes, I'd told Mabon I'd send him a quote for the cover of the dragon book, hadn't I? I hadn't had time to read it properly, but I'd skimmed it. It was all pretty sound information and quite amusing. Although it had taught me very little specifically about the dragons, other than they seemed to have the same damn problems as everyone else.

I thought about it for a moment. "Can you send him a message for me? Tell him I think he should say, 'We all need good advice now and then. Peggy's is excellent, and not only for dragons.'"

"Shall I make it sound more like Mabon?"

"Sure. How would you do that?"

In a perfect imitation of Mabon's voice, I heard, "Excellent advice we all need. Read the bluddy book, even if a dragon you're not."

I laughed, she'd nailed it. "Yep, send him that version, please."

"Finn, have we finalised the names for the Rainbow Council? I want to schedule the first meeting towards the end of this month. That should give everyone enough notice to free up time to come here. I can summon them if they wish."

I glanced around the Gateway while I gave Finn time to line up his reply. It was quiet today with only a few damp-looking travellers. I caught a slightly panicky look as it passed across Finn's face. "Red, Blue and Yellow are all confirmed. But Orange and Green ..." He shook his head and looked hopefully at Fi.

Fi stepped straight in, "Green is half fine; the Hobs are back from their honeymoon. Crane hasn't confirmed yet, but I'm sure he will. He might feel he needs to check with his Headwoman, and Lis Hob went through to Galicia the other day. I don't know when she's due back. But we're still one short."

"But Kari Halvor agreed to it. Has she backed out?" I wouldn't be amused if she had after her sanctuary claim. We'd negotiated. She'd agreed.

"Oh, no, but she said she can't represent both Viking and Caledonia. They have such different needs. I thought it would be easier to find someone for Green than to find another Viking while they're locked down. Did I make the wrong call?"

"No, Fi, you didn't. Kari's correct too, isn't she?" I was the one who hadn't thought it through. "OK, Kari for Viking, and we're one short for Scotland? You and I might need to put our heads together on this, Fi."

She nodded. "Niki, Orange." She sighed theatrically. "The emperor wants a meeting with you. I've reminded him several times I'm now in charge of the Trade Desk, but he keeps asking for you. He went over my head to Dola."

I wasn't sure Dola was "over Fi's head," not as far as trade was concerned. I said this, and Fi gave me a relieved smile. "Well, Dola agreed with you. She forwarded his email to me, copied him in and added a patronising note."

I smirked. "Oh, do tell?"

Fi grinned back and, in an unctuous tone, said, "She was so sorry he'd been unable to keep up with recent developments on the Trade Desk. Perhaps it would be easier for him now that, thanks solely to the extremely busy Recorder, Natalia was happily married to the correct man? But could she introduce

Fiona Glendinning to him as the correct person to deal with all trade enquiries henceforth?"

"Henceforth? Wow, she was cross." I laughed. The emperor had known Fi for twenty years. What was he playing at? I called, "Go, Dola!"

"Seriously, though, what's his problem? And what does it have to do with the Galician representatives for the council?"

"He cut me off. He said he'd discuss his representatives personally with the Recorder when he could schedule a meeting with her about his trade concerns."

"Hmm, I don't like that kind of politicking. I won't be blackmailed. At least not without doing it back. The matters are unconnected. Let's see how he likes unconnected matters giving him a roadblock."

At Fi's raised eyebrows, I said, "If we can find the last person for Caledonia, that gives us everyone else. Perhaps we'll hold the first meeting without the representatives from Galicia." Then I started laughing.

"What? You just had a wicked idea, didn't you?" Fi looked gleeful. The emperor must have upset her. I didn't like the idea that he thought he could do that to my staff.

"What if we add a note on the Portal about the council? Phrase it far more politely than this. But say,

'Sadly, the emperor couldn't get his act together. We can't delay all the other realms for his convenience. Perhaps he'll be able to complete the arduous task of suggesting two representatives to join the council at some unspecified time in the future? But, sadly, it will mean we'll be unable to help with their bandwidth problem if they don't have any representatives on the council. We apologise to the Galician citizens, but they must contact their emperor if they need help to fix their tech problems. Perhaps a clearer understanding of the problem will assist him in choosing the right people.'"

Fi started laughing.

Finn looked relieved, then he laughed too. "Uncle Alphonse as tech support would be worth watching. Alejandro might set up a livestream for us?"

Dola said, "I shall email a draft of the post for your approval. Perhaps if we put it up now, he will send us the names of his people before the first meeting."

"Good plan."

We moved on, and once we'd dealt with everything else, I said, "Quick word please, Caitlin."

When I asked her if the blue power had settled OK, she said, "Sure. Shared it with Ma and Juna. We're solid."

And that seemed to be it, as far as she was concerned. She looked well though.

"Is this new?" I pointed at her cheek piercing.

"Yeah, I'm twenty-five this year. Birthday portraits and all the slag that goes along with it." At my confused expression, she added, "Traditional time for the heir apparent to start wearing the heir's half-crown piercing. Stupid slagging strictures."

I told her I planned to summon Troels at noon and watched as a gleeful expression spread over her face.

"Can I stab him this time?"

"If he gives me any grief at all, yes, but not fatally. He's not getting off so easily. And I'll leave Tilly with Dola. I'm not giving him another chance at her. It'll be one less thing for us to worry about."

FORTY-SIX

At 10.30 a.m. on the dot, the back door opened to admit Ti'Anna wearing her old lady glamour. I gestured, "Come through to Stane Parlour," and led her to my new office.

The vista along the Solway Firth coastline fascinated her as she gazed through the wide windows. "Is it the actual view? It doesn't feel like an illusion."

"Dola says it's the view we would have if the house had two more storeys."

"Oh, how clever of her. You'll have a window onto the spring equinox celebrations. Although I expect you'll be there, won't you? Aren't you close to Mabon?"

I nodded. But what did the view from here have to do with the spring equinox? My face must have betrayed my ignorance because she pointed through the window. "He always holds it by the Lochmaben stane, Mabon's own stone. It's egg-shaped, you see. Picnic in the afternoon and then watch the sun go down on the last day of winter. He'll hope for a visit from Ēostre; she always liked his stone. It's usually a pleasant day, and he shields against the spies so we can all relax."

I thought before we got into any more meanderings about spies, I'd move on to what I'd invited her to discuss. So we poured coffee and cut ourselves a slice of a delicious pistachio cake with cream cheese frosting. It didn't seem to have any magical qualities, so it wasn't one of Juniper's. I wondered if it was one of the Glendinning family recipes that Fi and Mrs Glendinning had given Dola for her 1400th birthday? It was incredibly good.

Ti'Anna and I relaxed into the comfortable chairs to watch the view. "You said you had news, Recorder?"

"I do, but it seems you weren't honest with me."

She frowned, a dark expression crossing her face.

"I know you didn't lie. But attempting to mislead anyone as thoroughly as you did me is a hair's width from lying, Ti'Anna. And yet, you specifically told me I could trust you in this matter. I'm wondering, have you been gone from home too long?"

Now she looked frightened. Damn, I'd gone too far. The Book told me if I sent her home, she'd have to go. Citizens from the realms could only stay in Caledonia with the Recorder's consent. I'd meant to hint at my unhappiness, to make her stop bullshitting me, not threaten her. Blast!

Well, I'd done it now. I couldn't take it back without loss of face, and, with the Fae, loss of face was worse than being a bully.

"I specifically asked you to tell me the what, when, why, how, where and who." I was certain that was exactly what I'd said. Because, at the time, I'd smiled at myself when I realised I was inadvertently quoting an old poem about honest serving men. "Instead, you limited your response solely to Jamie and his well-being. Do you believe so tight a focus was being as trustworthy as you assured me you were in this matter?"

She gazed at me but didn't speak.

"Because Glais'Nee and Ad'Rian, when I spoke with them, suggested you had shaved the truth too finely to be considered honourable with an ally. So, if you don't consider me an ally, why were you requesting—no, why were you insisting on my help?" I folded my hands in my lap in my best librarian pose and waited to see how she might dig herself out of what was, to any Fae, an appalling breach of etiquette.

And I waited.

She started to speak several times but never managed to make it past, "I …"

I waited her out until eventually she found her words.

"I promised my sister," she paused and made the sign for *May she reach the Summerlands with joy and without hindrance*, but didn't speak the words. As I bowed my head, she looked surprised but continued, "I would look out for her child. We *knew* during her gestation, she wouldn't live long past his birth. We all agreed to do whatever we could to see he reached manhood alive. It was a tangled web we wove. But we succeeded. He is alive. But he doesn't live, not truly live."

Puzzle pieces started to come together in my brain.

Perhaps once I'd have rushed in. But I was learning, even if I often felt I was learning too slowly. I sipped my coffee and waited.

"Le'Anna was the brightest of us. You seem to know something of my people. More than Elsie did, anyway. The brightest often burn out too fast. Our passions need to be banked, not permitted to flare like dragons. But she adored Jonvar. There was no sense, no order, and no balance to be had from her once their bond locked. They were bonded. It was fated. All that was left for us to do for her was protect her son."

Oh, Gods and Goddesses, did she mean …? Now I felt like fireworks were going off in my head.

"You're his aunt?"

One eyebrow twitched as though I'd surprised her. "I am. His aunt and his goddess-given mother."

She was Rollo's godmother? "But what the hell does it have to do with Jamie? And why were you rabbiting on about central heating for a community hall? Why didn't you just tell me?"

De'Anna, L'eon's mother; Ti'Anna, my local Fae; and Le'Anna, Rollo's late mother were three of the sisters Ad'Rian had mentioned. There was an older sister too, but even in my own mind I didn't want to think about *her*. The younger three had been inseparable until Le'Anna's bond with Jonvar.

Suddenly, I lost all patience with the woman. I had things to do today. I wrapped all my private business behind my shields, left Rollo, Troels and all the Viking nonsense on the outside of my mind, and then tapped on her mind politely. I may have been thinking *you stupid, stupid woman*, but I did it politely.

Her expression when I tapped at the door to her mind was very un-Faelike. It was probably best described as gobsmacked. But she said, "I consent," and completed the connection.

I offered her the public events of the last week with her nephew and godson.

I felt her trying to probe much deeper than the

information I'd offered and broke the connection. "*That* is how you repay my trust, Ti'Anna?" I stood up. "We're done here. Do not return until you've reconsidered your unforgivable breach of etiquette and your vulnerable position and how best to make amends."

I moved towards the door, sincerely shocked. I'd thought she was Fae enough not to abuse the link. My gullibility made me angry with myself.

She stammered, "I sensed my nephew in your head. I lost sight of my position. I …" She sighed. "Probably I should pay a visit home. I seem to have misjudged you, Niki."

"Do. I'm not threatening you, Ti'Anna; I think you need the support of family. You feel out of balance. Go, reconnect with family. Speak to Ad'Rian. You and I can try again. But be warned, I have a two strikes and you're out rule. It used to be three strikes, but people around here abuse that, so now it's two. And you're one and a half down. I'm only giving the partial lack of honesty half a strike, but abusing a mind link …" I trailed off as words actually failed me. The etiquette around an offered mind link that Ad'Rian taught me as a child was as clear now as it was when I was seven.

She nodded. "I had a vision. I have some of the power of the seer."

Well, she'd been right about Jamie being in danger, so I paused before I opened the door for her.

"My nephew was in danger. He was in the dark and injured, and men were discussing killing him. That's why I breeched beyond politeness when I felt you had knowledge of him. We made a death oath, the three of us, to our sister. I would have been forsworn if I had not tried to look."

Actually, that made sense—well, it made no damn sense, but it was true. The Fae took promises made to the dying seriously, even forty years later. Forty years was no length of time to a race as long-lived as the Fae.

"Did you get any sense of the timing of your vision?"

"It felt soon, next week perhaps? That's why I planned to visit home, to speak with De'Anna."

"OK. Are you going through now? Or do you need to return home first?"

Ti'Anna replied, "No, Heli will deal with my house for a few days."

Heli? Did I have another Fae in the village I didn't know about? "Heli?"

"Heli Hob, my housekeeper." Oh, that was fine. Although I didn't know a Heli, did I?

We walked together to the Gateway. As we neared it, I asked, "Why on earth were you so concerned to save Jamie? Either of us could provide some new central heating. I could donate it in Gran's name, couldn't I?" This central heating nonsense had never made sense to me.

"Of course we could. I thought we may need Jamie. He is Troels' son, you know. We could track Troels through his blood."

"Troels has several hundred kids, if these petitions are to be believed. I'm sure a dozen of them would donate blood if I asked."

"Yes, indeed. But Jamie is," she glanced sideways at me as we strolled down the path, "already guilty."

I stopped walking and looked at her, allowing my confusion to show. "So?"

Her face calm now, she said, "So he is disposable. Close blood relatives' entrails can be most helpful if someone is trying to hide."

I still felt queasy after she'd passed through the violet gate. I asked Dola to brief Ad'Rian on our conversation and added in the entrails bit from our walk over. Had she been trying to freak out the Recorder? But, no, she'd looked perfectly serene and serious.

Some of these people were totally batshit crazy.

Crazy or not, her vision about Jamie had been accurate. I needed to get Troels here so he was unable to cause any more damage, and then find Rollo before anything awful happened to him. My stomach hurt now. The problem was my stomach had hurt with one thing and another for the entire last freaking week. I'd lost all perspective on what it might be trying to warn me about and was wondering if I should try to eat more healthily. Or perhaps just more regularly?

I stood behind the anvil, wrapped in power. Caitlin had drawn her sword. HRH waited on her plinth, ready for the show.

I placed the star in the indentation. "I summon the Rightful King of the Vikings to the centre of the Rainbow."

I breathed in and waited with my heart almost in my mouth.

But it wasn't King Troels who arrived.

Instead, a sack-wrapped bundle thudded wetly onto the floor in the centre of the Gateway.

Caitlin only just stopped herself from sticking her sword in it, and then she swore loudly, colourfully, and with heat. It'd been a very long time since I'd heard language that foul.

She was already on her knees as I rounded the anvil to see what had arrived. The colour must have drained out of my face because I felt like I was about to pass out.

Only the thought I couldn't do that yet kept me on my feet as I looked down at Rollo.

The sacking was filthy and wet with large red-brown patches. Rollo's face was grey under the bruising. His head looked misshapen, eyes swollen shut, and his right arm looked very wrong. Bloody patches around his torso and one of his legs were getting larger as I watched.

What was the use of having the power and the link with him if I hadn't known this was happening? I'd checked in on him this morning, and, other than my Gift nagging at me, I'd had no idea there was a problem. But they hadn't done this to him in a few minutes.

"He's alive, just." Caitlin blew out a breath as she removed her fingers from the pulse point in his throat. "Best get the Fae. Ad'Rian, ya think?"

But the pit of my stomach clenched as I looked at the sorry bundle of bloody rags on the floor, and I *knew* with a leaden certainty Ad'Rian would be too drained after all the multiple healings he'd given Dai so recently to help with injuries this critical.

He was probably still working on Dai and pulling in any spare energy from his healers to help, because he didn't want to disappoint Mabon again.

Crap.

There were other healers, but would I trust them with Rollo?

My Gift said Ad'Rian wasn't the answer. Then what the hell was? Could I time travel back and prevent this?

Probably not. The Book had been extremely clear on the dangers of time travelling to save a life. The power really didn't like me doing it, and I thought it would prevent me from going, as it had when Finn was taken. I needed a better plan.

My stomach roiled. My brain had frozen into a loop. It wasn't helping. It went, shit, shit, shit, oh, Rollo, shit, shit.

How the hell had this happened?

"Caitlin, you heard me summon Troels, right?"

Her voice was laden with fury, but not, I thought, at me. Damn, I wouldn't want to be whoever had done this to Rollo. Because she'd have to fight me for the right to deal with them, and I would win, but I'd take her along as my second, and we'd leave them in pieces.

"No," she almost spat. "You summoned the Rightful King of the Vikings."

The fury in her eyes hurt to look at. Her look said, *catch the slagging hell up.*

Well, double crap! That thrice-damned cat had known.

When I get my hands on her ...

I know you're all cursing me right now, aren't you? But Seeing Red and Code Yellow were always going to be **very** closely connected. Check the news section for more info about a forthcoming preview which might help you to hate me less.

Thank you so much for reading my book. I really hope you enjoyed the continuation of Niki's adventures.

I know (sigh, truly so sorry), but book reviews on every book are **ridiculously important** to me as such a new author.

Please do it for me? Even a one-line review has enormous weight within the Amazon system. As I write this it's **barely a year** since I published my first book.

Your reviews have made all the difference in the world to enable me to continue doing something I love—during what was supposed to be my retirement! This is far more fun and I'm *profoundly* grateful for each and every review. Pretty please?

Review wherever you prefer but please, review.

NEWS

We've covered reviews already, haven't we? But I could add another please if it would help? Or a thank you? Or a respectful bow?

Niki returns in 2024 in books 5 and 6.

Her adventures continue, and the publication dates will be confirmed on my Facebook author page and in my newsletter.

There's more now if you want it. You can claim three free bonus epilogues. And a preview of the next book is coming in October. You also gain access to future free short stories if you subscribe to my newsletter.

Get your free bonuses from <u>linziday.com/news letter</u>.

Release dates will also show when the Amazon Midlife Recorder Series page updates here.

Book 5 - *Code Yellow in Gretna Green*

My newsletter subscribers will be able to access a two-chapter preview of Code Yellow in October.

In Gateway terminology, a 'Code Yellow' signifies a missing person. Niki figures out how to summon the missing King Troels to an arbitration. Thanks to Dola's latest brainwave, he's unable to leave.

However, the problem of what to do with him now that they have him sets our key characters off on a new path, with a whole new set of problems. The power struggles in Viking following his removal bring new faces and fresh problems into the Recorder's orbit.

The stakes ramp up when Breanna hosts her book club, and Aysha and Autumn encounter a problem of their own.

And then the Viking rebellion begins.

Code Yellow in Gretna Green is filled with intrigue, humour, and life-changing developments.

Book 6 - *Market Forces in Gretna Green*

Insights from Rosie Hob, combined with Mabon's misery, spur Niki into overhauling the Gateway's part of the inter-realm commerce situation. Over-turning her gran's one-in, one-out rule hasn't resulted in the hoped-for free trade between the realms. She's going to need more creative solutions.

Fi tries to take the reins in her new role as the head of the trade desk but meets with opposition. Finn is hopelessly distracted by the joys of first love.

Now, Niki needs to take a hard look at her own priorities and consider the wider future for the realms.

Mags Hob, Caitlin, and Rhiannon—No, enough! You'll need to wait for more until you've read Yellow.

I'm shooting for early summer for Code Yellow and later in 2024 for Market Forces. Please note the 'shooting,' though. Very new author, remember? But I'm writing and editing as fast as I can. After all, Seeing Red came out six weeks early, so fingers crossed.

In the meantime, I'd love to stay in touch with you. I'm regularly on Facebook (LinziDayAuthor), TikTok, and Goodreads.

Made in United States
Troutdale, OR
01/21/2024

17037084R00387